PASSION'S PRISONER

Alexander caught her hands and held them high above her head as he imprisoned her body with his own. "What are you doing out here all by yourself, Elizabeth?" he asked softly. "Someone should have told you it isn't safe."

"Someone did," she admitted. "I just didn't listen. Besides, I was told you'd been chased out of the county."

Alexander grinned. "I wasn't. But, I'm not the one you need fear."

"Aren't you?"

Alexander looked down at the wary expression on her face, and his smile broadened. The Tory belle acted as if she expected him to ravish her. Well, he'd never been one to disappoint a lady. "Now that I think about it, maybe you are in some danger."

The touch of his lips on hers made Elizabeth gasp. He felt it too. She knew he did. He jerked away as if he'd been burned. But only for a moment. Then his mouth crushed against hers so suddenly, so intently, she forgot to struggle, or protest at all. . . .

THE BEST IN HISTORICAL ROMANCES

TIME-KEPT PROMISES   (2422, $3.95)
by Constance O'Day Flannery
Sean O'Mara froze when he saw his wife Christina standing before him. She had vanished and the news had been written about in all of the papers—he had even been charged with her murder! But now he had living proof of his innocence, and Sean was not about to let her get away. No matter that the woman was claiming to be someone named Kristine; she still caused his blood to boil.

PASSION'S PRISONER   (2573, $3.95)
by Casey Stewart
When Cassandra Lansing put on men's clothing and entered the Rawlings saloon she didn't expect to lose anything—in fact she was sure that she would win back her prized horse Rapscallion that her grandfather lost in a card game. She almost got a smug satisfaction at the thought of fooling the gamblers into believing that she was a man. But once she caught a glimpse of the virile Josh Rawlings, Cassandra wanted to be the woman in his embrace!

ANGEL HEART   (2426, $3.95)
by Victoria Thompson
Ever since Angelica's father died, Harlan Snyder had been angling to get his hands on her ranch, the Diamond R. And now, just when she had an important government contract to fulfill, she couldn't find a single cowhand to hire—all because of Snyder's threats. It was only a matter of time before the legendary gunfighter Kid Collins turned up on her doorstep, badly wounded. Angelica assessed his firmly muscled physique and stared into his startling blue eyes. Beneath all that blood and dirt he was the handsomest man she had ever seen, and the one person who could help beat Snyder at his own game.

Available wherever paperbacks are sold, or order direct from the Publisher. Send cover price plus 50¢ per copy for mailing and handling to Zebra Books, Dept. 2916, 475 Park Avenue South, New York, N.Y. 10016. Residents of New York, New Jersey and Pennsylvania must include sales tax. DO NOT SEND CASH.

TRAITOR'S EMBRACE

Christine Dorsey

ZEBRA BOOKS
KENSINGTON PUBLISHING CORP.

ZEBRA BOOKS

are published by

Kensington Publishing Corp.
475 Park Avenue South
New York, NY 10016

First printing: March, 1990

Printed in the United States of America

To Chip
Thank you for the shopping, the cooking, the critiquing — the love and support.

"The sun never shined on a cause of greater worth."
— Thomas Paine, *Common Sense,* 1776

Chapter One

July, 1777
Landon Hall,
Maryland's Eastern Shore

"What of this Major Knox? He appears to be causing his share of trouble in the area. I trust he won't be a problem."

Elizabeth Lancaster paused outside the library, drawn not so much by the words she'd overheard as by the clipped British accent of the speaker. She brushed an errant, raven curl off her brow and peered through the doorway into the spacious book-lined room. A dozen men were seated at the far end of the library, apparently discussing the rebellion.

"That devil has been a thorn in our side, but I'm told he disappeared when he heard General Howe was in the bay." Elizabeth recognized the voice as belonging to Henry Clayton, who owned the manor across the creek from Landon Hall.

"Devil he may be, but let's give him his due, Henry. I don't believe Alexander Knox would hightail it just when things were beginning to prove interesting, and I don't think you do either." Adam Farrel, another of her Uncle Jordan's neighbors leaned forward in his chair to emphasize his thoughts, but Elizabeth barely noticed his movement or his sentiments.

Whomever they were talking about could wait. She was interested in getting a look at the man whose voice she'd heard first. Not that she really cared, but her cousin Rebecca was bound to ask if she'd seen Colonel Robert Littleton, and it would be easier to answer in the affirmative.

The men were so intent on their discussion of this Alexander Knox, they didn't notice her edge into the room. Elizabeth assumed by the tone of the conversation that the subject of their discourse was one of the many traitors to the crown who were now causing such a commotion with their futile rebellion. She pressed against the cherrywood highboy, hoping that attired in her brown riding habit she'd blend in with the furniture.

"What Adam says has some truth to it. Alexander Knox is a lot of things, but a coward . . ." Jordan Landon, Elizabeth's uncle, let his words drift off. "He raided the First Battalion of Maryland Loyalists' bivouac up by the Sassafras River in broad daylight. Got away with enough horses so he doesn't need to worry about where his next mount will come from, and he did it without losing a man."

"He's nothing but a sneak thief!"

The words were fraught with loathing, and Elizabeth glanced toward Benjamin Suteland, her cousin's betrothed, and the man whose wedding she and her father had traveled from their home in Philadelphia to witness. His face was red with rage, and he looked as if he would dearly love the opportunity to throttle the "sneak thief."

"Now I wasn't meaning anything by it, Ben. No one here is blaming you for what happened. I was just trying to let Jonathan and the colonel know what we've been up against."

Elizabeth didn't see her father's reaction to having the situation explained to him, because she suddenly remembered why she'd come into the library. The man who must be Colonel Littleton sat beside Ben Suteland, studying him as thoroughly as he himself was now being studied by Elizabeth. She watched as the British officer steepled his fingers under his chin, and decided she had to agree with Rebecca. Colonel Littleton was a handsome man. Elizabeth was starting to back toward the doorway—after all, she'd seen what she'd come to see—when the colonel spoke again.

"You were in charge of the battalion the day Major Knox attacked?"

The question was sharp edged, and Elizabeth couldn't help feeling a twinge of pity for Rebecca's fiancé. Though she'd never been overly fond of him, he had courageously volunteered when the first Loyalist corps had been formed and had even been elected captain.

"I was." Ben Suteland's response was terse and

crisp.

"And have you an explanation for what happened?"

"Now see here, Littleton," Jordan Landon surged into the fray in defense of his future son-in-law, "there was nothing Ben or any of the others could do."

The colonel's brown eyes flashed to her uncle, and Elizabeth thought she could almost see the older man quake in his shoes.

"This is exactly the type of thing I've been sent to see does not happen. When Lord Howe lands his army, he expects cooperation from the inhabitants, not trouble from some pesky partisan fighter. Now, Captain Suteland, I will have your explanation."

It occurred to Elizabeth that this conversation was not one any of the participants would like overheard by her. As yet, no one had noticed her presence, but it was only a matter of time till one of the men looked toward the doorway. For now, they all seemed intent upon Ben's account of the fateful day he'd encountered the infamous Alexander Knox. Slowly, carefully, Elizabeth backed out of the room. She would have made it, too, except that Adam Farrel chose that moment to reach behind him for the wine decanter.

"Elizabeth?"

Elizabeth felt heat seep up her face and pool in her cheeks as she turned her large gray eyes toward her father. Adam Farrel's start of surprise when he'd seen her standing in the doorway had drawn Jonathan Lancaster's, as well as everybody else's, attention. Her father stood now, looking at her expectantly, and Elizabeth's blush deepened with the realization that she'd been caught eavesdropping.

"Yes, Father?" Elizabeth dared not glance to the left, for fear of encountering the stare of Colonel Littleton.

"Have you come to fetch me for something?"

Elizabeth flashed her father a grateful smile. She had a feeling he knew what she'd been about, but he was acting as if she'd been caught just walking into the library, instead of trying to sneak out. If she was to benefit from her father's chicanery, Elizabeth had to think fast. The wedding! There was nothing so dear to the hearts of her relatives and friends as a celebration, and a surreptitious look at the mantel clock showed Elizabeth that excuse would work.

"Yes, Father. I've been sent to remind you 'tis a wedding we've come for, and the time for that event is fast approaching." Elizabeth was purposely vague about who may have sent her on such a task.

Luckily, no one questioned it. Uncle Jordan pulled out his pocket watch and flipped it open with a flourish. "Ho! It is time we were getting ready. Rebecca would skin me alive if I let talk of the war interfere with her wedding. I hope you understand, Colonel Littleton."

"Of course. No explanations are necessary. I am completely at your service to continue this discussion at a later time."

Though his words were accommodating, Elizabeth felt a chill run through her at the colonel's tone. It was obvious he had not welcomed the interruption.

She used this opportunity to study him again. He'd stood, as had everyone else in the room, when Elizabeth's presence had been discovered. He wasn't near as tall as she'd first thought—nor quite as handsome either. Still, he looked dashing in his scarlet tunic.

Talk in the room was now centered about a convenient time to resume the meeting, and since everyone seemed to have forgotten her, Elizabeth decided to slip away. But before she could, her father was by her side, taking her hand, and leading her toward the colonel.

"Elizabeth, I don't believe you've met Jordan's guest, Colonel Littleton."

Elizabeth cringed inwardly as she smiled into the colonel's lean face. It was bad enough that the British officer had seen her at all, for she'd been riding and was certain her hair and clothes must look a fright, but to have to talk to him! Elizabeth could only imagine what the impeccably dressed man must think. Still, he was charming, and by the time the introductions were over and Elizabeth had escaped from the library, she'd decided she could overlook the colonel's lack of stature. But she wished she had ignored Rebecca's suggestion that she try to see the British officer.

Thoughts of the robe *à la française* she planned to wear to the wedding ball that night filled her mind as Elizabeth climbed the wide central hallway. It wasn't till she'd almost reached the top that she realized her father had followed her from the library.

"You've been riding again, and I'll wager you took no groom with you," he said without preamble.

"I would have, but none was available, and I—"

"Elizabeth, you must pay more heed to your safety. This isn't Philadelphia."

He sounded so agitated Elizabeth was almost sorry she'd sent the groom on a needless mission while she rode out of the stables. But she'd been doing it for so long, she decided to point this out to her father. "I've always ridden over the grounds alone. Why, even when I was a child, and we'd visit, I rode by my—"

"Dammit Lizzie, we weren't at war then!"

Elizabeth didn't know which shocked her more, her father's slip into profanity in her presence, or his calling her Lizzie. Since he rarely, if ever, did the former and had stopped the latter over four years ago at her request, Elizabeth knew he was truly upset.

It was this silly war. The rebellion had caused her father more trouble than he deserved. She knew it was constantly on his mind. If he wasn't worried about how it would affect her, he was thinking about their life in Philadelphia.

Most of their neighbors had not been kind when they'd discovered Jonathan Lancaster's loyalty to the king could not be swayed. There had been jeers and taunts, and some had stopped dealing with his trading company. That had been one of the reasons Elizabeth had looked forward to their trip south.

But even here, where she had spent so many

15

carefree days as a child, the talk of war never ceased. At least at Landon Hall, all were of the same mind as her father. There were no hot-tempered Whigs with whom to argue. But there was the rebel everyone in the library had been discussing.

"It's that man you're upset about. What is his name?" Elizabeth remembered and answered her own question. "Alexander Knox, that's it, isn't it? Is he the reason I must stay indoors like some helpless female?"

"You must stay indoors like a helpless female because you *are* a helpless female." Her father obviously recognized a defiant glint in her eye. "Now don't unleash your temper on me, Elizabeth. When it comes to men like Alexander Knox, you are helpless."

"Do you know him?" Elizabeth couldn't help being a little curious about the man who inspired so much discussion, even though she could not understand why any man worth knowing about would fight against England.

"I know *of* him." Jonathan Lancaster paused. "But this is not a topic that need concern you. Simply take someone with you when riding, and stay within sight of the house."

Within sight of the house! Elizabeth began to protest, but one look at her father told her the effort would be useless. Already it was past noon, and the wedding was scheduled to begin at three o'clock. There really was no time to argue with him. Maybe tomorrow he'd be more receptive to her pleas.

Elizabeth turned toward the bedroom she shared with Rebecca, but her father stopped her. "And Elizabeth," he began with a hint of laughter in his voice, "the next time you've a mind to steal a peek at someone, don't lurk around in doorways. There are those who do not take kindly to being spied upon."

Spied upon indeed! Elizabeth slanted a wry look over her shoulder in time to see her father, shaking with suppressed laughter, disappear around the corner of the hall. So he'd known all along what she was doing. She'd guessed as much. But the idea of spying was silly. Elizabeth didn't give a fig about what she'd overheard.

Still, as she stood in the hall, her hand resting upon the smooth surface of the brass doorknob, her mind strayed back to the things she'd heard about Alexander Knox. For some reason she couldn't explain, he fascinated her. Maybe it was because the men in the library had been so worried about him.

Yes, now that she thought about it, there had been real concern in their voices when they'd discussed him. Her Uncle Jordan had tried to conceal it by acting almost as if he admired the colonial. Benjamin had espoused self-righteous anger. And the colonel had affected cool detachment, but apprehension had been there. It was almost as if they were afraid of the man. What had her father said? "When it comes to men like Alexander Knox, you are helpless." Did these men feel helpless, too?

But that couldn't be. True, Uncle Jordan probably couldn't do too much fighting, but Benjamin Suteland was young and strong. He was a captain in the First Maryland Loyalists Brigade. And even if he had been bested once by Major Knox, Elizabeth was certain it couldn't happen again.

Then there was Colonel Littleton. Surely he had nothing to fear. He had the entire British army to back him.

"Did you see him?"

Elizabeth barely entered the bedroom before Rebecca flung this question at her. Thinking as she was about Alexander Knox, Elizabeth's first reaction was to say no. Then she remembered who Rebecca had sent her to see.

"Yes." Elizabeth began unbuttoning the jacket of her brown riding habit.

"Well, what did you think?" Rebecca sank onto the dressing table bench and looked at Elizabeth, her blue eyes wide in anticipation.

"You were right."

Rebecca jumped up, setting the ruffles of her silk wrapper aflutter. "I send you to see the most handsome man — other than my Benjamin — on the entire manor and that's all you have to say? 'You were right'?"

Elizabeth sighed. She usually found Rebecca's enthusiasm contagious, but at this moment she was a little put off by it. "I simply meant that you were right about his looks. He is very attractive."

This remark seemed to placate Rebecca, for she sat back down. But it was as though all the starch had been rinsed from her, and it struck Elizabeth how very unlike her cousin this was. She tossed her jacket onto the bed, and sat down on the bench beside Rebecca. As her cousin looked up, their eyes met in the mirror.

"Something's bothering you." Elizabeth touched the bright yellow curls that as a child she'd coveted, and was surprised when Rebecca's head fell against her shoulder.

"You smell like a horse."

This comment brought a peal of laughter from Elizabeth. Whatever was bothering her cousin couldn't be all that serious if she still had the inclination to comment on Elizabeth's fragrance. "No doubt, since I've been riding. However as soon as you tell me what's troubling you, I'll bathe. Then I shall smell like a lavender garden."

"Well, that will be a vast improvement." Rebecca wrinkled her pert nose and leaned her elbows on the dressing table.

"You're stalling, Becca." Elizabeth slipped into the nickname she'd used when she and her cousin were children. They had been Becca and Lizzie then, two carefree little girls. But as much as Elizabeth might wish otherwise, those days were gone.

" 'Tis nothing. Truly, I'm fine."

Her words said one thing, but the silent pleading in the depths of her pale blue eyes spoke more eloquently. Elizabeth cocked her head and examined her cousin. "If you don't hurry and tell me, the water will get cold. That is my bath, is it not?" Elizabeth motioned toward the tub in the corner of the room. At Rebecca's nod, she continued. "You know how I abhor chilled water. I may just decide 'tis not worth the discomfort and forego cleaning up. But then I don't suppose you'd mind my bringing the scent of the stables to your wedding."

"Oh, Lizzie." Rebecca giggled, "You always could make me laugh, but I can't tell you. You're so sensible. I know you'll think I'm just a silly goose."

Elizabeth shook her head. "No I won't," she said firmly, but she wasn't entirely certain that was true. Elizabeth didn't exactly consider herself sensible, but she knew everyone else at Landon Hall did. Maybe it was because, compared to her flighty cousin, she was.

Not that she didn't love Rebecca; she did. She also felt a fierce loyalty to her. But neither of those feelings meant that she wasn't going to think Rebecca's problem silly. After all, in less than three hours her cousin was marrying a man she professed to love more than life itself. An awful thought seized Elizabeth. "It's not Ben? I mean he hasn't changed his mind?"

"Don't be ridiculous!"

Rebecca's unabashed amazement that anyone could think such a thing made Elizabeth feel foolish. It was unthinkable that Benjamin Suteland would even consider not marrying Rebecca. After all, he was not only gaining a handsome dowry, for Uncle Jordan was a very wealthy and generous man, he was gaining Rebecca. With her blond curls, blue eyes and rosebud mouth she had the appeal of a perfect China doll. What man wouldn't deem himself extremely lucky to be marrying her?

Elizabeth brushed aside an untidy lock of her

own inky, black hair and sighed. She was hot and sweaty, wanting nothing more than to sink into the tub of refreshing water. And for all she'd said it as a tease, Elizabeth really didn't like cold bath water.

"Well, if it isn't Ben, what is it?" Exasperation stained her voice, but when she saw Rebecca's hurt expression, Elizabeth was immediately sorry.

"If you must know, it's tonight," Rebecca said before propping her chin in her hand and affecting a pout.

Elizabeth was confused and didn't mind admitting it. "Tonight, you mean the ball? Has something gone wrong? The musicians . . ." Elizabeth couldn't imagine what else could be amiss. For weeks the house servants had been cleaning till everything sparkled and shone. Elizabeth herself had supervised the kitchen, so she knew there was plenty of food. Yesterday the dressmaker had finished the final fittings on both their gowns.

Rebecca's annoyed voice interrupted Elizabeth's musings. "I'm not worried about the ball, silly. It's after the ball that concerns me."

"Oh, that." Elizabeth felt as young and naive as she had the time Rebecca explained to her what people did to make children.

"Yes that," Rebecca answered hesitantly. "Do you realize I'll be doing *that* tonight?"

"I hadn't really thought about it."

"Well, I have. And I'm worried. I wouldn't speak of it, Lizzie, except I know I can talk to you about anything."

"Of course you can." This time when Elizabeth

put her arm around her cousin there was no mention of horses. "Have you talked to Ben about this?"

Rebecca pulled away, aghast. "Oh, I couldn't tell him!"

"Why not? He's going to be your husband, and it seems to me what we're talking about will affect him as much as you." Elizabeth, for all her seemingly sound advice, could not bring herself to define exactly what it was they were talking about.

"It's different for a man."

"I see." But of course, Elizabeth didn't see at all. If she ever fell in love, she'd want it to be just the same for the man as it was for her. Still, even with the realization that all was not perfect for Rebecca, Elizabeth envied her. Not that she had any desire at all for Ben Suteland. That was one area where Elizabeth questioned her cousin's taste, but there were times she yearned for the love she knew this pair shared.

Elizabeth had been present the first time Rebecca saw Ben. Actually it hadn't been the first time. The three of them had practically grown up together. Ben was older by a half-dozen years, and had mostly ignored the little girls from the neighboring manor, but he had been around often. Elizabeth, who had stayed with her aunt and uncle those years after her own mother died, had thought it *too* often. But he came to visit Charles, Rebecca's older brother, so there wasn't much Elizabeth could do about it. He went to school in England—a move for which Elizabeth was exceedingly grateful. But by that time, she was living in Philadelphia, visiting

Landon Hall only when her father could get away from his import business, so Ben's absence really hadn't mattered much.

Ben had been away from home for over five years, and when he'd returned, Elizabeth hardly recognized him. Gone was the gangly youth who had teased her about her riding ability, and in his place was a pleasant looking young man—a man Rebecca professed to fall in love with at first glance.

Elizabeth found that unlikely, though she had to admit from that moment on, her usually flirtatious cousin had eyes for no one but Benjamin.

That was one of the reasons Elizabeth found it difficult to understand Rebecca's reluctance about the night to come. She'd have thought her cousin would be anxious to make herself one with the man she loved, and told her so.

"Of course I am. I mean it's not as if he hasn't been practically begging me to make love with him since our betrothal—and there have been times I've been sorely tempted. It's just that I imagine Ben has had all kinds of experience, and I, well, haven't. I'm afraid I won't know what to do."

Elizabeth bit her bottom lip to keep from smiling. "I think Ben will probably help you with that part, don't you?"

"I suppose so, but I want to be such a good wife to him."

"Ben knows that. Don't tell me my self-assured cousin Rebecca is doubting herself?" Elizabeth caught Rebecca's eye, and they both laughed.

By the time Elizabeth shed her dust-covered riding skirt and slipped into the lavender-scented water, it was tepid at best. She could have ignored the temperature and luxuriated in the soothing fragrance, but time had gotten away from her. The hairdresser Uncle Jordan had brought from Annapolis was already working on Rebecca's golden tresses. Elizabeth washed quickly, relieved that she didn't have to carry out her threat and go to the wedding smelling of the stables. For all she enjoyed riding, she didn't wish to smell like her horse.

Lacey, one of the house servants had come in to help Elizabeth dress. After that Elizabeth barely had time to think as her body was pushed and prodded into the elaborate open robe she'd had made for the wedding and ball.

It was a delicate, lilac silk with an open bodice worn over a stomacher that Elizabeth had embroidered herself. The robings of pleats that hung from her bared shoulders did much to camouflage her tall, slender frame according to Aunt Mary, Rebecca's mother. "She's willowy," Rebecca had said in defense of Elizabeth's figure, but Elizabeth tended to agree with Aunt Mary.

"Are you sure you don't want to wear my bosom's friend?" Rebecca was admiring the way her own breasts plumped above the décolletage of her sky blue gown. Fashioned with a closed bodice, the overskirt was bunched into three puffs of fabric that draped over a silver tissue petticoat, resplendent with flounces and furbelows.

Though she had to admit that Rebecca's petite, rounded form did wonders for the gown, Elizabeth

24

declined the offer of extra padding for her own chest.

When her cousin's hair was done to perfection, Elizabeth donned a powder jacket and sat on the bench, ready to submit to the ordeal. She usually wore her long black hair, which had a definite mind of its own, tied back in a ribbon. But for an affair such as this, that would never do. Her hair was pulled straight off her brow and raised over a pad, which to Elizabeth's way of thinking only served to make her appear taller. But Rebecca raved over the effect and before Elizabeth knew it, the hairdresser was instructing her to cover her face with a mask, so she could apply white starch to the creation.

"Rebecca?" Elizabeth coughed once, and swiped a cloud of white powder away from her face. "Have you ever heard of a man named Alexander Knox?" Elizabeth had considered asking her cousin about him ever since she'd come into the room; however, if she could have anticipated Rebecca's reaction, she'd never have given in to the urge. "What's wrong?" Rebecca's lovely face with its carefully applied rice powder was positively apoplectic.

"Where did you hear that name?"

"Someone said it earlier. Why?" Elizabeth wasn't about to tell her how she'd heard it.

"Don't mention it in front of Ben. He absolutely hates the man. Just hearing that name sets him off into all kinds of wild rages." Rebecca snapped open her fan and used it to cool her flushed cheeks.

"What did he do?" Elizabeth thought she had a pretty good idea, but if anyone knew local gossip, and loved to tell it, it was her cousin, Rebecca.

"I'm really not sure, though I've heard enough whisperings to agree with Ben's perception of him."

"Well?" The hairdresser had gone, leaving the two girls momentarily alone.

Rebecca bent over as far as her gown and hair would allow, and responded in hushed tones, "Ben thinks he's a spawn of the devil."

"Oh, Rebecca!" Elizabeth, who was hoping for some true enlightenment, could only laugh at what she heard.

Rebecca had the wherewithal to look a little embarrassed, but she shook her head, sending a fine mist of powder into the air, before speaking. "I'm not saying he is, mind you; however, it is very strange."

"What is?" Elizabeth had the feeling she was going to hear something interesting now.

"The way Alexander Knox always knows what's going on. He attacked Ben's company when most of the men were away. And they can never find a trace of his camp. 'Tis said no Loyalist is safe around him."

Elizabeth was denied asking any more about him by the entrance of her Aunt Mary. "How beautiful you are!" Though her words seemed to encompass them both, her gaze remained on her daughter. "It's time to go downstairs." She seemed every bit as apprehensive as Rebecca.

The wedding was to be held in the salon, since it was the only room besides the ballroom large enough to accommodate all the guests. The room had been filled to overflowing with late summer blooms from the garden. There were gladiolus and zinnias in large urns, and roses of every hue—their sweet, simple fragrance perfuming the air.

Elizabeth watched as the Reverend Mr. Morgan read from the Book of Common Prayer. Once, Elizabeth felt as if someone was looking at her. She glanced to the side and met Colonel Littleton's brown eyes. He smiled and nodded before Elizabeth could turn away.

When Rebecca and her Ben were happily wed, and the rush of well-wishers had subsided, everyone retired to the dining room for an elaborate wedding feast. The Chesapeake Bay and Mary Landon had done themselves proud. The table groaned under the bounty of each. The great estuary provided oysters and crabs, fresh and succulent, that Landon Hall's mistress had turned into stews and cakes. There were water fowl, basted in their own juices and turned to perfection. And for those with a sweet tooth, the sideboard boasted an array of pies, puddings, and tarts. By the end of the meal there were few ladies present who did not wish they'd refrained from giving their stay ties that extra tug. Elizabeth was one who regretted doing so.

But there was naught to be done about it now, for as the filmy veil of twilight shrouded the manor house, it was time for the dancing to begin. The ballroom, too, had been gilded for the occasion. The myriad prisms of the lusters had been cleaned with vinegar till they sparkled in the candlelight, sending flashes of light adance on the cream-colored walls. At one end of the ballroom a platform had been built, and it was there that the musicians, playing violins and French horns, began a lively country tune.

"Now what do you think of Colonel Littleton?" Rebecca rushed into a bedroom after Elizabeth, who had gone there to have a small tear in her hem repaired. It was the first time the two had been alone since the wedding.

"I told you before, Rebecca, I think he's very handsome."

"Don't think I haven't noticed how many times you've been his partner. Why, it's almost indecent."

Elizabeth laughed. "It is not. He's only asked me to dance three times." Though she chided her cousin, Elizabeth knew Rebecca was right. Three were a lot of dances to share with a man she'd just met. And that didn't count the time he'd accompanied her onto the wide west portico. Elizabeth decided if she told Rebecca that, the new bride would have them betrothed before the evening was spent. Even without such knowledge, Rebecca seemed prone to make more of the relationship than was possible.

"I knew this would work out as soon as I saw him. You two were meant for each other," Rebecca stated emphatically.

"Don't be silly. I shall very likely never see him again after he leaves Landon Hall." Rebecca was taking wedded bliss too seriously.

"That's where you're wrong."

Elizabeth narrowed her eyes and stared at Rebecca

who suddenly looked as if she were the cat who'd gotten the cream.

"He's going to Philadelphia."

Elizabeth couldn't hide her look of surprise. "Colonel Littleton is?" Philadelphia was a staunch Whig city. Why it was the capital of the rebellion. What would a British officer be doing in such a place, unless . . . ?

"That's why he's here, to ready the area for General Howe to land his troops. The British are going to reclaim Philadelphia. Ssshh. Not a word of this to anyone."

Martha Webster entered the room, and Elizabeth was left with her questions unanswered. She wondered if the news were true. It certainly made sense. Elizabeth had often wondered why the king had allowed the rebels to hold the city for so long.

As soon as Elizabeth returned to the ballroom Robert Littleton approached her. He was very dashing in his gleaming white breeches and scarlet jacket, and Elizabeth found she enjoyed his attentions. He led her onto the dance floor to the opening strains of a quadrille. They had just taken their places when the music stopped.

Elizabeth glanced at her partner, whose face was now white as his periwig, before turning to follow the path of his gaze. Amid gasps of disbelief, the dancers, whose gaiety and laughter had moments ago filled the room, shrank away from the entrance. And that's when she saw him.

Chapter Two

Major Alexander Knox strode into Landon Hall's ballroom, his steely blue eyes searching for the telltale scarlet of a British uniform. To his right, he heard a muffled cry, a swish of silk, and Alexander turned to see a middle-aged matron collapse against her escort. Her companion, a man of less weight and greater years than she, buckled beneath this unexpected onslaught before lowering her unceremoniously to the floor.

Alexander's scowl deepened, and a tiny muscle began to throb beneath his sun-darkened cheek. He had no desire to frighten women and old men. The realization that he would had almost made him abandon this plan to capture Howe's emissary. But such side effects of war were unavoidable, and this was the safest time for him and his men to enter this hornet's nest of Tories. That had to be his first consideration. He would not risk the lives of the brave Patriots who fought by his side to spare the sensibilities of a few British sympathizers. Besides, a little scare might make them think twice before offering aid to the English.

Another movement caught his attention, but before he could signal any of his men, who'd positioned themselves against the walls of the elaborate ballroom, one of the guests rushed through the French doors at the far end of the room. Alexander's lips twitched as he tried to suppress a smile while he watched the spot where the man had exited. Alexander didn't have long to wait. Suddenly the doorway seemed filled with a redheaded giant of a man, who clutched the shoulders of the would-be escapee with two beefy hands.

"You want this one to get away, Major?"

"Not particularly," Alexander responded, keeping the amusement out of his voice with difficulty. He hadn't known for certain that Otis was out on the terrace, but when he hadn't noticed the burly frontiersman in the room, he'd assumed that was the case.

"Didn't think so," the giant began. "That's why I caught him for ya. He's a pesky little fellow though. Think I ought to hold on to him for a while?"

"I'll leave that decision to you, Lieutenant."

Elizabeth looked from where the huge, roughly dressed colonial held Ben Suteland back to the man who was obviously the leader of this band of barbarians. She had no doubt he was the Alexander Knox everyone had been talking about. Her cousin's reference to him as the "spawn of the devil" came to mind as she stared at him. He was tall, nearly the

31

height of the redhead, but where that man was husky, his leader was lean and muscular. But it was Knox's coloring that reminded Elizabeth of Rebecca's description. He was dark. His hair so black, that as he moved, the candle's glow seemed to catch in its deep waves, reflecting blue highlights. That her own hair was of nearly the same hue, did not detract her from comparing the traitor to all that was evil.

He walked toward her now, his gait easy and confident, and it took Elizabeth a moment to realize it was not really she, he approached, but her partner. Since the instant this drama began, Elizabeth hadn't given Robert Littleton a thought. She turned toward him, noticing his hand tighten on the hilt of the sword hanging by his side.

"I wouldn't recommend it, Colonel."

Knox stood in front of them, and Elizabeth realized by his words he'd noted the British officer's slight movement.

For what seemed an eternity, Littleton fingered the burnished gold of the hilt, while Knox stared at him. Finally, Littleton let his hand drop away from the weapon.

"A wise move, Colonel. Though 'tis only a ceremonial piece, I'm certain its edge is sharp. You wouldn't wish to be the cause of harm befalling your lady friend."

Because of his reference to her, Alexander Knox glanced toward Elizabeth. At that moment, when his startling blue eyes met hers, all thoughts of devils flew from Elizabeth's mind. His was the most arresting face she'd ever seen. The nose was straight, the mouth wide and sensual, but it was the eyes that held her attention. They were the deep blue of the late afternoon sky, and when he looked away, Elizabeth let out a breath she didn't realize she'd been holding, and felt a sense of loss. That feeling annoyed her almost as much as the major's bold arrival at the ball. How dare this impertinent rebel not only intrigue her with tales of his daring escapades, but send a current of electricity racing through her with but one glance. To make matters worse, it was obvious by the casual way he had dismissed her, that there'd been no similar spark for him.

"You are Colonel Robert Littleton, are you not?" Alexander reluctantly turned back to the British officer. He'd not been at all prepared for the allure of the woman's gray eyes. Though he by no means cared for the frivolous type she appeared, nor did he find her particularly beautiful, still she aroused his interest. He silently vowed to avail himself of a barmaid he knew in Chestertown the next time he passed through that burg. Obviously, he was in dire need of some feminine company if this thin, powdered wench excited him.

"I am." Colonel Littleton's voice was tight with barely controlled hostility. "And who, may I ask, are you?" The question was voiced with the utmost disdain.

Alexander grinned and let his gaze stray back toward the woman. She didn't appear quite as haughty as the colonel, but then Alexander took her

33

for the daughter of one of the local Tories and not someone Littleton had brought from England. Continuing to look at her, Alexander bowed. "Major Alexander Knox of the Continental Army, at your service. And you, sir," he focused his attention onto Littleton, "are my prisoner."

The man was incorrigible! Elizabeth felt resentment swell inside her at his words. The arrogant rebel thought he could just march into her uncle's home and take someone away. Why he wasn't even holding his pistol, but had it jammed into the waistband of his breeches. He needed to be told that this simply was not done, but there didn't seem to be anybody willing or able to do it.

Since his unruly band had entered the room, no one had resisted him. Oh, there was Ben, but Elizabeth wasn't sure his act had been motivated by heroism. Where was Uncle Jordan? Where was her father? And Colonel Littleton, was he so afraid of this rebel that he'd allow himself to be taken with nary a word? Before she could think about the possible repercussions, Elizabeth stepped forward, drawing Knox's attention to her once more.

"You cannot do this. I won't allow it!" She thought she heard a gasp from someone in the crowd, and she certainly felt Colonel Littleton's restraining hand on her arm, but she shrugged it off. Only one person held her interest, and he looked at her with a mixture of disbelief and amusement.

"But, madam," he said as his azure eyes raked quickly down her body, "I've no doubt you can find another partner when I take away your colonel." The words were spoken with just enough sarcasm to indicate he did have a doubt or two about Elizabeth's desirability as a dance partner. She bristled under the implication, but there was more at stake here than her dignity.

She raised her chin. "The colonel is not mine; however, he is a guest in my uncle's house, and as such, is under our protection." Whatever made her make such a claim, she did not know, but Alexander Knox's reaction to her proclamation was so immediate, Elizabeth had no time to retract her impetuous statement.

With his hands resting on his narrow buckskin-clad hips, he threw back his head and laughed. The action exposed his strong, sun-darkened neck and the black chest hair that curled up toward the loosely tied opening of his linen shirt.

When he stopped laughing, and it was a while till he did, he grinned at Elizabeth, his blue eyes full of gaiety. "Do you propose to fight me for him? 'Twould hardly seem an equal contest, but I'm more than willing to give you choice of weapons." Alexander let his gaze drift down her body more slowly this time, lingering when it encountered an interesting curve. There weren't that many, for Elizabeth was quite slender, and the dress she wore did nothing to enhance any feminine roundness she might possess. Still, he thought, it might be interesting to check for himself. . . .

"You, sir, are an uncivilized barbarian!"

Alexander felt certain her outburst was a result of

his appraisal of her body rather than his offer to fight her for the colonel. Her face glowed with angry color, her large gray eyes glaring at him from beneath a thick fringe of long black lashes. As she jutted her determined chin at him, Alexander noticed the intriguing cleft that marked its center, and had an unaccountable urge to touch it. But he didn't have to guess what her reaction would be to that! He could only thank heaven her spirit was not a universal quality in the Tories he'd encountered.

"This has gone far enough. Elizabeth, you forget yourself."

Elizabeth turned on Colonel Littleton, angry at his patronizing tone, and then she realized how caught up in her battle of words she'd been. Sometime during the sally she'd stepped toward the major till she now stood within arm's length of his tall, virile body. She was close enough to smell the rich scent of leather and outdoors that clung to him. As if she found the fragrance repulsive rather than pleasant, Elizabeth backed away.

"I wondered how long you'd let a woman speak for you, Colonel?"

Elizabeth imagined the rebel's words were meant to rile, and by the look of Littleton's tightly clenched fists she knew they had. What he intended to say in rebuttal, she would never know, for at that moment a skinny, towheaded boy burst into the room.

"They's comin', Major. Press just rode up and said there's a whole passel of them blood-suckin' Tories done comin' up the road."

Alexander listened to Billy Chew's breathless disclosure and grimaced. The major and his men had been one step ahead of a company of Tories for days. He'd assumed they'd shaken them by backtracking at Weston's Creek, but apparently they hadn't. He cursed himself for underestimating his pursuer's trailing ability. Now it was too late to take Littleton with them. The Englishman would just slow his band down. He should never have taken the time to banter with the woman, no matter how much he'd enjoyed it.

"Well, Colonel, it looks as if this day belongs to you. But I'm certain we'll meet again."

"I'll look forward to it, Major."

Alexander began backing toward the entrance, but he couldn't resist one final glance at Littleton's companion. "Enjoy your ball, Miss Elizabeth," he grinned, nodding his head in an ever so slight bow.

Elizabeth gasped. How dare the brute use her given name? Of course, she was beginning to realize he dared just about anything. She also realized that when he smiled, a most charming and beguiling dimple appeared in his left cheek. Realizing that she'd noticed this insignificant detail made her dislike him all the more.

For a moment after Knox and his men vanished through the door, everyone stood in stunned silence. Colonel Littleton recovered his wits first.

"Captain Suteland," he yelled at Ben, who leaned against the wall close to the French door. "Gather as many men as are available. We'll follow the bastard. This time he won't get away."

No one seemed to take offense at the colonel's slip into profanity when describing the rebel leader. Elizabeth watched as most of the younger men who'd attended the wedding, and even some who were no longer young, rushed to find their weapons. With relief she noticed that her father was not one of them. She didn't wish to think of him combing the countryside for the elusive Major Knox.

Before the men could assemble, there was a thunderous pounding on the front door. Elizabeth, startled by the clamor, left the ballroom and moved to the hall in time to see the leader of the Loyalist regiment that had been tracking Knox questioning Colonel Littleton. Together they hurried out the front door, followed by the volunteers from the ball.

"Whatever possessed you to talk to that horrid man like that?" Elizabeth still watched the empty doorway, wondering if the Loyalists had a chance of capturing the traitor when she heard Rebecca's question. "He could have shot you!"

Elizabeth smiled at her. "I don't think there was much chance of that happening." Though her heated words to the rebel major had been impetuous, and she hadn't given any thought to her safety, she'd not feared that he'd shoot her. It came to her that she knew he'd never harm her, but Elizabeth dismissed that as ridiculous. He was the enemy, after all, and they were at war.

"But, Elizabeth, you insulted him."

Rebecca fluttered her fan, and Elizabeth thought her cousin might swoon. Not that Elizabeth would blame her if she did. This had been a very trying day. Not many weddings that Elizabeth could recall ended with an invasion of armed men and the groom riding off.

"Come on, Rebecca, let's find some place to sit." Elizabeth led her into the library.

"I just don't know how you could say those things to him. He was so awful."

"He wasn't that awful." The sentiment was out of her mouth before Elizabeth could stop it. By the expression on Rebecca's face, she realized her cousin was shocked. "I mean," Elizabeth hastened to amend, "well, like you said, he could have shot me, and he didn't. And he really didn't act offended when I insulted him. He seemed rather amused."

"Amused? Elizabeth, he's a rebel, a traitor to the King! Why, do you realize at this very moment he could be killing my Ben?"

Elizabeth didn't think that very likely. She imagined Alexander Knox would be directing most of his energies toward escaping, however she wrapped her arm around Rebecca and comforted her. "Don't cry, Becca. I really wasn't defending him." But even as she denied it, Elizabeth realized she had been doing that very thing. Was it because she found him so very appealing? *Goodness, why did these thoughts keep popping into her mind?* With a shake of her head Elizabeth continued, "I'm certain Ben will catch Major Knox, and come back to you quickly."

"Oh, do you really think so, Elizabeth?" Rebecca turned her tear-stained face toward her cousin.

"Of course I do," Elizabeth assured, but there was a little part of her that hoped when Ben returned it would not be with a captive rebel major.

"There you are."

Elizabeth looked around to see her father standing in the library doorway. He walked across the Turkish carpet toward her, then sank into the winged chair across from the loveseat she and Rebecca occupied.

"Is she all right?" Jonathan Lancaster motioned to Rebecca who was wiping her eyes on a delicately embroidered handkerchief.

Elizabeth nodded. "She's understandably upset, but other than that, she's fine. Aren't you, Becca?"

Elizabeth interpreted silence punctuated by a hiccup as a positive response from her cousin.

"I want to talk to you about what happened earlier." Jonathan's words were addressed to his daughter. "You should never have antagonized that man."

Elizabeth cringed. Hysterical rantings from her cousin she could deal with, but when her father used this tone with her, it was serious. "I really didn't plan to," Elizabeth began in way of explanation. "He just made me so angry."

"That's hardly an excuse. The man's a desperate rebel. There was no predicting what he might do."

"He could have shot her," Rebecca conjectured in a muffled tone from out of her handkerchief.

"I doubt that. However, regardless of the possible consequences, you were ill advised to provoke him." Jonathan Lancaster crossed his legs and studied his daughter through narrowed eyes.

"I know, Father, and it shan't happen a—"

"It's your own good I'm thinking of, Elizabeth. I promised your mother I'd take care of you."

"You have." Elizabeth abandoned her seat on the couch, and sank onto the floor in front of her father. "You've always been wonderful to me." She truly hated to see him this upset.

Jonathan rose, pulling Elizabeth up by his side. "I sometimes worry that I've been too protective of you. There are times you don't seem to realize the consequences of what you do."

Elizabeth lowered her eyes. "You mean my riding about the manor?"

"That does come to mind." Jonathan responded. "You needn't look so contrite. My lecture is over. Just please try to remember what I've said. Now why don't you take Rebecca upstairs. It appears you both could use some rest."

Elizabeth, considering herself fortunate that she'd escaped a more lengthy discussion of her transgressions, hustled Rebecca up the wide, spiral staircase. This wasn't the first time, nor even the second, she'd raised her father's ire by acting before she thought. Nor was it the first time he'd blamed himself for not being a good enough parent. His being off to the north fighting Indians when Elizabeth's mother died had something to do with it, she guessed. But it wasn't as if he hadn't come back and seen her safely settled at Landon Hall before he'd returned to the war. And when the fighting had ended, he'd settled in Philadelphia, sending for her right away.

"Would you stop pushing? I'm about to trip over my petticoats."

"I'm sorry." Elizabeth forced her attention back to the present. She'd been so busy resolving to consider the consequences of her future actions before acting that she'd forgotten what she was doing.

Elizabeth stayed with Rebecca till the men returned. The women cleaned the powder from their hair and donned fresh clothes; Rebecca, a lacy night-rail, and Elizabeth, a loose-fitting sack dress, since she'd have to leave the room when Ben came back.

They were sitting by the cold fireplace, their forgotten sewing in their laps, when through the open window came the sound of horses' hooves crunching the oyster shell drive.

"They're back!" Rebecca jumped up and peered out the window. "There's Ben. Oh, Elizabeth, you were right. He's safe."

"Of course he is, silly." It took a great deal of restraint for Elizabeth to remain sitting. She tried to sound indifferent as she asked, "Do they have the rebel with them?" As much as she wished it were otherwise, Elizabeth had spent most of her time hoping Major Knox would make good his escape.

"I can't tell. It's too dark." Rebecca leaned further over the window sash. "They're bringing torches now. I see Colonel Littleton. He appears to be safe." Rebecca stuck her head inside and gave Elizabeth a smile.

"Good." Elizabeth *was* glad everyone had returned unharmed, but she wanted to scream, "What about that arrogant Patriot? Did his luck hold?" Of course she didn't. She even forced herself to make a few stitches in the pillow slip on her lap, knowing full well she'd have to tear them out on the morrow because they were uneven.

"I don't see him." Rebecca bent out the window again. "He must have gotten away."

Elizabeth let out a pent-up breath and rose. Picking a thread off her skirt, she started toward the door.

"Where are you going?"

"To my room. Now that everyone is back, I think I'll go to bed."

"But what about me?" Rebecca took a step toward her.

"Becca." Elizabeth shook her head. "Ben's home. This is your wedding night, and he certainly doesn't want to find *me* in his bedroom."

"Don't you want to hear what happened?"

"I'll find out in the morning." Elizabeth had a strong feeling that Rebecca was more concerned about the impending night with her new husband than with her cousin's hearing all the details of the chase. She gave her a motherly hug. "Remember, you love Ben, and he loves you. Everything will be fine."

Elizabeth lay among the rumpled linens of her bed and watched through the window as the dull pewter sky brightened to a pale mauve. If she'd slept at all last night, it had been little. It was warm, for nary a breeze stirred the dimity curtains, but she'd experienced many a hot night at Landon

43

Hall and had always been able to sleep.

No, it was her thoughts that had kept her awake. Though she tried to stop it, her mind constantly strayed to her encounter with Alexander Knox. She'd relived the meeting perhaps a hundred times since climbing the steps into the high tester bed, and each time her memory of him became more vivid.

"Enough." Elizabeth swung her slender legs over the side of the bed. She could stand it no more. There was absolutely no reason for her to be mooning over some ignorant misguided rebel, and she would put a stop to it. There was one way to clear her mind, and she intended to do it. Elizabeth didn't hesitate as she splashed tepid water on her face and tied her thick black hair at the nape of her neck with a scarlet ribbon. She donned an old riding habit. No one would see her anyway. The entire household had been up till past two o'clock, so she doubted there would be any early risers — except her, of course.

She would just take a short ride and be home and cleaned up before her father, or anyone else, awoke. Elizabeth felt better already.

She had no delays in the stables, and soon rode across the flat countryside on Hester, her favorite horse. They raced along a trail through loblolly pines, and stopped at a small brook for a drink. Then Elizabeth headed for the edge of the marsh. She loved to watch the new sun tinge the water with pastel shades as it filtered through trees behind her.

A mist was curling off the bay as Elizabeth tied Hester to a branch, and found a log near the shore to sit upon. It was cooler here, close to the water, but there could be no doubt it would be another sultry day. Elizabeth shrugged out of her jacket and loosened the stock at her neck. She considered removing her boots and dipping her feet into the water as she'd so often done as a child, but decided against it. She wasn't a little girl anymore. Instead, Elizabeth leaned back and enjoyed her solitude.

A breeze drifted off the bay, rattling through the cat-o'-nine-tails and sea oats, and lifting the curling tendrils of hair away from her face. Downstream an egret searching the shallow waters for its breakfast, reminded Elizabeth that she should be leaving. Reluctantly, she stood up, taking a deep breath to fill her lungs with the tang of the salt air.

For a moment Elizabeth stood still, listening for any unusual sound. Then she sniffed again. She was certain this time. Besides the expected peaty swamp smells, there was the unmistakable odor of smoke. A score of reasons why someone would have a fire on Landon property came to mind, and none of them were pleasant. Elizabeth began backing toward Hester. Ben had assured her, when she'd run into him in the hallway last night, that they'd chased the rebels into the next county. Now, as she felt a cold sweat break out on her upper lip, Elizabeth remembered all the times over the years Ben had been wrong.

She was almost to Hester when she heard a rustling in the brambles that twisted into large shrubs near the shore. She turned, and a cry of fear stuck in her throat.

Chapter Three

"Well, will ya look at this? What ya doin' out here all alone, girly?"

Elizabeth stared wide-eyed at the trio of men who'd thrust through the thorny vines into the clearing. She'd never seen any of them before. Their clothes were ragged and stiff with filth, but it was their surly expressions rather than their rough appearance that frightened her most. The man who'd spoken took a few tentative steps toward her, dragging his eyes away from the open *V* at the neck of her shirt with obvious reluctance, and looked around. When his gaze landed on Hester, casually grazing on some dried grass, his expression brightened.

"That your horse, girly?"

Elizabeth tried to swallow, found the process too painful, and stopped. Nothing in her sheltered life had prepared her for the fear she now felt. Though her mind told her to run or at least try to use her wits, her body refused to obey.

"I asked ya a question, girl." The man's tone turned angry as he stalked toward her.

Elizabeth backed up and nodded her head, frantically hoping he would stop. She stumbled over a rotting log, almost falling, but he grabbed her with a stocky hand, pulling her to him. While not overly tall, his weight was excessive, and though Elizabeth tried to pull away, she was pressed against his fat, sweating body.

"What'sa matter girl? Don't ya like ol' Zeke?"

"Aw, let her alone, Zeke. She ain't done nothin'."

Elizabeth flashed grateful eyes to the person who'd spoken. He couldn't be much older than she, and was as gaunt as his companion was obese.

"Shut your mouth, Pauly. Ya ain't out of leadin' strings long enough to want what this girl's got, that's your problem. But me, I aim to get my fill 'fore I leave." Zeke turned to the third man who was running his dirty hand down Hester's flank. "What 'bout you Luke? Ya be wantin' a piece of this 'fore we take that horse of hers?"

"Sure, Zeke. Anything ya say." Luke didn't take his eyes off the horse. "This is a fine-lookin' animal."

"This one ain't bad herself," Zeke said as his beady eyes stared at Elizabeth.

Zeke's fingers bit cruelly into Elizabeth's arm as his other hand squeezed her breast. Between the pain and humiliation, and the noxious odor of his unwashed body, Elizabeth thought she would be sick.

"Don't," Elizabeth sobbed as she tried to pull away from his exploring fingers. He'd torn her shirt and his hand groped at her delicate flesh.

"Stop fightin' me, girly. You're goin' to like this."

"I . . . I m not alone." It was a desperate lie, but Elizabeth was desperate. She'd hoped for some help from the one they called Pauly, but he seemed content now to toss pieces of bark into the water. She couldn't fight Zeke; he was simply too strong.

"Aw hell, Zeke. I told ya we should of left her alone. Let's just take the horse and go."

"And I told ya to keep your mouth shut, Pauly. She's lyin'. Ain't ya lyin', girl?" Zeke's hand tightened on her arm.

"No!" Elizabeth winced, and her knees buckled, but she forced herself to keep talking. "I . . . I'm meeting a friend here. He's very tough, and he'll . . . he'll kill you for touching me."

"Zeke." Pauly turned away from the marsh.

"Stop your whinin', Pauly. There ain't no friend."

Zeke's slobbery mouth muffled Elizabeth's scream of terror as he pushed her back against a tree. She shoved and tore at his skin, but he didn't seem to notice as he savagely plundered her mouth.

"Where's your friend now, girly?" His thick lips scraped across her cheek.

"I'm right here." The click of a pistol being cocked accompanied the deep baritone voice.

Though Zeke's body stiffened and pulled away, he kept his viselike grip on her arm. But Elizabeth no longer noticed the pain. She stared in disbelief at the man who'd entered the clearing. He was dressed much as he'd been last night, tight-fitting buckskin breeches jammed into high dust-covered riding boots. But today he wore no fringed jacket over his linen shirt. His midnight black hair was tousled, the thrust of his chin and unshaven jaw was bold, his determined face looked weary. But Elizabeth didn't think she'd ever seen a more beautiful sight.

Alexander Knox kept his eyes trained on the fat man, though he was cognizant of the man by the horse and the boy. He was also aware of the frightened gray eyes staring at him.

He'd somehow suspected it was the woman from the ball before she'd turned her face toward him. Maybe it was just because she'd been on his mind more than once during the long night of running, hiding, and doubling back. For whatever reason, when he'd investigated the voices he'd heard, Alexander wasn't surprised to see her. That didn't mean the sight of her being pawed by the fat bastard hadn't filled him with rage. By the look of the man, Alexander decided he must be one of the deserters who roamed the countryside. It had been all Alex could do not to tear into the clearing and yank the disgusting coward away from her. But reason and military discipline had won out.

"You her friend?" Zeke shifted his weight.

"That's what the lady said."

"You don't look much like her type." Zeke jerked Elizabeth forward.

Alexander's jaw clenched when he heard her small cry of pain. "I could say the same of you. Now why don't you take your filthy hands off her?"

"Well now, I would 'cept me and this *lady* was just startin' to get acquainted. And even though ya got that gun, there's three of us, and there ain't but one of you. Shoot it, and we'll be all over you like bees on honey."

Alexander's smile was grim. "You've got a point. And I am a notoriously poor shot." He paused, and his blue eyes narrowed. "That's why I always aim for the largest target." Alexander leveled the pistol he'd been holding in readiness at the center of the fat man's belly. "Let her go." These last words were spoken with a deadly intensity.

Except for the riotous chattering of a pair of blue jays the clearing was silent. Elizabeth tore her eyes away from Alexander's face and looked at Zeke. Beneath several layers of dirt, he'd gone ghostly pale. Elizabeth never doubted that Alexander would carry out his threat, and it was obvious Zeke didn't either.

With a snarl, the fat deserter released her arm. Suddenly relieved of the pain and forced to support herself, Elizabeth felt her legs go weak, but she took a deep breath and locked her knees.

"Come here, Elizabeth." Alexander extended his free hand toward her and was pleased when she started toward him. She seemed so frightened, he'd been half afraid she'd be too scared to move.

Elizabeth looked at Alexander's hand. It was large and sun-darkened, firm and unwavering, and she knew she'd be safe if only she could reach it. She had taken no more than two steps when she felt a sharp pain between her shoulder blades. Zeke's blow sent her sprawling forward, and before she hit the spongy ground, Elizabeth noticed Alexander move to catch her. He didn't though. As Elizabeth landed, she heard a fierce growl, followed by a thump and a splash.

Alexander was bent forward when Zeke barreled into him. The force carried him back, knocked him to the ground and dislodged the pistol. It flew out of his hand and sailed into the brackish water. Alexander pushed as hard as he could, and managed to shove Zeke off him, but by that time the man who'd been standing by the horse joined the fight.

Ducking his head to the side, Alexander managed to avoid the newcomer's fist, but he found his own punch halted as his arms were grabbed from behind. Zeke was on his feet and had pinioned Alexander against his blubbery body in a bear hug. Unable to defend himself, Alexander took a vicious blow to the temple from the second man. During the fracas, a movement to the right caught Alexander's attention. He turned to see the youngest of the three miscreants start toward Elizabeth.

"Get the hell out of here!" Alexander yelled to her just before he was doubled over by a jab to his stomach.

Alexander's command spurred Elizabeth to action. She'd watched in horror as Zeke and Luke pummeled her rescuer. She had to get help, and fast! With a speed borne of fear, she gathered up her skirts and ran for her horse. By the time she reached Hester, Elizabeth knew why Alexander had yelled. Pauly, having followed her, clutched at her ankles as she tried to gain her seat on the mare. If not for a well-placed kick by Elizabeth, he would have succeeded in hauling her to the ground.

She slapped at Hester, and the frightened animal pawed the dirt before racing toward the path. Hazarding a backward glance, Elizabeth saw Alexander Knox jackknife his legs and kick Luke in the belly. What happened next was lost in a blur of foliage as the horse galloped out of the clearing.

Alexander used the momentary lapse in Zeke's concentration, caused by Luke's grunt of pain, to twist out of the fat man's grasp. With one fluid motion, he turned on Zeke and shot out his fist. It landed with bone-crushing satisfaction on a saggy jaw. Alexander wiped the sweat from his eyes with his shirtsleeve, and spun on Luke. The man had recovered from the blow to his middle, and now advanced on Alexander, his expression full of hatred.

"Leave it be, Luke! That girl went for help," Zeke wailed as he staggered to his feet and lurched through the underbrush.

Luke started to follow, but Alexander lunged forward tackling him around the legs. They crashed to the ground, neither noticing Pauly as he scurried past them.

Elizabeth, having ridden no more than a quarter of a mile, pulled back hard on Hester's reins. The horse skidded to a stop amid clouds of sandy soil. *Just who at Landon Hall was going to lift a finger to save Alexander Knox?* The thought had struck her like a blow. More than likely, if she burst into the manor house begging for aid, Colonel Littleton would send a detachment of troops to capture the bold rebel. After what he'd done for her, Elizabeth couldn't allow that, even if he was the enemy.

Determinedly, she turned Hester, and galloped back toward the marsh. If Alexander Knox was to be saved, she must do it herself. Elizabeth dismounted and tied the mare a short distance from the clearing. She peered through a screen of holly leaves, deciding nothing would be gained by rushing into the struggle and getting captured.

Except for Alexander and Luke who were rolling around on the ground, locked in combat, the area appeared empty. Elizabeth gave one more quick look around before picking up a sturdy branch and stealing toward them. Alexander was on the bottom as Elizabeth lifted her makeshift weapon high. With all the force she could muster, she swung the branch, aiming for the back of Luke's dirty blond head.

The split second before her blow landed, Elizabeth realized the men had exchanged places, and the shiny raven locks of Alexander Knox would absorb the wallop. She tried to pull back, but it was too late. With a thud, the branch smacked his skull, and the man who'd managed to handle his adversaries fine without her, rolled onto his back at Elizabeth's feet, unconscious.

It was difficult to determine who was more surprised by what had happened, Elizabeth or Luke. He blinked up at her several times in disbelief, his eyes swollen and discolored. Then, apparently realizing he should thank fate rather than question it, scurried to his feet and out of the clearing.

Elizabeth gaped down at Alexander. He still lived. She could see the rise and fall of his powerful chest through the tears in his once-white shirt. Elizabeth tried to decide what to do. Aunt Mary often took care of injuries on the manor, but she'd never shown any desire to take her niece with her when she did so, thus Elizabeth had no idea what to do. After several minutes of indecision, she tore a strip from her petticoat and dampened it at the edge of the marsh.

The rebel was so big she had a difficult time turning him enough to see the back of his head. As she'd imagined, blood oozed from a cut near his crown. Gingerly, she touched the spot with the wet rag.

When the salty water made contact with Alexander's open wound, a searing pain jogged him to consciousness. Reaching behind him, toward the source of his discomfort, he grabbed the person causing it, and flipped her over him and to the ground. Before he took the time to see who it was, Alexander had pinned his tormentor beneath his own body.

"What the hell!" He glared down into Elizabeth's startled face. "Why did *you* come back?"

The breath had whooshed from Elizabeth's lungs when she'd landed on her back, and the weight of his body, which Major Knox seemed in no hurry to remove, kept her from regaining it. She sucked in air and tried to calm her rapidly beating heart. "I

. . . I came back to help," she finally managed to gasp.

"Help?" He sounded skeptical. Alexander shifted his weight in order to reach the back of his head, but he still made no move to get off her. He winced as his fingers explored the tender lump on his scalp. "What happened to my head?"

Elizabeth worried her full bottom lip, and stared up into his blue eyes. She felt totally at his mercy as snatches of observations she'd heard about him came flooding back. What had Rebecca called him? A spawn of the devil. Elizabeth had laughed then at its absurdity, but now, with his strong manly body pressing her into the bed of pine needles, and his sinfully handsome face only inches from hers, she wasn't so sure.

What would he do when he realized who'd hurt him? Elizabeth felt tears of apprehension swell in her eyes, but she resolutely blinked them back. There was nothing to do but tell him the truth. "I hit you with a branch," she blurted out.

Instead of the rage she'd expected, the rebel seemed genuinely surprised and perplexed.

"Why in the hell did you do that?"

"I didn't mean to," Elizabeth rushed to explain. "I tried to hit Luke, but you rolled over so quickly, I got you instead. He ran away," she added in a low voice.

"And *that's* what you call help?"

The tone of his question infuriated Elizabeth. Nothing had gone right since she'd met the man, and now he seemed to be making light of her attempt to rescue him. After all, she hadn't had to come back. "Obviously, I shouldn't have bothered. To be truthful, I can't imagine why I did."

"Can't you now?" The corners of Alexander's lips turned up in the beginnings of a smile, and a dimple teased his cheek.

"No, I can't!" Elizabeth wriggled under his weight and flailed at him with her fists. "Get off me!" He was even more insolent than he'd been the previous night. How had she gotten herself into this?

"Now, now, Elizabeth." Alexander caught her hands with ridiculous ease and held them high above her head. The motion thrust her breasts against the delicate fabric of her shift; a fact that Alexander was quick to notice. "I do appreciate the thought," he paused, "if not the result."

Elizabeth swallowed and lowered her eyes. The way he said Elizabeth, not to mention the expression on his face when his gaze raked over her torn shirt, did funny things to the pit of her stomach. "Please get off me." The words came out barely above a whisper, and if he heard them, he made no move to comply.

"What were you doing out here all by yourself, Elizabeth? Didn't your colonel tell you it wasn't safe?"

"He isn't my colonel."

"So you said last night."

"It's true." Why she felt compelled to convince this traitor there was nothing between herself and Colonel Littleton, Elizabeth hadn't the slightest idea.

"Even so, someone should have told you."

"Someone did," Elizabeth admitted. "I just didn't listen. Besides, I was told you'd been chased out of the county."

Alexander grinned. "I wasn't. But, I'm not the one you need fear."

"Aren't you?"

Alexander looked down into her face. Last evening she'd appeared the epitome of the type of woman he disliked, with her powdered hair and expensive gown, and yet he'd been intrigued by those silvery gray eyes. She stared up at him now, a wary expression on her face, and his smile broadened. The Tory belle acted as if she expected him to take up where the deserters had left off. Well, he'd never been one to disappoint a lady. "Now that I think about it, maybe you are in some danger."

Alexander let loose her hands, and traced a finger over one of her straight black brows. It was silky smooth, like her hair. He trailed his hand into her thick raven tresses. When he'd seen them before, their color had been hidden. Such a waste. The curls spilled over the forest floor like a shining obsidian puddle. A scarlet ribbon was tangled in an unruly wave, and he reached across and plucked it out.

"Please don't." Elizabeth lay very still, hoping he wouldn't notice the effect his touch had on her. Tiny shivers of excitement sluiced through her, shattering her composure. "I . . . I want to go back."

He'd only meant to tease her about the danger, but by the way his body responded to her softness,

Alexander wasn't certain they both wouldn't be in a lot of trouble if she stayed. "You'd better go home."

Elizabeth endured the moments it took for him to let her up with a strange ambivalence born of relief and reluctance. A part of her longed to wrap her arms around his muscular body and hold him to her. How could she feel that way about a man she'd just met, a traitor?

Her lower lip caught his attention. She'd nervously run the tip of her tongue across it, gilding its rosy fullness with a dewy sheen too inviting to resist. Oh hell, he thought. What harm can one little kiss do?

The touch of his lips on hers made Elizabeth gasp. It reminded her of the first time he'd looked at her. She'd thought then the jolt that shot through her couldn't be matched. Now she knew differently.

He felt it too. Elizabeth knew he did. He jerked away as if he'd been burned. But only for a moment. Then his mouth crushed against hers so suddenly, so intently, she forgot to struggle or protest at all. She just lay there, her hands still above her head, luxuriating in the feel of his bold kiss. The whiskers he'd had no time to shave, during his night of outwitting the Loyalists, chafed her chin, deliciously. His tongue wet the seam of her lips, then prodded and plunged till her resistance gave way and she opened to his invasion.

The passionate groan rumbled deep in his chest, vibrated through her breasts as they pressed against him. It excited her. It scared her. Too much was happening, too fast. She ached, but there was no pain. She couldn't think, yet her mind registered every sweet sensual sound of the marsh, every nuance of movement his body made. Every touch. Every taste.

His lips tore away from hers to blaze kisses along her cheek, her chin. His tongue touched the tiny indentation there, and then he was nuzzling the side of her neck, and lower. Elizabeth's breath came in short raspy gasps that matched the rapid thumping of her heart.

"Oooh . . ." The sound escaped her as the moist heat of Alexander's mouth covered one of her straining nipples. Through the thin linen of her shift, she could feel his tongue tease the hard tip, forcing it to swell even more.

She grabbed his head, and dug her fingers toward his scalp, holding him to her. His hair was thick and slightly coarse, sticky and—

"God . . ."

The rest of his mumbled curse was lost to her as Alexander jerked up and rolled onto the ground. Elizabeth's eyes flew open, then squinted shut against the sun's glare. A timid breeze from the bay flitted across her body, cooling her heated skin.

She sat up and looked at him. Sprawled flat on his back, he had one arm stacked under his head, the other thrown over his face. His shirt was plastered to his chest, and Elizabeth watched as it stretched and expanded with each rapid breath he took.

"What's wrong?" She tried to hide the anguish in her voice, but one second he was atop her, giving her pleasures she'd never imagined, and the next . . .

"Nothing." He didn't sound convincing, and he didn't lift the arm that covered his eyes.

"But something must be . . ." Elizabeth shifted onto her knees, and that's when she noticed her hands. Her fingers were covered with a sticky red substance. His blood. "Oh my!" She crawled toward him. "I've hurt your head again."

Alexander peeked out from under his arm. She looked so distressed, he couldn't keep the grin from spreading across his face. "You can thank your lucky stars you did." If the sudden pain hadn't brought him to his senses she'd probably be stark naked right now, and he'd be buried deep in her hot, moist sheath. The thought made him moan.

Elizabeth heard the sound and leaned closer, shimmering tears turning her eyes an iridescent silver. "I never meant to hurt you."

" 'Tis all right, Elizabeth." Alexander reached over and touched her knee. "Believe me. Other parts of my body pain far more than my head."

Elizabeth followed the path of his gaze, and her face blossomed with embarrassed color. The blatant bulge on the front of his breeches was large, and strained against the tight buckskin. With more difficulty than she cared to admit, Elizabeth tore her eyes away and looked out over the bay. She took a deep, calming breath and rose to her feet. "I must go." Seeing the proof of his passion made her realize how close he'd been to taking her—how close she'd been to letting him. Her father was right. She *didn't* consider the consequences of her actions.

Alexander stood up, slowly, shaking his head to free it from dizziness. "I'll ride along to see you safely back."

"No!" Elizabeth stopped brushing dirt from her riding habit and whirled to face him. Was he insane? What if someone should see him?

A scowl darkened Alexander's countenance. "Have you learned nothing from this experience? Don't glare at me like that," he ordered. "I may not be around the next time you need rescuing. Then where would you be?"

Elizabeth raised her chin. "I've survived eighteen years without your assistance, Major Knox."

"Aren't you forgetting this morning?" Alexander stepped toward her, his expression ominous.

Elizabeth resisted the urge to back up. "Of course not. I shall always be grateful for your assistance, however . . ."

"However what, Miss Elizabeth?"

There was no denying that he was angry, or that she was the cause. Elizabeth wondered briefly if this was one of those times to think before she acted, but she didn't. "It seems to me I was in as much danger of being ravished after your rescue as before."

"Ha!" Alexander's eyes narrowed till naught but slits of blazing blue could be seen. "If I'd had a mind to *ravish* you, you'd have damn well been ravished. Besides, my proper Miss Elizabeth, I don't recall your fighting off my advances." The wench behaved as if she hadn't been a party to their little

61

tussle. She may be inexperienced, but she wasn't unwilling. Why, he'd bet even now, he could . . .

Elizabeth's cheeks flamed. "You sir, are a rogue!"

"No doubt."

His last words were accompanied by a smug smile that infuriated Elizabeth. Her anger was fueled by the fact that he was right. She hadn't resisted him. Moreover, she'd participated and even been disappointed when he'd stopped. But she'd never let him know *that*.

Elizabeth turned abruptly, sending her long unbound hair swirling round her shoulders like an angry black thundercloud, and marched toward her horse. "I'm leaving. And if you know what's good for you, you'll do the same. Colonel Littleton and Captain Suteland are bound to find you if you stay here."

"Careful, you'll have me quaking with fear."

Elizabeth glared over her shoulder in response to his sarcastic tone and her heart gave a lurch. His long legs were spread apart, his hands rested on narrow hips, and a devilish grin played across his sensual lips. To make matters worse, when she averted her eyes, she noticed the spot where his body had pressed hers into the soft soil. The indentation was still there. "Oh, I hope they do catch you! And string you up by your toes! And I shall be only too glad to know I'll never have to see you again, you . . . you rebel!"

His laughter echoed through the oaks and willows as she mounted Hester and raced off toward Landon Hall.

Chapter Four

October, 1777
Philadelphia

"Ouch," Elizabeth dropped the needle onto the quilted petticoat covering her lap, and glared at her finger. A single crimson drop beaded on its tip, marring the pale skin. Impatiently she blotted the blood with her handkerchief. Stabbing the needle into the shirt she'd been mending, she rose and walked toward the window.

"Are you tired of sewing, Elizabeth?" Jonathan Lancaster glanced at his daughter over the top of his book.

"I'm tired of the cannon fire," Elizabeth answered, looking back across the library to where her father sat in a wing chair. For nearly three weeks the rumbling boom of heavy artillery was the first sound Elizabeth heard upon waking, the last sound she heard at night.

"It's only the English firing on Mud Island Battery."

"I know." Elizabeth leaned her forehead against the cold windowpane and sighed. She could feel the glass vibrate as the continued shelling shook the house. "I know," she repeated. "I just wish they'd stop."

Jonathan closed his book. "The worst is over, Elizabeth."

She continued to stare out the window at the cold, dreary, autumn afternoon. She and her father had returned to their home on the corner of Fourth and Locust streets in late September, shortly after General Howe had forced Washington's troops from the city.

It had happened just as Rebecca had told her it would, that evening of the wedding ball. The British fleet had landed at Head of Elk, at the northern end of the Chesapeake Bay, and marched overland to reclaim Philadelphia for England. Of course, their task hadn't been easy. The Americans had impeded Howe's progress at every turn. It hadn't been until after Washington's defeat at Brandywine Creek that the British had been able to enter Philadelphia.

Elizabeth felt her father's hand on her shoulder and looked up. Her mind had been so occupied, she hadn't even noticed that he'd risen and crossed the room to her.

"It has been hard on you, I know." Jonathan brushed aside a stray, midnight black curl that had escaped Elizabeth's ribbon. "You could have stayed at Landon Hall as I suggested. Because my business

64

required that I return to Philadelphia didn't mean you had to accompany me."

"But I wanted to." Elizabeth grabbed her father's hand, squeezing it. "If I weren't here, who would remind you when it was time to eat, or to retire for the night?" She gave her father a mischievous grin. "You'd do nothing but sit in your chair reading or talking politics with your friends."

Jonathan laughed. "You're probably right, daughter. But I'm still sorry you had to leave Maryland. I know how much you've always loved it there."

Elizabeth stared back out the window. "It had changed."

"Aye." Jonathan patted Elizabeth's arm, and then walked toward the warmth of the crackling fire in the hearth. "War has a way of spoiling our most idyllic settings."

"Yes," Elizabeth agreed, but in her heart she knew it wasn't the rebellion that had soured Landon Hall for her. It was Alexander Knox.

In Maryland, she had encountered the arrogant major at every turn. Oh, she hadn't actually seen him since that dreadful morning by the marsh, but she'd been unable to escape his powerful presence. His name had littered the joyous news of Howe's landing. It appeared that Major Knox and his men were everywhere at once. He'd attacked and destroyed a British foraging detail. He'd stolen into a British camp one night and in a single swoop, liberated the horses it had taken the Hessians two weeks to gather.

And Alexander Knox had seemed to have a personal vendetta against the First Maryland Loyalists. Elizabeth bit her lip to suppress a smile as she remembered the expression on Ben Suteland's face when he'd burst into the dining room at Landon Hall, announcing he would "run the bastard through" the next time the rebel raided the Loyalists' ammunition dump. At the time, it had been all Elizabeth could do not to remind her cousin's husband that he'd have to catch the infamous Major Knox first.

Elizabeth cringed. That had been one of the problems with being in Maryland. She had rooted the major. Silently of course, and even reluctantly, but she'd done it all the same. She, Elizabeth Lancaster, daughter of a prominent Loyalist, had wanted Alexander Knox, her enemy, to escape capture. And worse, she had even enjoyed hearing of his exploits against the British.

Elizabeth had tried telling herself her concern for him was only due to his having saved her life, but she knew there was more to it. Her memory of his rescue dimmed in comparison to the vivid mind-picture she had of his sensual blue eyes. She could close her own eyes even now and feel the delicious tremor that had shaken her body when he'd kissed her. And his touch . . . Elizabeth shook her head to dispel the thought, running her palms down the flowered brocade skirt of her gown. This mooning over a rebel who was miles away in Maryland was ridiculous, and she'd do it no more.

"Do you truly think the worst is over?" Elizabeth wrapped her shawl more tightly around her shoulders and faced her father. Maybe if she kept her mind occupied, her thoughts wouldn't so easily stray.

"American casualties ran high at Germantown. The British are still bringing in prisoners and rebel wounded." Jonathan moved the fire screen and added another log to the blaze. "I can't believe Washington will strike again any time soon."

"Yet, the Americans still hold on to the battery, and harass any attempts to open the river to shipping," Elizabeth said, referring to the rebel positions on islands in the Delaware River.

"Oh, I didn't say Washington would hightail it and run. The rebels are a tenacious group. They'll just find someplace close-by to lick their wounds."

A sudden picture of Alexander Knox's cocky grin flashed through her mind. *I wasn't. That was what the arrogant major had replied when she'd told him Colonel Littleton had assured her that Knox had been chased from the county.*

Elizabeth tilted her head, studying her father. "You almost sound as if you admire the traitorous, misguided lot of them."

"Respect your enemy, Elizabeth," Jonathan laughed. "Misguided they may be, but they won't give up easily. They've proved that time and again."

"But they continue to lose," Elizabeth sighed. "The British are even occupying their so-called capital."

"Ah, but Congress still meets. The fledgling country continues to exist."

"Yes, but where? First it was Lancaster, now York. Congress has had little time to do ought but flee."

Jonathan chuckled. "Spoken like a true Loyalist."

Elizabeth sank into the chair by the window, ignoring her father's jest. They both knew Elizabeth's political views were not overly strong. "I just want it to stop," she said. "The shelling." She motioned toward the window, the cannon fire continuing to rattle the panes. "The war. The wagon loads of wounded and dead."

"I know you do, daughter." Jonathan crossed back to her. "I should not have made light of your concern."

Elizabeth smiled up at her father. "No, 'tis I who should be sorry. Lamenting this rebellion will do no good. Besides, we are lucky. Thankfully the Americans didn't imprison you before they left Philadelphia."

"That's most likely because I wasn't here. We should be grateful to Rebecca for planning her wedding when she did." Jonathan leaned around the chair and peered out the window. "Now who can that be?"

Elizabeth followed her father's gaze. She watched as a gentleman in a scarlet tunic dismounted in front of their house. "Why, it appears to be Colonel Littleton. What would he be doing here?"

"I'd heard he'd arrived in Philadelphia." Jonathan moved toward the door. "Perhaps he can give us some news from Germantown."

Elizabeth was certain she had all the information *she* needed about the rebels most recent attempt to cause trouble, but she listened anyway.

"We soundly defeated the rabble," bragged the colonel after he'd been seated and offered refreshment. "I don't expect they'll try attacking a British encampment again." He smiled at Elizabeth over the rim of his teacup.

"Do you think they're ready to give up then? Go home to their families, perhaps?" Elizabeth lowered her lashes, conscious of the colonel's brown-eyed stare. She had found him attractive in Maryland, had even enjoyed flirting with him at Rebecca's wedding, but now his attentions seemed . . . awkward.

"I wish that were true, Mistress Lancaster. But I fear 'tis not." Robert Littleton set his cup on the candle stand beside his chair. "Some of the rebels will probably head for their homes before the weather turns, but I doubt if Washington or the main body of his army wander far from Philadelphia."

"I see." Elizabeth picked up her mending. Colonel Littleton's words came close to echoing her father's.

"But you needn't concern yourself, Mistress Lancaster," the colonel continued. "The coming winter should take a bit of starch out of the rebels. And you shall be quite safe in Philadelphia."

"Then Howe plans to take up winter quarters in our fair city?" Jonathan Lancaster interjected.

"He does." Colonel Littleton's gaze shifted from Elizabeth to her father. "I'm certain that relieves your mind, sir."

"Oh, most assuredly. Nothing would please me more than to have His Majesty's troops enjoy the hospitality of our humble town."

"Excellent. I was certain you'd feel this way. That's why your home was my first choice."

Elizabeth glanced up from her mending, and wondered why the expression in the colonel's eyes didn't change when he smiled. "First choice for what, Colonel?" She had a feeling she wasn't going to like his answer.

"To use as my residence during our occupation of the city." Apparently the colonel noticed Elizabeth's shock, for he continued. "Certainly you've heard that Howe's officers are to be quartered in private homes."

"Of course," Elizabeth began. "I just assumed we'd—"

"We'd be honored to have you stay with us." Jonathan interrupted. "My daughter and I want you to consider this your home for as long as you wish. Isn't that correct, Elizabeth?"

Elizabeth recognized her father's tone. It broached no argument. Not that she planned to give him one, even though she was so inclined. Colonel Littleton had been not so much asking their permission as telling them he planned to stay. The best course of action was to accept it willingly. Still, part of Elizabeth secretly rebelled as she answered. "Yes, Father."

"Good. I shall take up residence by the end of the week. I shall require a chamber for sleeping, and one for my baggage. My servant can probably use that room also, if it is large enough."

"Don't trouble yourself with the details, Colonel," Jonathan said. "Send your man around tomorrow,

70

and we'll see that everything is arranged to your satisfaction."

Elizabeth thought her father a little too accommodating in light of the colonel's overbearing attitude, but she supposed her sire had his reasons. She just didn't like the idea of Colonel Littleton staying with them.

Every day she'd have to look upon him, talk to him, sup and take tea with him. Elizabeth found the prospect unnerving as well as unpleasant. The colonel shifted in his chair, and the firelight reflected off the gold gorget, or ornamental collar, he wore around his neck.

There was no question that Colonel Littleton was impeccably dressed. His white stockings were spotless and fit his calves smoothly. They contrasted with the bright scarlet of his coat. Gold thread and buttons attested to his rank and wealth.

Elizabeth continued her covert inspection of the colonel while he faced her father. Colonel Littleton was giving Jonathan a more detailed account of a battle which Elizabeth assumed to be the attack on Germantown. Why had she ever considered the younger man handsome? Granted, his features were regular, and he had no deformity to detract from his appearance, still . . . Elizabeth's gaze rose to his light brown hair that he wore neatly tied back in a velvet bow, then went back down to his face. What was it about him?

She had it. Colonel Littleton was too neat and tidy. He was almost pretty. A handsome man would look stronger, be taller, bigger. Elizabeth glanced again at the colonel's hair. It was too pale. A handsome man would have dark hair and blue eyes—

Elizabeth sucked in her breath when she realized who she was describing. She stabbed the needle through the bleached linen with a vengeance. Damn the impertinent rebel! Must he constantly invade her thoughts?

"This should interest you, Mistress Lancaster."

The colonel's words, directed at her, brought Elizabeth's attention back to the conversation. She looked at him and smiled. Did he know how *un*interesting she found this discussion? Could he tell what she'd been thinking?

"Do you remember that rebel major who broke into the ball at Landon Hall?"

Remember! She seemed destined never to forget. "Yes, I believe I recall the incident."

Colonel Littleton chuckled, raising a lace-trimmed handkerchief to his mouth. "I must tell you, mistress, that at the time I was shocked by your defiance of the rascal, and more than a little annoyed," he added, conspiratorially leaning toward Elizabeth. "But in retrospect, I find it amusing. Not that I'd recommend you make a habit of arguing with the traitors, but when I think of the expression on that scoundrel's face when you stood up to him." The colonel began laughing again.

Elizabeth had little trouble picturing Major Knox at the ball, but unlike the colonel, she found nothing laughable about the picture her mind's eye conjured up. Granted, Alexander Knox had seemed momentarily stunned by Elizabeth's boldness, but he'd recovered soon enough. And even though she'd been the object of his quick wit, Elizabeth had found she'd enjoyed their sally.

But why had Robert Littleton brought up the major's name? Certainly he planned to do more than reminisce about what he obviously considered to be an amusing episode. Elizabeth could wait no longer to find out. "What about Major Knox?" she asked.

"Oh." The colonel wiped at his emotionless eyes with his handkerchief. "I have news of him which may amuse you, since you obviously took an immediate dislike to the fellow."

Is that what she'd done? Somehow it didn't feel like that. But what was the colonel trying to say? The hair on the back of Elizabeth's neck stood on end, and she could feel her heart racing inside her chest. Against her better judgment, she forced herself to ask. "What did you think I would enjoy knowing?"

"He's dead."

No. Elizabeth bit her lip to prevent the denial that screamed through her head from escaping. It couldn't be. He couldn't be dead. Alexander Knox fought off three men single-handed, he danced in and out of Tory camps, and he fooled the British time and time again. A man like that didn't just die. There must be some mistake. Elizabeth forced herself to listen to the colonel's accounting.

"It happened in September, but I just recently received confirmation of his death. Knox was with Washington when the general tried to hold together the New Hampshire troops near Scanneltown. We were attacking in force, and the whole American line seemed about to crumble." Robert Littleton paused, taking a sip of his now-tepid tea. "From what I'm told the rebel major, in his usual reckless manner, charged right into the foray, taking a musket ball in the leg for his trouble."

In his leg? A ray of hope brightened Elizabeth's heart. Leg wounds were serious, but not always mortal. Apparently her father was of a like mind, for he mentioned it to the colonel.

"Certainly, there are some who survive wounds of that nature," the colonel answered. "I myself have sustained similar injuries, and obviously have lived."

Colonel Littleton smiled at her, and Elizabeth did her best to return the gesture. It wouldn't do to let him know how much the fate of one rebel major mattered to her. Carefully she smoothed out the shirt she'd been mending, hoping no one had noticed how she'd clutched it into a tight wad.

"Well, perhaps Major Knox also survived." Elizabeth tried to appear only casually interested.

"You needn't fear that rebel ever interrupting a ball again, Mistress Lancaster. I've received word through my intelligence system that the major's wound was indeed fatal." Littleton leaned forward to share the remainder of his news. "Apparently Knox was an acquaintance of Washington, through his father I believe, and old George is much saddened by the loss. The general's wife was even seen to shed a tear."

"I see." Black dots floated in front of Elizabeth's eyes, and she blinked to dispel them.

"You don't appear overly pleased by my news, Mistress Lancaster." The colonel steepled his fingers and peered at her over the tips. "I'd expected a tad more enthusiasm. After all, the major not only ruined your cousin's ball, but he was extremely impertinent to you."

"I . . ." Elizabeth tried to answer, but a ringing began in her ears. She had a strange light-headed sensation, and feared she might faint.

"My daughter has been under a tremendous strain."

Her father's voice penetrated the fog filling Elizabeth's brain, and she was thankful that the colonel's attention shifted away from her.

"That encounter with Knox was, as you implied, dreadful, and then our move to Philadelphia." Jonathan shook his head. "I thought the fighting was over, or I would never have allowed Elizabeth to accompany me. She's very fragile, a true gentlewoman."

"I quite understand."

The colonel's gaze shifted back to Elizabeth, and she tried to appear delicate, gentle — anything but devastated.

"Please forgive me, my dear." The colonel took her hand, and Elizabeth wondered if he noticed how cold it was. "I've been too long in the company of soldiers. I'm afraid my manners are deplorable."

"No, really . . ." Elizabeth tried to extricate her hand, but the colonel held tight.

"I should never have come in to your home bringing news of death, no matter how much I suspected your dislike of the rogue."

His thumb traced tiny circles on Elizabeth's palm. She gritted her teeth till her jaw hurt.

"I need to reestablish my ties with the gentler side of life," Littleton continued. "I'm counting on you to help me with that, Mistress Lancaster."

How she got through the remainder of the visit, Elizabeth wasn't certain. Thankfully it was short, and her father and Colonel Littleton did most of the talking. As soon as the colonel left, with the promise to send his servant around on the morrow, Elizabeth headed for the stairs.

"Are you all right, Elizabeth?"

Her father's words stopped her as she stepped onto the bottom riser. Elizabeth clutched the newel. "Yes, I'm fine." She didn't turn around. Probably a mistake, she thought as her father moved along the other side of the banister till he could see her face.

"You look pale."

"It's the shelling, I—"

"The news of that Major Knox's death upset you. Now don't try to deny it. I think I know my own daughter." Jonathan raised his hand when Elizabeth opened her mouth to speak.

She spoke anyway. "I wasn't going to deny anything. Of course, I was momentarily unsettled. Even though I'd only seen the man once, I don't like to hear of anyone's death." Elizabeth had never realized what an accomplished actress she was. Or was she just a good liar? She'd been getting practice since the day at the marsh, for she'd never told anyone, including her father, of her second encounter with

76

the bold rebel.

Elizabeth didn't know if her father was convinced by what she said, but at least he dropped the subject.

"I know you're not pleased about the idea of Colonel Littleton living with us, but at least we're fortunate that we know him."

"I suppose you're right." Elizabeth turned and sank down on the step. The skirt of her gown billowed, and then drifted slowly about her. "Just look what the Evanses have to endure." Elizabeth's friend, Hannah, and her family were housing Hessian officers whose lack of sobriety and late hours sorely vexed the Quaker views of their hosts.

"Exactly." Jonathan leaned against the railing. "Besides, it truly isn't too much to ask of us. After all, the King has sent these men to protect us. The least we can do is offer them shelter."

"You're right," Elizabeth sighed and folded her hands in her lap. "There were simply so many people at Landon Hall, I thought perhaps a little peace and quiet would be nice." An explosion sounded from the direction of the river, and Elizabeth shook her head. "Obviously, a foolish notion."

Jonathan chuckled. "The assembly tomorrow night will make you forget the cannons."

Elizabeth began to stand. Certainly she had chatted with her father long enough to assure him, at least, that she was all right. Now all she wanted to do was go to her room, and examine her feelings in solitude. Then she'd forget all about Major Knox, she told herself. Suddenly she realized what her father had said.

"What assembly?" she asked.

"I had a suspicion you weren't listening. You really should try and curb that tendency of yours to let your mind wander," Jonathan admonished. "Colonel Littleton invited both of us to an assembly planned to honor Howe's defeat of the Americans at Germantown."

A ball. Elizabeth did think she recalled the colonel mentioning something about it, but it hadn't been long after he'd told her about Alexander Knox. She felt foolish tears swell in the back of her throat, and swallowed to dispel them. "I don't really feel much like attending an assembly," Elizabeth began.

"It would probably be prudent if we did, Elizabeth."

Something in her father's tone made Elizabeth sink back down on the step. "Why?"

Jonathan sat down beside his daughter. "We don't want to give the British any reason to doubt our allegiance."

"But that's ridiculous," Elizabeth insisted. "Why would they ever question you? If there has been one man in Philadelphia who has supported the King since the beginning of this rebellion, it's been you."

"I know that."

"And in Maryland you gave the British information that helped them with their landing."

"Now calm yourself, Elizabeth. I didn't say they suspected my fidelity. However, we *are* Americans, and I'm not certain the British trust even the most loyal of us completely."

"I see." Elizabeth rose and smoothed down her

skirt. "So we placate them by attending their parties."

Jonathan stood. "No. We attend their balls, and enjoy ourselves. And," Jonathan touched the tip of his daughter's nose, "we watch our impertinent tongues."

Elizabeth's thick, black lashes fluttered shut. "I'm sorry, Papa." She looked up into his kind face. She could never allow her feelings for a dead Patriot to endanger her father. "Of course we shall attend the ball."

"And enjoy ourselves?"

Elizabeth smiled. "Most certainly. I shall even dance with Colonel Littleton, and assure him of how much I look forward to his stay with us."

"That would be an excellent idea; however, you shall have to wait for another time. Colonel Littleton will not be at the assembly."

Elizabeth looked over her shoulder as she started up the stairs. "Won't *his* loyalty be suspect?" she asked with a saucy tilt of her dimpled chin.

"Lizzie!" Jonathan shook his head, and started to climb the stairs. "The colonel will be in Germantown inspecting the troops."

That piece of information made the prospect of attending the assembly a little more appealing. If only she hadn't heard of Major Knox's death . . . Elizabeth had thought it unlikely she'd ever see him again, but now the certainty of that sent her emotions reeling.

She felt the tears welling again, and turned toward her room. "I think I shall rest until dinner."

79

If only I could, Elizabeth thought an hour later as she sat by the window. She stared out into the garden, past the summerhouse. An early frost had killed the flowers, and the only color came from the flaming red and gold maple leaves. She leaned her forehead against the window, and her breath marbled the glass, obscuring even that.

It did not make sense to mourn someone you had only seen twice, Elizabeth tried to tell herself. Especially during a war. Casualties were as much a part of life as the changing seasons. Then why couldn't she just accept the fact that Alexander Knox was dead?

"I shall," Elizabeth mumbled to herself. She rose and walked to the china basin. The cold water she splashed on her face caused her to catch her breath, but it washed away the salty tearstains on her cheeks.

If there was a scarcity of candles, it couldn't be proven by the glowing windows of David Dreschler's house, Elizabeth thought as she alighted from the carriage the next night. Dreschler's large Georgian home had recently become General Howe's headquarters in Philadelphia.

"Smile, Elizabeth," Jonathan Lancaster said as he guided his daughter up the three steps to the front door.

Before she could respond to his request, the portal was opened by a large black man dressed in spotless green livery. Elizabeth and her father were bathed in a puddle of light from inside. As they walked down the central hall toward the ballroom, Elizabeth could hear the violins' melodic strains, mingled with the sounds of laughter.

It appeared that all loyal Philadelphians had turned out for the affair to welcome the British. Elizabeth recognized many of their friends. There were also many scarlet-clad officers whom she did not know. Her father seemed acquainted with many of them, however, and Elizabeth soon found her mind saturated with names and faces.

"I am very impressed with the hospitality of your fair city."

Elizabeth nodded her head in acknowledgment of her partner's comment. The bewigged Major Chalmers, or was it Chalder — Elizabeth couldn't remember — asked her to dance shortly after her father had introduced them.

The steps of the minuet separated them, so Elizabeth was spared thinking of a witty response. The British officer seemed pleasant enough, however, Elizabeth was relieved when the music stopped and he escorted her back to the large potted plant by the window where she'd been standing.

Jonathan Lancaster was no longer there. Elizabeth assumed he'd abandoned his role as charmer of the various ladies standing nearby to pursue an occupation more interesting to him — discussing politics. She scanned the crowd, and smiled as she spotted him, fellow Loyalist David Dreschler, and several British officers heading out of the ballroom. They would probably spend the remainder of the evening closeted in the library discussing the progress of the war.

Which leaves me to find my own amusement, Elizabeth thought. She almost envied her neighbor Hannah Evans. No one expected her to attend these affairs. Dancing and music were as much against the Society of Friends beliefs as was taking an oath. Of course, that refusal to swear allegiance to the Continental government had prompted the imprisonment of several Quakers, including Hannah's father. When Congress left town, they had taken these prisoners with them.

Elizabeth opened her carved ivory fan, using it to cool herself in the overly warm room. The war had taken a toll on so many. Her thoughts wandered again to the tall, handsome Patriot who'd saved her from the deserters. Elizabeth sighed, and turned toward the gentleman to her right, an aide-de-camp of General Howe. She *would not* think of Alexander Knox.

So great was her resolve to forget the rebel, Elizabeth had a difficult time registering what she saw as her gaze drifted beyond the general's aide at her side. Less than ten feet away, leaning against a doorjamb, stood an elegantly dressed gentleman. He was taller than most, broad-shouldered and lean, and he was staring at her with the same blue eyes she'd thought never to see again.

Chapter Five

Elizabeth froze. Like a startled doe, she could do naught but return Alexander Knox's mesmerizing stare. It was the stare of a hunter who'd found his prey. If there had been any question in her mind as to his identity, Elizabeth might have been able to free her gaze to examine him more thoroughly. But there was no doubt. Her mind had assimilated enough when he'd first snagged her attention to know that very little of his appearance remained the same.

The rough buckskins of their earlier encounter had been replaced by costly, fashionably tailored silk. His midnight black hair was now covered with a white periwig. Even his demeanor was different. He leaned against the entranceway with none of the cocky assurance Elizabeth knew to be so much a part of his nature.

He might change his clothes, disguise his hair, even affect nonchalance, but he could never mask those eyes. They had captivated Elizabeth when she'd first seen them, had haunted her since she'd heard of his death. . . .

Elizabeth felt light-headed when she realized the obvious. He wasn't dead. Somehow Colonel Littleton had been mistaken. Alexander Knox was alive and well, attending a ball in the heart of British-occupied Philadelphia—a ball to honor William Howe.

"Mistress Lancaster, are you quite all right?"

Elizabeth heard the voice of the man at her side, even recognized the desperation in his tone, but she could not free her eyes to look at him until he touched her. The aide's grip on her arm, below the lace flounce of her sleeve, was unrelenting. Reluctantly she gave him her attention.

"What . . . ? Oh, yes. I'm fine." Elizabeth tried to brush off his concern, and his hand.

"But, Mistress Lancaster, your fan."

Elizabeth's gaze dropped to the delicately carved ivory clutched in her hands. It was mangled beyond use. Had she done that?

Of course, she had. And who wouldn't? She'd just discovered a man she thought to be dead was alive, and more, he was lurking where he didn't belong.

Tell someone, Elizabeth's mind screamed to her. She gripped the fan more tightly. *Tell General Howe's aide-de-camp that the infamous Alexander Knox is right under his nose.* She felt the fragile ivory snap between her fingers. Horrified, Elizabeth looked down at her hands. Slowly she began backing away from the man who'd caused her agitation.

"Elizabeth."

The familiar, deep baritone voice stopped her. Alexander Knox spoke her name in the same tone he'd used to coax her from the side of Zeke, the deserter. He had commanded her attention then, as he did now.

Alexander smiled at her flirtatiously. To anyone who might see him, he appeared to be a slightly bored, wealthy gentleman engaged in amorous play. Elizabeth would almost believe it herself if it weren't for his eyes. They were deadly serious.

"How wonderful to see you again." Alexander surprised himself with the ease with which he delivered the lie. She was the last person he'd wanted to encounter at this ball.

Safe in Maryland. That's where he liked to think of her. And to his great annoyance, he did think of her—often. In his imaginings Elizabeth Lancaster rode her horse like the wind, her long black hair streaming behind her; or she faced him, fire in her eyes; or she sighed and writhed beneath him as . . . Realizing his body's reaction to his wayward thoughts, Alex feigned nonchalance.

"I haven't seen you since . . . let me see . . . your cousin's wedding, wasn't it? How is the happy couple?" Alexander focused his attention on Elizabeth, who had yet to speak and looked as if she'd seen a ghost. Yet, he was quite aware of the man by her side. Captain Christopher Bently, General Howe's aide-de-camp was regarding him suspiciously—and the last thing Alexander wanted to do was draw attention to himself. He must get Elizabeth away from the British officer.

Obviously she hadn't said anything to reveal his identity—yet. After all, he was still alive. Alexander had little doubt as to the outcome if this room full of Redcoats should suddenly find out that Major Knox was in their midst. He wasn't even armed.

Alexander took Elizabeth's hand. It was as cold as ice. He resisted the impulse to rub the soft skin between his palms, and warm it. "Do me the honor of dancing with me, Elizabeth. We have so much to discuss." Alexander tugged gently on her hand, and was pleased when she stepped toward him. "You'll excuse us please, Captain."

"Just a moment, sir."

Alexander tried to keep annoyance from marring his expression as he turned back to Howe's aide. Why did Elizabeth always have to surround herself with British officers? "Yes?"

"I'm not certain the lady wishes to accompany you."

Alexander smiled. There was nothing to do but brazen this out. "Well, why don't you ask the lady?" His grip on Elizabeth's hand tightened.

"Mistress Lancaster, do you know this man?"

Elizabeth looked at the captain. He stood with his feet spread, his hand resting on the hilt of his sword. He seemed almost ready to do battle. All she'd have to do was tell him, and the British would no longer need to worry about the infamous Major Knox. "Yes, I know him." Her voice seemed to come from far away.

"And you wish to dance with him?"

Elizabeth quickly studied Alexander. She could sense his anxiety. They both knew what she could do with just one word. But could she say that word, sentence him to the very death she had feared he'd already embraced? "Of course I wish to dance with him, Captain. He's an old friend of the family—the Maryland branch." Elizabeth was surprised at the calmness of her voice. Her heart beat like a drum inside her chest.

"Well spoken, Elizabeth," Alexander said once they were out of earshot. "Now if you'd stop looking as if you intend to swoon, your captain might be convinced. He's still watching us."

Memory of the last time this rebel referred to someone as "hers" flooded Elizabeth's senses, stiffening her spine. Did the foolish man think she laid claim to everyone who happened to stand beside her? She felt angry color rise to her cheeks, and she stopped, halting their progress toward the dancers. "I doubt my reaction is unusual for someone who has just encountered a ghost."

"A ghost!" Alexander's bark of laughter was spontaneous. "I'm hardly that."

He squeezed her hand, and Elizabeth—to her dismay—found herself returning the pressure. She jerked away and joined the lively country dance. Amused, Alexander took his place by her side.

"Why did you refer to me as an apparition?" He leaned close to Elizabeth. His breath fanned fine, white powder from her curls into the air.

"I was told you were dead," Elizabeth stated, not

87

looking up at him. She could feel his nearness through her entire body.

"Oh, really. By whom?"

Up and down the dance line couples separated. Elizabeth hoped Alexander would forget his question by the time the music brought them together again. She was reluctant to tell him who had given her the news.

"Who told you I was dead, Elizabeth?" Alexander repeated his query as soon as he returned to her side.

Elizabeth hesitated, and then answered quickly, "Colonel Littleton."

The faintest of smiles touched Alexander's sensual mouth. His dimple teased his left cheek. "So, you and your colonel are still acquainted."

Elizabeth didn't care for Alexander's expression, or the suggestive way he'd said that. *And* he'd called Colonel Littleton hers again. She wished she could slap that smug look from his handsome face. Instead she stamped on his foot with the heel of her leather shoe. Hard. He barely missed a step. The broadening of his smile was his only reaction.

"Now, Elizabeth, there is no need for violence. I simply—"

"I've seen Colonel Littleton once since we left Maryland!" Why she felt compelled to explain this to the traitor, Elizabeth did not know. "The only reason he stopped by the other day was to announce that he'd be quartering with us."

"How convenient—for both of you."

Elizabeth gasped. She turned on her heel, leaving

the dance floor in a swirl of blue silk. Let people wonder about her behavior. She didn't care. Maybe one of the myriad British soldiers in the room would take a closer look at the partner she was abandoning and recognize him. Then she wouldn't have to endure his innuendos.

Before she had walked three steps Elizabeth felt Alexander's hand clamp on to her elbow.

"It *is* warm in here. Take some air with me in the garden."

"I will not." Elizabeth tried to pull her arm free, to no avail.

"All right. I apologize. My remark was uncalled for. It is certainly none of my concern if Colonel Littleton dwells at your home." Or even in your bed, Alexander tried to tell himself, though that thought made him inexplicably angry.

Somehow he managed to maneuver her into the deserted hallway. Apparently their hasty departure had gone undetected. At least no one seemed to be rushing to her rescue. If indeed she needed rescuing. At this point Elizabeth wasn't certain.

"I promise not to kidnap you."

Could he read her mind? Elizabeth hoped not, for at this moment, looking into his fathomless blue eyes, she wondered if having him whisk her away would be so terrible.

"I won't even hold a knife to your throat," he teased. With one tanned finger he traced the gentle curve of the collarbone just above the bodice of her dress. He'd thought about this neck often. It was long and graceful, and the memory of how soft and sweet smelling it was, had helped him through many an uncomfortable night.

He must have replayed that morning with her beside the marsh a hundred times in his head as he'd lain wounded. He could remember exactly how she'd tasted right there . . . Alexander touched the pulse point on her neck, and watched it flutter. Reluctantly he pulled his hand away. This was no time to indulge in a flirtation with a Tory. But he *would* like to know what Colonel Littleton told her about his supposed death.

"Come outside with me, Elizabeth. I won't hurt you, and we'll only stay a moment."

Oh, I am so foolish, Elizabeth silently chided herself as she followed him down the hall. Who but she would leave the protection of a room full of soldiers to enter the unknown with the enemy?

Elizabeth lifted her skirts and stepped through the doorway. After the heat of the crowded ballroom, the night air felt good. Yesterday's dreary weather had broken, and tonight's sky glittered with hundreds of low-hanging stars.

"Are you cold?"

Alexander's voice came to her from out of the darkness. Peering ahead, aided by the sliver of silvery moon, Elizabeth made out his large form. She followed the brick path until she reached the garden bench where he stood. "No. The temperature is actually quite mild."

Elizabeth thought he nodded, but it was impossible to tell in the dim light. She should go back. Loyalist ladies did not stand in a dark garden discussing the weather with rebels. She should tell him she couldn't stay, walk back to the house. Elizabeth sank slowly onto the bench.

Alexander sat beside her, realizing immediately his mistake. The bench was small. By necessity his leg brushed against hers. Through all the layers of petticoats and ruffles, he felt that contact like a bolt of lightning.

It affected her, too. He could tell by the way she studiously ignored him, looking instead at something in her lap. Alexander forced his gaze away from the intriguing shadows her long lashes cast upon her cheek.

"What is this?" He lifted the mangled ivory from her hand.

"My fan." Elizabeth kept her eyes lowered.

Alexander pried open the carved blades. Most of them were broken. "Were you wont to use this as a weapon?"

"No." Elizabeth glanced up in spite of herself. The sight of him dangling the broken fan from his strong fingers was humorous, and she almost laughed. "I twisted it when I first saw you in the house. Accidentally," she added.

"I see. You no doubt wished it had been my neck in your hands instead of a fan."

"Oh, no." Elizabeth did laugh this time. "I didn't even realize what I was doing until it cracked."

Alexander stuck the broken fan in his frock-coat pocket. "Since I'm responsible for the destruction of such an innocent article, I shall replace it."

"That isn't necessary. I have others."

"I'm certain you do. However this one must be special, or you wouldn't have chosen to carry it to General Howe's ball."

Elizabeth decided against explaining that she had grabbed it only as an afterthought this evening. It would certainly be unwise to reveal that her mind had been on the man by her side the entire time she'd been dressing for the ball. "I should be going back inside." *I should never have come out in the first place.*

"Of course." Why in the hell had he brought her out here? He'd never been an advocate of self-torture, but that was what he was about right now. Sitting this close to her, he could smell the sweet lavender scent of her body, and when she looked up at him her gray eyes shone silver in the moonlight. He could remember the way she felt lying beneath him. . . . Alexander forced his mind back to the problem at hand.

He should be inside, too, gathering information. Also, later this evening he would meet his new contact. Even though he didn't know this person's identity, the chances were good it wasn't Mistress Elizabeth Lancaster.

Alexander began to stand, then remembered why he'd wanted to talk to her—at least the reason he'd given himself. "When Colonel Littleton reported my death to you, did he give any details?"

"Oh, yes. He was well pleased about your demise."

Alexander chuckled and leaned back against the bench's wooden slats. "I imagined he would be."

"Imagined?" Elizabeth twisted around in her seat and stared at him. "You planned for Colonel Littleton to think you were dead?"

He shrugged. "Let's just say I hoped he'd hear the sorrowful tale sooner or later."

"But why?"

"Now that, my dear Elizabeth, I cannot tell you." Alexander grinned, resting his arm on the back of the bench. From there it seemed only natural to reach out and touch her cheek.

Elizabeth tried to ignore the warmth spreading through her. "He said you were wounded . . . in the leg."

"So I was."

Elizabeth's eyes drifted to his silk-covered thigh — the one pressed against her skirt. The fine material did little to disguise the firm muscles there. "You took a musket ball, as he said?" She did a poor job of keeping the anxiety from her voice.

" 'Twas only a flesh wound." He shrugged again. "I was lucky that it hit no bone."

Elizabeth resisted the urge to reach out and examine the leg for herself, just to make certain it was truly healed. But even if it was, the thought of him wounded, in pain, tightened her stomach. She recalled the words Colonel Littleton had used to describe Alexander's actions the day he was wounded — "in his usual reckless way."

"You should strive to be more careful," she said, and almost immediately wished she hadn't. It sounded too much as if she cared what happened to him.

"This is war, Elizabeth. People are wounded; many of them die."

"I'm aware of that." She had seen the wagonloads of wounded, both British and rebel, brought into Philadelphia. Many of them had died on the steps of the State House before a surgeon could see them. Elizabeth closed her eyes in an attempt to block out the thought of that fate befalling Alexander.

"Colonel Littleton made it sound so real." Elizabeth realized her voice was little more than a whisper, and that Alexander had leaned closer to her so he could hear. She turned her face to the side. His breath wafted across her cheek as he spoke.

"My death?"

Elizabeth nodded. "I didn't believe him at first." She smiled. "You seem rather indestructible. But then he said that General Washington mourned you." Elizabeth looked back at Alexander. He was so close that even in the dim light she could make out his features, feel the heat of his skin. She swallowed. "Mrs. Washington was supposedly upset."

"What of you, Elizabeth? Did you mourn my passing?"

"Naturally, I was saddened — slightly," she quickly added, wondering if he knew what a lie that was. "You did save me from those awful men at the marsh, and —"

"Is that why you didn't tell anyone inside who I was — because I'd rescued you?" Alexander could tell by her expression and the quiver in her voice that she'd been deeply troubled when she'd thought him dead. When he'd devised this scheme to rid himself of Major Alexander Knox's name and reputation, it had never occurred to him that Elizabeth would find out — or care.

Elizabeth bit her bottom lip and turned away from his intense scrutiny. She wanted to move away from him, but the wooden bench arm stopped her. To stand seemed a coward's retreat. But she did not want him to know how often she'd thought of him since that day, or how she cried, alone in her room, when she thought him dead. There was a strong possibility he'd chide her for her foolishness. Not that she hadn't accused herself of the same thing often enough, but she didn't think she could bear to hear him say it.

She lifted her chin, and turned back, staring him in the eye. "I was too stunned when I saw you to—"

"Elizabeth," his low, silky voice interrupted. "Granted you were shocked to see me. Your face was nearly as white as the ghost you thought me to be; however, you had plenty of time to recover from your surprise before we left the ballroom."

Of course she had, and they both knew it. "I could still tell someone." Oh, how stupid could she be? As soon as the words escaped, she wanted them back. Threatening to reveal him could be dangerous, especially after he'd gone to the trouble of convincing people he was dead.

She wasn't a small woman, but his size made her feel she was. With very little effort he could make certain she never revealed his secret. Elizabeth was sure he'd killed before. As he'd said, this was war.

She couldn't imagine him hurting a woman, but if he considered his own life at stake . . . She really knew very little about him.

Elizabeth searched his face, certain she'd see hostility stamped on his handsome features. Instead, mirth was reflected in his eyes.

"Don't worry, Elizabeth. I'm not going to harm you." The finger that had earlier caressed her cheek now played with the garnet earring dangling from her ear. "I shan't even threaten you, though you seem inclined to worry me." Alexander touched the spot on her jaw where the tiny red stone sent sparkling reflections from the stars. "I don't think you'll tell anyone that you saw me."

"Why?" Elizabeth could barely speak. His nearness sent her heart racing. The hand on her neck had the magical effect of warming not only the spot it touched, but her entire body. She sucked in her breath as he leaned closer.

"Because, Elizabeth, you remember the marsh as well as I do."

Elizabeth's breath escaped on a puff of air as his lips brushed hers. The kiss was brief, fleeting, but the festive sounds from inside the house ceased, and Elizabeth could swear she heard the breeze rattling through cat-o-nine-tails. She closed her eyes, and the peaty smell of land washed by brackish tidewater permeated her senses. It was as if they'd never stopped touching.

Alexander pulled back, moved as much by this kiss as he had been when he'd first seen her standing by Littleton. The thought reminded him that though he didn't consider her a threat, she was still a Tory. "We better go inside."

"Oh, yes," Elizabeth agreed, but she didn't move. She couldn't. His intense eyes held her hostage.

Alexander didn't plan to kiss Elizabeth again. What needed to be done was clear in his mind. He must take her back to the ball, and be ready to meet his contact when the time came. He knew that. Then why was the space between them slowly disappearing?

Elizabeth knew he was going to kiss her again — knew she should stop him. But when his warm mouth pressed against hers she could only give a small sigh of welcome. Hands that had been content to stay folded in her lap now found their way around Alexander's neck. She wished he weren't wearing that silly wig. His own hair was so thick and rich, and she longed to weave her fingers through it.

By the swamp, she'd needed tutoring in the ways of a kiss, but no more. She had learned the lesson well. No sooner did Alexander nip gently at her bottom lip, than she opened her mouth for him. His tongue plunged inside, caressing the honeyed interior.

Alexander slid his hands around her slim, silk-clad body. He could feel the whalebone corset beneath her gown. With a finger, he followed the stays around to the front of her dress. Her breast fit his palm perfectly. He squeezed it gently, then, as he felt the nipple tighten, more firmly. But it was too easy to remember the feel of it in his mouth. He

97

cradled Elizabeth's head with his free hand as his lips left hers to travel down her neck and lower.

"Ooh." Elizabeth couldn't suppress the moan of delight that welled up from deep inside her. His tongue wet the rounded flesh of her breasts above her gown, and teased the crevice between them. She grasped his shoulders, and arched her body toward him in what she could only imagine was wanton abandon. Her skin was hot — as hot as that summer day by the marsh. Elizabeth had the insane desire to strip the bodice of her gown away. When he nudged away her shift's ruffle with the tingling roughness of his chin, she knew he had the same thought.

"Alexander," she whispered through the sensual fog that surrounded her. But did she call his name to beg him cease or to urge him further? Elizabeth wasn't sure.

The sound of his name vibrated through Alexander as he rested his cheek against Elizabeth's soft breast. It was a wild, sweet siren's call — it was the voice of reason.

What in the hell did he think he was doing? This was no tavern wench or loose woman who traded favors for a bit of coin. Elizabeth Lancaster's father was one of the most influential Tories in the colony. It was a piece of bad luck that he'd run into her here — very bad luck. Alexander didn't think she would betray him — he had saved, if not her life, at least her virtue last summer. But taking that same innocence for himself was certainly no way to insure her silence. Who knew what she would do if he gave in to the rash impulses that drove him when he was near her?

Slowly, he raised his head. But he couldn't resist pressing his lips against the dimple in her chin, the corner of her mouth, before he pulled away. With the hand that had, moments ago, been trying to find its way beneath her skirt, he smoothed out the polonaise flounce.

"Please accept my apologies, Mistress Lancaster. I have no excuse for my actions, however you may rest assured they shall never be repeated."

Never? Elizabeth wondered why the night had suddenly grown so cold. When she'd been in Alexander's arms, when he'd been touching her, she'd felt warm and safe. Now the air seemed to hold a bite that sent shivers down her spine.

He watched her warily from eyes that seemed distant. Eyes she barely recognized. It occurred to Elizabeth that he awaited her response. But what could she say to him? It must have been perfectly obvious that he hadn't forced himself upon her. If the truth be known, she had wanted him as much, maybe more, than he had wanted her. After all, she hadn't been the one who pulled away.

Elizabeth tried to search his face once more in the grainy darkness before she lowered her lashes and stared at her folded hands. There must be something about her that had made him withdraw so suddenly. She hadn't responded correctly, or maybe . . . maybe he'd recalled, in that instant when he'd pushed her away, that she didn't possess the type of beauty he favored.

Hurt pride raised her chin, and Elizabeth looked

back at him. This time, however her gray eyes flashed with indignant silvery sparks. "No apologies are required, Major Knox. This entire unfortunate incident can be forgotten as soon as you take your leave."

Alexander couldn't stop the grin from spreading across his face. She was ordering him to leave, just as she had the first time he'd seen her. What a haughty little act she could fake. He considered giving in to his own desires and gathering her in his arms again. How long, he wondered, would it take those beautiful eyes to lose their fiery flare and become dark with desire once more.

He was laughing at her! Oh, she felt like such a fool. Not only had she mooned around and mourned the death of this insolent rebel, but every time she saw him she practically threw herself in his arms. She raised her chin a notch higher. "If you don't leave, I shall be forced to tell General Howe of your presence." Elizabeth didn't mention that she'd yet to meet the general. She hoped his name would add some credence to her threat. She should have known better.

Alexander's smile just broadened, and he shook his head at her threat. "Elizabeth, Elizabeth," he chided gently.

"Elizabeth!"

The added threat Elizabeth was about to hurl at Alexander froze on her lips when she heard her name being called from the direction of the house. She grabbed Alexander's sleeve. "That's my father. You simply must leave or he'll—"

"I'm not going anywhere."

"But, he'll recognize you," Elizabeth said in a frantic whisper. "And he'll turn you in. I know he will. He doesn't know what you did for me by the marsh . . . and I'm not certain it would even matter if it meant capturing you." Did he realize she was urging him to escape the fate with which she'd just threatened him?

Clasping the hand that gripped his sleeve, Alexander pulled her to her feet. "Don't worry, Elizabeth. It will be all right." He led her along the brick path toward the house.

"But —"

"Your father didn't get near as good a look at me at Landon Hall as you did," Alexander explained. "And we both know he wasn't at the marsh."

Elizabeth could have sworn Alexander turned and winked at her, but she couldn't believe even *he* would be so cavalier in a situation such as this.

Elizabeth's father had called once more, but he hadn't started down into the boxwood garden. He stood near the house watching Alexander and Elizabeth approach him.

Alexander wished he were as certain that Jonathan Lancaster wouldn't recognize him as he'd pretended. His present assignment depended on his being able to pass as a loyal Englishman recently returned from the mother country. Obviously his disguise hadn't worked with Elizabeth. Now he must see if it would work at all.

"You had me worried, daughter." These words spoken by Elizabeth's father greeted Alexander and his reluctant companion when they reached the door. Jonathan Lancaster turned and entered the house, apparently not willing to spend any more time than necessary in the night air.

Alexander would have preferred holding this little interview shrouded by darkness, but he followed Jonathan and Elizabeth into the house. The back hall was still deserted. Brass wall sconces afforded the light Alexander had hoped to avoid.

Elizabeth could not believe the three of them were standing, staring at each other. She had to say something to distract her father's attention from Alexander. On an inspiration, she remembered all the times her cousin Rebecca had feigned illness — and with satisfactory results. "I thought I was going to swoon," Elizabeth blurted out. She had the satisfaction of seeing Alexander's gaze shift to her, as well as her father's.

"What did you say?" her father asked.

Elizabeth twisted her hands. "In the ballroom. I felt ill, and . . ." She hesitated. Of course Alexander wouldn't be using his real name, but she had no idea what to call him. ". . . This gentleman escorted me outside for some air."

"I'm in your debt, sir." Her father appeared to study Alexander with a great deal of interest. "Perhaps you will have a glass of Madeira with me later, Mr. . . . ?"

"Weston, Alexander Weston, at your service, sir," Alexander supplied. "I would enjoy that very much."

"I still don't feel very well. Maybe we should go

home." Elizabeth could not understand why Alexander agreed to see her father. Did he *want* to be caught?

"Come, daughter. A cup of punch will probably revive you," Jonathan said as he took her elbow, leading her toward the ballroom. "The evening is still young, and we don't wish to miss any of it."

Pretending to be sick hadn't worked out well at all, Elizabeth thought sometime later. The funny thing was that she really *didn't* feel very well. Her stomach seemed tied in a thousand knots that tightened every time she spied Alexander.

Much to her unease, he stayed at the ball. She noticed him dancing a reel with a lady whose hair and headdress must have been two feet tall. When Alexander's eyes met hers, he gave Elizabeth a quick smile, but she looked away.

He was so foolish not to heed her advice about leaving — and her father . . . Alexander simply couldn't meet with him. Elizabeth decided she had to speak with Alexander again to convince him that she knew best. But she could never devise a way to accomplish this. Her father, breaking a long standing tradition, remained by her side until late in the evening. When he did finally excuse himself, Elizabeth searched the room, but could find no trace of Alexander.

She settled into a chair in an alcove, and sighed. At least Alexander was gone.

Alexander grimaced as the door that led into the

small study creaked open. Stealthily, he crept into the room. At first he thought it empty. Perhaps he was early for this meeting, or his contact was late. Then he noticed a movement by the desk in the far corner, away from the flickering glow of the dying embers in the fireplace. Instinctively, Alexander reached for his sword, not remembering until his hand grasped silk that he was unarmed.

"Man is born free," said the voice from the shadows, and Alexander relaxed his stance.

"But everywhere is enslaved," he answered, completing the quotation from Rousseau that was to be the method for recognizing his fellow spy.

"I wasn't certain you'd be able to make this meeting tonight, Major Knox."

"I said I would come." The contact's voice sounded vaguely familiar. Alexander peered into the darkness. Although his eyes had adjusted to the lack of light in the room, he could make out no more than the silhouette of a man. Friend or foe, Alexander's military training preached caution. It was not prudent to be seen without having the same advantage. "Come out of the shadows, fellow Patriot, that I may know to whom I speak."

"As you wish, Major."

Alexander wondered if the shock showed on his face as the man stepped into the dim light. He'd never imagined this man would be his contact. Alexander recovered quickly. "Have you any information for me?"

"Very little. Troop and weapons numbers are written here." He handed Alexander a folded piece of paper. "Not much has happened since Germantown. There are rumors of a new British offensive, but as yet, they are unconfirmed."

"You will inform me if you hear more of this?" Alex quickly slipped the paper into a small tear in the lining of his waistcoat.

The man shrugged. "Of course. How shall I get in touch with you?"

"For the most part, I'll be contacting you every few days. Affairs such as these should offer us a good opportunity to meet. If you have urgent information that cannot wait until we meet, you may drop it by my temporary residence at number 220 South Eighth Street. You'll find a man there named Samuel Brown who can get word to me."

"That sounds fine. I should have more for you next time. A high-ranking British officer is billeting in my home, and General Howe appears eager to include Loyalists in his plans for the city."

"Good. I shall see that these figures reach the proper people." Alexander patted his coat where he'd secreted the paper. "If there is nothing else." He turned toward the door.

"There is one more thing, Major Knox."

"And that is."

"My request that you stay away from Elizabeth. My daughter knows nothing of my true allegiance, and I do not want her involved in any of this."

Chapter Six

"I'm not certain about this."

"Thee will do fine, Elizabeth."

Elizabeth gripped her basket of lint and bandages more tightly as she walked along Chestnut Street toward the State House. She glanced over at her friend and neighbor Hannah Evans. "My knowledge of treating wounds is very limited." Her mind started to wander to the time she had tried to help Alexander Knox with his cut head, but she pulled her thoughts back to the present.

"So thee has said, Elizabeth. Several times."

Elizabeth grimaced, knowing she deserved Hannah's mild rebuke. "Well, I just thought you should know."

"I doubt thee shall be called upon to perform surgery; however, if thee wishes to turn toward home I shall understand."

"No," Elizabeth stated with more conviction than she felt. "I want to help . . . with more than just supplies."

"The food thee has sent to the hospitals has been sorely needed by the wounded."

Elizabeth lifted her skirts, stepping around a patch of ice on the sidewalk. "Yes, but as you said, I could do more."

"Thee said that, Elizabeth, not I," Hannah reminded her companion.

"You didn't disagree," Elizabeth said stubbornly.

Elizabeth and Hannah stopped. They had reached their destination. The large brick building in which the Declaration of Independence had been signed now housed wounded American prisoners from the Battle of Germantown.

"There is much suffering inside these walls, Elizabeth."

"I know." The wind whistled around the corner of the building, and Elizabeth gathered her cloak more securely with her free hand. She had thought about coming to the hospital before, but her father had been against her becoming involved. He and several of his Loyalist friends had left yesterday on a packet bound for British-held New York. When he returned, Elizabeth told herself, she would simply tell him she planned to continue her visits. In the meantime, she had to prove to herself that she could do this.

With a determined step, Elizabeth walked up the front stairs and opened the double, paneled doors. The stench hit her immediately. Her hand flew to cover her nose, and she peered over the top of her glove at Hannah, who seemed to be taking the odor in stride.

"Part of the suffering, Elizabeth," she explained. "The British do not have enough doctors to care for their own wounded. They have little to spare for the enemy."

Elizabeth entered the lofty hall. Even here, men lay on makeshift pallets of straw on the cold brick floor. Some enjoyed the luxury of a blanket; some did not.

Shivering beneath her wool dress and cloak, Elizabeth stared in amazement at the scene before her. These were her countrymen. Perhaps their beliefs were different from hers, but they fought for the same cause as Alexander. He had been wounded near Brandywine Creek. Had he lain, as did these men, on a crude bed of straw, waiting for some relief from his suffering?

Slowly Elizabeth moved toward the soldier nearest her. He didn't appear to be much older than she, though with his pallor and several days' growth of beard, it was difficult to tell. A crude, blood-soaked bandage covered a stump that had once been his leg. Elizabeth forced herself not to look away as she dropped to her knees beside the man. Tentatively she reached out and touched his cheek.

"He's so cold." Panic uncoiled inside Elizabeth as her hand skimmed over the prickly whiskers to his mouth. It was still. No air escaped it or his nose. "Hannah!" Elizabeth knew her attempt to keep her voice calm failed miserably. "I think—" Elizabeth stopped when she felt her friend's hand on her arm.

"Come away, Elizabeth. There is naught thee can

108

do for him."

"But . . . Tears ran unchecked down Elizabeth's cheeks, and she brushed a lock of brownish blond hair off the forehead of the dead young man.

"Elizabeth!" Hannah's grip tightened. "Thee has come to relieve the misery of the living. This man suffers no more."

Elizabeth's breath caught on a sob. Hannah was right. The hospital was no place for a hysterical woman, and Elizabeth felt very close to becoming one. But she wouldn't. Rubbing her sleeve across her eyes, she stood. "I'm sorry. I don't seem to be doing a very good job." She glanced down at the nameless, dead soldier.

"It is hard at first." Hannah squeezed Elizabeth's arm. "I cannot even tell thee it will get easier, and I'm not certain thee would want it to. We simply do what must be done."

Swallowing past the lump in her throat, Elizabeth nodded.

"Is thee all right?"

"Yes." Elizabeth's gaze fell again to the man at her feet. She couldn't help wondering if he had a wife or sweetheart to mourn his passing. And his mother. Certainly the woman who had once held this man-child to her breast must grieve for the loss of his young life. But then, the unfortunate woman probably didn't even know. She might not realize her son was dead until he failed to return to his family. "Shouldn't we do something?" Elizabeth whispered.

"People come through, gathering the dead. He shall be cared for."

Elizabeth had heard of the shallow trenches where the bodies were dumped, and supposed that fate awaited this man. It seemed so unfair. "Perhaps we should cover him." It was such a small thing, but Elizabeth wished to protect his mutilated body from the gaze of others.

"The blankets are needed to shelter the living from the cold, Elizabeth. This man need not fear the elements any longer."

"You are right, of course." Elizabeth offered a silent prayer for his soul, and turned away. There really was no more she could do for him.

"I need to take some of these supplies to Friend Sarah Drinker in the back of the building," Hannah said. "Does thee wish to come with me?"

Elizabeth hesitated. It would be so much easier to handle foodstuff and linens. Maybe that was all she *could* do. She took a deep breath. "I shall stay here."

"Is thee certain?"

"Yes."

There were occasions during the following hours when Elizabeth wished she had gone to the kitchens to prepare food, or had even stayed at home. By the time she and Hannah left for the Evanses' home, where Elizabeth was staying while her father was away, both women were bone tired.

"Thee can rest on the morrow," Hannah said as they climbed the back stairs to the bedroom they shared. Two Hessian soldiers had taken over the front rooms.

"Why? Aren't we returning to the hospital?" Elizabeth dropped her cape across a chair, and began unfastening her gown, too weary to summon a servant to help.

"I must attend meeting in the morning, and then I have promised to visit the Widow Mason. Thee may accompany me if thee wishes."

Elizabeth cringed. The Widow Mason's voice rambled nonstop from the time you arrived at her home till you could manage a retreat. On her last visit to the elderly lady it had been all Elizabeth could do not to jump up and scream. "I doubt the Widow Mason wants to see me."

"Now, Elizabeth, I am certain she has forgiven thee thy abrupt departure last time." Hannah laughed.

"Perhaps." Elizabeth's words were muffled as she pulled the soiled dress over her head. "However, I don't think she possesses enough Christian charity to overlook the way I fear I would behave *this* time. Besides, I had planned to work at the hospital tomorrow."

"Thee doesn't need to go every day."

"I know." Elizabeth flopped down on top of the quilted coverlet and shut her eyes. "But I think I should."

All day, as Elizabeth had moved among the men, she had felt more and more as if she were actually offering them some relief from their suffering. At first, she'd done no more than press a cup to thirsty lips or cover a shivering body. As time passed

111

though, she had discovered she could change a bandage, and even pack a wound with lint.

The sight of blood still bothered her. And she had to fight to keep at bay the vision of her mother, weak and ghostly white, propped on pillows. "There's nothing that can be done," the midwife had told the five-year-old Elizabeth. "She wants to say good-bye to you." Elizabeth had tried to be brave as the midwife bid her, but as she stood beside the bed, a crimson stain began to seep through the sheet that covered her mother, and it kept creeping closer. . . .

"Elizabeth."

Elizabeth's eyes opened. She blinked, and smiled in relief to see Hannah staring down at her.

"Thee had drifted off to sleep, and it is time for supper."

The Hessian officers joined the family for dinner. Elizabeth found their accents difficult to understand, though they both spoke English. They left the house immediately after the meal.

"Let us hope they return before dawn," said Friend Evans, Hannah's mother. "It would be a blessing if they were also sober."

Elizabeth knew the Hessians caused the Evans family many problems. It hardly seemed fair that Friend Evans was forced to quarter soldiers at all. Her husband had been imprisoned by Congress for refusing to sign an oath denouncing the King and swearing allegiance to the new government. He was now being held in Carlisle because he had upheld the conscientious conviction of his religion against the taking of oaths.

112

Hannah's mother had received a letter from him that day, delivered by a member of the Society of Friends, who had arrived in Philadelphia from the south. Friend Evans read it to her family and Elizabeth as they gathered around the small stove in the parlor.

So much suffering, Elizabeth thought to herself as she snuggled beneath the quilt later that night. John Evans taken from the bosom of his family, the poor men at the State House, and for what? She rubbed her forehead. If she understood why the rebels fought, maybe the whole thing would make more sense to her.

"I could ask Alexander," she whispered to herself, almost biting her tongue in disbelief. She glanced over at Hannah's still form. Apparently her friend was asleep. At least she hadn't heard, but how could Elizabeth even think such a thing? She never intended to see Major Knox again. While she stayed with the Evanses she need not attend any assemblies or concerts where he might appear. And by the time her father returned to Philadelphia, Elizabeth hoped the brash rebel would be long gone.

It still worried her that she hadn't told anyone of his presence at the ball last week. Elizabeth had gone to her father's study before he'd departed to tell him, but at the last minute, a vision of Alexander, his hands tied behind his back, a noose around his neck, invaded her mind. Instead she hugged her father, bid him a safe trip, then ran to her room, full of guilt for harboring a spy, yet unable to do anything about it.

113

Elizabeth wriggled onto her side, yanking her long, black braid from beneath her. If she planned to accomplish anything at the hospital tomorrow, she needed sleep. This thinking of Alexander Knox had to stop. But even in sleep he haunted her, and when Elizabeth woke the next morning it was with the memory of his kiss fresh in her mind.

She dressed quickly, and hurried to her own home. Colonel Littleton spent a great deal of time in Germantown, and Elizabeth was relieved to find he hadn't been at her house for several days.

Summoning Jane and Polly, two of the Lancasters' indentured servants, to follow her, Elizabeth marched into the larder.

"Where you taking all this food?" Polly asked, stuffing a ham into a basket.

"To the hospital." Elizabeth reached for a burlap bag full of coffee beans. She doubted any of the American wounded would drink English tea, though she considered it the superior drink.

"But, if you take all our food, we'll starve."

Elizabeth brushed the hair out of her face, sparing her buxom servant a stern glance. She bit back a retort suggesting that hardly seemed likely. "I shall save plenty for us." Elizabeth heaved a bag of flour onto her pile. "Jane, go upstairs and gather all the blankets we can spare. And Polly, go tell Daniel to ready the push cart, and that I shall require his assistance."

An hour later, Elizabeth arrived at the hospital. Today there was no hesitancy as she entered. She checked on several of the men she'd seen the previous day before climbing the staircase. At the landing Elizabeth looked out the Palladian window at the city before continuing to the main hall of the second floor. Here, as below, the floor was strewn with the wounded and dying.

"Lady."

Elizabeth had just risen to stretch her aching back when she heard the childlike voice. Though she didn't know the time, the lengthening shadows, and the gnawing hunger in the pit of her stomach convinced her it had grown late. She glanced around to see who had called her.

"I need a drink, lady."

Elizabeth followed the sound to a bundle of rags on the floor. On them lay a youth, a child actually. Elizabeth estimated he couldn't be much older than twelve. His urchin's face was covered with freckles and dirt, and was topped with an unruly shock of carrot-colored hair.

Carefully sliding her arm beneath his thin shoulders, Elizabeth helped him to sit enough to drink from the tin cup. "Do you want more?"

"No, I reckon that'll hold me for a while."

Elizabeth tried to make him comfortable, then sat back on her heels. "You're a little young to be a soldier, aren't you?"

"I ain't that young." His brown eyes flashed. "Be fourteen my next birthday."

"Really?" Elizabeth sounded skeptical.

"Well, birthday after next anyway," he growled. "But I'm old enough to be the man of the family. Pa told me I was before he left last spring."

"I'm certain you are." Elizabeth straightened his blanket. "Still it must be difficult for a b—man of your age to be in charge of a family. I'm sure you'll be glad when your pa gets back."

"He ain't coming back. Took a British ball at Paoli. Died." He blinked. "But you can bet he took a lot of Lobster Backs with him. My pa weren't one to give up without a fight."

Elizabeth swallowed back tears. "I'm certain he wasn't."

"He'd be mad at me though. Whup me good if he was here."

Elizabeth looked down at the pitiful child lying in the straw. "Whatever for?"

"Leaving my ma like I done," the boy admitted with obvious reluctance. "I should of never done that."

"Is she alone?"

"No. But Nancy ain't much help, and the youngins." He made a noise that Elizabeth took to mean he was dismissing them. "The worst of it is that ma'll be thinking I ain't coming back neither. She'll be real upset. Losing Pa . . . then me."

"But you're not . . . you'll be able to go home." Elizabeth pulled down the blanket to examine his wound. A linen bandage was wrapped around his thin waist. Without removing it, she couldn't tell the extent of his injuries, but there was no fresh blood, and when she touched the boy's face he seemed free of fever. Still, it would be some time till he could return to his family.

Elizabeth thought about the first man she'd seen

116

at the hospital yesterday, and wondered again if his mother knew he was dead. And this boy's mother . . . what did she think?

"How were you wounded?" The boy coughed, and Elizabeth pulled the blanket back over his body.

"Some Red Coat tried stabbing me with one of them bayonets, and me not even carrying no gun, just my drum. Good thing I can move pretty quick."

Elizabeth smiled. "It certainly is."

"He got me anyway, but only in the side." The boy's countenance sobered, and his bottom lip quivered. "I sure wish Ma knew that."

"Try not to worry." Elizabeth started to rise. The poor child was so upset. She wished there were something she could do, but outside of providing him with food and water, she was helpless. "You can tell your mother all about your adventures when you go home to . . . where do you live?"

"Little past Frankford. My Pa has . . . we have a farm out that way."

"Really." Elizabeth sank back down in the straw. "I used to ride to Frankford and back all the time before the war." Actually, she had only done it when her father had been away, because he'd been against her riding so far without an escort. But she'd always enjoyed it. The freedom she'd felt had reminded her of galloping across the countryside near Landon Hall.

"Maybe I seen you riding by when I was helping Pa in the fields." He paused, and Elizabeth saw tears well in his brown eyes. "I guess Ma will be thinking she's got to do the planting herself come

117

spring."

An idea began to blossom in Elizabeth's mind. "Exactly where is this farm of yours?" She'd ridden to Frankford before. She could do it now.

"Off Nice Town Lane, past the Rising Sun Tavern."

Elizabeth's heart sank. The Rising Sun Tavern kept by the Widow Nice was several miles past Frankford, and if the farm was farther than that, it might be too far for her to travel in one day, especially without someone missing her. "How far past the tavern?"

"Couple of miles. Why?"

Elizabeth did some quick calculating. It would take her most of a day to go and return, but if she thought up an excuse for being away from the Evanses' house that long . . . and if Hannah would cover for her . . . she could do it.

"Tell me . . ." Elizabeth realized she didn't even know who the boy was, "what is your name?"

"Jacob, Jacob Anderson."

Elizabeth smiled and nodded her head in a modified bow. "Well, Mr. Anderson, I am Elizabeth Lancaster, and I'd like you to tell me how I will recognize this farm of yours."

"You!" Jacob tried to sit up, but Elizabeth grabbed his shoulders and pushed him back into the straw.

"Yes, I. Now will you please lie still, or you'll open your wound."

"But you can't go to my farm."

"And just why not? I thought you wished your

118

mother's mind relieved."

"Well, I do. But, but," Jacob stuttered, "you're a woman."

Elizabeth sighed in frustration. "I can, and have made the journey to Frankford by myself."

"Them Redcoats ain't gonna let a nice American lady like you through the lines."

"You let me worry about that," said Elizabeth as she brushed straw from her skirt. "Just tell me how I'm to find the Anderson farm."

"Thee cannot do this thing, Elizabeth."

Elizabeth hung the lantern on a nail in her father's stable. She had hoped to dress and sneak away from the Evanses' house without waking Hannah. Apparently she'd failed, for her Quaker friend had just walked in on her. She threw a blanket over Hester's back. The horse snorted, and Elizabeth patted her neck, speaking to the mare in a soothing tone before turning to her friend.

"Why did you come here, Hannah?"

"Someone must make thee see reason."

Elizabeth lifted the saddle onto the dapple gray. It was heavy, but the hour was just before dawn, and Elizabeth hadn't wanted to wake a servant. Reaching under Hester's belly for the girth, Elizabeth spoke with more calm than she felt, "We discussed this yesterday."

"And thee said thee would carefully consider thy actions."

"I have." Elizabeth led Hester out of her stall.

"An officer at General Howe's headquarters was kind enough to issue me a pass through the British lines."

Hannah touched Elizabeth's arm. "Has thee forgotten what is beyond those lines?"

Hannah's question echoed in Elizabeth's head some time later as she trotted along the Nice Town Lane. Apparently, there was nothing beyond the British lines. The only people she had encountered since she'd passed the periphery of the city were local farmers, and they'd paid little enough attention to her.

Oh, near the flour mill in Frankford, several men had watched her ride by, but they certainly hadn't been soldiers. They had worn the simple homespun jackets of farmers. Their lingering stares had made her nervous, though. Elizabeth had felt, more than seen, them peering at her from beneath the cocked, felt hats they wore.

She shook her head to dispel the memory. Hannah's question was making her fear trouble where there was none. No, Washington's ragtag band of defeated soldiers was not a worry. If she encountered a problem at all, it would come from the weather.

Clutching her cape more tightly around her, Elizabeth studied the western horizon. Directly ahead the sky darkened ominously to a gun-metal gray. There was going to be a storm, and judging by the bitter, knife-edged wind that whipped through her cape, a bad one.

When the feeble, mauve-tinged sunrise had been

obscured by the heavy clouds earlier this morning, Elizabeth had considered turning back. Nor'easters were nothing to tamper with. But when she thought about Jacob's mother grieving for both husband *and* son, she kept going. With luck, she'd be back, safe and snug, in Philadelphia before the storm hit.

Elizabeth touched Hester's flank with the crop, forcing the horse into a canter. They'd passed Widow Nice's tavern what seemed like hours ago. How much further could it be to the covered bridge Jacob had described? Maybe she'd be able to see it when she cleared this copse of birch trees.

"Halt."

Elizabeth was so shocked by the order, and the men that seemed to materialize from nowhere, that her body went rigid. Hester, obviously as frightened as she, reared, and it took all Elizabeth's strength to deal with the immediate problem — keeping her seat. Elizabeth's heart pounded inside her chest, and her legs quivered from the effort of staying on her horse. Pulling on the reins, she managed to calm the mare, though Hester snorted steam into the frigid air, and pranced restlessly.

Now Elizabeth could spare the men who had stopped her some attention. The fact that they sat their own mounts, offering her no assistance, did not escape her notice. She imagined, as she met their stares, that they'd have been just as pleased if she had fallen in an ignominious heap on the frozen ground.

She raised her chin. The action caused her hood to slip off her head, but she didn't bother to pull it up. "What is the meaning of this? I insist that you let me pass at once." Trying to calm her breathing, she realized her indignant speech had had no affect on the men.

One of the five, whom Elizabeth took to be their leader, sidled his horse closer to Hester. He could have been one of the men from the mill, though Elizabeth wasn't certain. His clothes were similar, but then all of the men were dressed in rough homespun garb.

"What you doing out in weather like this, and in such an all-fired hurry?" His dumpling-dough face seemed to fit without benefit of neck on an equally misshapen body. He reached a mitted hand toward the dapple gray's neck.

Elizabeth pulled on Hester's reins, wrenching them from the man's grasp. "I don't see where that is any of your concern."

"Well, maybe we're making it our business. Right, boys?"

He appeared to be speaking for the others as they bunched in even more tightly around her. Hester pawed the rutted road as the leader's horse brushed against her. Fear churned Elizabeth's stomach, but she kept her voice calm as she asked, "By whose authority do you stop and harass innocent travelers?"

"We ain't so sure you are innocent." The man's words filtered through his woolen scarf. "Can't think of no good reason for a woman to be ridin' out here all alone, times bein' like they is." He paused, and his gaze raked Elizabeth. " 'Cept maybe if you was carrying some important message or something. That it? You some kind of spy?"

Elizabeth tried to laugh at the absurdity of his question, but the sound she made only betrayed her nervousness. "I assure you that nothing could be further from the truth. Now may I pass?"

The leader leaned over, whispering something to one of the other men—something that Elizabeth could not hear. When he turned back to her, his watery blue eyes were narrowed. "You gonna tell us where you're bound?"

The wind caught Elizabeth's hair, flinging it across her face. Impatiently, she swiped it away. The time for righteous indignation had passed. Perhaps if she revealed the reason for her journey they'd let her proceed. Surely no one could find fault with relieving a mother's mind—no matter what his political persuasion. She wasn't certain whether these waylayers were rebels or Loyalists.

Elizabeth cleared her throat, and looked the leader straight in the eye. "I am on my way to the Anderson farm. Young Jacob Anderson lies wounded in Philadelphia, and I carry word to his family."

The leader looked around at the other men, and for the first time one of them spoke. "Eb Anderson's got a little place few miles up the road," he explained. "Heard he got hisself killed, but I don't know nothing about his son."

Elizabeth bristled. "I just told you about Jacob." All the while the men delayed her, the wind grew stronger, rattling ominously through the naked trees.

The leader shook his head. "Don't rightly make sense to me that a fine lady like you'd be braving this cold just to do a turn for some poor farmers. I'm thinking we should take you back to the Committee of Safety, and see what they say."

Before Elizabeth could protest, the leader grabbed again for Hester's reins. The horse, unused to such rough treatment, whinnied, stomping her front hooves. Elizabeth hit at the man's hand with her crop, but missed, and the leather tip swatted the mare's neck. Hester bolted, scattering the ring of stunned men, and took off down the road at a hard gallop. Her reins lost, Elizabeth grabbed handfuls of coarse gray mane, and held on for dear life.

"Guess this is where we part company, Major." Lieutenant Otis McFarland twisted in the saddle, and buried his red beard deeper into the fur collar of his buckskin jacket. "Wish I could ride out this storm lounging by a cozy hearth in some Tory parlor." He rubbed his hands together. "Sure would beat the hell outta trying to stay warm in one of them tents by White Marsh."

Alexander Knox grinned at the giant of a man riding beside him. "Anytime you want to trade places with me, Lieutenant, just let me know."

"Aw, Major, you know I'm no good at this spy thing. I just ain't cut out for it."

"Yes, but think of the food you're missing, and the women." Alex chuckled. "Some of those Tory ladies are mighty fine to look at."

Otis gave his commander a good-natured slap on the arm. "I ain't interested in no powdered-up Loyalist hussy. Now the food—that's something else again. You say they've got sugar?"

"Some. But things are getting pretty scarce. The British are working frantically to clear the river of the chevaux-de-frise we sank so they can bring their ships up to Philadelphia."

"Well, we'll have to see how hard we can make that for them, hey, Major."

Alex laughed. "They're not going to get much done once this storm breaks." Feeling the first sprinkles of icy snow he saluted his friend. "I'd better get back to town. Give my regards to the men, and I'll report back in about a week." Alex watched Otis ride away, then turned his mount toward the Nice Town Lane. If he was lucky, he'd be able to slip into Philadelphia before the snow became too heavy.

Alex grimaced. He wished it were as easy to slip into his role as Alexander Weston as it was to pass back and forth through the British lines. Counterintelligence was something at which he excelled, however it was not something he particularly enjoyed. Contrary to what Otis might think, Alex would prefer to be in camp with the rest of his men, even if it meant sharing their meager supplies. But Washington had learned through experience that he needed spies to keep him abreast of the enemy's movements.

Alex had been introduced by Washington to Nathaniel Sackett, and had worked with Sackett in New York. When Sackett had shifted his operation to Philadelphia, he'd asked for Alex's help.

The clip-clop pounding of hooves racing across frozen ground attracted Alex's attention, and he berated himself for letting his mind wander and dropping his guard. Looking across the countryside toward the Nice Town Lane, he spotted the horse. He couldn't tell if the woman rider had lost control of the animal or not, but she was going too fast for safety.

Alexander started off across the meadow at a right angle to the road, hoping to cut her off before she reached the next curve. It wasn't till he'd nearly reached the lane that he noticed the group of riders lumbering up the road after her. No wonder she rode like a crazy woman.

The wind sliced through his coat and whistled around his ears as Alex bent low, urging his horse to gallop faster. The woman's cape billowed, and her black hair streamed behind her in a blur. It was obvious now she had no control of her horse. Having the angle on them, Alex gained ground quickly. When he was abreast of her he reached out, wrapping his arm around her middle, and yanked her off her precarious perch. The force of her momentum almost unsaddled Alex, and he squeezed his thighs taut against his mount's belly in order to keep from falling.

It took several minutes to stop his horse, the task made more difficult by the struggles of the woman he held clamped to his side. When he slipped them from the saddle, she pounded his chest with her fists, and kicked at his legs.

"Ouch!" Alexander grasped her shoulders, holding her safely at arm's length as one of her well-placed kicks landed above his boot. He swiped away the thick tangle of windblown hair covering her face.

He could only assume his expression was as shocked as hers. "What in the hell are *you* doing here?"

Chapter Seven

Elizabeth grabbed hold of a strong, muscular arm to steady her shaking knees. She stopped struggling when she heard Alexander's words, staring at him in astonishment. "What am I doing here?" she sputtered, spitting out a lock of hair. "What are *you* doing here?" She hadn't been able to see who'd pulled her off her horse, but even at the time she'd been amazed that one of the colonials who'd stopped her could accomplish such a feat. And that had been before she'd found herself hauled against a rock-hard body.

Resting his hands on his hips, Alexander shook his head, barely able to conceal his amusement at her disheveled appearance. "Saving your pretty neck, it would seem. What in the hell were you doing?"

Elizabeth tried to jerk away when he began stuffing her hair under the woolen hood, fighting the powerful surges of wind that whipped about them.

He ignored her feeble efforts so she lashed out with her tongue instead. "I suppose you expect my thanks for dragging me off my horse and flinging me across yours, but the truth is I would have gained control of Hester momentarily." Elizabeth ignored Alexander's grunt of disbelief. "And besides, I was attempting to escape."

"From them?" Alexander cocked his head toward the men who'd finally caught up and were milling about, apparently trying to decide upon their best course of action.

"Yes, from them." Elizabeth resisted the urge to step behind Alexander when she noticed the expression in the leader's pale blue eyes. Obviously, he hadn't enjoyed the little romp down the lane. He dismounted with the same lack of finesse with which he rode.

Alexander took quick inventory of the men who'd been chasing Elizabeth. They were obviously farmers, or tradesmen, and unused to wild rides of pursuit. Only one of the five had gotten off his horse, and he approached with an unsteady, but belligerent gait. "What did you do to these men?" Alexander asked as he inconspicuously slid his hand inside the buckskin jacket of his uniform, wrapping it around the butt of his pistol.

"Nothing, I just . . ." The pressure of Alexander's arm around her shoulders quieted Elizabeth.

"Well, I see you caught our spy for us." The leader said, casting a wary eye toward Alex.

"Spy?" Alexander's raven brow arched questioningly.

Elizabeth wondered if the man realized he backed up before answering Alex. "Yeah. We caught this woman riding along all by herself."

"I see." Alex appeared to consider this information. "But you mentioned spying."

Opening her mouth to defend herself, Elizabeth clamped it shut when Alexander shot her a quelling look.

"Well, we weren't exactly sure about that." The colonial had the decency to appear sheepish. "But she didn't have no good reason to be out in this weather. Then, of course, we knowed she was guilty of something when she took off like she done."

Alexander nodded his head. "What you say certainly sounds incriminating." He tightened his fingers on Elizabeth's caped shoulder when he felt her stiffen beside him. "However, there's just one problem."

The man who had moments before appeared relieved by Alexander's agreement now seemed deflated. He glanced behind him as if looking for support. "What's that?"

"I know this woman, and she's no spy. As a matter of fact, I'm the reason she was on this road alone." Alexander folded Elizabeth more firmly into the curve of his body, grinning down into her surprised countenance. "We were supposed to meet at a tavern right outside of Philadelphia, but I got waylaid. A meeting with General Washington," Alex added, leaning toward the man confidentially.

Alexander straightened, and gave the colonial a broad wink. "I guess she was just too anxious to see me to wait."

Elizabeth watched in disbelief as the man who'd harassed her earlier, now looked at her and smirked.

He rubbed his beefy jaw with a mitted hand. "Still don't understand why she didn't tell us that plain out."

"Embarrassed probably," Alex explained. "You know how women are?" Alex tried not to grimace when he felt Elizabeth's boot heel grind into his instep. She might let him do the talking now, but he had a feeling, there was going to be hell to pay later.

"Yeah," the man agreed. "This makes a lot more sense than that story she told us about taking a message to the Anderson farm."

Alexander slapped the man on the shoulder. "I hope she didn't cause you too much of a problem. Lizzie can be a little feisty sometimes, but then that's not all bad, is it?" Alex winked again before turning Elizabeth back toward his horse. "Come on, honey," he said, letting his hand drop from her shoulder to her waist. "I only have a twenty-four hour pass, and we don't want to spend it stuck out in this storm."

Elizabeth shook with rage. She wanted to call out to the man who was now rejoining his mounted companions, tell him that it was all a lie. She hadn't ridden out of Philadelphia to have an illicit meeting with this soldier. She really was going to the Anderson farm. But for once common sense prevailed. The men were leaving her alone, and as soon as she got rid of Alexander . . .

Elizabeth jerked away when she felt him pat her

bottom.

"Careful, honey," he quipped. "You wouldn't want them to see you treating me in an unfriendly manner."

"Oh, you . . . you beast," Elizabeth hissed, but she was careful not to say it loud enough to be heard by the departing men.

Alexander's laughter only fueled her anger. "How could you deliberately make that man think . . . think that we . . ." Words failed her.

"That we are lovers?" Alex finished for her.

Elizabeth only glared at him, then gathered up the skirts the wind seemed intent upon twisting about her legs, and trudged up the road.

Alex grabbed his horse's reins, falling into step beside her. "I never actually said we were. He just assumed it."

There was still laughter in his voice, and Elizabeth ignored him as she scanned the horizon, looking for Hester.

"Besides, what would you have had me do, shoot him?"

Elizabeth stopped short, swirling to face him. "Don't act as if the thought never occurred to you. I saw you reach inside that jacket for your gun."

"Quite observant," he commended with a slight nod. "But I never really thought I'd have to use force. Those men were only trying to protect their homes."

"From me?" Elizabeth's eyes widened in amazement.

"I admit they were a little zealous."

"A little? Those men treated me as if I were some sort of criminal. And for doing nothing more than traveling along this road." Elizabeth kicked a clod of frozen dirt with the tip of her boot, ignoring the tingling pain that shot up her leg from her cold foot.

"I said they were overzealous, but I doubt they would have done much of anything if you hadn't tried to escape."

"I didn't," Elizabeth mumbled, starting off along the lane again.

"What? But that man said you—"

"I tried to hit him with my crop. Well, he was grabbing for my reins," Elizabeth explained when she noticed his shocked expression. "Anyway, I missed, and hit my horse instead. She spooked, and I went flying down the road, with those men in pursuit." Elizabeth studied Alex's face. "Don't laugh," she warned.

"I wouldn't consider it." Alex did his best to appear sober, but the thought of Elizabeth fighting off that doltish farmer with her crop was just too amusing. No wonder the man had looked as angry as he had.

"You're thinking about laughing. I can tell."

"Am not," Alex lied.

"You are." Elizabeth accused sternly, poking her finger at Alexander's buckskin clad chest. Though she tried not to, a corner of her mouth tilted upward, then, before she could stifle it, a giggle escaped, and another. The whole situation *had* been funny—now that it was over. "Oh, go ahead and

133

laugh. I'm afraid you'll burst if you don't."

When they had both stopped laughing, Elizabeth shook her head. "I should have thanked you right away for coming to my rescue." She sighed. "I really couldn't get control of Hester, and I'm sure you saved me a considerable amount of trouble from those men."

"It was my pleasure, Elizabeth." When she smiled at him like that, her serious gray eyes lit with silvery sparks that made him feel warm inside. The sensation only emphasized the frigid afternoon. Alex flung his arms around himself, slapping them against the cold.

"We'd better get back to Philadelphia before the snow picks up." He paused, realizing she wasn't listening to him, and watched her turn slowly in a half-circle. "What are you looking for?"

"My horse. I didn't think she'd wander too far, but I don't see her." A sadness settled over Elizabeth at the thought of losing Hester.

"Wind most likely scared her." Alex decided not to mention the slap on the neck. "Some soldier in Washington's army will probably find her, and be glad of it." Alex mounted, and reached down for Elizabeth's hand. "We can ride double. You'll have to sit up here." Alex indicated his lap. "I don't have a pillion."

Elizabeth eyed the saddle dubiously. The space available for her to sit was practically nonexistent. She was going to have to be pressed intimately against him, of that there was no doubt. Her mind fervently replayed the other times she'd found herself in similar situations, and the results of them. Not that she thought riding pillion behind him would be much better. Then she'd have to wrap her arms around his firm middle.

"Well, come on," Alex said impatiently. "We'll be lucky to make Philadelphia before the snow starts in earnest as it is."

Elizabeth began to reach toward him, then pulled away as his words registered. "Oh, I can't go back to the city yet."

"What?" His horse snorted, then danced to the side, as Alex turned him in a tight circle. "What do you mean you can't go back? For God's sake, Elizabeth do you want to get stuck out here in a snowstorm?"

"Of course not." Elizabeth tilted her head and stared up at him. The angry gray sky made a fitting backdrop for him as he scowled down at her, reminding her of her cousin Rebecca's words: *'Tis said Alexander Knox is a spawn of the devil*. Clasping her hands beneath the cloak, Elizabeth sucked in a deep breath of icy cold air. "I promised Jacob Anderson I'd get word to his mother."

Alexander sighed in frustration. "The Anderson farm, right?"

"Yes. You didn't think I'd made that up, did you?"

Alex shrugged. "I really hadn't given it much thought — till now."

"But, you see I really must go there. Mrs. Anderson just lost her husband, and now she thinks her son is dead, too, but he's not." Elizabeth took

135

another deep breath. "And I promised I'd tell her." Without thinking, she reached out and touched his leg.

Elizabeth's face was chapped from the wind, and strands of raven hair escaped her hood. She hardly appeared the pampered Tory he'd once thought her to be. But then Alex had realized long ago that she was different from his first impression of her. Reluctantly, he looked away from her pleading, gray eyes and examined the sky. The impending storm gave the feeling of twilight, even though it couldn't be much past noon. Already snow flurries swirled around on currents of icy air. But it was going to really snow soon, and snow hard.

"Hell," Alex mumbled under his breath. When had he become susceptible to a woman's whim? He bent down and grabbed Elizabeth's hands before she could protest, pulling her up in front of him. "We'd never make it to Philadelphia ahead of the storm anyway. Maybe we can sit out the worst of it at this Anderson farm. Where is it?"

Elizabeth smiled into his face. "You really aren't anything like a devil, you know."

"What?" Maybe the girl was going soft in the head. First she'd risked herself by coming into the countryside alone, and then she'd spoken of Satan. So what did that say about him for going along with her scheme?

"Oh, 'twas nothing." Elizabeth decided this was not the time to voice her cousin's concerns, especially when they were so unfounded. She wriggled on the saddle, trying to pull her cloak from beneath

136

her.

Alexander swallowed a moan as Elizabeth's soft bottom, squirmed against a part of him that was fast becoming anything but soft. "What are you doing now?" His voice was gruff and slightly husky.

"My cloak . . . stuck. . . ." Elizabeth closed her eyes in embarrassment. She had accidentally rubbed against his hard body, and now she couldn't string words together into a coherent sentence. He must think her such a foolish girl.

Alex blew out air between his clenched teeth. "I'm going to lift you. When I do, free your cloak, and skirts, and anything else you need. Do you understand?"

Too mortified to speak, Elizabeth simply nodded. He sounded so exasperated with her, as well he might.

Alex leaned back, and reached under Elizabeth's woolen cape, trying to grasp her around her narrow waist. At the same moment, Elizabeth turned, presumably to assist him. Instead of a corseted side, Alex's hand closed around something infinitely softer. Elizabeth's breast. It seemed to swell to fit his hand, and Alex could swear he felt the nipple harden against his palm. Gently he squeezed the soft flesh, memories of other times he'd touched her thus still strong in his mind.

Elizabeth gasped. Flashes of heat coursed through her, welling in an area below her stomach. Slowly, she raised her head, meeting Alexander's dark blue stare.

"Please accept my apologies." Alex yanked his

hand away, abruptly, and blinked. How long had he sat lost in Elizabeth's silvery gray eyes, fondling her breast? He had no idea. And if his horse hadn't started pawing the ground, he'd probably still be doing it.

Alex reached again for her waist, and this time his aim was truer. "When I lift you, yank the cloak."

"No, really. It is fine the way it is." Elizabeth tried to wriggle out of his grasp. Even his touch about her waist was unsettling.

"Damn it, Elizabeth, would you sit still? Just do what I say."

Alexander settled Elizabeth back against him, hoping she wouldn't notice his arousal, which was, by this time, out of control. "Are you comfortable now?"

Elizabeth ignored the sarcasm in his voice. "Yes, quite," she managed to get out, though her breathing was still somewhat unsteady.

"Then tell me how I'm to get to this farm." Alex squeezed his thighs and the horse began trotting down the road.

Though Elizabeth tried to sit erect, back straight, the rhythmic jostling caused by the horse's brisk gait proved her undoing. Besides it was so much warmer nestled against Alexander's chest. He smelled of leather and outdoors and that unique fragrance she'd come to associate with him. His arms bracketed her body, making her feel comforted and safe, and after she'd given him directions, Elizabeth couldn't keep her eyes open.

"Elizabeth." The voice came to her as from a

dream.

"Mmmm." Elizabeth snuggled closer to the warmth.

"Elizabeth." Her name didn't sound as dreamlike this time.

"What?" She jerked awake, and sat up abruptly, coming very near to slipping off the horse. If it hadn't been for Alexander's quick hands, she would have.

"We're approaching the covered bridge."

Elizabeth blinked, and pushed back her hood. Icy crystals propelled by the fierce wind, pelted her face. "It's snowing harder."

Alexander pulled her back against him. "It has been for some time. I'm anxious to reach that farm."

"It shouldn't be much farther." At least Elizabeth hoped it wasn't. The part of her that rested against Alexander was comfortable enough, but her legs and feet were burning from the cold. She imagined Alexander, wearing his fringed, buckskin jacket and felt hat, was equally chilled.

The sides of the covered bridge offered some relief from the howling wind. But the echoing clatter of the horse's hooves hitting wood, lasted only a short time, and then they were again buffeted by the storm.

"I think that's smoke from a chimney over that way." Alex pointed off to their left.

Elizabeth squinted. She could hardly see anything through the blowing snow. "Jacob said his place was just past the bridge." The wind seemed to snatch

139

her words and carry them away, but Alexander must have heard because he turned off the road.

The farmhouse appeared to be little more than a one-room shack. A feeble yellow glow filtering through the window and the faint odor of wood smoke were the only signs of life.

Alexander dismounted, then lowered Elizabeth to the frozen ground. "Stay here," he ordered, pulling her around to the side of the house that offered some protection from the storm.

"But why?" All Elizabeth wanted to do was warm herself by a roaring fire. She didn't think she'd ever been so cold. Alexander ignored her, scanning the area, and the few dilapidated outbuildings. He removed his gloves, and blew on his fingers, before reaching inside his coat.

"What are you doing?" Elizabeth grabbed his arm when she saw the pistol.

Alexander looked down, seeming to remember her presence. "Just stay here a minute." He pushed her closer to the wall, into the V formed by the chimney and the house. "I don't know what it is, but something doesn't seem right."

He was gone before Elizabeth could insist on an explanation. Oh, what a frustrating man. She wrapped the cloak around her more tightly, and huddled in the niche, leaning against the jagged edges of the stones. The heat that permeated through them from the fireplace offered some relief from the cold, but not much. How long she stood there, hunched against the storm, Elizabeth wasn't certain. She considered ignoring Alex's advice. What did he think he was doing, ordering her around? She had almost decided to follow him into the house, when she felt his hand on her shoulder.

"Where have you been?" she demanded. "I'm freezing. I want to—" Elizabeth stopped midsentence, concern erasing the shadows of anger from her face. "What is it? What's wrong?"

"They're sick."

Sick? Elizabeth searched Alex's dark eyes. "Well, I have to help them." She turned, starting for the front of the house, but two large hands clamped over her arms, stopping her. She swirled around to face him. "What's the matter with you? If they're ill, I need to—"

"It's smallpox, Elizabeth."

"Smallpox." Elizabeth's gloved hand flew to her mouth. "Are you certain?" she whispered.

Alexander stomped his feet, trying to warm them, and nodded. "I saw enough of it at Washington's camp in Morristown so that I wouldn't mistake it."

"But there must be something we can do. Who's down with it?"

"A boy about five, and a young girl named Nancy are pretty sick. But Mrs. Anderson seems to be fine." Alex brushed snow off Elizabeth's hood. "They have plenty of food and water, and I'm going to bring in enough firewood to see them through this storm. Other than that there's nothing we can do." Alex turned his head, staring into the swirling snow. "I'll try to get a doctor to come out here, but . . ."

Elizabeth didn't need Alex to finish his sentence.

141

She knew, as well as he that doctors were scarce. She'd certainly learned that lesson when she'd worked with the wounded soldiers at the State House.

"Alexander, I think perhaps we can do more for them. I don't know very much about nursing sick people but I'm certain I could—"

"You're not to go in that house!" Alexander grabbed Elizabeth's shoulders. He didn't realize the force of his grip till he noticed the mingled shock and pain in her eyes. He relaxed his hands, but did not let them drop. "You are not to go in that house," he repeated more softly. "I've seen what can happen. The affliction spreads from person to person like a fire out of control."

"What about you? You were in there. Or do you consider yourself too indestructible to be afflicted?" There was a part of Elizabeth that enjoyed Alexander's concern for her well-being, although standing outside in this storm hardly contributed to her comfort. But another part of her bristled at his authoritative attitude.

A corner of Alex's mouth lifted, his dimple deepened. She wasn't easily intimidated. Of course, he'd known that. Slowly he let go of her shoulders, and tightened the drawstring of her hood about her wind-chapped face.

"I've seen stronger men than I felled by smallpox," he said. "But I've had the inoculation and am immune to the ravages of the disease." A sudden thought crossed his mind. "Perhaps you have had the inoculation?"

Elizabeth lowered her eyes, and shook her head. "I thought not."

"Then what are we going to do, about the Andersons . . . about us?" Elizabeth hated to show concern for herself when the family inside the cabin was so sorely plagued. It was just that she didn't think she could survive the storm huddled in the corner formed by the chimney and the house. Even now she wondered if all of her would ever thaw.

"The Andersons are as well off as we can make them for now—or will be when I carry in the wood. I told Mrs. Anderson about her son, and that news greatly relieved her mind." Alex noticed Elizabeth's smile, and returned it. "As for us, we'll have to find shelter before nightfall."

"But where?" To Elizabeth's recollection, the closest inn was the Rising Sun Tavern, but certainly they couldn't make it there. If she hadn't known how sudden, and intense, his reaction would be, she would have suggested they stay with the Andersons. She was almost too cold to worry about the consequences.

"I noticed a small house before we crossed the bridge. According to Mrs. Anderson, no one lives there now, but it's still fairly weather tight. We shouldn't have too much trouble finding it."

An abandoned farmhouse? That was where they were going to spend the night? Together. Alone. Elizabeth cleared her throat. "I don't recall seeing another cabin."

"You, Elizabeth, were asleep."

Embarrassment for the way she had nestled

against him flooded her cheeks. She looked away, catching sight of the outbuilding the family obviously used as a barn. "Couldn't we stay there?"

"No way to build a fire" was his succinct reply. "But you and my horse will be more comfortable there while I stack up the firewood." Alex took Elizabeth's arm and led her across the snow-covered yard.

Once inside, Elizabeth had to agree with him. It wouldn't be a very comfortable place to wait out a storm. Wind whistled through the cracks between the boards, and sifted snow was already piled in one corner of the structure. She studied the gaping hole in the roof, and decided that Jacob's father hadn't been very handy with a hammer and nails.

To fill the time Elizabeth fed and watered — breaking the ice in the bucket with a rake handle — the Anderson's work horse, as well as the sleek animal that belonged to the rebel major. She felt guilty taking some of the meager supply of grain, but she decided to leave Mrs. Anderson a coin in payment.

Elizabeth had almost finished rubbing down Alexander's mount when his owner appeared in the doorway. "I think that should keep them," Alex said, taking off his hat, and knocking the thick layer of snow off the felt. "Thank you for seeing to George."

"George?"

"My horse," Alex explained. "His name is George."

"Oh, really?" Elizabeth threw a blanket over the stallion. "Which George is he named for, our King

144

or your exalted general?"

Alex took the saddle Elizabeth had earlier pulled from the horse's back. "Maybe I just like the name," he said, a twinkle in the depths of his blue eyes.

Elizabeth doubted that was the case, but she let the subject drop, especially since she imagined there was a number following the horse's name, and that naming the horse for the King hadn't been as a compliment.

Alex boosted Elizabeth into the saddle, and led the horse through the shed door.

"Aren't you riding?" Elizabeth yelled down at him when she noticed Alexander made no attempt to mount.

Alex tightened his grip on the reins when George twisted his head, apparently not relishing the thought of being out in the weather again. "I think we'll make better time if I walk him. It's not far," he added, hoping it was true. Now that he'd come back out into the storm, he wondered if he was doing the right thing.

Maybe they should stay here. Not everyone got smallpox. Perhaps Elizabeth was one of those people who'd be spared. Besides, what if he couldn't find the deserted cabin? Was he sparing Elizabeth one form of death to risk her life on another?

Alex glanced at Elizabeth. She had her cloak wrapped tightly about her, but she sat up straight, and her eyes met his without wavering. Alex turned around and bent his head against the fury of the wind. He'd find that cabin, and see her safely through this storm. Then he'd take her back to

Philadelphia, and tell her father to lock her in her room for the rest of the war.

It seemed forever till they reached the shelter of the covered bridge. When they did, Alex slid down the wooden side for a moment's rest.

"Are you all right?" Elizabeth slipped out of the saddle, landing on the planked floor. The sides and roof offered some relief from the wind and snow, but none from the cold. She rushed over to where Alexander sat, leaning against a support beam. His head rested on his drawn-up knees, and he didn't seem to have heard her.

"Major?" Elizabeth tried again, brushing the snow off his shoulders.

"I'm all right, Elizabeth. Just need a little rest." He started to stand.

"We could stay here a while," Elizabeth offered. She had no doubt the poor man was near exhaustion. The constant battering of the wind had tired her, and she wasn't even trying to walk against it, or trudging through the ankle-deep snow.

"We need to get to the cabin before dark. Come on." He stood, and reached for Elizabeth's waist, but she brushed his hands away.

"Let me walk, too. It will be easier on George."

"No." Alex insisted as he helped her onto the horse's back. "Your skirts would trip you up in the snow. He'll have plenty of time to rest once we get there. Besides, it's not much farther."

Elizabeth wanted to scream at him that she wasn't a child who had to be coddled. He'd been telling her it wasn't much farther since they'd started. She bit back her anger as the icy wind hit her face. An argument now would do neither of them any good. Elizabeth only hoped they really were close to the cabin, because she didn't know how much longer either of them could keep going.

Chapter Eight

"There it is."

The words, carried to her by the ice-lashed wind, forced Elizabeth to sit straight in the saddle. Anxiously, she peered into the gathering gloom. She had no way of knowing the time. Was it really near nightfall, or did the swirling snow only make it seem thus? Elizabeth knew it couldn't be true, but it seemed they'd been traveling forever. And for all she could see, the journey was not over.

"Where?" Elizabeth yelled, not surprised when Alexander didn't answer. He'd already veered off between the tall trees that lined the road like shadowy, silent sentinels.

"Oh, I see it! I do." Tears of relief welled in Elizabeth's eyes as she spotted the dark shape nestled in a small clearing. She brushed them away impatiently. Now wasn't the time to give way to foolish crying.

Lifting Elizabeth from the horse, Alex carried her to the front door. She shivered uncontrollably, and again he wondered if he'd done the right thing by taking her away from the Andersons'.

"It isn't necessary for you to hold me. I can stand." Alex smiled when Elizabeth's breath warmed his cheek.

"You're protecting me from the wind, while I search for the latch string," he teased. Alex gave the rope a pull, and the door swung open.

Inside it was nearly as cold as outside. "It's so dark," Elizabeth said after Alex had shut the door against the relentless wind and snow.

"Just stand still," he answered, putting her down but wrapping an arm around her to keep her close. "Your eyes will adjust to the lack of light soon."

Elizabeth pressed herself against the bulwark of his body. She could hear his heartbeat, and took great comfort in its strong, steady sound.

"There's the fireplace." Alex moved toward the large, fieldstone structure, keeping Elizabeth by his side. "Now we have to get a fire started."

"How are we going to do that?" Elizabeth hated to be so pessimistic. However, now that she could see more clearly, it was evident that the one-room cabin was empty. Whoever had lived in it had taken everything with them when they'd left.

"There's probably a woodpile outside. You stay inside while I check."

Before Elizabeth had time to protest, she found herself alone. Alex was right, of course. They must have a fire. But she felt so much safer when he was with her. She slid down the rough, wooden wall, to sit on the floor, trying to ignore the cold that seeped through her cloak.

Tiny scritch-scratching noises drifted to her from the far corner of the room. Elizabeth sucked in breath to scream, stopping herself just in time. Alexander didn't need to come racing to her rescue again. Especially over a few field mice — at least, that was what Elizabeth hoped made the noise. She refused to think it might be rats — or worse. But she stood up, just in case.

"I found some wood." Alex burst through the door, dropping a pile of split logs and kindling near the fireplace.

He seemed so pleased with himself, that Elizabeth decided against telling him that the cabin had at least one other inhabitant. Once they had a fire going, and could see better, would be soon enough. Besides, he was already back outside before she could say anything.

Elizabeth leaned over, brushing snow off the logs. She wished there was something else she could do, but she couldn't think of anything. So she tucked her hands under her arms, and waited.

When Alexander entered the cabin again, he carried with him supplies from his saddle. He dropped his blanket roll, linen haversack, and canteen in a pile on the floor. His "brown Bess" rifle, cartridge box, and powder horn, he took care to stack in the corner.

"There's a lean-to out back for George. I need to see to him directly, but I thought a fire would be appreciated first."

Elizabeth moved to where he sat by the fireplace. "The wood is none too dry," she commented as she watched him pull wads of straw from his pockets.

"It will have to do." Alex took the camp hatchet from his belt, and chipped pieces off a log. Then he hunched over the straw, striking his flint till a spark caught. Blowing gently, he carefully began feeding splinters of wood to the infant blaze. Initially, when he added a log, the hearth spewed out more smoke than warmth, but within minutes, the wood caught. A lively orange glow chased the shadows from all but the farthest corners of the room.

Alex stood with his back to the fire, absorbing the heat. "I need to see to my horse now," he said. "While I'm gone, I want you to get out of those wet clothes. You can wrap up in my blanket."

"Take off my . . ." Elizabeth didn't think she'd heard him correctly. She hoped she hadn't. "My clothes aren't wet," she argued.

"They will be, as soon as the ice starts to melt."

Elizabeth glanced down at her cloak. Standing by the fireplace for just this short time had caused large wet splotches to appear. She didn't even have to look at her skirt. She could feel the dampness against her cold legs.

Still . . . It was bad enough that circumstances, mostly of her own making, Elizabeth admitted, forced her to share a cabin with Major Knox, unchaperoned. However, that didn't mean she had to undress for him. Well, maybe it wasn't exactly for him, but . . . "I think I'll just stand by the fire, and let my clothes dry," Elizabeth said with a shy smile.

"You'll catch a chill, Elizabeth." Alex tapped the tiny dimple in her chin before pulling his gloves back on. "Heed me without argument this once . . . please."

Elizabeth stood staring at the door long after he disappeared through it. The wool blanket he'd stuck in her hands before leaving felt prickly, but dry. What was she to do? An involuntary shiver ran through her, and she remembered Alex's prediction about catching a chill.

Oh, for goodness' sake. He was right. But she'd only take off her cloak and riding habit. Certainly they were all that was wet.

Elizabeth draped her cloak across the floor, close to the hearth and unbuttoned her jacket. To her dismay, not only the waistcoat, but the shirt under it were damp. She stepped out of her skirts, deciding that no matter how cold she might be, or how great her chances of catching a chill, she was not going to take off her shift. She wrapped the blanket around her thin, linen chemise, and bent over to unlace her Moroccan half boots and then take off her wool stockings. She placed these close to the fireplace, hoping they would dry quickly so she could dress.

"How do your feet feel?"

Elizabeth ignored his question, clutching the blanket more tightly against the draft from the open door as well as against the major's curious eye when he again entered the cabin. He stomped the snow off his boots, and pulled in the latch string.

"Do they hurt?" Alex glanced down at the little

pink toes peeking out from beneath the gray wool.

"If I didn't know better, I'd think some evil wizard was sticking needles into my flesh."

"That's good. It means you haven't lost feeling in them." Alex bent down, whipping back the bottom of the blanket, and enfolding one of her feet in his hands.

"Don't . . . " Elizabeth tried pulling her foot from his grasp, but he tightened his fingers around her ankle.

"Now, Elizabeth. I'm just checking for signs of frostbite." He examined one foot, then the other, slowly running his finger along the arch of her instep. "Well, I see no evidence your skin isn't perfectly healthy." He grinned up into her face, across the expanse of her blanket-covered body. "Perhaps a trifle ticklish," he added, "but healthy all the same."

"Thank you," Elizabeth mumbled. She let out a breath she hadn't noticed she was holding when he tucked her feet back under the blanket, and rose. Her ankle still burned where he'd touched it, idly rubbing the bone with his thumb. Elizabeth wondered if Alexander knew what effect his touch had on her? She pushed the thought from her mind. While they were here there would be no more touching. She would simply make certain that Major Knox kept his distance.

She glanced up. "You're going to . . . undress?" What a stupid question. He'd already taken off his fringed jacket, and was pulling his hunting shirt over his head.

"Don't worry," he said, letting his amused gaze rake over her. "I won't strip further than my shift."

What was he talking about? Men didn't wear shifts. Elizabeth, made uncomfortable by his stare, looked down at herself. Abruptly she grabbed together the ends of the blanket she'd let fall open. From neck to waist he had seen her covered by no more than the gauzy-thin material of her chemise. Elizabeth felt her breasts tighten at the thought. "You could have told me the blanket had slipped," she said, more angry with her body's reaction to him than with his lack of chivalry.

"And deprive myself of such a delightful view?" Alex chuckled. "Not very likely."

"Oh, you . . . you—"

"Uncivilized barbarian," Alex supplied, remembering what she'd called him the first time they'd met in Maryland.

Color flooded Elizabeth's cheeks, and unable to meet his gaze, she let her lashes drift down. Since she'd pronounced those words, she'd learned that he was neither. Whatever his political beliefs were, he'd proved that he could be both cultured and humane. Elizabeth hated to think where she'd be right now if it weren't for his willingness to help a fellow human being.

"I don't think you're a barbarian . . . or uncivilized."

"Ah, so I've risen in your esteem," Alex teased.

"Oh, yes. I think you—"

"What's wrong?"

Elizabeth's eyes flashed up to meet his, then

skittered away. She swallowed, or more accurately tried to swallow, but her mouth was suddenly dry. "Nothing . . . nothing is wrong." At some time, while she'd been absorbed studying her lap, he'd taken off his linen shirt. When she'd looked up to answer him, he'd stood before her bare chested.

She'd seen glimpses of his chest before, that morning at the marsh, and she'd even allowed her mind to conjure up images of what he might look like beneath his buckskin shirt. But she hadn't been prepared for the reality of his body, or her reaction to it.

His shoulders were broad, and well muscled—no need for padding under *his* clothes. Curly, black hair covered the area around and between his flat, male nipples, then arrowed toward his breeches. His skin, darker than hers by several shades, was a rich bronze color that accentuated the planes and ridges of his body.

"Are you certain you're all right?"

"Yes," Elizabeth got out. Then she turned her head and coughed to disguise the weakness in her voice.

Alex added more logs to the fire. It hissed and crackled as the flames engulfed them. "If you're cold, move closer to the warmth."

If I move any closer, Elizabeth thought, I'll be sitting in the fireplace. Besides, she didn't feel the least bit chilled. Heat had spread through her, originating from the most interesting places.

Alex shrugged, and bent over to tug off his boots, no simple job without a bootjack. But the task gave him something to occupy his mind other than a practically naked Elizabeth. There was no help for their being here, alone, but damn if it wasn't going to be a test of just how civilized and unbarbaric he was. Mistress Elizabeth Lancaster would be shocked to the bottoms of her dainty, little toes if she knew the thoughts that were running wild through his mind.

But he didn't make a practice of seducing innocent women, even if he did think about what it would be like to strip this particular woman of her innocence.

Alex wondered what Elizabeth's father would say if he could see her and his rebel contact now. This probably wasn't what Lancaster had had in mind when he'd told Alex to stay away from his daughter. Well, Alex certainly hadn't planned this. If Lancaster would keep a closer eye on his daughter, Alex wouldn't have to run around rescuing her so often. Maybe then he could forget about how soft her skin was, or how her gray eyes sparkled when she was angry or when he kissed—

"Damn it!" Alex gave his second boot a ferocious jerk. He just had to stop thinking about kissing Elizabeth, because that led to thinking about doing lots of other things with her. Things he had no right to even think about. There was no place in his life for a respectable woman—especially a Tory woman. All Alex had to do was remember that.

"Are yours all right?" Elizabeth slanted Alex a glance from under her lashes. "Your feet, I mean." His back was as powerfully built as his front, and she found the play of the well-honed muscles across his shoulders fascinating.

"They're cold, but fine other than that."

"I'm glad," Elizabeth whispered. She tried not to look at his stockingless lower legs and feet, but it seemed the harder she tried, the more her eyes were drawn to examine his body. Curly, dark hair, matching that on his chest, grew on his legs, and even across the tops of his feet and toes. Must even his toes be so devastatingly male?

"Are you hungry?" Alex couldn't keep the amusement from his voice. He wondered if Elizabeth realized how intently she stared at him.

It took Elizabeth a moment to notice Alex had asked her a question. Slowly her eyes traveled up to meet his. It was obvious from the expression on his face that he'd been aware she was looking at him. Elizabeth hoped she didn't appear as embarrassed as she felt.

What had he asked her? Was she hungry? She was starved! Elizabeth tried to remember when she'd last eaten. This morning she'd been in too much of a rush to eat breakfast. Even last night, she'd merely picked at her food because she'd been so edgy about her plans for this day. But, after their ordeal in the storm, Elizabeth assumed just being relatively dry and warm was enough. The wind still howled angrily outside, and she shivered to think what might have happened to them if the major hadn't found this shelter. It was simply too much to hope that he might also have food.

But he did! Elizabeth watched, trying not to

appear too anxious, as he took a cloth from his haversack, and unwrapped four biscuits and a small chunk of corned beef.

"This isn't much," Alex said, handing Elizabeth a hard biscuit. "But then I'd planned to dine in Philadelphia tonight." This was to be his nooning, but he'd never gotten a chance to eat it. He fashioned a point on a stick with his knife, and rammed the partially thawed meat on it. Holding the meat over the flames, Alex turned to Elizabeth and grinned. "I'm certain this isn't what you're used to, but it should stave off starvation."

The meat sputtered and sizzled as Alex turned the stick. Wondrous aromas drifted from it, and Elizabeth swallowed in anticipation despite the small portion they would share. She took a bite of her biscuit—and almost choked. Never before had she tasted anything so dry.

Alex glanced over his shoulder. "There's something to drink in the canteen."

Elizabeth merely nodded, unable to speak with the powdery substance in her mouth. She took a large swig of what she assumed to be water, nearly spitting out the foul-tasting liquid. Her eyes watered, and her throat burned, but at least she was able to swallow the biscuit.

"I'd use caution when drinking that. You're probably not used to"—Alex shifted around, and upon seeing Elizabeth's face, her streaming eyes and flushed cheeks, knew his warning was too late— "whiskey," he finished lamely.

"Why . . ." Elizabeth's voice croaked. She started

158

over. "Why do you have *that* in your canteen?"

"It's my allotment from the quartermaster." Alex forced his attention, reluctantly, back to the meat. Elizabeth had let the blanket slip again, and he didn't want to be caught staring when she became conscious of her error. Besides, his awareness of being alone with her bordered on the obsessive. Any more observing the way the firelight burnished her bare shoulders or played in the obsidian depths of her hair, and he'd be sorely tempted to forget caution. Hell, he was more than tempted now!

Elizabeth licked her lips, deciding the whiskey's taste was not nearly so bad when it was taken in by droplets. A rush of warmth spread through her, and she blinked once to clear the dizziness in her head. Carrying the canteen, she moved back toward the fireplace, drawn by Alexander and the smell of the roasting beef.

"Do you want some of this?" She held the canteen out to Alex as he hunched over on his knees, slowly turning the meat over the fire.

Alex started to shake his head, then caught sight of her out of the corner of his eye. Against his better judgment, he turned to look at her. She'd let the damn blanket drop even further. He could clearly see the outline of her breasts through her shift. How could he have ever thought her without womanly curves?

Granted, the word buxom could hardly be used to describe her, but then had he ever cared for overly endowed women? Alex couldn't remember. He only knew that the soft, subtle flow of Elizabeth's body

159

made his mouth dry. He reached out, taking the canteen, and swallowed a fiery gulp that he felt burn its way to the pit of his stomach. Unfortunately, it did nothing to relieve the cotton-dry feeling in his mouth.

"Is that almost ready?" Elizabeth motioned toward the meat, trying to divert Alexander's attention from herself. The major's staring made her uncomfortable. No, Elizabeth admitted to herself, not uncomfortable—excited. Yes that was how she felt when his blue eyes raked over her, seeming to sear her flesh.

Without answering, Alex pulled the stick from the flames, and spread the meat on the cloth in which it had been wrapped. Cooking had shrunk the scrap of beef till it seemed hardly large enough to toss to a dog.

Elizabeth looked down at the corned beef that the major had placed between them, and then up at him. "Is this your allotment from the quartermaster, also?"

"Yes."

"Perhaps he would be wiser to spend more time procuring meat, and less time buying from the local tavern."

"Usually the army does the best it can with what it can find." Inexplicably, Alex was annoyed with his paltry offering, and with her reaction to it.

Elizabeth didn't like to think of Alexander having nothing to eat but dry biscuits and a leaving of meat. "But certainly, with a little ingenuity your army could be supplied with more ample fare than

160

this. I've lived in this area long enough to know that it's rich in farmland and—"

"And what are we to use as enticement for the farmers to sell their beef to us, Elizabeth?" Alex realized he'd raised his voice and lowered it. "None but the most dedicated Patriot will take continental scrip in payment, especially when the British wag their fine, shiny gold under the farmers' noses." Alex leaned back against the wall, running his fingers through his hair. "And who can blame them? They have families to feed and clothe, and it's hardly a secret that our scrip is worth little more than the paper it's printed on."

"I'm sorry." Elizabeth sank down on her knees, eyes fastened on her folded hands. "I didn't know."

Of course she didn't know. How could she? A stab of guilt for the way he'd lashed out at her ran through Alex. "No, Elizabeth." He sighed, resting his head against the splintery wall. " 'Tis I who should be apologizing. I'd no right to raise my voice to you, and the problems of General Washington's army are obviously none of your concern."

Then why did she feel they should be? Elizabeth didn't know for certain, but she assumed a lot of her interest revolved around this man before her. Somehow, between the time she'd first encountered him and now, his concerns had become her concerns. Slowly, her eyes rose till they met his. The now-familiar jolt of excitement rushed through her. "At least you get enough to eat while you're in Philadelphia." Even though foodstuffs were in short supply because of the American blockage of the

161

Delaware River, there was enough to keep people from going hungry in the city.

"Aye." Alex laughed mirthlessly. "I get my belly full in Philadelphia."

Instinctively, Elizabeth knew he didn't speak of just food. "You don't like what you do in Philadelphia very much, do you?"

The corners of Alex's mouth tilted upward, the dimple teased his cheek. "Exactly what do you think I do in Philadelphia, Elizabeth?"

"I'm not certain." She'd asked him what he'd been doing at General Howe's ball, but he'd refused to tell her. Since then her mind had been kept busy conjecturing. "I imagine your job involves gathering secrets."

Alex's bark of laughter apparently disturbed the animals nesting in the cabin. Elizabeth could hear them scurrying about, but Alexander appeared to ignore the sound so she did the same.

"Gathering secrets," Alex repeated her words slowly. "It sounds so much more genteel than spying."

"If it bothers you so much, why do you do it?"

"Who said I don't enjoy it immensely?" Her gray eyes regarded him unwaveringly. They seemed able to delve beyond the surface, into his thoughts and dreams. He looked away. "It's necessary."

"And dangerous."

Her eyes snagged his again. "Very few professions during time of war are entirely safe."

"But you . . ." Elizabeth hesitated. "You're so vulnerable."

162

"Why, Mistress Elizabeth, you sound almost as if you care," he chided. "Is this the same Tory firebrand who wished her British colonel would hang me by my toes?" Alex watched her eyes darken from the soft, gentle gray of the new dawn to the color of aged pewter. His flippant remark had annoyed her, as it was meant to do.

In that moment when her gaze had searched his soul, he had realized his vulnerability. Oh, not to the British. Alex was confident of his abilities against them. It was to her. Elizabeth Lancaster wielded power over him, and she didn't even know it. And that was the way Alex wanted to keep it. He didn't want to care about her or think about her—and he didn't want the responsibility of her caring about him.

Elizabeth had been right about one thing. Danger and death never strayed far from his side. He accepted that; he didn't think she could.

Elizabeth bristled, trying to hide her anger. She did care what happened to him, though she couldn't imagine why. He was such an insufferable man, making fun of her fears for him. She had felt so close to him earlier, closer than she'd ever felt to anyone. But it was obvious he hadn't experienced the same feeling. Elizabeth turned and stared into the bright orange flames of the fire, hoping its warmth would penetrate her suddenly chilled body.

"You'd best take a piece of that meat before it gets stone cold."

Elizabeth spared a glance over her shoulder at the shriveled-up meat, but ignored Alexander. "You eat it. I'm not hungry."

"Damn it, Elizabeth, take a piece of the meat."

"Don't swear at me, Major Knox. I don't want any of your meat. Besides, if I should take a piece, there'd be naught left for you."

Alexander whipped out the knife he'd used to whittle the stick, and for the length of a heartbeat, Elizabeth thought he might use it to force her to eat. He looked so ferocious. But it was the hapless beef that received the sharp cutting edge of the blade.

"There." Alex examined his handiwork, ignoring the stubborn woman glaring at him. "Half for you, and half for me." He added another biscuit to her pile, and began to eat.

Elizabeth cursed the hunger that drove her back to the food. Oh, how she wished she could simply stick her nose in the air and take no heed of the enticing aroma or the captivating drop of juice that rolled down Alexander's chin. She would eat quickly, then ignore him until they could leave this place.

Unfortunately, eating this beef, no matter how small the portion, was not something to be accomplished in haste. It was tough and stringy, unappetizingly burned on the outside, and almost raw near the center. But she ate it. She even managed to down the biscuit, needing more swallows from the canteen to accomplish it.

"I'll be glad to gather some snow to melt for you to drink," he'd offered, but Elizabeth had refused. She didn't want him doing anything else for her.

Now she sat leaning against the rough fieldstone fireplace, wishing she'd choked the food down without liquid. Her head tilted from side to side, twirling and spinning. The amazing thing was, this was happening without her actually moving.

"I'm going outside to get more firewood before we go to sleep."

Alexander's voice carried to her through the misty fog surrounding her brain. She turned her head cautiously, noticing that he had pulled his shirt back on, covering the manly breadth of his chest. Too bad, she thought, and began to giggle.

Alex peered at her, then shook his head. "I believe you're drunk Mistress Elizabeth."

Drunk? What was he talking about? "I feel fine."

"I'm certain you do." Alex bent over, grasping her under the arms to help her stand.

"What are you doing?" Elizabeth's hands stole around his neck, weaving deeply into the thick black hair that grew there. Whatever he was doing it felt wonderful to be held by him again. Elizabeth nestled closer, pressing her thinly clad breasts against his shirt.

Alexander's breath hissed between his clenched teeth. The blanket, lying in a pool at her feet, made no pretense of covering Elizabeth. His fingers, of their own volition, moved to her back till they traced the ruffled edging of her shift. The contrast between her silky smooth skin and the crisp linen filled his mind making him wonder what he was doing.

He tried to pull away. As much as he might want

to, taking advantage of Elizabeth while she wasn't in complete control of her faculties was not something he'd do. "I'm moving you away from the fire," Alex said, trying to keep his voice steady. The feel of her body against his caused a yearning he fought to suppress. "In your present state, you might just fall and be consumed by the flames." He dragged his hands away from her and reached behind his neck to unlock her fingers.

Elizabeth held on. What did he mean, she'd be consumed by flames? Wasn't she already? She touched her lips to the underside of Alexander's chin. His whiskers were abrasive, and she tentatively tested them with her tongue, tasting the salty tang of his skin.

"Don't . . . Elizabeth. Stop that . . . please."

"Why?" Elizabeth felt his hands tighten on hers, his body stiffen. She wriggled up till her teeth teased the tip of his ear. "I like this, don't you?"

Like it, hell, he loved it. Wild currents of pleasure rushed through him, emanating from the spot where her mouth moistened his skin. But Alex hadn't missed the slur of her words, or the telltale unsteadiness of her movements. It might sound like Elizabeth talking, and it might feel like Elizabeth's soft, warm body, but it was the whiskey that had taken control of her. It had wiped out her good sense. She'd never act like this without the drink's influence.

Her fingers loosened, dropping away from behind his neck, and Alex let out a relieved sigh. But before he could pull away, her hands crept around his back, tugging on the buckskin.

"Take this off," she ordered in a low, sultry voice, pulling on his shirt. "And these," she giggled, letting her hands drift down across the bulge in the front of Alex's breeches, "are damp. You wouldn't want to catch a chill, would you?"

"Elizabeth!" Alex imprisoned her exploring fingers in a tight grip. What she was doing to him was tantamount to torture. "I think you'd better lie down." Alex tried to recall how much whiskey she'd had. Whatever the amount, it was way beyond what she could handle.

"Are you going to lie down, too?" Elizabeth asked as he swiped up the blanket and spread it on the floor.

"No." Alex folded his linen shirt for a pillow.

"Then I don't want to." Elizabeth raised her chin, staring at him defiantly.

Alex stared down at her. He'd dealt with his share of inebriated men, but had never experienced anything like this. "Listen, Elizabeth—" Whatever he'd meant to say was cut off when her lips pressed against his.

The whiskey certainly hadn't affected her ability to kiss. Her lips were moist and relaxed as they moved over his. Slowly . . . sensually. Alex heard himself moan as her tongue traced the outline of his mouth, then with an unhurried motion, eased its way between his teeth.

You must put a stop to this. But when Alex's hands finally moved, it was not to follow his mind's command. He wrapped his arms around Elizabeth's thinly clad body, pulling her into the cradle of his own.

Elizabeth felt as if she were floating through the most wonderful dream. She flew among the stars with Alexander. His touch was magic, his nearness was all she could ever want. It was wonderful. It was heavenly.

Then, abruptly, her stomach lurched, and reality came crashing in around her. She twisted away, and felt a cold sweat break out across her forehead.

"What is it, Elizabeth? What's wrong?"

Elizabeth could barely understand what Alexander had asked her. The spinning in her head interfered with her thinking. She leaned against his chest, but it didn't help. "I . . . I'm going to be sick."

Chapter Nine

Flickering firelight danced merrily on the white-washed wall, playing hide-and-seek with the shadows of predawn. Elizabeth awakened slowly, vaguely aware of the dull ache in her head, and the scratchy wool beneath her cheek. Where could she be? The solid warmth lodged against her back shifted, and realization flooded her senses.

She was stuck in an abandoned cabin somewhere on the road outside of Frankford, in a snowstorm. Elizabeth paused to listen. The steady sonorous sounds behind her vied with her pounding heart for dominance, but she could detect not the slightest hint of howling wind. The storm had abated.

However, before this knowledge could brighten her spirit, a hand, strong and sure, slid around her body. With an aim more true than any sharpshooter, it grasped hold of her breast.

A squeal escaped Elizabeth as she bolted from beneath the cover of her cloak. She couldn't be certain if its cause was the major's bold action or the feel of the cold floor under her feet. Whatever the reason the sound startled the major—who, Elizabeth now realized, had been asleep. While she watched in wide-eyed shock, he leaped from the makeshift pallet of blanket and straw, grabbing his pistol.

Firelight flashed off the cocked gun's burnished brass trim as Alexander's gaze darted about the room, freezing momentarily on Elizabeth, before finally settling on the door. His squared-off stance exuded pent-up power. The muscles of his back and shoulders—and lower body—were stretched taut. For long moments he stood that way, seemingly straining to detect the slightest sound.

"What is it? What did you hear?" His gravelly whisper was sleep tinged but firm. He accompanied it with a quick glance behind him to where Elizabeth stood quaking beside the fireplace.

"Nothing." The word, barely louder than a breath, drifted on the tense air.

"What?" He moved to the window, and peered out into the darkness.

Elizabeth cleared her throat. She clasped her hands, and said as calmly as she could, "I didn't hear anything." She knew the exact moment her words registered in his mind. He lowered the gun ever so slightly and turned till his eyes locked with hers.

"Then why in the hell did you scream?" Exasperation laced his question.

"I . . . I . . ." What was he so angry about?

170

None of this would have happened if he hadn't grabbed her in his sleep. "I didn't scream."

"You didn't . . ." Alex rubbed the heel of his hand over his gritty eyes, trying to clear his head. He couldn't have dreamed the sound of her anguished cry. It had been too real. "I heard you."

"It wasn't a scream," Elizabeth insisted. "Possibly a small cry—nothing more."

"Oh, pardon me, Miss Elizabeth." Alex's eyes narrowed. "How foolish of me to mistake a cry, a small cry," he amended, sarcastically, "for a scream."

Elizabeth bit her bottom lip. "You needn't use that tone with me."

She was going to cry. Damn! Alex raked his fingers through his sleep-tossed hair. She was right. He shouldn't be angry with her just because she'd jolted him out of the best damn dream he'd ever had. Could she help it that she looked just as she had in that dream, with her black curls tumbling around her shoulders? No. She couldn't even help it that the drawstring of her shift had slipped during the night, and the sight of her nearly bare breasts was frustrating the hell out of him.

Alex sighed. Something must have frightened her, and she was right. He hadn't been very sympathetic. "I'm sorry, Elizabeth. Now can you tell me what made you sc—cry out?"

She couldn't! She just couldn't tell him she'd precipitated all this trouble because he'd touched her breast in his sleep—especially since she'd allowed him to do the very same thing while they were both awake. Elizabeth's mind searched for some excuse, finally lighting on the one that was possible. "The floor was cold."

"The floor . . ." Alex's control broke. He'd been scared to death that something was hurting her when he'd awakened to her cry. "You caused me to lose ten years of my life because the damn floor was cold?" The hand that held the pistol dropped to his side.

Elizabeth tried not to follow the path of the gun—she really did. But it had been such a strain to keep her gaze trained above his waist, especially when she knew . . . Her eyes of their own volition drifted down.

"What is wrong with you now?" Her face looked as if the color had been drained from it, and she had a drop-jawed expression that confounded him.

His voice forced her eyes up to meet his. "You . . . you're naked."

Blue eyes shot down, then back up to meet Elizabeth's, as if daring her to look anywhere but his face. His ripe oath sounded mumbled as he jerked forward, swiping the blanket off the floor. Straw that he'd brought in from the lean-to last night to soften their bed sprayed up as he whipped the wool around his lean middle tucking in the excess.

Elizabeth thought she detected the slightest stain of heightened color brushing the chiseled planes of his cheeks, but that couldn't be. Nothing about his body should cause embarrassment. Granted she'd allowed herself but a moment to view its burnished perfection, however, the image seemed to have seared itself into her memory. Elizabeth had no doubt that in a year's time, ten year's time, she'd have naught to do but close her eyes, and the vision of him standing tall and proud before her would return.

She'd be able to see the dance of firelight play across the smooth ripple of well-honed muscles and dark-honey skin, see the sprinkling of hair that roughened his chest then arrowed down to form a nest for . . . Elizabeth's lashes drifted shut.

"Hell, you're not going to faint, are you?" The sight of him didn't usually have *that* effect on women. Irrationally, her behavior annoyed him— probably because the sight of her induced anything but that type of reaction in him. Just being this close to her partially clothed body was causing part of him to stiffen behind the scratchy wool.

"No." Elizabeth's eyes shot open as his large hands pressed into her upper arms. She hadn't heard him move, but now he stood so close she was aware of the faint smells of leather and outdoors that clung to him. She breathed deeply, letting the fragrance mingle with the sights in her mind.

"If seeing me nude bothered you so much, it would have been easier if you'd have just mentioned it to me earlier," he growled. She looked as if she would pass out any second.

Why was he yelling at her? He was the one who'd marched around without a stitch of covering, and she told him so.

Marching? "I was hardly marching. Like a fool, I thought you needed my protection — again."

Oh . . . His reference to her helplessness made her so angry. Her gray eyes turned stormy. "Well, perhaps you have helped me," honesty made her add, "a few times. But it was hardly necessary to remove your breeches to do it this time."

"They were wet." He bit out each word with a vengeance. "Besides, as sick as you were last night, I wouldn't have thought you'd notice."

Gossamer-soft memories of his holding her, comforting her, as she moaned in agony, drifted across her mind. Her misery had been her own fault. He'd told her to drink water instead of the whiskey, yet he'd taken care of her without a moment's complaint. Elizabeth opened her mouth to thank him, but he never gave her the chance.

His steely gaze raked her insolently. "You hardly appear the one to berate me for my lack of modesty. This bares more than it covers." Alex meant only to flick the wispy ribbon that maintained a precarious bow above her breasts, but his finger grazed the soft mound of flesh instead. He heard her small gasp, saw the delicate fluttering of her heartbeat, and he could not move his hand.

His touch tore through her body shattering all thought but her desire for him. She raised her hand, pressing his hand more firmly against her, feeling her nipple harden in his palm.

Molten blue eyes burned into her soul. "We can not do this, Elizabeth."

His words warred with the mesmerizing movement of his hand. Elizabeth moaned, leaning into him, willing him to continue. He'd resisted her last night when the whiskey had made her daring. Would he do the same now? Unable to stop herself, Elizabeth searched for and found the end of the ribbon. With a single movement she released the bow. The shift slipped lower, catching on the crests of her breasts, forcing them into further prominence.

The crush of his mouth against hers forced the air from her. His tongue filled her mouth, his taste and smell filled her senses. Elizabeth's arms wove around his waist, following the curves of his sturdy ribs. His skin burned hot against hers. She luxuriated in the heat.

Skin as soft and silky as a butterfly's wing drew Alex's fingers. He traced the curve of her small, tight breast, her smooth stomach and lower, pushing the shift ahead of his greedy hand. When the linen drifted on a silent wisp of air to form a circling, white pool at her feet, Alex pulled back, allowing his eyes to feast upon her fragile beauty.

Blood rushed through Elizabeth's body, tinting the pale pearl of her skin a delicate, rosebud pink as his hungry gaze wandered over her, lingering on the swell of her breasts, the apex of her thighs.

"You're lovely." His words were a husky whisper. "More lovely than even *I* had thought possible, and I want you so much, but . . ."

His gravelly voice sent tingles racing down her spine, yet wrapped around the sentiment, buried but fighting its way to the surface was doubt—

hesitancy. Was he withdrawing from her? Heavy-lidded eyes, darker now than the deep blue of new-dyed indigo, stared into her own. What had he said? *We can not do this, Elizabeth.* He was thinking that. She could see the thought battling in his mind with the desire he could not quite resist.

But . . . His word hung heavy on the sizzling air between them, like a jagged bolt of lightning trapped in the prestorm sky. With those three letters, he offered her an escape. The intrepid major who allowed no quarter to the enemy had tendered her release from his passion.

But did she want it? Could she—did she—wish to resist the boiling caldron of emotion he evoked in her? Would turning her back now, pulling up the shreds of her modesty with a whisper of linen, erase him from her mind?

Never. The answer came quickly. He lived in her thoughts, in her heart . . . he would always. Since the moment she'd seen him stride into the ballroom at Landon Hall, part of him had dwelled within her. The time had come to have all of him.

The separating space melted away as Elizabeth, her decision made, molded her body to the iron-hard contours of his. She heard his sharp intake of breath, the deep, rumbling moan that followed. The sounds echoed through her head, intensifying till they pounded in harmony with her raging pulse, obliterating all thoughts but one. Love. She did love him. Foolish as it was, impossible as it was, there could be no denying it.

Love had made her wanton, shamelessly longing

for his touch, at the marsh. She had mourned, as only a woman in love could, when she'd thought him dead, and that same love had restrained her from revealing his presence at General Howe's ball. Love. Foolish, impossible love. The word permeated her mind until his lips touched hers, and then even that thought disappeared.

Strong fingers tilted her head back, seeking better purchase for the onslaught of his kiss. Elizabeth's hair grazed, whisper soft, across the swell of her buttocks. How could the feel of her own curls be so invitingly sensual? The reason could only be Alexander. He'd awakened her senses, filling them with the sights, the sounds, the smells that aroused her.

"Elizabeth." He whispered her name as his lips left hers to trail kisses, warm and sweet, down her neck. His whiskers bristled, abrading her delicate skin, but there was no discomfort. Quite the contrary, the sensations his manly texture produced sent shivers of anticipation singing through her veins.

Lower his mouth traced, skimming over the swell of her breast, clamping greedily to its crest. He suckled, teasing the turgid tip with his tongue, and Elizabeth's legs lost their ability to support her. She clung to his broad shoulders, the pillar of his neck, thankful for the arms that held her tightly against him.

His blanket slipped, its makeshift tuck of wool no match for their eager bodies. Now Elizabeth could feel the strong, corded muscles of his thighs.

They cradled hers, drawing her against the rock-hard proof of his passion. Raw need swept through her, pooling in the depths of her womanhood, forcing a shameless plea of desire to her lips.

"Please . . . oh, please." Elizabeth's small fists flexed spasmodically as she begged for the unknown.

Her breathless cry filtered through to the tiny scrap of reason that Alex's mind maintained. God, what was he doing? This was no woman to be toyed with. This was Elizabeth. He dug his fingers in the thick satin of her hair, his thumbs smoothing the straight line of her brow, the baby-fine curls at her temple. His hair-roughened chest expanded and contracted rhythmically, as he strove to regain control. "You don't know what you're asking for, Elizabeth." Eyes bold and blue searched hers, willed her to understand. "You deserve more than to be taken on a straw-covered floor."

"But it's all we have." Elizabeth's voice held a note of desperation. Her hand outlined the firm curve of his jaw; her eyes, silvery and luminous with desire, beseeched. "It's all we may ever have."

Turning his head into her palm, Alex kissed the satin-smooth skin. This *was* all they could have, and he wanted it—her—more than he'd ever wanted anything. Slowly, allowing her time to change her mind, Alex spread the blanket over the straw, and lowered her onto it. His heart pounded in his chest as she raised her arms invitingly.

Eager and magnificently ready, Alex hesitated but a moment before sinking down beside her. He kissed her eyes, her cheek, the tiny, intriguing cleft in her chin. "I don't want you to be sorry."

"I never will."

The breath from her words fanned across his face, warmed his soul. But honesty forced him to tell her the truth. "When the dawn comes, I will take you back to Philadelphia . . . leave you . . . forget . . ." Alex's voice faltered as he gazed into the silvery depths of her eyes. He took a deep breath. "I'll have to forget you, Elizabeth. I can offer you noth—"

Elizabeth's mouth silenced him as she wound her arms around his neck, tugging Alexander's lips down to meet hers. With that touch, his hesitancy disappeared. Wild and sensual, his tongue plundered her mouth, meeting hers in an intoxicating dance old as the ages. His fingers stroked her flesh, following the gentle curves of her body till they tangled in the soft thatch of midnight black below her stomach. Warm and moist she drew him, tantalizing him with the promise of fulfillment.

Writhing with desire, Elizabeth arched against the sweet torture of his hand. The longing ache inside intensified until she thought she could bear it no more. Then with the brilliance of a splendid sunset, the release burst upon her.

Still tingling with the aftermath of her surrender, Elizabeth welcomed Alexander's weight as he rolled atop her. His mat of soft chest hair skimmed across her breasts, sending new tremors spinning through her body. Alexander's arms, muscles bunched, quivered with suppressed strength, as he

179

stared into her eyes.

With a bold thrust, he imbedded himself within her. Elizabeth's small gasp of pain was soon forgotten as her body stretched to accommodate his size. Moving slowly at first, then plunging deeper, Alex tutored her body to the ways of pleasure.

Elizabeth embraced him with her legs, her arms, the curve of her body. She moved with him, instinctively, loving the length of his hardness inside her. Feeling—knowing—that this was how it should be.

Helpless cries escaped her as his movements grew more frenzied. She clutched at his sweat-slicked skin, scoring the bronzed flesh with her short nails. Tighter, the sweet ache inside her grew, until with one powerful plunge, he sent her spinning breathlessly into a world of flashing colors, and dizzying dreams.

On a ragged gasp of breath, Alex collapsed on top of Elizabeth. He buried his face in her soft breasts, savoring the hint of lavender that clung to her skin. Never before had he experienced anything to compare with what had just happened. His soul felt shattered, splintered into a thousand pieces that only Elizabeth could reunite. "This changes nothing," he said more to himself than her. "It can't."

"I know," Elizabeth lied as he rolled to her side, gathering her body firmly in the crook of his arm. How could anything ever be the same? She was fragmented, shamelessly, helplessly in love. But she couldn't tell him. Alexander had made his position very clear from the beginning. He wanted no ties to bind them. Even the intimacy they'd just shared had not swayed him. His resolve was unalterable, strict and unmoving as the lines of battle between the British and the Patriots. But certainly this would not last forever. History had proven that wars ended, breaches healed, people lived together in peace once more.

"Alexander, perhaps when this war is over, we—"

"Don't!" Alexander rolled over, propping himself on his elbow, searching the clear gray of her eyes. "This war will not end. At least no time soon. General Washington is not about to surrender—and neither am I." His voice softened. "Please don't harbor any dream of tomorrows that can never be."

His expression was so sad, Elizabeth could almost believe he regretted the sentiment as much as she. She swallowed past the lump in her throat, and nodded. "I shan't." The steadiness of her voice made Elizabeth wonder at her ability to be so convincing. "Chances are we shall never meet again. And that is, after all, for the best."

"Yes," he agreed. "For the best." In the fireplace a log shifted, scattering a spray of sparks onto the hearth. For an instant, they burned brightly, then faded and died. Alex leaned forward, kissing the dimpled chin. "Go to sleep, Elizabeth. The storm has blown itself out. We'll leave for Philadelphia at first light."

How long she lay there, cuddled in Alexander's strong arms, willing herself to sleep, Elizabeth didn't know. His steady breathing soothed her, but her mind could not rest. What was she going to

181

do? Could she possibly go home and forget about him? The answer to that was clear. She'd tried it before to no avail. She wasn't completely certain that he'd be able to put her from his mind either. If only there were no war . . .

"Alexander?" She whispered his name on a breath of air.

"Hmmm?"

He couldn't sleep. The realization warmed Elizabeth's heart. "Why do you do it?"

"Do what?"

"Fight the British, your own people?" Elizabeth's hair formed a lacy cocoon separating them from the outside world as she sat up and leaned over him. "Oh, I know some of the reasons that men give. I've read one of Mr. Paine's pamphlets." At his look of surprise, she explained. "I found it in my father's library. He doesn't know I saw it. He'd be furious if he did."

"What did you think of it, *Common Sense* I mean?"

"I couldn't believe anyone would actually do as he advocated, I mean it was so radical . . . but they did."

"Declaring ourselves a free and independent nation hardly seems alien to me."

"Perhaps not." Elizabeth sighed. "But to separate ourselves from England. Oh, I realize that King George isn't always completely just, but he is our sovereign. Don't we owe him our allegiance?"

He returned her searching stare, his blue eyes unwavering.

"No, I don't suppose you think we do," Elizabeth answered her own question.

Alex tugged gently on a raven curl, pulling her back into the shelter of his arms. "I didn't ask for this war, Elizabeth, but yes, I believe as Thomas Paine does. The time has passed for us to follow blindly where a tyrant might lead us."

"A noble sentiment, but what will words do to help Mrs. Anderson and her family."

"Don't blame the Revolution for smallpox, Elizabeth. It's hardly fair."

"You're right, of course. But I *can* charge the war with the death of her husband, the imprisonment of her son." Elizabeth sat, turning her back to Alexander, and stared into the dying fire.

Alex reached up to touch a shoulder that peeked, pearly white, from beneath the obsidian veil of her hair. "Mr. Anderson was a free man who chose his path."

"Perhaps." Elizabeth rested her cheek on his hand. "But I wonder, in that moment before death claimed him, was it Thomas Paine's lofty ideals he spoke, or a prayer for peace."

"Elizabeth!" Alex jerked her around to face him. "I shall do what I can for the Andersons, but this war demands sacrifices from us all."

Ah, was this what she'd waited to hear him say all along? Did he consider giving her up a sacrifice? Her eyes shone silver bright as she challenged him. "I hope it's worth it."

"It is. I have to believe it is."

Elizabeth's head fell forward on his chest, all the

fight drained from her. His heartbeat resounded strong and steady against her ear, his hand smoothed the tangles from her hair.

"Elizabeth." Alex brushed a whisper-soft kiss upon her brow and felt her snuggle closer. "Just till the dawn, would you help me forget the sacrifices, the war . . . once more?"

Together they sank onto the woolen blanket. How could she deny him?

The banging of the door woke Elizabeth. She sat up, blinking her eyes against the bright sunshine that spilled through the open portal. Alexander stomped snow from his boots as he entered the cabin.

"You're awake." A grin lit his face as he viewed her tumbled hair, her naked breasts. "I would never have guessed you were such a lazybones."

"Lazybones, indeed. Why didn't you wake me?" Elizabeth noticed the direction of his gaze, and yanked her cloak up to her chin. A reaction that Alexander apparently thought very amusing.

"Maybe I just like to watch you sleep," he chuckled, reaching down to grab Elizabeth around the waist and pulling her to her feet. "Now hurry and get dressed. The road is passable and we shouldn't have much trouble reaching Philadelphia by afternoon."

Elizabeth clutched the cloak that kept threatening to slip, especially when Alexander leaned down and kissed her soundly. His spirits were much improved this morning, as were hers. Why he'd returned to his usual roguish self she couldn't say, but Elizabeth's own good mood resulted from a decision she'd made last night. After they'd made love for the second time, she'd decided to find some way for them to be together. Not today, of course, but sometime. She refused to believe differently.

The trip back to Philadelphia was uneventful. Today's sky, so different from yesterday's, sparkled a sharp vivid blue. Stacked limestone fences lined the road as Elizabeth and Alexander rode double down the frozen lane. Bordered by pines, their boughs weighed down with snow, the brilliant white fields shone in the sunlight. Even in the hamlet of Frankford, there were no gawking spectators to mark their passing.

Elizabeth leaned back into Alexander's chest, happy for the protection of his arms. With every passing mile that brought them closer to Philadelphia, her melancholy returned. It was all well and good to decide in her heart that she'd never give him up, but now that the moment of parting was close—

"Whoa." Alex pulled on the reins, and slid from the saddle.

Shading her eyes with the back of her hand, Elizabeth glanced around. "Why are we stopping?"

"It's time for us to part company, Elizabeth." He reached up, settling her back into the saddle.

"But . . . we're not in Philadelphia yet." Surely he wasn't leaving her now, not now.

185

"I'm aware of that." He untied his canteen and haversack. "The problem is, we could be running into British sentries at any time now."

"I have a pass."

Alex grinned up at her, his eyes twinkling as blue as the winter sky. "Well, I don't."

"But how will you get back if I have your horse?"

"Always trying to learn my secrets, aren't you, Elizabeth? Maybe that colonial was right the other day. Maybe you are a spy?"

She was in no mood for his teasing. "I'm serious, Alexander. We're at least five miles out of town, and this isn't exactly Sunday strolling weather."

"Don't worry, Elizabeth. I'll be fine. Much better off, mind you, than I would be if a Redcoat spied me riding along in uniform."

"But—"

"You'll be all right. Another mile or two down this road, and you'll come across the first British outpost. Show them your pass, and you'll have no trouble. And Elizabeth." He paused, resting his buckskin-covered forearms against the horse's side. "If there are any questions about last night, explain that you took refuge from the storm at the Rising Sun Inn . . . alone. I'll see that the Widow Nice corroborates your story."

So they really were going to forget . . . pretend that last night had never happened. Elizabeth blinked, fighting back the tears that threatened to spill over her lashes.

"Do you understand?"

She nodded. "Yes. I was at the Rising Sun Inn, alone. Pray tell, did I dine on chicken or stew?"

"For heaven's sake, Elizabeth. This is for the best."

"I know." She turned her head away. "How am I to return George to you?"

"I'm staying at number 220 South Eighth Street. If you ever need me, for any reason, get in touch with me there." Alex checked the landscape. Two miles from the nearest British outpost they might be, but the Queen's Rangers guarded this area, and he'd feel safer when he left the road. He'd only stayed with Elizabeth this long because he wanted to make certain she'd be safe.

"I . . . I'll see that your horse is delivered there."

Alexander touched her leg. Even through the skirts and cloak, he felt her shudder. "Elizabeth." He willed her to look at him, and she did. "Don't concern yourself about the horse. Simply get safely home, and stay there."

"I shall." Before she could no longer control her tears, Elizabeth kicked at the stallion's flanks, sending the great beast trotting down the road in a spray of snow.

Uncaring of the possible danger, Alex watched her ride away. When she was no more than a dot on the horizon, he shouldered his brown Bess, and faded into the woods at the side of the road.

Chapter Ten

Elizabeth hesitated in front of the imposing, red-brick house. She had no desire to join Sarah Chamberlain for tea, but had no choice. "Part of my penitence," Elizabeth mumbled to herself as her mind returned to the day, two weeks past, when her father had returned from New York.

Friend Evans, for all her seeming acceptance of Elizabeth's little adventure during the snowstorm, had wasted not a moment in relating the tale to Jonathan Lancaster. Elizabeth had suspected her father would be upset, but nothing had prepared her for his reaction.

She could still see the protruding tendons of his neck, the bloodred hue of his countenance, as he listened to the Quakeress. "Elizabeth," he had said, when Friend Evans finally folded her hands in her lap, her story complete, "take yourself home this moment, and go to your room." His voice had been calm—too calm—as in that electricity-charged moment before the storm.

And storm there had been. A short time later, her father had burst into Elizabeth's room, hardly waiting for an answer to his knock, demanding to know exactly what had possessed her to do such a foolish thing. Jacob Anderson's tale of woe seemed to affect him not at all. "At the very most, you could have sent someone else to relieve the poor woman's mind," he'd said. "But to go yourself into enemy-held territory . . . good lord, daughter, I gave you credit for having more sense than that."

Elizabeth had sat, thankful for the lie about the Rising Sun Inn, as he'd clutched a post of her high tester bed while berating her impetuous nature.

Alexander had been right about telling people she'd stayed the night with the Widow Nice. Elizabeth couldn't imagine how much worse the situation would be if her father knew the truth. *Actually, Father, while the storm raged, I lay, quite content, in the arms of the infamous Major Knox.*

"Elizabeth! Are you listening to me?" her father had bellowed, effectively cutting short her daydream about the strongly muscled arms of the handsome rebel.

"Yes, of course, Father," she'd answered, wondering how many of her punishments she'd missed hearing about while her thoughts had strayed to Alexander.

There was to be no more riding—period. If she felt the need to travel farther than she could walk, she was to take the coach, but only if she was escorted.

It took a multitude of tears and promises of good behavior to override her father's decree that she could no longer visit the hospital. But in the end, he'd capitulated, allowing her to spend some time there each week.

"And furthermore, daughter, it is my understanding that you've been sending your regrets when asked to take tea with the ladies of this town. That policy is to cease immediately."

That was the reason Elizabeth stood now, on this first day of December, in front of Sarah Chamberlain's house. The young, vivacious wife of elderly Zachary Chamberlain had invited Elizabeth to tea, and she dared not refuse.

Elizabeth sighed, and marched up the front steps like a soldier going to battle. "I wonder if father knows of all the lovers Mistress Chamberlain is purported to have?" Elizabeth murmured as she lifted the brass knocker. It was an ill-kept secret that while old Zachary occupied himself with helping the British, his lovely wife kept busy dallying with a succession of young, handsome men. Well, if her father did know, Elizabeth admitted to herself, he probably didn't care, as long as Sarah and her lovers were staunch Loyalists.

"Oh, Elizabeth dear, I'm so glad you could come." Sarah's voice, sweeter than the gooey inside of a honeycomb, drifted down the staircase as an indentured servant let Elizabeth into the hallway.

Watching her hostess descend in a cloud of pink lace, Elizabeth regretted her own decision to dress for warmth rather than style. Not that her gown wasn't becoming, but the quilted petticoat and heavy satin material seemed much too serviceable next to the furbelows and ribbons Sarah wore.

"You look well," Sarah remarked as the servant took Elizabeth's red wool cloak. "I hope you've recovered from your illness."

"Oh, yes. I'm feeling much better," Elizabeth answered with a smile, remembering just in time the excuse she'd used the last time she'd been invited to tea.

"Is that handsome Colonel Littleton still quartering with you? I swear, Elizabeth," Sarah cooed, "you do have all the luck."

Elizabeth hardly considered the British officer's staying in her house luck, certainly not of the good variety. But at least he absented himself often. Elizabeth mentioned this as Sarah linked her arm with Elizabeth's and started back the wainscoted hallway.

"Oh, what a shame." Sarah affected a moue. "But I have a surprise for you." Sarah stopped before a closed door. "The most delicious man is in my parlor. You understand, of course, that he's mine, but I thought you might enjoy hearing some of his stories about England. He's just recently come from there."

Elizabeth couldn't imagine anything more boring than meeting one of Sarah's lovers, however there seemed no help for it. Feigning interest, Elizabeth asked, "Is he a soldier?"

Powdered curls bobbed beguilingly as Sarah cocked her head. "Nothing so mundane as that. He's . . . Do you know, I haven't the vaguest idea what he is, except that he's frightfully rich, and more handsome than the devil himself."

Sarah opened the paneled door with a flourish, stepping inside, not waiting to see if Elizabeth followed. And she didn't. Elizabeth stood, as if rooted to the spot, her eyes trained on the tall, broad-shouldered back of Sarah's latest lover. As she watched him turn to the sound of Sarah's voice, Elizabeth told herself that, at least this time, she'd be prepared for the impact of his eyes.

But she wasn't. The moment Alexander's blue gaze scanned, then snagged on her own, Elizabeth felt the air rush from her body. Knees, weak as a new babe's, refused to propel her into the parlor, but, oh, how they longed to take her racing back down the hall and out of this house.

How could he? Not that the major hadn't made it quite clear that there was nothing between him and Elizabeth, but must he choose Sarah Chamberlain? She was so . . . Elizabeth watched the dainty green-eyed woman tug on Alexander's silk sleeve. Beautiful. That's what Sarah Chamberlain was, beautiful. A band around Elizabeth's heart tightened. It had formed when she'd seen him leaning against the marble mantel. No, it had started earlier, when Sarah had mentioned the word devil, for somehow Elizabeth had known even then.

"Oh, look, Alex dear, someone has come to join us for tea. And we're so fortunate to have her. Poor Elizabeth has been ill, but she's better now. Aren't you dear?" Sarah tore her eyes away from Alexander long enough to glance Elizabeth's way. "Though she does appear a trifle pale. Come inside, Elizabeth, and close the door. There's a frightful draft coming from the hall."

Until this moment Alexander's intense gaze had remained locked with Elizabeth's. Now he severed the stare, glancing about the room, then moving to stand beside a chair. "Perhaps you should sit down."

His words sounded innocent enough, but to Elizabeth they carried all the strength of a military command. She obeyed. Crimson, satin skirts crinkled as she sank into the Chippendale armchair.

"Goodness, Elizabeth, you look horrid. Maybe you should lie down. I can have a servant take you to a bedroom."

"No. . . . No, please, I'm fine." Did she really look horrid? Elizabeth wished she could pinch some color into her cheeks.

"I don't think it necessary for her to take to a bed. Some tea, though, might help."

"Oh, of course you're right Alex." Sarah sat behind the delicate cabriole-legged table, and poured steaming water from the silver teakettle. "In all the excitement of her entrance, I have been neglecting my duties as a hostess." Sarah leaned forward, allowing a more advantageous view of her bountiful attributes evident above the décolletage of her gown. "Dear Alex, this poor child is Elizabeth Lan—"

"Mistress Lancaster and I are acquainted." Alex's deep baritone interrupted Sarah's prattle.

"You are?" Sarah's voice registered surprise.

"Yes. We met at General Howe's ball."

"Oh." Sarah balanced the eggshell-thin china cup on a saucer. "Why, Elizabeth Lancaster, you let me go on and on about Alex, and you never said a word."

"As I recall," Elizabeth was amazed by her own calm demeanor. "You never mentioned your . . . guest by name." Had she almost said lover?

"I didn't?" She handed the tea to Elizabeth. "You're right. Silly me. No, sit here, Alex." Sarah patted the seat beside her on the settee. "It will be cozier."

Elizabeth sipped her tea, ignoring the pain as it burned her tongue as studiously as she ignored the sight of Alexander settling down beside Sarah.

"Have you been ill, Mistress Lancaster?"

"What?" Elizabeth's gaze shot up to Alexander's handsome face. Had he addressed her?

"Your health? Sarah mentioned you'd been ill. Were you?"

"No." Elizabeth heard Sarah's startled gasp. "I

194

mean . . . yes, but not seriously."

"Good. We've had some nasty weather here of late. I wouldn't want to think it had caused you any lasting discomfort."

"No, it has not." He sounded so concerned. Elizabeth could almost believe he cared, except for the way his strong body fit snugly against the rounded curves of Sarah's.

"The weather has been dreadful, hasn't it? And now there's talk that our dear troops will have to leave the comfort of their fires and chase after that rebel Washington. Oh!" Sarah's ringed hand flew to her mouth. "Zachary told me not to mention that. But I'm certain my secret is safe with you." She tapped Alexander's sleeve.

"I shan't tell a soul, save Washington himself."

Elizabeth's heart skipped a beat at Alexander's words. What was he trying to do, arouse suspicion?

But Sarah simply laughed. "Oh, you tease. I can't imagine why I find you so irresistible."

Elizabeth nearly choked on her tea. By the way Sarah's eyes devoured the man at her side, it was very obvious why—why any woman would. The salmon silk and cascades of snowy white lace did nothing to disguise his tall, powerful body.

Elizabeth wondered again how anyone mistook him for a British dandy. Even dressed as he was in silk stockings and silver buckled shoes, it was easy to imagine him garbed in his rugged buckskin uniform, the wind mussing his raven hair. Or with

195

his linen shirt open, exposing a breadth of hair-roughened, sweat-slicked chest. Or standing, proud and bold, clothed in only his desire for her.

"Would you care for more tea, Elizabeth . . . or Alex?"

"No, thank you. I . . ."

Elizabeth's voice faded away when she noticed that Sarah wasn't paying the slightest attention to her answer. Instead, she smiled sweetly at Alexander who merely shook his head at her offer.

"Thank heavens we shall have all the tea we want now that General Howe has cleared the river of those pesky rebels. Imagine them clinging to that ramshackle fort in the river, thinking they could stifle honest British shipping." Sarah sipped her tea delicately.

"They are hard to understand at times." Alex's eyes met Elizabeth's. "The rebels, I mean."

"Hard?" Sarah's curls bounced as she slanted him a look. "It is positively impossible to comprehend what motivates them. You'd think they'd have better things to do than march around the countryside, following that madman." She waved her hand, as if in dismissal. "But we won't have to worry about them for much longer."

"Oh?" Alex tried his best to sound only casually interested.

"Yes." Sarah leaned toward Alex, conspiratorially. "Zachary assures me that in but a few days' time the rebel army will be no more."

Alex leaned back in his seat. "I fear I've heard

that boast before."

"But this time 'tis true. When Howe surprises Washington's army at Whitemarsh, they'll be soundly defeated, and then . . ." Sarah shrugged. "No more silly rebellion."

"It can't be over soon enough for me." Alex crossed his ankles. "The whole thing is becoming quite tiresome."

"Well, you shall have to wait a few days, darling. Zachary wasn't certain when the troops were marching, but he did say it would be soon."

Elizabeth watched in disbelief as Sarah told all she knew about Howe's secret plans to the Patriot spy. The poor woman just didn't know what she was doing. But Alexander did. It appeared to be so easy for him. He simply stared into Sarah's eyes, gave her his heart-stopping smile, and gently prodded till she all but gave him the information on a silver salver.

Somehow, Elizabeth had always thought Alexander gathered his secrets listening at the keyholes of British officers, or stealing coded messages. She'd never considered that his clandestine activities might take place in a drawing room, or worse, a bedroom. Sarah's possessive hold on Alexander's arm made the possibility of the latter seem all too plausible.

Tears Elizabeth was too proud to shed welled in her eyes as images of Alexander and Sarah together flashed through her mind. Alexander had warned her. She had to grant him that. *Don't*

197

build dreams that can never be. But she had. In the long weeks since she'd seen him last, Elizabeth had woven intricate fantasies of what their life would be like when the rebellion was over. When they would be together.

Of course, they would marry, have children, and he would love her as completely, as passionately, as she loved him. Her plans, however, never included Sarah Chamberlain or anyone like her. Foolishly, Elizabeth had thought the war the main obstacle to their happiness. But that was when she'd thought the daring Patriot cared for her.

A new thought entered Elizabeth's mind. What if he'd used her, too? She was the daughter of a prominent Loyalist, a Loyalist who was privy to secret information. Perhaps Alexander thought she could also tell him of troop movements and such. He had no way of knowing that her father told her nothing—that she asked nothing.

Slowly, Elizabeth raised her eyes from the contemplation of her teacup to Alexander. Her breath caught in her throat when she met his steely blue gaze. He stared at her with an expression she could not fathom. Stared at her with an intensity she could not resist. While Sarah prattled on about Elizabeth cared not what, the tall case clock in the corner ticked away the seconds. And still he did not look away. Could he read her mind?

She could bear it no more. What he was doing to her, to her body, with just the power of his eyes overwhelmed her. So abruptly that her cup teetered, spilling droplets of tea into the saucer, Elizabeth rose. "I must be going," she announced, startling Sarah, and interrupting her story about General Cornwallis.

"Oh, but you can't leave yet," Sarah pleaded. "I promised Alex some entertainment this afternoon. And you know how dreadfully I play the harpsichord." Sarah gave Elizabeth her complete attention for the first time since they'd sat down. "Please stay and play for us. You'd like to hear her, wouldn't you, Alex?"

Elizabeth didn't even wait for Alexander's reply. She set her tea upon the table, and walked toward the harpsichord. Her senses were inundated with Alexander, her heart was breaking, and she was in no mood to argue with Sarah. One piece was all she'd play. Then she'd leave — go home and allow herself the luxury of being upset in private.

The ivory felt cool beneath her fingers as Elizabeth began to play. Though she'd tried to demur, Alexander had insisted upon turning the pages of the music for her. She felt his presence as surely as a touch.

Sarah's enthusiastic clapping drowned out the echoes of the last tingly notes. "That was wonderful." She sidled up to Alex, linking her arm with his, and leaning her rounded body against him. "It's too bad we don't have your violin here, darling. You and Elizabeth could play something together." She smiled down at Elizabeth. "Alex played for me when I was at his house the other night."

That did it. Argument or no, Elizabeth was leaving. It was bad enough that her imagination had conjured up visions of Alexander's long, hard body entwined with Sarah. She did not wish to hear of their affair firsthand.

"I really must leave." Elizabeth turned to her hostess. "I am feeling a bit ill—perhaps a relapse," she lied, with more ease than she liked to admit to herself.

"Oh, dear."

"I'll see you home, Mistress Lancaster."

"No!" Elizabeth realized she'd nearly shouted her response, and lowered her voice. "I don't wish to interrupt your tea. There is no need for an escort."

"But if you're not feeling well, I don't think you should venture out alone." Sarah was obviously torn between wanting Alex to stay, and a desire to do the right thing.

"Please." Elizabeth smoothed her gown's quilted petticoat, and walked to the door. "I will be fine. Fresh air is probably all I need."

"Elizabeth."

Startled by the sound of the major's voice, Elizabeth turned, her hand clutching the brass doorknob. He stared at her again with such intensity that tears stung the underside of her eyelids. "Please," she repeated. "I don't want you to come with me, Alexander."

The icy drizzle that enveloped the city gave her an excuse to hurry along Walnut Street, but in truth Elizabeth barely noticed the inclement weather. Too busy chastising herself for her past foolish dreams of Alexander, she simply drew her hood higher and all but raced home.

"It's my own fault," Elizabeth mumbled on a sob, as she let herself in the wide front door of her Locust Street home. Alexander had never pretended to be anything other than what he was—at least not to her. She'd known from the first that he was a rebel—and it hadn't mattered. Had known since coming to Philadelphia that he was a spy—and it hadn't mattered. So why was she all of a sudden so upset?

I can't stand to think of Alexander with another woman, she admitted to herself. Not the way he was with me. Elizabeth leaned against the banister at the bottom of the stairway, and shut her eyes. Visions of him paraded through her mind. Alexander, his strong muscles burnished by firelight. Alexander, the dip of his dimple teasing his cheek when he smiled. His long, callused fingers touching, tantalizing, as they skimmed down soft, pale skin . . .

Elizabeth's eyes flew open; then, clutching the newel, she squeezed them shut. It wasn't she! The woman in her mind's picture, the one Alexander made love to, was Sarah Chamberlain!

"Miss Elizabeth."

Elizabeth let go of the polished mahogany, and twirled around at the sound of the indentured servant's voice. "What . . . what is it, Polly?"

"Are you all right, miss?" Under her mob cap, the girl's freckled face wrinkled in concern.

"Yes . . . yes I'm fine."

Polly shrugged. "I have a message for you from that colonel."

It took a moment for Elizabeth to realize who Polly was talking about. "Oh, you mean Colonel Littleton?"

"Yes, miss. He sent his aide 'round to say that he'd be taking supper with you tonight."

Elizabeth sighed. "Thank you, Polly." How could she ever endure Colonel Littleton tonight? She started up the stairs, stopped, and called to Polly before the girl disappeared into the back of the house. "Is my father home, Polly?"

"No, miss, he's at Mr. Dreschler's house. Said to tell you he'd be home late this afternoon."

Howe's headquarters. Her father spent much of his time there lately. Elizabeth shook her head. It was too bad Major Knox couldn't dupe her father into revealing what he knew as easily as he had Sarah Chamberlain. Elizabeth was certain Jonathan Lancaster could tell the rebel spy plenty. Of course, he never would. Her father's loyalties were squarely with the British, and he was too clever to let any information slip.

Elizabeth remembered Polly standing in the hallway below. "Thank you, and please set the table

202

for one extra."

"Do you wish to be changing the menu any?"

"No. No, what I planned this morning will be fine." She had no intention of putting on a fancy feast for the colonel. Maybe if he was unimpressed with the fare, he'd make his visits even less frequent. Elizabeth knew she really shouldn't complain. Luckily, the colonel spent most of his time at headquarters, or traveling between New York and Philadelphia. If they must have an officer quartered in their house—and it appeared they did—then Robert Littleton was not a bad choice. If only he weren't coming tonight.

Climbing the stairs to the second floor, Elizabeth shed her damp cloak, and peered out the window at the dreary afternoon. She was tired of winter, and wished for the sweet blossoms of spring. But that was a long way off. Besides, if she were honest with herself, it wasn't the weather that bothered her. Flowers of every hue could greet her gaze, and she'd still feel as if her heart were breaking.

"Maybe I should return to Maryland," she whispered to the garden below. At least there'd be no chance of running into Alexander there. Just last week she'd received a post from Rebecca practically begging her to come. Elizabeth let her breath out slowly. She couldn't leave her father. Besides, she would feel like a coward running away. And the hospital. People needed her there.

She turned away from the window. That was

where she'd go. Being of help there never failed to revive her spirits. And she had as much as promised Jacob Anderson she'd be there on this day.

He seemed to improve every time she saw him. But Elizabeth was unsure if that was boon or curse. No longer ill enough to be a patient, he'd soon become a prisoner. A shudder ran through her as she thought what that could mean to the lad. Poor Jacob. He didn't even know of the curse that had befallen his family. Alexander emphatically declared that she should not tell a soul of the Andersons' plight.

"Do you understand me, Elizabeth?" he'd insisted on the road outside of Philadelphia, before he'd left her. "You are not to breathe a word to anyone that you've been near the Anderson farm."

His demanding tone had surprised her. "But surely I can tell Jacob. He's—"

"No one, Elizabeth. There's naught that young Anderson can do but worry, and no reason to make people wonder if you've been exposed to smallpox."

Alexander had been right about Jacob, Elizabeth realized as she took a dry cloak, a dark gray wool trimmed with silver fox, from her clothespress. Jacob had enough concerns without burdening him with the woes of his family. Upon returning to Philadelphia, she had told the youth only that she'd sent a messenger to his farm. Since he'd never expected her to make the dangerous journey herself, Jacob had accepted the lie easily enough.

Elizabeth stopped in the kitchen for the extra loaves of bread she'd asked the cook to bake. Stuffing them in her basket, she noticed the mince tarts destined to be tonight's dessert. Quickly, she gathered up two, tucking them beneath the calico napkin. Elizabeth could almost see the expression on Jacob's face when she gave him the sweets.

The rain had stopped, but a low, clinging fog rolled in from the river as Elizabeth stepped out the kitchen door. Hurrying through the garden and out the picket fence, she started down Sixth Street.

"It took you long enough to come back out. I thought perhaps I'd be forced to climb the lattice to your bedroom window."

A startled gasp escaped Elizabeth as she turned, in a swirl of satin and wool, to face Alexander. "What are you doing here?"

"Waiting for you, obviously. I don't make a habit of hanging around street corners, at least not in weather like this."

"But . . . but how did you know?"

"Where you lived or that you'd be coming back out?"

Elizabeth could do naught but stare at him with her wide gray eyes.

"You make a habit of visiting the State House. That is where you're off to, isn't it?" He glanced at the basket she sheltered beneath her cloak.

"Yes, but—"

"And as far as where you lived, you knew I was aware of that."

Elizabeth lowered her eyes. "Yes, thank you for returning my horse." The moment she walked into the stables two days after returning to Philadelphia, and had seen Hester in her stall, Elizabeth had known Alexander had been there. That knowledge had given her a warm feeling about him — until today.

Alex shrugged. "You returned mine." He wasn't sure exactly why he'd gone out of his way to find and return her mare, but he had.

"I'd told you I would." Because she felt foolish standing on the sidewalk while groups of scarlet-clad soldiers passed them by, Elizabeth began walking. Alexander fell into step beside her.

"Why did you run away from Sarah Chamberlain's?"

Elizabeth wasn't certain what she'd expected when she'd seen him outside her house, but it hadn't been this. His question took her by surprise. She forced her pace to remain steady. "I didn't run."

"Oh, didn't you? It took a bit of ingenuity for me to come up with a feasible reason to excuse myself. I didn't imagine Sarah, for all her fluff-filled head, would believe we'd both suddenly been taken ill." Alexander smiled and nodded to a British officer who hailed him by the name he'd given her father at General Howe's ball. "When I'd managed to disengage myself, you were nowhere to be seen."

"I didn't run," Elizabeth insisted under her

breath. "Besides, there was no reason for you to interrupt your . . . your tea with Sarah Chamberlain. Did you fear that I would run to General Howe and inform him of your presence?"

"No, I never thought that." Alex was at a loss to know why he had gone chasing after her. He only knew he'd felt compelled to do so.

Elizabeth's heels clicked on the damp brick sidewalk. "You needn't worry on that count. I owe you my life, several times over. I shan't be the cause of you losing yours." She slowed her pace. "You should know, however, that I have no information. My father offers no talk of battle plans or troop movements over dinner, and I ask for none."

"I'm afraid I don't understand."

Why must he make this so difficult? Elizabeth lowered her head against the damp chill. Clutching her hands tightly beneath her cloak she explained. "I'm not so blind I couldn't see how you were exploiting . . . Never mind. It's simply that being . . . nice to me will do you no good. I can't tell you when Howe's troops are leaving Philadelphia, or even if they are leaving."

The bite of his fingers into her arm was so unexpected Elizabeth didn't resist when he pulled her behind him into the alley. The basket knocked against her leg as she nearly ran to keep up with him. With little fanfare, Alexander stopped, using his body to back her against the side of a carriage house.

"Just what in the hell is that supposed to mean?"

Elizabeth's chest rose and fell as she dragged in air. She tried to calm her racing pulse, tried not to notice the feel of his long, taut body pressed against hers.

"Well?" He was obviously impatient — and angry.

As Elizabeth stared, wide-eyed, into his scowling countenance, her cousin's words came back to her. *'Tis said Alexander Knox is a spawn of the devil.* She shook her head to dispel the fanciful notion. She knew him to be no devil, but a man of flesh and blood. But if he was angry, so was she.

Even as her chin rose defiantly, Alex couldn't help admiring the tiny cleft that marked its center. If he weren't so incensed by her implication, he might have smiled at the way her eyes sparkled silver in that animated face. "I meant, Major Knox, that though some women, Sarah Chamberlain to be exact, might be tempted to pass you secrets across a pillow, I shall not."

"Across a pillow?" The dark shelf of his brows lowered, till they all but overshadowed the intensity of his steely blue eyes. "I assume you mean in bed?"

"Yes." Elizabeth swallowed, compulsively. She hadn't missed the throbbing muscle in his taut cheek, nor the clipped tone with which he spoke. "Let me assure you, I care not to whom you make love . . . I mean . . . how you collect your secrets. It's just—"

"Don't expect them from you. Right?"

Elizabeth nodded.

"So then it would appear the time and effort I invested in you while we were stuck in that storm was wasted." He heard her sharp intake of breath, noticed the shimmering of tears that glazed her eyes, and knew he'd hurt her. But what in the hell did she mean, implying that he'd made love to her in hopes of getting information?

Elizabeth tried to squirm away from him, but he used his body to trap her. "Oh, no you don't, Elizabeth. You're not getting away that easily. Tell me first what secrets I've tried to pry out of you."

Elizabeth stood perfectly still as the fog rolled around her skirts. She was very aware of the effect his nearness had on her.

"Well, Elizabeth?"

"None. . . . You've asked me nothing," she admitted in a breathy whisper.

"Ah! Nothing." He pressed closer, wondering again at how easily he could become lost in her softness. "I've asked nothing, nor will I ever. Then perhaps . . . just perhaps, what happened between us in that cabin had nothing to do with the war — or anything else except that I wanted you." Still want you, he added to himself.

Elizabeth felt the want, the need, radiate from him like the sun on a spring day, but she couldn't forget Sarah. She turned her head away from the intensity of his stare. "I suppose you tell Sarah the same thing before you . . . you . . ."

"Sarah and I aren't lovers, Elizabeth."

Her eyes shot back to his. "But she said she was at your house . . . you played the violin for her."

"Lizzie, Lizzie." Anger drained from him as his hands left her shoulders to tangle in the thick black hair inside her hood. "I hosted a musical. True, Sarah Chamberlain was there, but so were her husband and twenty or so others. I would have invited you, but I didn't think you'd appreciate the gesture. It was *business*."

"Collecting secrets?" Relief and desire battled for prominence as his thumbs caressed the sensitive skin below her ears.

"Yes, but not from bored matrons who repeat only rumor. I prefer to discover what's going on at the source."

Odd, but now that she knew the truth, Elizabeth was almost sorry. How much safer he would be dealing with the likes of Sarah Chamberlain than with whomever he considered to be the source.

He wanted to kiss her. Alex almost gave in to his desire to cradle her body against the whitewashed boards and taste again those sensual lips. But someone had come out of a dwelling to hush the dog that had barked incessantly since he'd pulled Elizabeth into the alley, and Alex didn't think it a good idea to remain.

"Come on. I'll see you to the State House." He noticed regret flash in her eyes as he withdrew the shelter of his body—regret that matched his own.

"I've mince tarts in my basket for Jacob."
They'd walked along in silence for what seemed an eternity, each contemplating what had transpired in the alley, and what might have. Elizabeth had spoken more to fill the void than to impart information, so she was doubly surprised at his response.

"Jacob isn't at the State House."

"Where is he? Has he been transferred to the prison?" Elizabeth's hand fluttered to her throat.

"No." Alex shook his head. "He's not rotting away on some prison ship in the harbor. It seems the lad escaped last night."

"You helped him." It wasn't a question.

Alex slanted her a look beneath his tricornered hat, and grinned. "Perhaps I had a hand in it. Anyway he's resting comfortably until it's safe for him to return home."

"He knows then . . . about his family?"

"I thought it best to tell him. But the news was not all bad. Both his brother and sister were much improved when I stopped by last week."

"I'm so glad." Alexander had gone back to help, as he'd promised.

They stood now in front of the State House. "I suppose I should go inside."

"Yes." Alex stuffed his hands inside the pockets of his caped coat. "And I should be going."

"Alexander." Elizabeth called his name as he turned to leave. He looked back. "If you'd had to climb the trellis, how would you have known

211

which room was mine?" The question had nagged her since he'd mentioned it when she'd come out of her house.

His smile creased the dimple in his cheek. "I know your window, Elizabeth. You've a fondness for viewing the garden through its panes. As you did earlier today." Alex chuckled and used a finger to close her dropped jaw. "You shouldn't be so surprised, Elizabeth. I am, after all, a spy."

Chapter Eleven

Darling Alexander,

My love for you will soon be confirmed. Ever since that night we met at General Howe's ball, my desires have attacked my common sense. I wished nothing more than that the white gown I wore would disappear, leaving me naked in your arms. I have tried to marshal my strength, but to no avail.

Please meet me at my home on December fourth, as my husband will be in New York.

I must warn you, that I await the moment with great anticipation. Just think, if it weren't for that awful Washington, we might never have met. Till then, dearest.

Love,
J.

The message had arrived as only the faintest brush of dawn streaked the winter sky. Alex, unable to sleep, had been awake to answer the door himself. After giving the boy who'd brought the letter a copper, he'd torn open the seal. Reading it through quickly, he'd smiled. This was what he'd been awaiting.

As a precaution, Alex locked the door to his study, and closed the heavy brocade drapes. The underside of his desk felt rough and splintery as he searched for the hidden knob. It opened with a satisfying click. Alex unrolled the sheet of paper that fell into his hand. The mask contained a pattern of oblong holes. Carefully he positioned it over the love letter and read the exposed words.

Confirmed. Howe attack white marsh, December fourth. Warn Washington. J.

Rumors of a British surprise attack on Washington's position at Whitemarsh, had been flying about the city for days. Even Sarah Chamberlain had heard them. Alex shook his head as that brought thoughts of Elizabeth to his mind. He had no time to waste on fantasizing. Apparently Jonathan Lancaster had discovered the reliability of the rumors, and the date the attack was to be carried out. Now Alex's task was clear.

Experience had taught Alex that unnecessary haste often led to errors. Carefully, he rerolled the mask, concealing the paper in its hiding place before holding the letter over the candle's flickering flame. The sudden burst of light as the parchment caught fire burned as bright as Howe's dreams of a complete and decisive victory over the American army. Alex watched with satisfaction as the spent ash drift onto the polished mahogany desk top.

Within minutes Alex rapped on Samuel Brown's bedroom door, quietly, to avoid waking the servants. "I'll be gone for several hours this morning," he began without preamble. "If anyone should call, say I'm indisposed. That shouldn't be hard to believe considering the state of poor Alexander Weston when he parted company with his fellow revelers last night." Alex laughed sarcastically.

He'd spent the evening with a small group of high-ranking British officers, playing his roll of bored English dandy to the hilt. The rum had flowed, tongues had wagged, but no one had divulged the information he'd sought. Alex wondered briefly about Jonathan Lancaster's source, but he knew better than to question it. The older man had a reputation, a deserved one, among the Patriots for the accuracy of his information.

"You've found out when it's to be then?" Samuel rubbed the sleep from his eyes, and scratched the balding pate under his nightcap.

"Yes," came Alex's succinct reply.

"Sure wish I could be there to join in the

welcome old Georgie Washington will have for them lobsterbacks." Sergeant Brown's eyes burned bright with anticipation.

"So do I, Sam. So do I."

The frigid December air sliced its way into Alex's lungs, frosting his breath as he made his way through the thin light to the stables. After saddling George, Alex flung himself onto the horse's back. Getting past the sentries was ridiculously easy, if you knew how—and Alex did.

By the time the weak, winter sun split the horizon, Alex had covered much of the distance between British-held Philadelphia, and Washington's camp at Whitemarsh.

"Blast those bloody rebels to hell!"

The outburst, easily heard over the violins and French horns playing a sedate minuet at the far end of the ballroom, caused a momentary hush among the dancers. Gentlemen, many of them resplendent in scarlet, paused before paying the next outlandish compliment to the silk-clad lady at their side. No giggle or tinkle of glass could be heard as heads, powdered and curled, turned to stare at the portly general who had voiced what many of them were thinking.

George Washington's ragtag army had done it again. If he hadn't made the British Army a laughingstock, he'd at least wounded their pride.

When they'd arrived at Whitemarsh to mount their surprise attack, the British had found primed Yankee cannon, and the rebels armed and waiting.

With his usual wariness, Howe had retreated, nary a shot being fired. Two days later, the knowledge apparently still galled.

"It's a momentary reprieve at best, General Warner," Elizabeth heard her father say as she stood by his side. "No one can honestly believe that Washington will keep his army together through the winter."

"You're right, of course, Jonathan. But it is just so . . . frustrating."

Elizabeth imagined the general planned to swear again, but his bulging eyes had shifted to her, and he didn't. Deciding that she, like Howe, should execute a strategic retreat, Elizabeth smiled at the group of middle-aged men. "Father, gentlemen, I've just noticed that Sarah Chamberlain has arrived, and I do so need to speak to her. Please excuse me."

They had been only too glad to forgive her departure, Elizabeth thought as she wended her way toward the opposite side of the ballroom. Now they could talk politics and war plans to their hearts' content. She probably wouldn't have stayed at her father's side as long as she had, except that she was curious about what had happened at Whitemarsh. Curious, too, as to how the Americans knew of the proposed attack. Could

Alexander have had something to do with it? Somehow Elizabeth had little doubt that he had been involved.

Elizabeth skirted away from the gaggle of young dandies surrounding Sarah. She had no desire to see or talk to the flirtatious woman. Though it might be interesting to inquire how she balanced her head when it sported a wig complete with a replica of one of His Majesty's frigates. Elizabeth wondered if it might sail away in a good rain.

She tried to stifle a smile behind her fan as the small orchestra began a country dance.

"Do you find something humorous?"

"Yes, Sarah Chamberlain's he—" Elizabeth had begun to respond without thinking. Silk and gossamer-thin linen swirled around her slender body as she turned toward the voice. "What are you doing here?"

"I thought it had already been established that you could expect to see me often at affairs such as this."

"Well, yes," Elizabeth began. "But I didn't see you earlier." Her heart fluttered madly, whether from pleasure or anxiety she could not tell, and she wondered if Alexander could hear its fitful cadence.

"I've been here only a short time. Few observed my arrival, thanks to General Warner's undignified outburst." He grinned, and his dimple deepened. "Should I be flattered into thinking you took note of my absence because you wished to see me?" Alexander's eyes twinkled as he noticed the twin dots of color that bloomed on Elizabeth's cheeks.

"Certainly not." Her chin tilted up. "I only wondered if you'd have the audacity to show your face after what you'd done."

The raven brow that Alex cocked did nothing to hide the mix of pride and amusement registered upon his face. "After what *I've* done?"

"Don't play innocent with me. 'Tis very unconvincing. I know you had something to do with the failure of Howe's surprise attack." The pressure of his hand, through the ruffled ecru lace of her sleeve, caused heat to flow through her body. She allowed him to maneuver her toward an alcove formed by a large bay window that looked out over the gardens. In the spring and summer, with the aid of the sun, it formed a pleasant nook from which to view the intricately designed rows of boxwood. Now the small-paned glass simply acted as a midnight-lined mirror, reflecting the opulence of the ballroom.

"You suspect *me*. First you bemoan my absence, then you try to flatter me. You must be careful how much encouragement you give a man such as I."

Now that he had her in a relatively secluded area, out of earshot of the British soldiers and sympathizers, Alex found himself enjoying the serious manner in which she chastised him. He could imagine her trying to admonish a beloved son for putting a frog in his sister's bed. Her sweet face would strive for sobriety, as it did now, but her underlying admiration for the audacity of the act would be difficult to smother.

"Oooh." He was laughing at her. The irreverent rebel disguised as an English dandy was making light of her concerns—and she could barely keep from laughing herself. When Elizabeth had first heard what had happened at Whitemarsh, her thoughts had flashed to Alexander. She'd had no doubts then, nor did she now, that he'd had something to do with Washington's advance warning. But her main concern had been for the rebel major's safety. Now that he stood before her, safe and sound, and strikingly handsome in a blue silk waistcoat that nearly matched the color of his eyes, she could relax. But she didn't think she'd allow him the same privilege—not just yet.

"I know 'twas you who warned Washington. Somehow or other, you found out when the British planned their attack, and you let the Americans know."

"I only wish it were true," Alex lamented. "But, alas, poor Alexander Weston had overindulged in spirits, and was able to do naught about the situation. I do have a theory as to who the true hero, or shall I say heroine, is." Alex leaned toward Elizabeth, more to luxuriate in her lavender scent than to make it easier for her to hear.

Not for one minute did Elizabeth believe his ridiculous denial, but he was so close that his breath fanned across her cheek. She would play along with his game, if for no other reason than to keep him near. "Who?" Her voice was a breathy whisper.

"Sarah Chamberlain," Alex said with all the sobriety of a judge.

"Sarah . . ." Elizabeth could not restrain the laughter that bubbled up. It was so utterly absurd. Elizabeth leaned against Alexander, straightening, and biting her lip to muffle her mirth when she noticed several heads turn her way.

"Now listen to my theory before you disregard it as having no merit." Alex had almost hugged her to him. He had been so close that his fingers itched from denied fulfillment. Elizabeth was completely captivating when she laughed. Her eyes sparkled, reflecting the light like a thousand prisms, and her sensual mouth turned up at the corners in a way he found altogether delightful.

He considered asking her to join him in the garden. It was cold as sin outside. He doubted either of them would notice for long, but there was her father to consider. The older man had disappeared toward the back of the house with a few Tories before Alex had approached Elizabeth, but he'd be back. It wouldn't pay for Alex to antagonize his most valuable contact. Alex must remember his priorities.

Besides, he had no desire to be involved with a woman, and he was already too entangled with Elizabeth as it was. If he had any sense he'd walk away from her this moment and never look back. I 'd forget about the lavender, the haunting gray eyes, the cleft chin. He'd—

"Well, what is it?"

Alex cocked his head questioningly, wondering if he could forget the creamy texture of her skin.

"Your theory. I'm curious as to how you arrived at your conclusion that she is our traitor."

Alex smiled. "Traitor is a rather nebulous term, depending upon your loyalties, but I'll let that pass. As to why I'm convinced that Sarah is our *heroine,* it is simple. You yourself heard her relate secret information to a questionable character. And what better way to smuggle information could one devise than inside her charming coiffure?"

Elizabeth's composure broke as she dissolved into fits of helpless laughter. Turning her back to the room, she stared into the star-spangled sky. "You're incorrigible," she gasped, when she could finally catch her breath. "Poor Sarah probably spent all afternoon with a hairdresser, trying to look her best, and then you make light of the results."

Alex feigned shock. "You mistake my motive, dear Elizabeth. Ridicule of the lovely Mistress Chamberlain was never my intention. I simply tried to relate to you my admiration of her innovative spying methods. Besides," Alex raised his brows, questioningly, "was it not you I discovered laughing behind your fan at Sarah's hair?"

Color blossomed in Elizabeth's cheeks, but though she raised her chin haughtily, her eyes danced with silver light. "No manner of torture could persuade me to admit any such thing."

Alex smiled down at her. She was rather tall for a woman, yet easily dwarfed by him. Just the right size for him actually, he caught himself thinking. Suggesting a stroll in the garden snagged at his mind again. Or the drapes. Alex studied the heavy brocade window hangings. With very little effort he could undo the tiebacks. The drapes would swish shut, closing Elizabeth and him off from view. Then he could kiss her, just kiss her.

"Hell!"

"What's the matter?" Elizabeth was astonished. One minute he'd been looking at her with an intensity that made it difficult for her to breathe, and the next he'd backed up, cursing.

"Nothing's wrong." Damned if he hadn't come close to taking her in his arms, tasting her lips. "I think we'd better dance." He shouldn't be over here having an intimate conversation with her anyway.

"Well, perhaps I don't want to—" Elizabeth began. Her protest ceased when it became apparent that want to or not she was being maneuvered into a lineup for a quadrille. Elizabeth glared at

223

Alexander over the three feet that separated them, but he only smiled back benignly. The music began, and Elizabeth had to concentrate upon the intricate steps instead of wondering what had caused her partner's abrupt change in attitude.

She had no idea what could have happened. All she knew was that every time his hand touched hers, she could feel the tension in him—feel the thrill of excitement he sparked in her.

"I'd almost forgotten," Alex began. "I've a message for you." The dance's pattern brought them together, so close that Alex could smell the clean lavender-laced fragrance of her hair. She wore it curled, but unpowdered, entwined with a garnet-colored ribbon that matched the love knot at her throat. The rich raven locks shone in the candlelight afforded by the silver lusters overhead.

"From whom?" Elizabeth tilted her head, slanting him an inquiring look from beneath her thick, black lashes.

Alex peered down at her and smiled. Elizabeth's manner was natural, with none of the practiced coquettish wiles of some women. It made her all the more charming. "From a mutual friend of ours, a lad of fourteen."

"Jacob." Elizabeth reached out to touch Alexander's hand, then recalled where she was and stopped. "How is he?"

"Resting comfortably with acquaintances of mine, members of the Society of Friends."

Couples shifted, and Alex watched Elizabeth gracefully weave her way through the dancers before he turned to bestow a courteous smile on his new partner, Sarah Chamberlain.

"Alex," she cooed, fluttering her beringed hand toward her breast. She'd placed twin velvet patches in the shape of half moons on the nearly exposed mounds. "I'm crushed that you didn't even say hello to me when you arrived."

"But my darling, Sarah," Alex said, affecting the speech of a flirtatious fob, "crushed is what I'd have been if I'd tried to fight my way through that mob of admirers surrounding you." Alex watched her preen under the false flattery.

"Oh, you are such a devil," Sarah said, sidling closer to Alex than the dance steps dictated. "I should be angry with you, especially since I noticed you found time to speak with poor Elizabeth Lancaster."

"Simply inquiring as to her health," Alex lied as the strains of violin and French horn moved the dancers along. Elizabeth appeared before him like a breath of fresh air.

"What is my message?"

Alex had wondered if Elizabeth would make any comment about his talking with Sarah or her nearness, but she didn't. Inexplicably this annoyed him. "He asked me to tell you he was doing well, and to thank you."

"You didn't tell him that I—"

225

"No." Alex chuckled. "He doesn't know about your little escapade in the snowstorm. I believe he is appreciative of the kindness you showed him at the State House."

"I see." The final echoes of the tune drifted about them as Alex offered Elizabeth his arm to escort her off the dance floor. "Will he be able to go home soon, do you think?"

"Hopefully, for a visit." Alex had meant to escort her to a group of women sitting along the wall on Queen Anne chairs, but instead he found himself guiding her toward the same alcove they'd departed before the dance. It would be impolite to leave her there alone, but then, he realized suddenly, he didn't want to leave her.

"I don't understand." Elizabeth's eyes searched his. "Why would he see his family for only a visit?"

"He'll stay at home for a while, till he regains his strength, of course, then he'll return to General Washington's army."

"What?" Elizabeth clutched Alexander's sleeve, as fear for Jacob came over her. "You can't let him do that. He's only a boy. You once said he was fourteen. He told you that, didn't he?" Elizabeth didn't give Alexander time to respond. "Well, he lied. He's only thirteen. A boy. A boy who's already been wounded once and who's lost his father. What further sacrifice do you want from—"

"Elizabeth!" Alex's hands closed over her shoulders, and he pulled her further back into the alcove, hoping no one had noticed her emotional outburst. He wanted to take her in his arms, to soothe away her worry and tell her everything would be all right. Tell her that there would be no more sacrifices to be made on the altar of liberty, but he couldn't. He could only try to explain the harsh realities of life to her.

"The decision was not mine, but Jacob's."

"But you could influence him. What am I saying? You probably already have." At this moment Elizabeth hated his cause so much, a cause that would take young boys from the bosom of their families, that she wondered if that hate spread to Alexander.

Alex felt as if she'd slapped him. His eyes narrowed till naught but steely blue slits appeared. "That is unfair, Elizabeth. I have done nothing to prejudice his decision. The seeds of freedom were sown upon his soul long before I met him."

"Words, Alexander. That's all they are. Powerful words that lead men—and boys—to their deaths." Tears blurred her eyes as she whirled away from him, her skirts billowing softly. He let her go, and she turned the corner of the alcove, running straight into her father.

"What is wrong with you, Elizabeth?" Jonathan Lancaster's voice was low but intense as he looked from his daughter's stricken face to the stoic countenance of Alexander Knox.

"Nothing." Elizabeth fought for control. "I . . . I was just discussing . . . the progress of the war with Ma—Mr. Weston."

"I've never known you to care strongly about the war, Elizabeth. Why are you so distraught now?"

"I believe your daughter's reaction comes from her disappointment that Howe didn't effectively eliminate Washington's entire army at White-marsh." Alex turned on his heel and strode away.

Elizabeth watched him wend his way through the dancers, all too aware of her father's presence by her side. It didn't take him long to reintroduce the subject.

"What did that man say to you, Elizabeth?"

"Nothing," she repeated, though her voice was stronger this time. "We danced, spoke briefly of General Howe's aborted plans, and I started to leave."

"Colliding with me in the process."

Elizabeth said nothing.

"Has he threatened to harm you in any way?"

"Alexander?" She was so shocked by the query, she forgot to use his last name. "Of course not. Why should he?" As soon as the words were out of her mouth, Elizabeth regretted them. She wanted to drop the conversation about Alexander, not perpetuate it with questions.

If he recognized Alexander as the brash rebel major from Landon Hall, her father might suspect him of menacing her. But that didn't make any sense. If Jonathan Lancaster suspected Alexander, he'd be alerting the scores of British officers attending the ball, not questioning her.

"I've no reason to think he would." Her father kept his eyes trained on the spot where Alexander had disappeared into the hallway. "Simply stay clear of the man. I don't want you around him."

Because her father had rarely—never, if she remembered correctly—voiced such an ultimatum to her, she longed to ask why. Yet she dared not. Instead she contented herself with studying his expression. Etched white lines of tension radiated from his eyes and the thin taut slash of his bloodless lips. They made the brackets surrounding his mouth appear deeper, the curve of his jaw more sagging. He looks older, Elizabeth thought with a frown of her own. Is it the war that has aged him so?

To further worry her, he looked up quickly—Elizabeth barely had time to disguise her careful scrutiny of him—and suggested they go home.

"Are you all right, Papa?" Elizabeth touched his sleeve.

"Yes, yes, Elizabeth. Just a bit weary, and I can't help but think you'd enjoy a quiet evening at home, also."

Of course she would. She hadn't wanted to come in the first place. Elizabeth let her gaze wander over the ballroom and spotted Alexander

229

talking with Sarah Chamberlain. He was possibly the only man in the room who didn't appear upstaged by her wig. Alexander must have felt Elizabeth's stare for he glanced her way, allowing their eyes to catch for just a moment before turning his attention back to Sarah.

"I think returning home would be an excellent idea," Elizabeth said. "I shall get my cloak."

When she reentered the central hall of City Tavern, where balls were held almost weekly, Elizabeth found not only Jonathan Lancaster but General Warner. She shied back, not wishing to interrupt their conversation, hoping her father would not forget his promise to escort her home.

"There she is." The British officer's booming voice beckoned her to join them. "I was just apologizing to your father, but you are the one I really want to see." He smiled, revealing prominent teeth to match his bulging eyes. "You must forgive my earlier outburst about our aborted surprise at Whitemarsh." He took her hand.

Elizabeth, wishing she'd taken the time to put on her gloves, tried not to notice how damp they were. "There's nothing to forgive, General." She flashed him her sweetest smile, hoping he would be convinced and would let her hand go.

"Such a lovely girl." Warner patted her captured fingers. "You must be very proud of her, Jonathan."

"Yes, quite."

The general smiled again. "I would never have said anything to insult your sensibilities, dear girl, except that I am so frustrated. General Washington always seems to know our plans before we do. I'm certain there is a very clever spy operating in Philadelphia."

Elizabeth wondered if the general noticed her hand turn to ice. "No doubt more than one," her father put in.

The general shrugged, the gold fringes of his epaulets shimmering in the candlelight. "There will always be spies. They are a necessary evil of war, are they not? But the man I'm speaking of is more dangerous than most. It shall be all the more challenging to capture him."

"Capture him?" Elizabeth pulled her hand away.

"Of course. It is only a matter of time. We are almost certain of his identity. We only await the moment when we've given him enough rope to hang himself."

Elizabeth took a deep breath, replenishing the air that had escaped her when she heard the general's words. "You plan to hang him?" She tried not to think of Alexander swinging at the end of a twisted rope.

"Naturally. Can you think of a more fitting punishment for a traitor?"

Chapter Twelve

Muted sounds, strange and ominous, surrounded Elizabeth like a shroud. She had never considered herself one to be afraid of the dark. At home, safe within the familiar confines of her room, she'd often welcomed the quiet tranquility of deepest night. Now she wondered if it had been another of her impetuous acts to stuff pillows under her sheets and steal out into the darkness.

It was recalling General Warner's words that had spurred her to action. She must warn Alexander. They knew his identity. Even now the British could be springing the trap that would send him to an ignominious death.

Elizabeth hugged her cloak around her shivering form, and tried to stop her teeth from chattering. Though the night was cold, she knew it was fear more than the temperature that caused this reaction. "I am not afraid. I am not afraid." Elizabeth whispered the words like a liturgy over and over again as she made her way down Arch Street.

She knew the way. Alexander had given her his address the day he'd brought her back to Philadelphia, and she had walked past it once. Hannah had been with her, and had wondered aloud why they were taking this roundabout way to the hospital. Elizabeth tried now to remember the excuse she had given, but couldn't. Whatever it had been, Hannah had seemed satisfied, or at least had stopped questioning her.

Somewhere nearby a cat screeched, and Elizabeth bit her lip to keep an answering scream at bay. Oh, I am no good at this, she thought. No good at all.

The pavement veered around a corner, and Elizabeth allowed herself a sigh of relief. Eighth Street. She turned south, searching the shadowy shapes for Alexander's house.

"Two o'clock and all is well."

Elizabeth heard the crier before she saw him, before he saw her. Quickly she moved away from the meager light of the street lamps and melted into the darkness between two brick buildings. Her hastily constructed plans did contain an excuse to use if someone, a sentry or other official, confronted her. She'd say a friend had taken ill and she was on her way to offer succor. But Elizabeth didn't want to use this, since it sounded flimsy

233

at best.

Finally. She peered through the darkness at the large Georgian style house. It had looked different in the kind light of day—friendlier, less forboding. Heavy drapes were drawn against the night air, and Elizabeth could not tell if any candles burned within.

Now, a whole new set of fears occurred to her. What if Alexander weren't here? He could be anywhere. Days ago he had told her that he and Sarah weren't lovers, but that may have changed. Elizabeth hadn't missed the intimate way they had talked at the ball that very night, or how Sarah had leaned against his arm when they'd danced. At this very moment Alexander could be in Sarah's bed—her husband *was* out of town. Or worse, Sarah could be in Alexander's bed!

Fresh shivers shook her as she tried to dispel the vision of Alexander and Sarah wrapped in each other's arms, laughing at her.

"Stop it," Elizabeth admonished herself. "You have come to warn him, now do it."

"You expecting someone, Major?"

Alex glanced over at Samuel and shook his head, as surprised by the knock on the front door as the other man. They were sitting in the library of the house on Eighth Street, sharing a glass of Madeira and talk of the war before retiring. It was late, but Alex hadn't been home long and he felt too restless to sleep. He'd been grateful for his sergeant's company.

He unfolded his long frame from the chair, motioning toward the hallway. "Perhaps you better see who is about this time of night, Sergeant."

Samuel Brown nodded. He reached down and patted the hunting knife strapped inside his boot. "Sure thing, Major."

Glancing around the room for his waistcoat, Alex spied it atop the desk, along with his wig and cravat. He'd removed them quickly thirty minutes hence, when he'd returned from the ball, and tossed them there. The jacket was wrinkled and dusted with fine white powder from the wig. Alex began brushing it off when Samuel entered the library.

"It's a lady, Major."

"A what?" Alex dropped the waistcoat, sprinkling powder onto the Turkish carpet. He'd thought it might be Jonathan, or one of his other contacts, but none of them were women.

"A mighty pretty one, too. Says she has to see you right away."

"Damn!"

"Beg your pardon, Major?"

Alex glanced up at Samuel and waved his hand. "Never mind. Send the *lady* in. Oh, and, Sergeant, stay close. I'll need you to escort Mistress Chamberlain home." Alex ran his fingers through his hair. Sarah Chamberlain had asked him to visit her tonight, mentioning in a none too subtle way that her husband was not in town. He'd refused, gently, feigning regret, offering the excuse of fatigue, trying to believe it himself.

He wasn't exactly sure why he'd declined her offer, or the others that had been tossed his way. He was, after all, playing the part of a British dandy. In New York he'd enjoyed the favors of several ladies, wives of wealthy Tories or English officers. Why not now? What had changed?

Alex stared into the fireplace, trying to deny the answer that kept flashing into his mind. No, he thought, as he turned toward the opening library door. He absolutely refused to believe the reason was . . . "Elizabeth!" He blurted out her name without thinking. Was his imagination conjuring her up? He blinked, but she still stood there, clutching the folds of a dark gray cloak, watching him with serious gray eyes. "What in the hell are you doing here?"

"Alexander, please forgive my coming here." She stepped forward, then glanced back at the other man who still stood behind her in the doorway. "I . . . I must talk to you."

Alex rushed toward her—he couldn't help himself. He'd told her to come if she ever needed him, if she were ever in trouble. "For God's sake, Elizabeth, are you all right?" He grabbed her shoulders to keep from enfolding her in his arms.

236

Her hood slid down, spilling forth masses of ebony hair.

"Yes, yes . . . . It is not I."

"Your father, then." Alex searched her face. "Has something happened to him?" Alex didn't like thinking about what the British would do if they discovered Jonathan in an incriminating situation.

"Father is fine. I imagine he's sound asleep. At least I pray 'tis so." Elizabeth had waited two hours after her house was quiet before she'd slipped out.

Relief washed over him. Elizabeth was all right. The British apparently had not captured Jonathan. Alex's eyes narrowed. "Then I repeat, what in the hell are you doing here?"

Elizabeth winced under the bite of his words. "Please, Alexander, if I could only see you a moment—alone." This wasn't happening at all the way she'd envisioned.

Alex inclined his head, signaling Samuel to leave them. He then let go of Elizabeth, and turned back toward the fireplace. He studied the blue and white tiles, depicting knights and their ladies that lined the fireplace opening, trying to contain his anger.

Elizabeth had endangered herself—again. Foolishly leaving her house in the dead of night. And for what? Alex heard the soft click of the closing door. He gripped the mantel, refusing to look

237

back at her. "*Now* will you let me know what is so important that you would risk your safety to tell me?"

"I hardly think my safety was ever at risk." Though she'd been truly frightened coming there, Elizabeth did not care for his condescending tone.

"You don't?" He turned toward her now, one raven brow cocked, questioningly. "Tell me, Elizabeth. Did you come alone?"

"Yes, but —"

"And have you not been warned of the gangs of armed Tories that roam the city at night?"

"Yes, but —"

"Perhaps you thought they might leave you in peace because you are also a Tory." He gave her no chance to even attempt an answer this time. "But I can assure you, Elizabeth, if they had come across you tonight, they would not have wasted time inquiring as to your political persuasion."

"Are you quite finished with your lecture?" Elizabeth glared at him defiantly. Perhaps she had not considered all the potential dangers in coming here; however, she had what she still considered to be a very good reason for doing so. And Alexander hadn't even allowed her to tell him what it was.

He shook his head. "I would address you on this subject from now until doomsday if I thought it would make you act more responsibly."

He was a fine one to be speaking about thinking of one's safety. It was not she who was a rebel spy operating in the midst of British-held Philadelphia. She told him as much in her haughtiest voice.

"We are not discussing me, Elizabeth."

"Oh, but we are." Elizabeth watched as he folded his arms in front of him. He seemed not to notice that his ruffled linen shirt was unfastened, revealing the strong muscles of his chest.

"In what way?"

"I heard General Warner telling my father that there was a spy in Philadelphia."

Alex shrugged. "That's hardly news."

"He bragged that he knew the identity of this person, and was only waiting for him to slip up." Even though Alexander didn't appear to be taking this as seriously as she would have liked, Elizabeth couldn't bring herself to repeat what the general had really said.

"Is that all?"

"What do you mean?" Elizabeth couldn't believe his reaction—or lack of it. She'd noticed his body tense slightly, but for the most part Alexander acted as if they were discussing which flavor of tea cake they preferred.

"Did he say anything else?" Alex asked. "Anything to make you think he suspected me?"

"Only that the spy was clever . . . and dangerous."

Alex sank into the chair and smiled. "And from

that you assumed he meant me? Should I be flattered?"

Flattered? Anger at his arrogance flashed within her. Marching up to Alexander, so close that the skirt of her gown brushed his knees, she glared down at him. "You should be careful. You should leave Philadelphia before . . . before . . ."

"Elizabeth." Alex reached up, grabbing her hand, and pulled her down on his lap. She went to him willingly, but kept her face turned away. Alex suspected it might be to hide the tears that he noticed beginning to mist her eyes. "Elizabeth," he repeated more gently, cupping her dimpled chin and turning her to him. He'd been right. Alex brushed away a tear. It sparkled, diamondlike on his fingertip.

Resting her head against his shoulder, Elizabeth let go of the tension that had wracked her since she'd heard General Warner's remark. It felt so wonderful to be sheltered by Alexander. She breathed deeply, filling herself with the masculine, musky smell of him. "Why won't you listen?" She wasn't even certain she'd voiced her concern until he answered.

"I did listen, Elizabeth. But you've known from the beginning that what I do is dangerous. I certainly can't run and hide every time some general decides he wants to sound important in front of a pretty woman."

"You weren't there. You didn't see his face. He

240

wasn't just showing off." She spoke against the soft linen of his shirt.

"But your father was there?"

Elizabeth sat up. "Yes, why?"

"No reason." Alex threaded his fingers through her hair, pressing her back against his chest. He rested his chin on the top of her shoulder. "I'm still angry with you for coming over here. Please don't do it again, unless you or your father are in serious trouble."

"I had to warn you." Elizabeth thought she felt a whisper-soft kiss on her forehead.

"Don't endanger yourself for me, Elizabeth."

How could she not do everything in her power to help him? She leaned into his body, listening to the steady rhythm of his heart. She loved the sound it made, the strong, even beat that vibrated through her. Tentatively, Elizabeth raised her hand, touching the hair-roughened skin where his shirt fell open. The cadence quickened. She savored his sharp intake of breath, the pressure of his lips on her brow. This time there could be no doubt that he kissed her.

Elizabeth lifted her head until she could look into his eyes. They were dark with passion, the blue of a late afternoon sky. A log shifted in the fireplace, hissing a sputtering complaint as it landed on the grate. And still they stared at each other.

"I have to take you home."

His breath fanned her cheek. "I know," she answered in a husky whisper.

Did he move or did she? Elizabeth wasn't sure, but the space between them disappeared. His lips molded hers, shaping them, devouring them. The kiss was hard and hungry. Made so in part by the fear they felt for one another. Though it had happened before, Elizabeth was shocked by the sudden explosion of desire that swept through her. Her tongue met his, plunging, learning the sensitive recesses of his mouth as intimately as he knew hers.

Alex pulled away, trying to catch his breath. It came in short, raspy gulps. "You . . . shouldn't have come here." The words, his lips, pressed hot and moist against her neck.

Elizabeth threw back her head, allowing him greater access.

"Promise me you won't do anything like this again." His tongue flicked the racing pulse at the base of her throat. "Please, Elizabeth." Shudders ran through her as he nipped her earlobe.

Instinctively, her arms wove around his shoulders. She didn't want to think of promises she feared she couldn't keep, didn't want to think at all. Her mind was going numb, her movements were intuitive, her only desire to fill the aching need inside her.

The rapping on the library door caught them both by surprise. Elizabeth jumped up. Alex had pushed aside her cloak, but she quickly gathered it tightly around her. By the time Alexander grumbled an irate "Come in" in the general direction of door, she was peering out the window into the darkness.

"Begging your pardon, sir, but may I see you a moment?"

Alex nodded at Samuel, both glad at and annoyed by the interruption. He had been on the verge of losing all control with Elizabeth. He glanced at her silhouette by the window, and had a sudden desire to dismiss Samuel, dismiss his duty, the war, everything from his mind. To simply take her—here, now, always. Giving himself a mental shake, Alex walked to the door.

"You got yourself another visitor, Major," Samuel informed him as soon as they were in the hall. "It's that Lancaster fellow. I put him in the front parlor."

Alex forced himself not to look in the direction of the library when Samuel spoke. What in the hell was Jonathan doing here? In their brief meeting earlier this evening, Lancaster had made it clear there was no news. There was always the chance he'd gotten wind of something between then and now, but somehow Alex doubted it. His mind strayed back to the woman in the library. Could Jonathan have followed Elizabeth here?

"You want me to take the lady home for you?"

"What? Oh, no. I'll do that myself after I see

what Lancaster wants." Alex started toward the parlor door, then retraced his steps. "Take the lady up to my room, Samuel, and let her rest. I don't know how long I'll be."

Samuel had lit a branch of candles in the parlor, but other than that the room was dark and cold. The fire had already been banked for the night. Alex found Lancaster standing by a window. Even though the drapes were drawn, blocking his view of the night, Jonathan's stance reminded Alex of Elizabeth. Well, this was her father. It seemed only natural they would have similar gestures, characteristics.

"I'm surprised to see you here," Alex began. "You normally send a message. This must be important."

"It is." Jonathan turned away from the window. Though Alex indicated a chair, Lancaster continued to stand. Alex did the same. "Are you threatening my daughter?" Jonathan began without preamble.

Surprised by the underlying hostility in the question, Alex countered with one of his own. "Why would I do that?"

"Damn it, Knox, don't play stupid with me. This isn't one of your little spy games. This is my daughter we're talking about. I recognized you as the rebel who broke into Landon Hall the moment I saw you, and I'm certain Elizabeth did, also. We both know why I haven't exposed your true identity."

"Ah, yes, *our* little spy games," Alex supplied dryly. What he was doing in Philadelphia was anything but a game to him. "But you are wondering why Elizabeth hasn't turned me over to the British?" Alex paused. "Perhaps you should ask *her?*"

"I'm asking you, damn it."

Alex studied the older man for a moment. "Of course you can't ask her, because then she might find out whose side you're really on in this war. What's the matter, Lancaster? Are you too ashamed of your allegiance to let Elizabeth know, or are you afraid she'd expose you?"

Jonathan started toward Alex, fists clenched, then apparently thought better of so foolish a move. "My reasons for secrecy are not the question here. Your threats against my daughter are."

A muscle in Alex's cheek throbbed. "I have not threatened Elizabeth."

"Me, then. Have you told her about me? Threatened to implicate me if she talks?"

Alex's eyes narrowed. "I have not threatened Elizabeth, period."

"But you haven't stayed away from her."

Alex met Lancaster's stare, but he didn't answer. He refused to lie, even if the proof weren't upstairs in his bedroom.

Suddenly Jonathan's demeanor changed. The anger left his eyes, and in its place came defeat. He

245

seemed to age in a matter of moments. "I don't understand any of this," he said, dropping his face into his hands.

Sighing, Alex indicated the chair again. This time Lancaster sat down. Alex poured him a glass of wine before seating himself. Compassion for Elizabeth's father had come upon him abruptly. Alex supposed, though they might go about it in different ways, they both had something in common—a desire to protect Elizabeth. He would relieve Lancaster's mind by giving him the truth—at least, part of it.

"Your daughter is protecting me because she thinks I saved her life."

Jonathan looked up, surprised. "And did you?"

"Possibly." Alex's eyes never wavered. "Elizabeth would probably have told you this, had you asked. The day after we raided Landon Hall Elizabeth took a ride to the marsh—by herself."

Jonathan's sharp gasp interrupted Alex's story. "Yes, you really should keep a better watch over her." Alex's thoughts strayed again to Elizabeth, waiting for him in his room. "Anyway, while she was there, three deserters came upon her."

"My God! She never said a thing."

"She wasn't hurt. Shaken up some, but luckily the Loyalists hadn't chased me very far, and I happened by."

"What . . . what did they do to her?"

"Nothing," Alex said firmly. "They didn't do

anything but scare her." He didn't think it necessary to mention what the deserters had planned to do. "Anyway, Elizabeth and I came to an understanding that morning. It was an unspoken understanding, but rather binding nonetheless."

Jonathan leaned back against the plaid cushion, becoming once again the shrewd intelligence agent. "How do I know what you're saying is true? Remember I saw Elizabeth's face tonight after you'd talked to her."

This is Elizabeth's father, Alex reminded himself, when he heard Lancaster questioning his veracity. Naturally he's concerned about his daughter. The thought kept Alex's tone civil. "I'm afraid you will simply have to take my word on it. Unless you wish to ask Elizabeth. But then, of course, she might wonder why you've allowed a Patriot spy to run loose in Philadelphia."

Jonathan's fists clenched again, however, his expression never changed. "Why was she so upset tonight?"

"We'd had a difference of opinion."

"About the war?"

Alex thought about Elizabeth's reaction to the news that Jacob would be rejoining Washington's army. "Yes, I suppose you could say that."

"And you wonder why I choose to keep my activities a secret from her." Jonathan shook his head. "She was raised by her aunt and uncle for the most part. Wonderful people, but there is no

247

questioning their allegiance to the Crown."

"You think Elizabeth has adopted their beliefs?"

"I know she has. Oh, she really doesn't become very involved with politics, but I know she agrees with her aunt and uncle. Her cousin, Rebecca, even married a captain with the Maryland Loyalists."

Alex remembered the wedding, or rather the post-wedding ball, well. But he wasn't as certain as Elizabeth's father seemed to be that any of that made her a Loyalist. "I don't believe Elizabeth cares as much about who wins the war as she does that it end quickly."

"You said yourself she argued with you about the war."

"Not the differing ideologies of it. 'Tis the human suffering caused by the war that she finds objectionable."

Jonathan sipped his wine. "What of you, Major? Do you find that aspect of war objectionable?"

"I'm not fond of killing, if that's your implication—or of the thought of being killed. However, I feel our cause is just and that sacrifices must be made."

"Well put, Major." Jonathan lifted the stemmed wine glass in salute. "I just don't want Elizabeth to become one of your sacrifices."

"Nor do I." Alex decided that though the Americans might need Lancaster, he didn't much like the man. Alex thought again of Elizabeth upstairs in his bedroom, and decided his own guilt might be affecting his judgment. Had he done his best not to become involved with her—not to allow her to become involved with him—a spy surrounded by danger? Granted he rarely went out of his way to seek her, well, not often anyway, but there was no denying the passion that flared between them when they were together. No denying that he'd allowed them both to be swept up by that passion.

Even now, as he sat with her father, Alex could not forget the kiss he and Elizabeth had shared in the library, or the fact that she was waiting for him in his bedroom.

He stood. Lancaster was right. He had to stop seeing Elizabeth, for her sake. "If you have nothing else to say, I'd suggest that you leave. It really wasn't wise for you to come here."

"No one saw me." Jonathan picked up the walking stick he'd leaned against the chair. "And I did need to know about Elizabeth."

"My advice remains the same. Keep an eye on her, or better yet, send her to Maryland. Philadelphia is too dangerous right now, with the British troops occupying the city, and will become even more so in the spring. My guess is that Washington will not allow the British to control the American capital any longer than he must." Yes, Maryland seemed the perfect solution for everyone.

"She refuses to go. But then maybe I haven't been insistent enough." Jonathan fitted his tricornered hat over his wig. "I shall be in touch."

Alex nodded, letting him out into the cold hallway. "Lancaster?" Alex recalled Elizabeth's warning. "Have you any reason to believe that the British suspect you . . . or me?"

Jonathan paused. "General Warner was boasting again this evening, but I don't think he really knows anything. Why?"

"No reason." Alex turned the brass key in the front door. "I mentioned that I didn't relish the thought of being killed. The idea of hanging as a spy has even less appeal."

Alex watched as Lancaster disappeared into the shadows beyond the first street lamp, then turned and bounded up the stairs. He'd give Jonathan time to get home and in bed, then he'd take Elizabeth to her house, and *order* her to stay there. Alex shook his head. Maybe he'd *beg* her to stay there. Until it was safe to take her home, he'd attempt to convince her to visit her aunt and uncle in Maryland.

His resolve stood firm until he opened the bedroom door and Elizabeth threw herself against him. Instinctively his arms wrapped around her, comforting, protecting, pressing her to him.

"I was so frightened," she whispered into his bare chest. Her breath played in the crisp curls there. "I heard yelling, and I feared—"

"Hush now, sweetheart." Alex buried his face in her hair, inhaling the fresh scent of lavender, wondering if he'd ever get enough of her fragrance. "It wasn't the British come to take me away."

Elizabeth thought to ask him who it had been, but decided perhaps she was better off not knowing. Besides, he was safe, and back with her. She nuzzled closer, trailing her lips upon the hair-roughened texture of his skin.

"Elizabeth." He meant to tell her to get her cloak, that they must leave, but the words never came out. She wasn't wearing stays. He could feel her soft, womanly curves through the silk of her gown. Smooth and inviting, the fabric held the warmth of her skin, and Alex couldn't seem to stop touching it—touching her. His hands slid slowly down her spine, pressing more firmly when they reached the swell of her buttocks.

"Oh, Alexander." Elizabeth moved against him, and even through the layers of her petticoats, she could feel the magnetic pull of his manhood, the answering need within her. She burned for him. Hands, made bold by the flame that seared inside her, brushed away the edges of his shirt, kneaded the coiled muscles of his back.

He took her mouth then, gently, his patience contrasting sharply with the throbbing heat she felt against her stomach, the fevered touch of his hands. Slowly, his tongue outlined the contours of her lips, teasing the corners, catching her breathy

251

sigh as she opened to him. And then his tongue plunged inside, any hint of self-control washed away by the force of his desire. The thrust of his tongue was erotic, a sensual motion, reminiscent of the way their bodies had joined before.

Elizabeth's gown buttoned up the front, and Alex made quick work of unfastening it. He slipped the bodice off her shoulders, stopping to brush her exposed flesh with a kiss before pushing it below her waist. The pale silk pooled around her ankles. A quick pull on her petticoat tapes, and linen sank onto the cushion of silk. Her shift of gossamer-thin gauze fell away, and Alex dropped to his knees to untie her garters, and strip away her stockings.

Primal need coursed through Elizabeth, as his mouth touched her stomach, her thigh . . . higher. She clutched at his hair, weaving her fingers through the thick, raven strands, thankful for the hands that cupped her buttocks. Without them she would surely fall—fall away from the liquid fire that was his tongue. And then she was falling—no flying—high above the clouds. Her body shuddered. Her knees gave way.

Scooping her into his arms, Alex covered the distance to the bed in long, greedy strides. He gently placed her on the heavy brocade coverlet, caressing her with his eyes. Her ebony hair, tangled and curled, fanned out from her face. Elizabeth was so beautiful, more so than he had remembered.

What had become of his exalted memory? He who could see a letter once, and remember every word, every comma; catch a glimpse of a map and reproduce it perfectly, had forgotten so much about her. How could he have forgotten the exact hue of her skin, its velvety softness. Or the gentle, delicate curve of her breast? Alex touched her cheek, and wide gray eyes, smoky dark with desire, opened up to him.

"You should not have come here." Foolish words, he knew with her lying naked on his bed.

"But I had to." Her fingers reached up to trace the line of his jaw. He shook his head, then kissed her nose, her eyes, the stubborn, dimpled chin.

"What am I to do with you, Elizabeth?"

"Love me," she answered, pulling him back to her. "Just love me."

Shedding his breeches, Alex sank onto the bed. Her legs opened to welcome him. Not allowing himself time to think about what he was doing, Alex thrust inside her. Hot and moist, her body surrounded him, offering a haven of pleasure from the harsh realities of life.

"Alexander." Elizabeth breathed his name against his lips as she moved with him, lifting herself off the cool coverlet, drawn always toward his heat. He pulsed within her, that iron-hard part of him that plunged deeper, and deeper, toward her very soul. She was near the precipice — she knew it.

Knew he took her there, knew they would fly off the edge together.

A ragged sound tore from him, blended with her soft cry of release, as his climax pulsed, hot and strong, flooding into her. His arms quivered, threatening to cave in with him, and Alex rolled onto his side, gathering her close.

It had been like this before with Elizabeth, this feeling that he belonged to her, and she to him. This intimacy. He felt it more often than he cared to admit, and not just when they made love. It scared him. Made him try to deny it.

He was a soldier, and worse, a spy. Such dangerous work rarely went undetected for long. Yet, he couldn't give it up, not when his country needed him.

But he'd already seen what living with the kind of man he was had done to one woman. His mother. Alex's father had been a scout for General Braddock during the French and Indian War. His mother hadn't been able to stand the uncertainty of her husband's life, and it had eventually killed her. A frail, fearful woman, she'd sunk into a melancholy when news of her husband's death had reached her. Nothing Alex could do had helped her.

Alex brushed curls away from Elizabeth's face. She wasn't weak like his mother had been, but she still couldn't handle the fear. He was sure of it. Her coming here tonight, wanting him to flee, had been proof enough.

"Elizabeth." She had fallen asleep, and he longed to let her stay, cuddled in the crook of his arm. But he couldn't. "Elizabeth, wake up." He could feel her awakening smile against his chest. "I must take you home."

Elizabeth sat up, more because of the tone of his voice than his words. Regardless of what had just happened between them, or maybe because of it, she felt a blush stain her cheeks. "I . . . I shall get dressed."

"We need to talk first."

What had happened to the passionate lover who moments ago had swept her to the heights of ecstasy? Now she stared into serious blue eyes that made her long to cover her nakedness. But she couldn't, not without seeming silly. So she simply met his stare, hoping whatever it was he wanted to say would be done quickly. And it was—too quickly.

"This can never happen again. I realize I've said this before, and yet, obviously, it has. But this time I mean it." He paused. "It would be best if you'd go back to Landon Hall."

"I won't." She sounded like a petulant child, even to herself.

Alex sighed wearily and sat up, leaning against a bolster. "I was afraid that would be your reaction, but I must tell you I can not meet with you again—not here, not at someone's house, not even

255

when surrounded by people as we were earlier tonight."

"Why?"

"I have a job to do, and you're interfering with it." Alex started to lift a curl off her shoulder, but she jerked away. It was probably best if she were angry.

"I see." Elizabeth threw her legs over the edge of the bed, and stood up. Scooping up her clothes, she began to dress. What difference did it make if he watched her? He didn't want anything to do with her. She loved him—had done everything she could to show him—and he wanted her gone from him. Elizabeth bit her lip to stem the tide of tears that threatened.

Alex thrust his legs into the silk breeches, trying not to look over at Elizabeth. Though she was obviously in a hurry, her movements were graceful and feminine. He jerked on his shirt. "Nothing could ever have come of this, you know."

"I said I understand. Please don't belabor the issue." She wrapped her cloak around her shoulders. "I can find my own way home."

"Don't be a fool." Alex moved in front of the door. His stare almost dared her to try to leave.

Elizabeth tossed her head, sending her hair tumbling around her shoulders, and sank into the chair by the fireplace. She wasn't so stupid as to think she could fight him and win.

"This is for you." Alex handed her a beautifully

256

painted fan. Elizabeth had noticed it while she waited for him, wondering to whom it belonged.

"I don't understand."

Alex shrugged into a greatcoat. "I bought it to replace the one you broke."

Anger, white hot and raging, swept through her. What was he trying to do? Was this trinket supposed to make everything fine? Her heart was breaking. She wanted him, and he offered . . . a fan. "I could still tell the British who you are."

He looked up, but there was no fear in his eyes, no surprise either. Had he expected her to say that? Shame surpassed the anger. Shame that she had been so predictable. Shame that she had threatened him with something she would never do. Elizabeth threw the carved ivory at him. Bouncing off his chest, it fell harmlessly to the floor.

"I don't want your fan. Just take me home, damn you!"

Chapter Thirteen

Alexander Knox, blast him, certainly was a man of his word! Elizabeth sat in her parlor, waiting for Hannah, and decided she could find no fault with him in that regard. He'd said they would have no further contact, and they hadn't. Through December, bleak and cold January, and now into February, their only communication had been a polite exchange of greetings at the theater.

She had accompanied her father to the Southwark Theater on South Street that evening. Major André was starring in the production, though Elizabeth couldn't, for the life of her, remember what play it had been. All thought flew from her mind the moment she'd turned and bumped into Alexander. It surprised him, too. There were other times when she'd seen him, at balls and assemblies; other times when she'd felt his gaze upon her only to look up and find it gone. But this contact was the closest she'd been to him since the night at his house—in his bedroom, in his bed.

Alexander had told her he'd come to the play because Major André was his friend. No. Elizabeth forced herself to be honest. He'd said that to her father. "You're looking well, Mistress Lancaster." That was all he'd said to her. Five words. Elizabeth caught her breath on a sob, and jumped to her feet. Marching to the window, she jerked back the heavy winter drapes.

Where was Hannah? She should have arrived ten minutes ago. If Elizabeth had known her friend would be late, she wouldn't have stopped organizing the larder so soon. That had been the day's project. The task that would keep her from thinking about Alexander. Nothing worked completely, but keeping busy helped. Then too, she'd seen him very little of late. Perhaps, in time, that would help her forget him. Though, for now, his absence at the Loyalist functions just piqued her curiosity.

Was he all right? Had the British truly discovered his identity? Or was it simply that cold weather had slowed the war effort? Did spies, like armies, go into winter quarters?

Elizabeth knew General Washington's army had. Before Christmas they'd moved to an area about twenty miles north of Philadelphia. Valley Forge, travelers had named the spot for the old forge on Valley Creek.

Word of Washington's encampment, and of Burgoyne's defeat in the North, was the only war news she'd heard this winter. Neither seemed to affect the British in Philadelphia. They continued to plan and attend balls, musicals, and theater productions.

Footsteps on the front porch caught Elizabeth's attention, and she rushed into the hallway, opening the door without giving Hannah time to use the brass knocker. "You're here at last," she said before she realized it wasn't Hannah but Colonel Littleton who stood on her porch.

"If this is to be my greeting, I shall return to your home more often," the British officer said, coming into the hall. He closed the door and took hold of Elizabeth's hands.

"I . . . I thought you were someone else." Elizabeth tugged gently on her hands.

"Oh, but I'm crushed, lovely lady."

Littleton's brown eyes remained on her as he pressed cold lips to her palms. Elizabeth tried not to cringe. She did however manage to free her hands. The colonel appeared only slightly taken aback by her action.

He whipped off his coat, tossing it across a chair in the hall. "I see you're planning to visit the rebel hospital again today, Elizabeth," he said, indicating the basket of food beside the door.

"If you've no objections." Elizabeth could not keep the sarcastic tone from her voice. The more she learned of Robert Littleton, the more she disliked him—and the more he seemed to pursue her. Elizabeth wasn't certain whether his attentions stemmed from a true desire to be with her or from the challenge of a potential conquest, but, in either case, she did nothing to encourage them.

"On the contrary, my dear. I find your humanitarian efforts quite admirable."

"I'm so relieved." Elizabeth went back into the parlor to stand by the window and wait for Hannah. Colonel Littleton followed.

"However, there *are* other hospitals in Philadelphia. Hospitals containing loyal troops of King George."

Elizabeth stopped her perusal of the street, and glanced over her shoulder. "Yes, I know."

"One wonders why you never visit any of those hospitals." He sat down, studying Elizabeth over steepled fingers.

"Perhaps I do. Or perhaps I simply choose to go where the suffering is greatest."

"Do not let sympathy for a group of misguided rabble affect your judgment, Elizabeth."

How dare he question her judgment. Elizabeth spun around, a scathing retort on her lips, but she stopped. Colonel Littleton stared at her above his fingertips, coolly assessing her next move. *He wants me to lash out at him.* Had her father been

261

right about their being suspect simply because they were Americans?

Elizabeth smiled sweetly. "I don't discuss politics with the prisoners."

"A wise move. We wouldn't want anyone to doubt your loyalty."

Elizabeth continued to stare at him as he rose, moving toward her with catlike stealth. She wondered at that moment how she had ever considered him anything but disgusting. He made her skin crawl.

"You really could use some protection, Elizabeth." He touched a lock of hair that had escaped her cap. "I could see to it that your allegiance is never questioned."

"Thank you." Could he tell how insincere her words were? "But I'm certain that isn't necessary."

"I wouldn't be so confident, Elizabeth. There are those in high places who, because of their penchant for listening to rumor and innuendo might already harbor doubts about you . . . even your father."

"That's ridiculous."

"You know that, and I know that, but . . ." He shrugged, then wound Elizabeth's curl around his finger. "You have lovely hair, Elizabeth. I've been impressed with it, and you, since we first met. It has long been my wish that we could become . . . shall we say, better acquainted."

Elizabeth swallowed. His meaning was all too

clear. Tiny shivers of pain radiated through her scalp as he tugged on the curl, wrapping it more tightly around his hand, but she refused to call out or let him know he hurt her. A minor victory, Elizabeth thought, for what could she say to counter his veiled threats?

Knocking on the front door saved her from responding.

"I imagine that will be your little Quaker friend." The colonel backed away from her, examining an imaginary speck of dust on his scarlet sleeve.

"Yes." Elizabeth forced her voice to remain calm, kept her step sedate as she escaped toward the door. "I must be going."

"Till tonight, Elizabeth."

Her hand on the brass knob, Elizabeth hesitated a moment, then left the room.

"What is wrong with thee?"

Elizabeth glanced over at Hannah, but did not slow her stride as they made their way down Sixth Street toward Chestnut. "I don't know what you mean?"

"Doesn't thee?"

Elizabeth ignored the remark and kept walking. She knew it silly to think putting distance between herself and Colonel Littleton would do any good, but at this moment that was all she could think

263

to do. He had threatened her, and her father, and, though it had been subtle, had given her a way to avoid those threats. A shiver of revulsion shuddered through her at the thought of what he'd suggested.

"It's cold," Elizabeth explained when she noticed Hannah watching her. She didn't think Hannah accepted her explanation; however, she could think of nothing else to say. As much as she wanted to confide in her friend, Elizabeth didn't want to burden Hannah with her problem. Besides, what could Hannah possibly do about it?

Telling her father wouldn't help either. He would become so angry with Littleton that there would be a row. Then the colonel would have to carry out his threats simply to save face in Philadelphia society.

Elizabeth was sorely tempted to turn across Arch Street toward Eighth. What a relief it would be to tell Alexander—to have him hold her in his strong arms. Hadn't he said to come to him if she were in trouble? But that had been months ago. What if he simply laughed, told her to give in to Littleton's demands? After all, he knew her to be no fainthearted maiden. Elizabeth dug her fingers into her cloak. No, Alexander would never suggest that.

But what could he do? Littleton would recognize him in an instant. Unlike her father, the colonel had gotten an excellent look at Major

Knox that night at Landon Hall. It hadn't taken Elizabeth long to realize that Alexander kept track of Littleton's comings and goings, so he never made the mistake of showing up at any function the colonel attended. Alexander had his own problems. She wouldn't add to them. This was something she'd have to take care of herself.

They were passing Market Street now, and though there was little in the way of produce to be had, and that at a dear price, there were more people here. Elizabeth pulled her basket tighter against her body. That's when she noticed the shock of bright red hair. Without thinking, she turned to follow it, wending her way through the noisy crowd.

"What is thee doing now? Elizabeth!" Hannah caught up and grabbed her shoulder, but Elizabeth kept her eyes fixed on the bright head that darted in and out of the crowd, never slowing her pace.

"I think I've spotted someone I know."

"Elizabeth?" Hannah's hand tightened, but Elizabeth shook it off.

"No. Go on to the State House. I'll meet you there later." It wasn't until she'd followed the redhead past the market with its smell of fish, toward the Center Commons that Elizabeth realized Hannah had stayed with her.

There were fewer people here, the British having finished their parading for the day, but now that she might have caught up with him, Elizabeth could find nary a trace of a carrot-topped head.

"Has . . . thee finished . . . running about?" Hannah asked, obviously winded.

"Did you see where he went?"

"Where *who* went?"

Elizabeth sighed. "The boy with red hair." She wasn't even certain it had been Jacob, and now it appeared she'd never know.

"The alleyway. I saw a lad dart in there, but I don't know if is the same one . . . Elizabeth?" Hannah found herself talking to thin air.

Littered with crates and barrels the alley was a treasure trove of hiding places. "Jacob." Elizabeth kicked at an overturned box with the tip of her shoe, barely suppressing a squeal when a cat jumped out, hissing. "Jacob, are you here?"

"You trying to bring the whole bloody Redcoat army down on me?"

"Jacob." Elizabeth hurried toward the sound of his voice. "I *knew* it was you." He'd crouched down behind a turned-over barrel that smelled of rancid meat. Deciding that he probably wouldn't appreciate a hug, Elizabeth grabbed his hands instead. They were ice-cold. "How are you? I've been so worried."

"Ow now, Mistress Lancaster, no need to fret. I gave the major a message for you. Didn't he tell you?"

"Oh, yes, he gave me your message. He also told me you were joining Washington's army."

"Rejoining. And keep it down. Who's that?" Jacob pointed a thin, chapped finger over Elizabeth's shoulder.

"She's a friend of mine. You needn't fear her. Now tell me about this decision of yours to *rejoin* the army. I thought you wanted to be with your family."

"You sound just like the major. He—"

"Major Knox tried to convince you to go home?" Elizabeth thought of the night, the last night they'd been together, and the way she'd accused Alexander of influencing Jacob to stay in the army.

"Till he was nigh blue in the face."

"Then why didn't you?" Her exasperation was only partly due to Jacob's decision. She wanted to be able to go to Alexander, tell him she knew he'd tried, ask for his forgiveness. Only she couldn't, of course.

Jacob shrugged his skinny shoulders. "Don't rightly know for sure. Guess I started thinking about why my pa joined up. He didn't much cotton to them British runnin' things over here."

Elizabeth shook her head. Jacob had become a dyed-in-the-wool rebel. "Be that as it may, they do."

"Not for long," he spoke up with all the conviction of youth. "Well, I got to be going now. It was real nice seeing you again, mistress. I ain't forgot what you done for me in that hospital."

267

Swallowing back tears, Elizabeth nodded, looking at him one last time while he stood. She couldn't be certain, but he seemed to have grown half a foot since she'd seen him last. Maybe that accounted for the ill fit of his garments, however not for their tattered appearance. She examined him more carefully. "Jacob, you have no stockings!"

"Aw, they wore out about Christmas time."

"But how do you stay warm?"

"Guess I'm kinda used to the cold by now. At least I got shoes."

Elizabeth glanced down at the raw leather covering his feet. She'd hardly go so far as to call them shoes. They were held together by tied rags. "Do you mean that some go barefoot . . . in this weather?" Her own feet were cold, and she had on sturdy leather shoes and woolen stockings.

"Yeah, life ain't exactly no picnic at Valley Forge. Though the general, he does his best for us."

Barefoot. In the snow. Elizabeth knew the rebel army to be poorly equipped in comparison to the British, but she'd never imagined them barefoot. Elizabeth's attention shifted back to Jacob.

"Got the itch," he said when he noticed Elizabeth watching him. "Sometimes, I think that's worse than the cold." Jacob emphasized his words by digging at his legs.

"Use brimstone. That should clear it up."

"Ain't got none."

"But your hospital at Valley Forge, surely they can treat you."

"Ow, they ain't got hardly nothin' there. Supplies are real dear." Jacob started backing down the alley. "I really got to be goin'."

"Just a minute. I have brimstone. You can come to my house, and—Wait. I forgot about Colonel Littleton. There's a British officer billeting with us. Hannah, how about your house. He could—"

"Has thee forgotten the Hessians?"

Elizabeth bit her lip. "That's right. I know. Tell me where you're staying, and I'll bring it there."

Jacob gave a sharp bark of laughter. "I ain't staying in town. Just come in to deliver some messages to the wives of some solders, and I really got to be going. Thanks again for all you done."

"But I haven't done anything," Elizabeth called after his retreating form.

"Let him go, Elizabeth. Thee is endangering him by making him stay."

"But," Elizabeth shook her head, "what he described is so awful. Someone should do something about it. Those poor men . . . boys."

"There are those that help." Hannah took Elizabeth's arm, turning her back toward the commons. "And this is not thy concern."

Elizabeth stopped walking and faced her friend.

"What did you mean by that?"

"Thee cares naught for the Whig cause."

"No, not that. You said there are those that help. How do you know? What do they do?"

"Nothing. I meant nothing."

"Hannah." Elizabeth searched the face under the plain gray bonnet. "Tell me."

"Thee is being unfair to ask."

"Then you do know. But, Hannah, how can you be sympathetic to their cause. They've imprisoned your father."

Hannah shrugged. "My father refused to sign the declaration of loyalty to the new government. That does not mean he did not believe in its ideals. He simply followed the dictates of the Meeting."

Hannah's family sided with the Patriots. Elizabeth could hardly believe it. But then . . . maybe she could. When had she begun to think the Americans' cause had merit? Elizabeth shook her head. She didn't—not really. Still . . . "I want to help." Elizabeth wasn't certain which of them was more surprised by her words. Yet once she'd spoken, she knew that was what she truly wanted.

"Thee can't."

"Why?" Elizabeth started after Hannah, who'd marched out of the alleyway. "Why can't I?" Elizabeth repeated when she'd caught up.

"Thy father for one thing."

"He won't have to know." Elizabeth smothered a

pang of guilt.

Hannah appeared shocked. " 'Tis not a game, Elizabeth. Men are dying from want."

Elizabeth's eyes met Hannah's and held. "All the more reason to accept my offer. Washington's army needs medical supplies. I have some."

"Oh, Elizabeth, I do not mean to hurt thy feelings, but what you keep in your home will help so few."

"Then I shall get more." Elizabeth turned left and began walking.

"Elizabeth, thee must not do anything foolish. Wait, this is not the way to the State House."

"I'm not visiting the rebel prison today. Colonel Littleton suggested I spend some time in the British hospital, and I think I shall."

It had been so easy. Elizabeth leaned back against the coach's soft leather cushion, amending her thought. It really hadn't been *that* easy, but she had managed it. For weeks she had divided her time between trips to the British hospitals at the German Reformed Church, and the Dutch Calvinist Church, and badgering Hannah. "Humph, that was a waste of time," Elizabeth mumbled to herself. Hannah hadn't budged at all until three days ago when Elizabeth had dragged her to the stable and shown her the stockpile of medical supplies stashed under the seats in the carriage.

"Where did thee get these things?" Hannah had asked, though she'd just as quickly added, "No don't tell me. I don't want to know."

Elizabeth had shrugged, pretending nonchalance. She would have loved to explain to Hannah how she'd managed to walk into the British hospital every day with a basketful of bread, and leave with medicines. But her own recent sleight of hand wasn't the point; getting Hannah to tell her how to get her bounty to Valley Forge was.

"Are you going to tell me how to take it to the rebels?" Elizabeth had asked.

"No."

"No? But Hannah I st—got all of this for them, for Jacob." Elizabeth didn't like to think of what she'd done as stealing. Sharing was the term she'd come up with to ease her mind. "Surely you aren't going to let it just sit here in my carriage house?"

"Thee has done a commendable job of *acquiring* this." Hannah motioned toward the coach seat that Elizabeth was covering back up with cushions. "However, I can't allow thee to endanger thyself anymore."

"But I have a plan. . . ."

Elizabeth smiled feeling the gentle sway of the well-sprung coach as it rolled along Second Street toward the outskirts of Philadelphia. Yes, getting Hannah to listen to her idea had been hard, convincing her even harder, but she'd done it. And now Elizabeth, British pass tucked safely inside her muff, rode toward her rendezvous with a farmer's wagon. A wagon that would take the supplies she was smuggling from the city, and would deliver them to the sick and wounded men in Washington's army.

Elizabeth dried her palms on the dark gray velvet of her riding coat as the coach stopped at the west gate of the city. A British sergeant, young and apple-cheeked, opened the door, and Elizabeth gave him her best imitation of an innocent smile.

"Where are you bound this fine winter day, mistress?"

The scarlet-clad soldier's attitude seemed more flirtatious than official, so Elizabeth opted for another smile. This time she accompanied it with a fluttering of her lashes. "My grandmother's house. She's taken ill."

The sergeant appeared to ponder her words, studying her with a keener eye than Elizabeth had initially thought he possessed. Her lungs began to burn, and she realized she'd been holding her breath. This had been one of Hannah's prime arguments. "And just how does thee plan to pass the barriers General Howe has erected across the roads?" All travelers and baggage were to be examined before entering or leaving the city, however it was no secret that this order was loosely obeyed — by most.

Have I happened across the one soldier who takes his duty to heart? Elizabeth thought. She leaned forward out of the shadows, interrupting his perusal of the coaches interior. "I have a pass through the lines."

"Are you traveling alone, mistress?"

"Well yes . . . except for my servants." Amos was driving and Charles was riding postilion, Elizabeth's concession to Hannah and to her own memory of what could happen to her when alone outside the city. Elizabeth tried to push that thought from her mind. There would be no snowstorm today. As the sergeant had said, it was a fine winter day — crystal clear and mild. And she wasn't going far. All she had to do was cross the ferry and travel to the home of the miller John Roberts, scarcely ten miles from town. But first she had to get past this guard.

"The countryside is crawling with rebels. I'm not sure it is safe for a young lady to be traveling alone. If you wait but a short time I can offer you my services as an escort."

The glint in his eye reminded her uncomfortably of Robert Littleton. She shook her head to dispel the notion. This man could demand nothing from her. But she did reassess her opinion of him. He hardly acted the dedicated soldier now, devoted to protecting the city at all costs. He leaned further into the coach, his fingers brushing her knee.

Elizabeth resisted the urge to slap his hand away. She drew herself up, indignation coloring her words. "My pass is signed by General Warner, a close friend of mine. Perhaps we should go to headquarters and see if he wishes his judgment questioned by a sergeant." The sudden pallor of the man's ruddy complexion was gratifying.

"Let the coach pass!" He yelled while giving the door a vicious slam.

Elizabeth clutched the sides of the cushions as the coach sprang forward. She extracted the rumpled pass from her muff, straightening it till the royal seal was flat. Squinting, she tried to read the scrawled signature. It was nearly illegible, however no one would mistake it for the words General Warner. Elizabeth shrugged, and stuffed the paper back into the furry warmth. Her nerves were too taut for her to speculate on what might have happened had the sergeant not been cowed by her bluff.

She probably shouldn't have chanced trying to trick him. Possibly a few more simpering smiles would have accomplished the same thing, her passage through the gate, but Elizabeth couldn't make herself do that. These last three weeks with Colonel Littleton in residence had been almost more than she could bear. He hadn't made any more overt threats, but then she'd managed never to be alone with him. And she had visited only the British hospitals, as he'd suggested, though he wouldn't be happy with her motivation for doing so. A tiny smile curled her lips as she settled more comfortably on the seat—the seat that hid a bounty of medical supplies.

She almost wished she could tell Littleton why she'd changed her routine. The colonel, doing his best to disconcert her, became bolder as time passed. Last night he'd even run his finger down the side of her face, smiling his wolfish grin all the while. Elizabeth shuddered at the memory. Her father had cleared his throat twice before Littleton glanced around at him and dropped his hand.

Perhaps she should go to Maryland. Papa had mentioned it several times recently, and Elizabeth was beginning to see a lot of merit in the idea. When she returned to Philadelphia this afternoon, she'd speak to her father, and have him make the arrangements. She refused to consider that this could mean she'd never see Alexander again.

They crossed the Schuylkill River at Upper Ferry without incident, and continued west. The road, rutted by recent rains, jostled the coach as they traveled across the countryside. Elizabeth was just beginning to wonder how far they had come, and if it would be much longer till she could stretch her travel-stiff legs, when she heard Amos yell at the horses. The coach lurched to a stop.

She pulled back the curtains and lowered the window, expecting to see a house and outbuildings. Instead, it was obvious they were still on the road. She stuck her head out the window. "Why did you stop?"

A large black stallion trotted into view. Elizabeth shaded her eyes, staring up at the imposing figure atop the horse. Her breath caught on a gasp.

"I told him to."

A month may have passed since she'd heard that voice, but she'd never, never forget it. The deep timbre sent tingles down her spine. And all she could do was sit, her head leaning out the window, and gape at Alexander as he dismounted.

He was dressed as Alexander Weston, in a black frock coat and breeches. His gleaming boots were mud splattered as was his horse, and Alexander brushed a dried clod off the stallion's flank as he approached the coach.

"If you'd allow me a word with you, Elizabeth?" His actions belied the mild-mannered tone of his question. Before Elizabeth knew what he was about, Alexander yanked open the door and lifted her from the conveyance. Skirting the muck by the roadside, he carried her several paces into the winter-dead grass, setting her down with such force that her teeth clicked together and her eyes flew open.

She looked at Alexander's grimacing countenance, and then up at Amos and Charles. They obviously didn't know what to do. Elizabeth gave

277

them a small smile, trying to convince them that she could handle the situation. She wished she felt as confident as she tried to look.

"Well, Mr. Weston, imagine meeting you here."

"Spare me the small talk, Elizabeth. I want to know what you think you're doing."

"Doing? Why I'm on my way to visit my grandmother. She's—"

"You have no living grandmother."

His remark caught Elizabeth off guard. "She's not actually my grandmother. More an old friend, but I think of her as—"

"I know what's in the coach."

Elizabeth examined his face. The scowl was darker, the crease between his raven brows deeper. What did he have to be so angry about? She planted hands on hips. "If you know, why are you harassing me? I assume you are also aware of my destination."

"Oh, I'm acutely aware of that. You're coming back to Philadelphia with me right now."

"I am not!" Of all the nerve. It wasn't enough that this arrogant rebel made her fall in love with him, then ignored her, but now . . . now he thought he could ride back into her life and order her about!

"Elizabeth." A nerve in Alex's cheek leaped compulsively. It was all he could do to keep from grabbing her shoulders and shaking some sense into her. For nearly two hours, ever since one of his contacts in the British army had casually mentioned the name of the woman smuggling medicine out of Philadelphia, Alex had been in a rage. And now after riding at breakneck speed, not to mention passing up dinner with several loose-tongued officers, Elizabeth had refused to listen to reason.

He kicked at a rock, stalking off a few paces before turning to face her again. "You don't seem to realize—"

"What? What don't I realize, Alexander? That there is a war going on?" Her eyes flashed angrily. "Is that what I don't know? Or is it that I don't seem to realize I'm supposed to obey you? Is that what it is, Alexander? I'm not obedient enough?"

"Hell, no. This has nothing to do with whether or not you listen to me."

"Good." Elizabeth turned on her heel. "Because I think I've done an admirable job of following your directives—until now." Hadn't she agreed without protest when he'd declared they were to have no further contact?

"Where are you going?" Alex grabbed Elizabeth's arm before she'd taken three steps.

"To meet a wagon." Elizabeth jerked away. She climbed into the coach, dragging mud with her, and slammed the door. But before she could signal the driver to proceed, the door flew open and Alexander bounded into the seat across from her. He pounded on the roof, and the coach

279

jumped forward.

"What are you doing?" Elizabeth's voice was breathless, he seemed to have taken up all the air in the coach.

"I would think that was obvious, Elizabeth." Alex leveled his eyes at her. "If you insist upon meeting the wagon, then I shall, too."

Chapter Fourteen

Silence surrounded her. Elizabeth tried not to notice. Certainly there were sounds to be heard. Where was the whir of the wheels, the plop-plop trod of the horses' hooves? Even her own breathing quieted till she could detect nary a whisper of air. Elizabeth's fingers laced tightly inside her muff. All noise couldn't disappear just because one man sat staring at her—silently.

"Why?"

His word split the silence like that first volley of musket fire to shatter the early morning calm. Elizabeth's gaze shot up to meet his, the contact exploding upon her senses. Starved for long weeks, inside the confines of the coach, she became inundated with the sight of him, the smell. She loved the way his midnight black hair fell across his brow, the impatient swipe he used to brush it aside. His manly, outdoors scent drew her, and Elizabeth pressed her spine against the soft leather squab to prevent herself from swaying toward him.

"Well, Elizabeth?"

She swallowed. "Well, what?"

Impatience marred the symmetry of his brow. "Why are you doing this? We both know you have no love for the rebel cause."

No love perhaps, yet no hate either. How could she tell him of the softening of the boundaries? She herself no longer knew where her loyalties ended, her enemies began. But that was not what he wanted to hear. The explanation he demanded had to do with motivation, not political ideology. "General Washington's army needs medical supplies."

"I see." He spoke calmly, the tight clenching his jaw the only outward sign of his disapproval. "So you took it upon yourself to steal provisions from the British."

"It wasn't stealing . . . exactly."

"I fear the British might question your interpretation of the word."

Elizabeth blanched. If Alexander had found out about her st—sharing, perhaps others had also. "Do they know what I've done, the British, I mean?"

It crossed Alex's mind not to answer her question. Perhaps letting her stew in her own juice would be an apt punishment, a deterrent against trying anything like this again. But he couldn't do it. Her wide gray eyes burned with unsuppressed fear, and though perfect white teeth bit at her lower lip, her dimpled chin quivered ever so slightly. He wanted to take her in his arms and protect her. That was all he'd ever wanted to do.

"No, they don't. At least no one of consequence knows. But you were seen," he added quickly. Her recovery from anxiety had been too abrupt for his liking. Alex didn't want her trying something like this again.

Oh, dear. She had thought herself so careful, and now to find out someone had observed her . . . "Why wasn't I reported to their superiors?"

"You were."

Fear tingled her skin. "But you said—"

"They work for me, Elizabeth."

"Oh." She relaxed enough to stare out the window at the winter landscape of muted browns and gray. "Why do you have spies in a hospital?"

"Philadelphia is an occupied city. General Washington has eyes and ears everywhere." Better not to tell her that the man who discovered she was taking drugs from the hospital wasn't a spy at all. The only reason he'd realized what she was up to was because he was doing the same thing. "There's very little you can do without my knowing."

"You have me watched?" Elizabeth's gaze shifted back to meet Alexander's.

He returned her stare. He hadn't meant to say that. She now thought he had someone watch her. Closer to the truth was that he kept an eye on her himself. He hadn't planned it that way. When he'd said good-bye to her in the predawn hours two months ago, his resolve had been firm. There'd be no further contact between them. It was best for both of them that way.

He'd only gone around in the garden below her window to make certain she got to her room without incident. But the soft glow of candlelight, the fleeting glimpse of her outline through the glass had been magnetic. Before he knew it, Alex found passing her house on his way home in the evening had become a routine.

"Well, do you?" Elizabeth inquired angrily. During all these weeks while he ignored her she was being spied upon.

"I—"

"Riders coming." Amos's voice, coming from the top of the coach, interrupted Alex. "Looks like a British patrol."

"Damn!"

Elizabeth ignored Alexander's outburst as she frantically searched her mind for the excuse she'd rehearsed for riding through the countryside. Grandmother. That's right, she was on her way to visit her grandmother. Elizabeth had to remember the British didn't know about the smuggled goods in her coach. Alexander had said as much. Alexander! What reason was she to give for his presence?

Before the question had completely formed, a blur of movement caught her eye. The unmistakable warmth of Alexander settled into the seat beside her, pressing her back against the cushions. "What are you do—"

Wrenching away was her first reaction. The last thing she'd expected from him was a kiss. Think. They had to devise some sort of plan. Already the coach slowed. The British would be upon them in a moment! Alexander's fingers fumbled with the clasp at her throat, pushing the heavy cloak away from her shoulders. His mouth dampened the sensitive skin at the base of her neck.

Had he gone mad? Elizabeth's arms flailed against Alexander's hard chest. She wriggled and twisted, managing only to tangle herself more thoroughly in her petticoats. "Stop." Her breathless plea went unanswered as his tongue tantalized the corner of her lips. "No, please," she sighed when it plunged inside her mouth.

Elizabeth's body softened, molding intimately against his. She thought she noticed a glimmer of triumph in the blue depths of his eyes before her lashes fluttered shut, but she was beyond caring. The feel of him, the taste of him were as much a part of her as her own heart. The heart that yearned only for him. For nearly two months she had held him only in her dreams. But now her fingers wove through his hair, her hands caressed the muscled back.

Alexander's palm cupped her breast, teasing the tight tip through the silk material, and Elizabeth arched toward him.

"You. Inside the coach. Step down."

Alex raised his head. "I think they mean us," he whispered, his voice husky with apparent passion.

"My God." Elizabeth's hands flew to her cheeks. How could she have forgotten the British? The coach had stopped, the only movement now a slight swaying as Alexander pulled away from her. She grabbed at his sleeve. "I can't let them see me like this." Her dress was wrinkled, the bodice askew. Thick ebony hair tumbled about her shoulders, set free of its ribbons by Alex's busy fingers. "Whatever will they think?"

The grin he flashed her sizzled with devilish intent. "They'll think you've been thoroughly kissed, and wonder what else. They'll think me damn lucky and fantasize about taking my place, but being good soldiers of the King they won't force the issue. They'll just wiggle uncomfortably in their saddles while they look at your reddened lips and tousled hair."

"You . . . you did this on purpose." Realization dawned on her in a blinding flash. Cold and calculating, his kiss had been one of premeditation rather than passion.

"Hell yes, I did it for a reason." Alex tried not

286

to be affected by the stricken expression on her face as he stopped to catch his breath. Maybe he'd started the kiss with nothing but fooling the British in his mind, but he'd been swept up in the emotion of it quick enough. The thought made him angry, with himself — with her. "Come on. And keep your mouth shut."

Elizabeth thought to refuse. She'd give herself up rather than parade in front of these men like a wanton. But Alexander was out the door, dragging her with him, before she could stop him. Frantically she stuffed her hair under her hood, trying to shield herself from the soldiers' eyes with her cloak. She didn't realize until too late that her actions only attracted more attention to herself.

"Sagler, is that you?" Alexander's voice boomed in her ear as he draped a seemingly lazy arm around her shoulders. The leader of the dozen men, a captain, nudged his horse forward. From beneath his hat, he peered at Alex. A moment later his round face split in a smile of recognition.

"Weston, you son of a . . ." His gaze slipped to Elizabeth then back to Alex. "What are you doing out here? The last I saw you that big Hessian, Gruber, had wagered he could drink you under the table."

Alex shrugged, letting his hand tangle in Elizabeth's hair. He felt her stiffen, and hoped she had the sense to take his advice and be quiet. "It's so difficult to find amusement in this godforsaken

287

land."

Sagler's horse pranced to the side, snorting, and he tightened the reins. "You seem to do all right." Small, pale eyes raked Elizabeth.

"I try." Alex pulled Elizabeth more tightly against his side. "But these interruptions are becoming tedious."

The British officer laughed so hard Elizabeth thought it possible he'd lose his seat. "Sorry, Weston," he chortled. "Just a moment more of your time, and I'll let you get back to your . . . amusement. Though it might be wise if you'd pick a safer place to indulge yourself."

"Safer? How could we be much safer than here where the brave king's men keep such a vigilant patrol?"

This question sent Sagler into another fit of laughter, and Elizabeth took the opportunity to examine the other soldiers. Their scarlet uniforms were relatively clean and seemed weather-tight. Not a one appeared to be suffering from the cold, for though the winter sun shone brightly today—a tease of the spring to come—the air still nipped as in late February. Elizabeth thought of the tattered rags Jacob had worn, and again wondered how the American army could ever hope to beat the King's finest. Her gaze traveled to their faces. As Alexander had predicted, to a man, they were watching her. Unconsciously she sidled closer to Alexander.

He tightened his arm around her, and listened to

Sagler describe how his patrol had just raided a storage dump for the rebels. A mantle of apprehension settled over Alex's shoulders as he questioned the captain. "Filthy rebels. When will they learn that their foolish acts simply prolong this stupid little war. What did you find, some grain hidden in an underground cache?"

"Not this time." Sagler's little-boy face beamed with pride. "About two miles from here, we came upon a miller at a very incriminating time. We've suspected him for a while, but we'd never caught him in the act, so to speak."

"Don't leave me in suspense. Do tell what happened?" Elizabeth thought Alexander's words belied his tone. If she didn't know better, she'd have sworn, he was totally bored with the entire discussion. For herself, Elizabeth could not keep at bay the nagging fear that a hitch had developed in her plan.

"We caught him red-handed with a wagon load of goods bound for the rebel army. Of course he denied it."

"Of course," Alex agreed dryly.

"But he didn't count upon his indentured servant being quite so loose with his tongue.

"I imagine a well-placed coin didn't hurt your cause either?"

Sagler leaned forward in his saddle. "I know how to deal with these traitors. They'd sell their own mother's soul for a sovereign."

"No doubt."

"But today all I wanted to gather was information, and the boy was full of that. The miller must have thought he could trust the youth."

"More fool he."

Sagler nodded. "Before he ran off, the lad even told us they were waiting for someone to deliver some stolen medicines before they left for Valley Forge."

Elizabeth felt certain her knees would buckle. They knew about the goods she was smuggling. But Alexander chose that moment to drop his hand off her shoulder and to trace the exposed tops of her breast with his finger. Annoyance with him stiffened her joints.

Sagler cleared his throat. "I can tell you're anxious to be back to your amusement, and I can't say as I blame you."

Alex looked up as if he'd just realized where his hand had been. He grinned at the British officer. "I'm more than ready. But wait." Alex stopped turning Elizabeth toward the coach. "You mentioned stolen medicines. Perhaps you'd like your men to search our coach?"

Was he crazy? Elizabeth's heart beat a frantic tattoo, and she wondered why everyone couldn't hear the loud, thumping beat.

Sagler's loud guffaw drew her attention. "I know better than to keep you from your pleasures, Weston. The next time we play whist, you'd leave me naught of my next quarter's allowance. Just heed my advice. You can't trust these rebels. Philadelphia is the safest place to be."

Elizabeth collapsed against the seat in relief when Alexander handed her into the carriage. But was it premature? Sagler called out to Alexander before he could follow her, and Elizabeth watched surreptitiously through the window as they talked. Curiosity overcame worry as the British officer leaned over his horse, slapping Alexander on the shoulder.

"What did he want?" Elizabeth couldn't help asking the question as soon as the coach jolted to a start. Alexander had forsaken his seat across from her in favor of squeezing beside her on the same cushion.

"You don't want to know." Alex resisted the urge to glance out the window to determine in which direction the patrol headed.

"What do you mean, I don't want to know?" Elizabeth was livid. "After you made me stand out there like a . . . a . . ." She shook her head in anger. "I insist you tell me."

Alex stared at her, taking in the flashing silver eyes, the thundercloud black hair. Perhaps it was better to let her know everything. The more repulsed she became by her little adventure, the less likely she'd be to repeat it. "He wanted an introduction." Alex watched her luscious mouth drop open. "To you. When I tire of you, of course. We must be gentlemen about this, you know."

At first she was speechless. Then she asked, "What did you say?"

Alex shrugged. "I mentioned that I still found you rather intriguing, so it might be a while till I could accommodate him."

"You . . ." Elizabeth drew in a deep breath, suddenly seething with rage. "You despicable devil, you animal, you—"

"Don't forget barbarian, Elizabeth."

"That too." Angry tears blurred her vision. "I can't believe you'd say such an awful thing about me."

"What would you have had me say?" Alex realized he was yelling to match her tone, and forced himself to lower his voice. "I could hardly tell him what we were really doing. And as for your insipid little story about a nonexistent grandmother—well, perhaps you think he'd have believed that, but I have serious doubts."

"But they think—"

"What the British think is of little consequence. War is reality, harsh reality. You would have found out exactly how harsh had Sagler discovered what is hidden beneath these cushions."

Elizabeth let her head fall back, and closed her eyes. He was right, of course, but somehow it didn't make her feel any better.

Alex stared at her, wishing for the hundredth time she were the type of woman who was content

292

to sit quietly in front of a warm fire making little stitches in whatever it was women made little stitches in. Wishing, too, that he didn't feel the tiniest seeds of pride that she was not.

"Elizabeth." His voice gentled, and he had to force himself not to touch the ebony curl lying across her breast. "We fooled them back there. They were looking for stolen goods, and it was right under their noses. Because of you, they didn't even notice."

Her lashes fluttered open, and Elizabeth cocked her head so she could see him. "I didn't do anything. You're just trying to make amends."

Alex smiled. She had no idea how irresistible she looked to him at that moment. "It wasn't I that kept them from noticing how low a supposedly empty coach sank in the mud."

"I did that?"

Her smile warmed him, then almost as quickly he noted the folly of his ways. What was he trying to do, convince her that she should take up smuggling? "You did, but don't get any glorious ideas. All of this would have been unnecessary had you not been out here in a carriage full of stolen medicines."

"Oh!" Elizabeth jerked around, showing him her back. She wished he'd move back to the other seat. Certainly they no longer had to worry about the British patrol noticing. She thought of moving herself, but refused to let him know that his nearness bothered her. It obviously had no effect upon him. All he could do was chastise her for the trouble she had caused. And she feared their troubles were not over yet. What was to happen when they reached the miller's house?

Alex jumped out of the carriage before it came to a complete stop in front of the two-story stone house belonging to the miller, John Roberts. "Stay here," he yelled over his shoulder to Elizabeth.

She let him shut the paneled front door behind him before she stepped from the coach and followed. Once on the wide front porch, she had a moment of doubt; however, she turned the brass knob and walked in as she had seen Alexander do. A wide hallway opened into a small parlor. Elizabeth stopped in the doorway, startled by the sight that met her eyes.

Alexander stood in the center of the room, his arms wrapped snugly around a woman. He opened his eyes, looking at Elizabeth over the woman's blond head, and his expression bordered on annoyance. Gently, he pushed the woman away, reaching in his pocket for a handkerchief.

"Dry your eyes, Abbey. You have company."

Oh, how Elizabeth wished she had listened to Alexander and stayed in the coach. The woman, he called Abbey turned tearstained eyes to her. Her loose saque dress did little to conceal her pregnancy.

"Elizabeth." Alex kept a comforting arm around

Abbey as he spoke. "This is Abigail Roberts. Her husband has just been imprisoned by the British."

"I'm so sorry." Elizabeth stepped forward. "Is there anything I can do?" Even as she said the words, Elizabeth realized how ridiculous they sounded. What could she possibly do?

"No . . . no thank you, mistress."

"Lancaster, I'm Elizabeth Lancaster," Elizabeth said realizing Alexander had not mentioned her name in the introduction. "Please call me Elizabeth."

"Thank you, Elizabeth." Abbey left Alex's side and sank into the closest chair. I'm not usually this weepy. Perhaps it's the babe." She rested a small, trembling hand on her rounded stomach.

"Don't be silly." Elizabeth sank onto her knees in front of Abbey. "You're being very brave." Empathy seeped through Elizabeth as she imagined herself in Abbey's place. What would she do if Alexander were captured? Her eyes met his. "Maybe something can be done to procure his release?"

Lifting his shoulders in a halfhearted shrug, Alex looked away from Elizabeth's probing gaze. "May I see you for a moment, Elizabeth? Outside."

Once they were out in the cold, crisp air Elizabeth said, "Why didn't you say something to that poor woman?" She paced across the far end of the porch, staying carefully out of earshot of the parlor window. They had left Abbey Roberts resting in the chair.

"Such as?"

"Tell her you'll find her husband, help him escape."

"I don't know if I can do that."

"But—"

Alex leaned his forearms across the porch railing. "I can't work miracles, Elizabeth. If I could this damn war would be over, and people like Abbey and John could live in peace *and* freedom."

What of us, Elizabeth wanted to ask as she watched him straighten? Could we live in peace . . . together?

"We'll grab a bite to eat here, and should be back in Philadelphia before nightfall."

"But what about Mr. Roberts?" Elizabeth stood, blocking his way.

"The sooner I get back to the city, the sooner I can do something to help him."

"Couldn't you get help for him at General Washington's headquarters?"

"Possibly, but . . ." Alex grabbed Elizabeth's shoulders, moving her aside. "Oh, no. I know what you're thinking, and the answer is no."

"Alexander, I can't take those supplies back to Philadelphia." Elizabeth followed him back into the hall, almost running to keep up with his long strides.

"We'll leave them here, then."

"It's too dangerous. What if the British patrol comes back and searches the mill again? They might arrest Abbey this time." Elizabeth almost bumped into his broad back when he stopped abruptly.

Alex turned, drilling her with his blue gaze. "I am not taking you to Valley Forge."

"I don't know why you're so angry."

Alex leaned back, stretching his long legs as best he could in the coach, and stared at Elizabeth. She sat across from him, her hands grasping the cushions against the constant jolting caused by the rough road. It crossed his mind that if he shared her seat, she wouldn't be jostled around quite so much. He remained where he was. "I'm not angry."

"You sound as if you are. This was the best solution, Alexander."

He didn't deign to respond, but merely broke the contact of their gaze. Since there was noplace else to look — he'd closed the curtains when they'd climbed into the carriage — Alex closed his eyes. It didn't help.

Even when he couldn't see her, her presence dominated his thoughts. The fragrance of lavender permeated the close confines, and he forced himself not to breathe deeply of the scent.

Damn it, he was angry with her — more angry

than he'd ever been with any woman. It seemed, despite his best efforts, she was determined to involve herself in dangerous dealings. Now they were on their way to Valley Forge. The rebel camp for God's sake! And she was a Tory.

"Do you think Abbey will be all right?"

Alex's eyes opened to lazy slits. "When and *if* she gets her husband back, she'll be fine."

"But the baby—"

"Isn't expected till spring."

"Oh." Elizabeth searched her mind for something else to say. She'd won. Against all his arguments, and she knew, his better judgment, Alexander had agreed to take her to Valley Forge. But somehow the victory seemed hollow. She had no desire to work against him. Part of the reason she was doing this was to help Alexander and Jacob.

Elizabeth glanced over at Alexander. His large body slouched across the seat, his muscular legs bracing the floorboards beside her. She had the strongest desire to kick him, pinch him, even bite him—anything to make him stop ignoring her. She opted for words instead. "It was sweet of Abbey's sister-in-law to come to the mill so quickly."

Elizabeth decided his response to this could best be described as a grunt. The sound grated on her nerves, annoyed her to no end. She did kick him then—not hard, but forcefully enough so that his eyes shot open and he looked at her.

"What the hell?"

"You're acting like a spoiled, little boy who didn't get his way." A violent lurch of the coach to one side marred the force of her words. She grabbed for the leather strap.

"*I'm* acting spoiled." Alex's short bark of a laugh echoed through the carriage. "I'm not the one who insists upon getting her own way no matter whom she hurts."

"I've hurt no one." Elizabeth insisted, indignantly.

"What about your father? What is he to think when you don't come home tonight?"

"Nothing. I left a note explaining that I was staying the night with my friend Hannah. I do it quite often anymore. He'll not think anything amiss." Elizabeth decided not to mention that she spent so much time with the Evanses because of Colonel Littleton.

So the wench had thought that far ahead? The knowledge didn't please Alex. "Well, you force others to worry about you."

"Who?"

"Me!" Alex jerked forward, his body straining so close to Elizabeth that she cringed against the squab. "You make *me* worry about you, and it's driving me crazy."

Elizabeth tried to swallow, but couldn't. His breath fanned across her cheek, and his blue gaze bore through her. "I . . . I never asked you to

299

concern yourself with me."

"Didn't you?"

"No, and you needn't yell." A foolish thing to say since her own voice vibrated with anger. How dare he imply that she had asked him to watch out for her. "You don't even care about me." Elizabeth's bosom heaved, and she stiffened her spine, leaning forward till they were nearly nose to nose. "You ignored me for over two months."

"For your own good!"

"Ha!"

"What in hell does that mean?" Alex clenched his fists to keep from grabbing her.

"A noble sentiment, Alexander, but I'm not naïve. I'd rather hear the truth."

"Which is?"

"You're tired of me." Elizabeth's voice was barely a whisper as she admitted to him what she'd tried to deny to herself all the long winter.

Had the woman lost her mind? Alex scanned the luminous gray eyes, the quivering bottom lip, and his control crumbled. He bracketed her slender body with his arms, and his mouth crushed against hers, claiming her with the heat of his desire.

Elizabeth's breath caught in her throat, and her heart raced as his tongue plunged, pillaging the soft recesses beyond her teeth. There was hunger in his kiss, a deep longing that Elizabeth could not mistake. It ignited the need within her, exploding upon her senses like a brilliant sunrise.

The kiss ended too soon. Alexander lifted his head till his lips barely grazed hers. His chest heaved against her breasts, and his eyes burned bright with desire.

"Does that feel as if I've tired of you, Elizabeth?"

The raspy words vibrated through her.

"No."

Her whisper drew him back, negating the breath of space that separated them. She touched his cheek, the sculptured line of his jaw, then moved to curl her hands around his broad shoulders. The feel of him beneath his jacket was intoxicating. Shamelessly she kneaded the muscles that bunched as he pressed her against the cushions. She reveled in the magnificent weight of his torso, the tangle of legs and petticoats as she dug her heels into the floorboards, arching toward his heat.

He couldn't stop touching her — had no patience with the fabric preventing his exploration of her soft, smooth skin. Alex tugged at her bodice, and the moist heat of his mouth surrounded the aroused nipple the instant the gown forfeited its hold. His tongue flicked the sensitive tip, wet the soft mounds of flesh as he sought — demanded — her other breast.

Her low, sultry moan was an echo of the one he heard in his dreams. Now, as then, it filled him with need, forced his life's blood toward that part of him that ached to plunge into her softness. His frenzied hands ruffled through layers of petticoats, not resting till one brushed the curling thatch guarding her sweetness. Moist heat greeted his finger as he traced, probed.

"Alexander, please." Elizabeth ground her body against his palm, completely fragmented by her yearning. Deserting his shoulders, her hands wriggled between their bodies on a desperate search. She found him, bulging rock-hard, caressed him through the nankeen breeches.

"My God, Elizabeth, the buttons."

She couldn't unfasten them fast enough. Her trembling fingers fumbled over the commonplace task. Free at last, he pulsed into her hand, velvet smooth and hot to the touch.

His first plunge was strong and bold, driving deep within her. Elizabeth cried out with the pure pleasure of it. Sure and true, the rhythm of his body escalated, stroking her, thrusting until raw need pulsed through her body. He allowed her no time to gather her defenses, but drove her higher, ever higher. Release, when it came, exploded upon her in a flood of fiery ecstasy. Colors flared, vibrant and rich, and Elizabeth gasped for breath, unable to fill her lungs fast enough.

They had soared so high that reality was slow to permeate their sated bodies. Minutes passed before the confines of the coach touched their senses advising them of their awkward positions. The lurching motion reminded Elizabeth that her head was cocked at an uncomfortable angle, wedged between the back cushion and arm rest. Alex's arms quivered with the effort of supporting his body's weight, and his long legs were cramped by the seats.

Slowly he levered himself free, collapsing on the seat across from Elizabeth. Carefully he straightened her skirts, and helped her sit. Her luminous eyes stared at him, reflecting the shock of what had just happened. Alex supposed an apology was due, or at the very least an explanation; yet he had none. It was only the obvious he could voice. "Never, never doubt my desire for you, Elizabeth."

Elizabeth twisted on the hard pallet, courting a slumber that would not come. Alexander had been right. She shouldn't have come here. She didn't belong.

Moonlight filtered through the tiny window in the thick, stone wall, and Elizabeth stared wide-eyed at the patterns of naked birch branches that played against the wall. Shelves, stacked neatly with clothing and books, lined the room. Mrs. Washington had told her how two soldiers, carpenters by trade, had built them for her when she'd first joined the general at his headquarters in Valley Forge.

"I asked only for something simple and service-

303

able," she'd said, "And look what they did. Lovely craftsmanship, don't you think?"

"Oh, yes," Elizabeth had agreed, fingering the smooth wood. "They did an excellent job."

"You rest now, my dear. Major Knox said he'd send a detail here early tomorrow morning to see you safely back to Philadelphia."

That was when Elizabeth had discovered Alexander wouldn't be taking her back. She'd smiled, thanked the short, motherly looking woman for all her kindness. Mrs. Washington had personally seen to her comfort from the moment Alexander had brought her to Valley Forge.

"Don't worry, Alexander, I'll take care of your young lady," she had said when Alexander had pleaded that duty forced him to decline her dinner invitation.

Alexander had bowed low over Mrs. Washington's hand, then winked, giving her a devilish grin. "I'd hoped I could count on your hospitality," he'd said.

To Elizabeth he'd said nothing. He'd only stared at her, his blue gaze so intense her face had blossomed with rosy color. Then he'd left.

"The general and I are very fond of Alexander. We knew his father . . . and his mother, too, poor dear." Mrs. Washington's face had reflected sorrow. She shook her ruffle-capped head. "I shan't bore you with talk of that unhappiness."

Elizabeth nestled further under her blanket,

wondering anew what Mrs. Washington had meant. The general's wife had assumed Elizabeth knew about Alexander's mother, but then Elizabeth had gotten the impression that Mrs. Washington thought she and Alexander were close.

Were they? Elizabeth wished she knew. There were times, when they made love . . . Is that what we did, Elizabeth wondered, make love? For her, there could be no doubt. Every time she looked at him, thought of him, it was with love. But, Alexander . . . what had he said? *Never doubt my desire for you.*

Erotic memories flooded her senses. He desired her, desired her passionately. But was that love?

Elizabeth squeezed her eyes shut, not liking the answer.

Chapter Fifteen

"Rebecca?" Elizabeth rose, her forgotten book sliding off her lap to land on the carpeted floor with a soft thump as her cousin swirled into the parlor. "Rebecca," she repeated in disbelief, rushing forward, "Is it really you?"

"Oh, Elizabeth, I've missed you so much. Please forgive me for coming like this, without a word."

"Forgive?" Elizabeth disentangled herself from the ruffled hug. "Don't be silly. I've missed you, too. I'm just so surprised. Come sit down." Elizabeth took Rebecca's gloved hand, and led her toward a chair, then settled back into her own seat. "Now tell me how it is you're in Philadelphia?"

"Well . . ." Rebecca patted her curls.

"Ben's all right, isn't he?"

"Oh, yes."

"And Aunt Mary and Uncle Jordan?"

"Yes, they're fine, too. Glad that spring is finally upon us, but fine."

Elizabeth sighed in relief. "Did you come alone? Does Father know you're here?"

"Elizabeth, if you'd just give me a moment to catch my breath, I'll tell you all." Rebecca's hand fluttered to her throat.

Leaning back in her chair, Elizabeth couldn't help but smile. She *had* missed Rebecca. It had been a long, lonely winter—made more so by Alexander's absence. She'd neither seen nor heard from him since he'd dropped her off at the Pott's house, Washington's headquarters at Valley Forge.

Several rumors were circulating among the Loyalists she knew. That Alexander Weston had returned to England seemed the most frequently voiced—and least likely in Elizabeth's opinion. Sarah Chamberlain had mentioned with a sly grin that he was in New York. Possible, and preferable to most other unpleasant alternatives Elizabeth's fertile imagination had conjured up. She simply refused to think of him as—

"Elizabeth!" The tone implied this was not the first time Rebecca had called the name. "You look as if you're a hundred miles away. Whatever were you thinking?"

"Only wondering what has brought you to Philadelphia," Elizabeth lied.

307

"Well, I came with Ben."

Elizabeth's gaze shifted to the doorway, and she noticed her indentured servant, Polly, standing there surrounded by baggage, obviously belonging to Rebecca.

"Oh, he's not here. Those are my things," Rebecca explained. "Ben has been assigned to the fort over on Jordan's Branch, just east of here."

Elizabeth had heard of the fort the Loyalists were building. The British helped supervise its location and construction, however it was to be manned solely by Loyalist troops. "I'm so glad you'll be staying in Philadelphia. You are staying, aren't you?" Elizabeth questioned, although as she went to the hallway and saw the rest of the baggage Rebecca brought, there could be little doubt.

"Yes, as long as Ben does. It is all right, isn't it? I mean I know I should have written to tell you, but I just couldn't resist seeing the astonished look on your face."

"It was a wonderful surprise. If I'd had any idea you'd come, I'd have asked you earlier." Elizabeth turned to Polly. "Mrs. Suteland will be staying in the room next to mine."

"But where am I to put all these things, mistress?"

"What won't fit in there can go in my room." Colonel Littleton's belongings, augmented by a shipment from his home in England, now occupied three extra rooms.

"Well, you simply must tell me everything that has happened to you since you left Maryland." Rebecca removed her stylish traveling hat, setting it on the cherry table beside her chair.

Elizabeth smiled. "Haven't you received my letters?"

"Of course, but that's not the same as your actually telling me. For instance, you never said why you refused to leave Philadelphia and visit Maryland."

"Yes, I did. My father—"

"Oh, posh." Rebecca's hand waved in the air. "You needn't pretend with me. I knew the moment I received your letter about Colonel Littleton billeting with you what the real reason was." Silk rustled as Rebecca leaned toward her cousin. "I'd hoped I might be able to help plan your wedding."

"My wed—" Elizabeth laughed, she simply couldn't help herself. True, Colonel Littleton had made several proposals to her this winter; however none of them included matrimony. Not that she would have even begun to entertain such a foolish notion. But one look at Rebecca's face convinced Elizabeth that her cousin didn't understand her amusement. She regained her composure with difficulty. "I'm not getting married, Rebecca."

"But you've been together all winter." Rebecca seemed crestfallen.

"Colonel Littleton is often absent and when he's

not—" Elizabeth decided there was no reason to explain to her cousin that when Littleton was around, she tried not to be. "Well, I'm afraid your matchmaking efforts at Landon Hall were all for naught."

Rebecca had not taken the news well.

"Do you suppose Colonel Littleton will be at the assembly tonight?" she asked.

"I don't know," Elizabeth answered for the tenth time as she watched Rebecca apply rice powder to her already pale complexion. Their eyes met in the beveled mirror, and Elizabeth knew her tone had been too sharp.

"Well, in case he is, you must be prepared." Rebecca twisted on the bench, obviously willing to let Elizabeth's snappishness pass.

"Prepared for what?"

"To win him, of course. Now I realize you probably haven't handled this well on your own, but don't worry. I'm here now, and I intend to devote all my time to you."

"That's very sweet of you, Rebecca, however I have no desire to marry Colonel Littleton." Even before her cousin began circling her, eyeing her appraisingly, Elizabeth knew her words had been wasted.

"Don't you powder your hair anymore?" Rebecca picked up a curl hanging over Elizabeth's shoulder, examining it critically.

"No, Al—I mean I prefer it natural."

Powdered curls bobbed as Rebecca shook her head. "Do you see what I mean? *No one* in England would go to a ball with their hair . . . well, it's no wonder he hasn't proposed."

"Rebecca . . ."

The knock at the door interrupted what Elizabeth was going to say, and she was just as glad. What could she do to convince her cousin to forget about Colonel Littleton?

"This package just arrived for you, mistress." Polly handed Elizabeth a small wrapped bundled tied up and sporting a pink bow.

"What is it?" Rebecca huddled closer.

"I don't know."

"Well, open it."

"I shall." Elizabeth moved toward the window, but Rebecca followed, obviously not to be deterred. The moment she pulled the ribbon and the paper fell away, Elizabeth's heart skipped a beat. Almost reverently she lifted the fan that Alexander had given her months ago in his room.

"Oh, it's beautiful. Let me see."

Resisting the urge to clutch the delicate carved ivory to her breast, Elizabeth handed it to her cousin.

Rebecca snapped it open with a well-practiced flourish. "Whoever sent you such a lovely gift?"

"I don't know," Elizabeth lied.

"Isn't there a note?"

"No." Elizabeth glanced down at the empty wrapping paper, her breath catching at what she saw. There was writing. The paper made a crinkly sound as she quickly wadded it up, stuffing it in her pocket.

"I'll wager it was Colonel Littleton."

"What makes you think that?" Elizabeth searched her mind for an excuse to leave so she could read the note. She had only seen part of it, and it didn't appear to be more than a few words. She was certain it was from Alexander.

"Who else could it be?" Rebecca said in exasperation. "Don't you think Colonel Littleton is the one who sent it?"

"No." Rebecca looked up, apparently startled by Elizabeth's tone. "I mean . . . it could have been, I suppose." If not him, who could she say sent it? Granted there was no note; however, Rebecca would expect her to have some idea.

"Oh, you sly thing. You tried to make me think—"

"I'm going to check on Father. Finish readying yourself, and I'll wait for you downstairs."

Rebecca turned away from the mirror. "Aren't you going to let me powder your hair?"

"Not tonight." Elizabeth rushed from the room, her hand clutched protectively over the crinkled paper in her pocket. The library was empty, blanketed in heavy shadows except where the light

312

from the flickering flames in the fireplace danced into the darkness. Brushing back her satin overskirt of rose and green stripes, Elizabeth leaned close to the fire.

John Roberts safe. Elizabeth read the words scrawled in large bold script, and smiled. Alexander had helped him escape; Abby's husband was safe. Elizabeth hoped that meant Roberts was also with his wife.

April had bloomed, warm and sweet with the fragrance of spring upon the land, but it had not escaped Elizabeth that Abby's child, due to be born this month, might come into the world fatherless.

Her thoughts strayed to Alexander. At least she knew he was alive, and probably in Philadelphia. And he had cared enough to ease her mind about John Roberts.

"What are you about, daughter?"

Elizabeth heard her father's voice from the doorway, and on impulse propelled the balled-up paper into the flames. It caught, instantly flaring to life and briefly illuminating the room.

"Father, I didn't hear you enter." She turned only when the last bit of paper became ash.

"I warrant not. You were so deep in thought, I imagine Washington's army could have invaded the city, and you would not have stirred."

"Oh, Father." Elizabeth tried to laugh, but apparently her throat had tightened when she'd heard

313

her father's voice, and it was slow to open. She wiped her palms against the ribbed satin of her petticoat. "I better see to Rebecca. She's so excited about the assembly tonight. I gather, from what she says that Landon Hall has been in near hibernation all winter. Can you imagine, no balls or musicals, hardly a visitor to break the monotony? How very dull it—"

"Is something wrong, daughter?"

"Of course not." Elizabeth bit her tongue when she realized how obvious her babbling had been. If seeing her throw something into the fireplace hadn't aroused her father's suspicions, then certainly singing the praises of the social whirl she'd tried to avoid all winter would.

"You seem tense."

"I'm not." Elizabeth smiled, though she wasn't certain that her father could discern her expression in the feeble light. She certainly couldn't read his.

"I realize these are not pleasant times. I've been often absent, and, well, we haven't had much opportunity to talk, but if there is something troubling you . . ."

"There isn't. I'm excited about Rebecca's visit 'tis all. Don't you think she looks grand?"

She'd made her escape, but even now, as she stood watching the gaily colored kaleidoscope of dancers whirl past her, Elizabeth's heart could trip from just thinking about it. She didn't enjoy fooling her father, didn't believe for one moment he'd been fooled. He knew she was hiding something, yet she doubted he guessed what.

Guilt flushed her cheeks, and she snapped open Alexander's fan to stir the air. She received notes from notorious American spies, and worse, at least to her father's way of thinking, her sympathies, nay loyalties, had shifted.

What would her father do if he knew she no longer embraced the Loyalists' beliefs? Elizabeth moved toward the window to her right, then stared out to the expanse of midnight black sky. He probably wouldn't think a thing of it, but would chalk up her Patriot fervor to a silly female whim.

"Your soft heart has interfered with your common sense," he would say. And perhaps he would be right. Certainly the suffering she'd witnessed at Valley Forge had done much to sway her beliefs. Hungry, cold, denied even the most essential necessities of life, the men of General Washington's army remained, clinging to the ideal of liberty.

Mrs. Washington had said it best. Elizabeth closed her eyes, and visions of the night she'd spent at the rebel camp paraded across her mind. "We do what we must," the general's wife had said. *What we must . . .*

Tinkling laughter interrupted Elizabeth's reverie, and she opened her eyes. Candlelight from the overhead lusters reflected brightly in the dark window panes, obscuring her view of the gardens. Flowing silks and taffetas of blue, green, and pink swirled by, mirrored in the glass, as the dancing continued. And scarlet, always the scarlet of the British, blemished the picture Elizabeth saw.

Feeling suddenly overwhelmed by it all, she made her way to the door. Scented candle wax and overly perfumed bodies stifled her breathing. A quick glance around the ballroom told her Rebecca was well occupied with a group of soldiers. Marriage hadn't dimmed her appeal to any noticeable degree.

Oh, how much sweeter the fragrance of spring. Elizabeth breathed deeply, drawing in the scent of hyacinths and plum blossoms to cleanse her soul. Her skirts, the pink and green of a spring bouquet, swayed gently, brushing the boxwood lining the path. Moonlight bathed her as she paused to open her fan.

"I see you've decided to accept my gift this time."

"Alexander," she breathed. The voice, so near and so unexpected in the quiet of the garden, should have startled Elizabeth, but it didn't. She turned to find him emerging from the shadows. A smile to match his spread across her face.

Though dressed as Alexander Weston, his clothes were informal, not nearly grand enough for a ball, Elizabeth noticed as he strode toward her. His dark hair gleamed in the moonlight, and she

316

thought she saw a twinkle in his blue eyes.

"You received my message, then?" Alex reluctantly shifted his gaze from Elizabeth's face to the fan. How was it possible that she became more beautiful every time he saw her?

"Yes." Elizabeth found her voice. "I'm so glad John Roberts is safe. Is he with Abby?"

"They're together, though not at the mill. It was too dangerous."

"And the baby?"

"Has yet to arrive."

Elizabeth lowered her lashes. It was simply too hard to look at him and not fall into his arms. "I'm glad John Roberts is safe," she repeated. She could feel his gaze on her, knew herself a coward not to meet it. She swallowed, trying to think of something to say. "Is that where you've been, rescuing Mr. Roberts?" Wanting to pull her words back, Elizabeth cringed. Better to have said nothing than to question him about his absence. After all, he'd made it clear there was nothing between them but passion.

"Stealing him back from the British didn't take long. I had lots of help. Mostly I've been in New York. I only returned to Philadelphia today."

"Oh." Elizabeth studied the snowy white fall of his cravat. "You've chosen a good evening to come back. The ball is—"

"I haven't come to attend the assembly. No one knows I'm here . . . except you. I thought to allow myself a small holiday."

"I see."

"Elizabeth, about the way I left you at Valley Forge—"

"You were perfectly right to do it. Mrs. Washington proved herself to be a wonderful hostess, very kind and—"

"I should have come back to say good-bye."

"The guard you sent was wonderful. They escorted me to the British lines without a hint of trouble," she told the silver button on his waistcoat.

"Still, I should have . . . Damn it, Elizabeth, would you look at me?"

"I am."

"My face, damn it. Look at my face so I can see your eyes." Alex grabbed her shoulder, conscious of the warmth of her skin beneath the silk. His hand drifted across her bare shoulders, nestling in the thick black curls at the nape of her neck. He tugged gently.

Slowly, Elizabeth raised her lashes, postponing the moment when the impact of his blue gaze would impact on her senses. She studied his face, while avoiding his stare. Midnight black hair waved around his forehead and ears, framing the high cheekbones, the blade of nose. His jaw clenched stubbornly and his sensual mouth thinned as he waited. He pulled on her hair again, his fingers twining with the curls and braided ribbons.

318

The magnetic eyes drew her, and the moment she gave in to temptation her knees softened and she swayed toward him. "Why did you come?"

"I knew you'd be here." No reason at all for his coming, Alex realized. He'd sent her the note. Surely, that was enough. Then why had he found himself walking in this garden, staring at the house? "I saw you standing in the window."

"I couldn't stand it in there. Everything is so . . . so opulent. Especially after seeing the men at Valley Forge." This last was muffled into his chest as he pulled her against him.

"Shh, Elizabeth. It's not your concern, remember." His hand held her head close, his thumb drawing lazy circles on her cheek.

"I know it's not supposed to be, but I can't forget." Elizabeth pulled away, now actively seeking his gaze. "Are things better? Certainly the warmer weather helps?"

"It does." Alex's arms tightened around her. "Even the hunger has abated. The shad ran early up the Schuylkill this year. I'm told men plunged into the river, spearing the fish with pitchforks, branches, anything they could find. They may tire of salted shad, but it beats dying of starvation."

Elizabeth snuggled closer.

"And, of course rumors of the French joining the fight have boosted morale."

Elizabeth left the shelter of his arms, and walked further along the path. She picked a box-

319

wood leaf, tracing the smooth foliage with her fingertip. She'd heard the rumors also, though in Philadelphia talk of the French allying themselves with the Americans had not been taken too seriously. Elizabeth had a feeling the British did not give the Americans enough credit for ingenuity.

"Is that what's going to happen? Are the French going to declare war on England?" She turned, her skirts swirling around her in a pastel cloud, and searched his face in the moonlight.

"Does that bother you so much?" he asked, closing the gap between them.

"The possibility of the British losing?" Elizabeth watched as Alexander nodded and then folded his arms across his broad chest. "Not really." She dropped the leaf, and it fluttered to the brick path. "Are you surprised?"

"No."

Her eyes shot up to meet his. "Am I that predictable, that you know my mind before even I do?" Her question was met with silence. "I suppose you knew I'd come outside to walk in the gardens, also. Is that why you came?"

"Elizabeth."

"Don't." But he seemed not to hear her command as he enfolded her in his arms. "Washington will never give up if he receives succor from the French."

"He won't surrender regardless."

"I know, oh, I know." Feeling utterly defeated

herself, Elizabeth wove her arms inside Alexander's jacket, clutching the smooth linen of his shirt. "And this war will go on forever."

"So this is where you are."

Elizabeth stiffened when she heard Rebecca's voice.

"I noticed you slip out of the ballroom, but never dreamed you'd be gone this long. Now I can see why."

Pulling away from Alexander, Elizabeth tried to shove him toward the shadows, before hurrying to her cousin. "Let's go back inside, Rebecca?"

"In just a moment." Rebecca shook off the arm Elizabeth had linked with hers. "I'd like to meet your young man. As your married cousin, I feel somewhat like a chaperone."

Elizabeth turned and discovered to her dismay that Alexander stood where she'd left him. Of course, she realized, he wouldn't know who Rebecca was. He probably hadn't noticed her at Landon Hall. But Elizabeth was certain Rebecca had seen him.

"I suppose he's the one that sent you the fan, too. And you let me think it was Colonel Littleton." Rebecca glanced back at her, and Elizabeth could do naught but stand, twisting her hands and waiting for the ax to fall. "Aren't you going to introduce us, Elizabeth?"

Elizabeth knew the exact moment when Rebecca recognized Alexander as Major Knox. A cloud that

321

had drifted over the moon filtered away, bathing the garden in silvery brightness.

"My God," Rebecca gasped, her hand going, in horror, to her mouth. She swayed, and Elizabeth rushed toward her, certain Rebecca would faint. "Do you know who this is?" she demanded, her voice shrill.

"Yes." Elizabeth's answer seemed quiet by comparison.

"My God," Rebecca repeated before twisting away from Elizabeth's supporting hands.

"Where are you going?" Elizabeth grabbed hold of her arm.

"To tell the general who is in his garden."

"Don't do it, Rebecca."

Rebecca jerked away, looking at her cousin as if she'd suddenly grown two heads. "Are you out of your mind, Elizabeth. This man is a rebel." She motioned toward Alexander who stood watching the scene unfold before him. Realizing who this woman must be, his mind groped for a solution to his dilemma. He didn't like the idea of kidnapping Elizabeth's cousin, but was beginning to wonder if he'd have a choice. "He tried to kill my Ben for heaven's sake," she continued.

"Don't do it, Rebecca," Elizabeth repeated, desperation creeping into her voice. She looked at Alexander. Why didn't he do something?

"Why, just tell me why?" Rebecca had taken three steps, then swirled back to face them.

322

"Because, I love him." The words were out of Elizabeth's mouth before she knew it, and her breast heaved with the import of her revelation. Elizabeth heard Rebecca gasp, and she could feel Alexander's surprised gaze burning into her skin.

"Have you lost your mind?" Rebecca gaped at her, her mouth hanging open.

"No." Elizabeth swallowed. "Just my heart. And I swear to you, Rebecca, if you betray him, I shall never forgive you."

"Elizabeth?" Rebecca moved back, grasping for her cousin's hands, trying to pull Elizabeth along. But Elizabeth stood firm, her eyes unwavering.

"Never, Rebecca."

And now Rebecca was leaving. Elizabeth lay in bed, staring up at the shadowy tester, wondering how it had come to this. Could she have changed anything?

She couldn't help loving Alexander. She'd tried, and it had done no good. She squeezed her eyes shut, cringing as she remembered how she'd blurted out her declaration of love. Whatever must he think? Looking back at him had been impossible after she'd said the words. Rebecca had glared at him, but Elizabeth couldn't face him, didn't know if she ever could again.

Recalling the evening, Elizabeth bunched the coverlet in her hands. She should have warned

Alexander immediately that Rebecca was in Philadelphia. He had no way of knowing a woman who could recognize him would be at the ball.

She sighed and glanced toward the window. Silvery moonlight filtered through the glass, gilding her room with soft light. She was vaguely aware that the wind had picked up. Oak branches, still bearing last summer's leaves, now brown and crinkled, grated against the panes.

Rebecca had said nothing as Elizabeth had marched into the gaily lit house and insisted that her father take them home. "Rebecca is unwell" was the excuse she'd given for the sudden departure. The expression on her cousin's face had given credence to the lie.

But once in the privacy of Elizabeth's room, Rebecca had regained her poise — and her voice. "I can't believe this, Elizabeth. Not of you."

"I hardly think it's that inconceivable," Elizabeth had said.

"Well, I can't stay here. I'm leaving in the morning. No, don't try to stop me," she'd ordered when Elizabeth had reached for her. "My father's sister has written, asking me to stay with her. I'll have my things moved there tomorrow."

Rebecca had turned then, sweeping toward the door, only to pause, her hand on the knob. "Whatever will your father think of this, Elizabeth? Have you given thought to his reaction if he knew you were in love with a rebel?"

The noise at the window grew more insistent, and Elizabeth wondered if a storm were brewing. But wouldn't clouds have dimmed the moonlight if that were true? It sounded again, rattling against the glass, and Elizabeth threw back the covers. That was no windswept branch.

Pushing up the sash, she stared down into the garden, gasping at what she saw. Dark as it was she could make out Alexander in the moonlight. He stood looking up at her, his hands full of pebbles.

Pushing open the window, she called down to him in a muffled voice. "What are you doing here?"

"I want to talk to you."

"No, go away," Elizabeth gritted through her teeth.

"Come down."

"No."

"Then I shall be forced to come to you." Elizabeth watched in horror, as the vine-covered trellis outside her window began to shake. He was climbing up.

"Alexander stop. You'll fall."

The rustling sound ceased. "Come down."

There was only a slight pause, his demand going unanswered by her, before she heard the ivy leaves rustling again.

"All right. I'll be there in a minute." Elizabeth drew her head inside, listening for any evidence

that Alexander's foolishness had awakened someone else. She heard nothing. Her father's room
was on the other side of the house, and Colonel
Littleton was away. But Rebecca slept next door.

Elizabeth grabbed a shawl, wrapping it around
her embroidered linen nightrail, stuck her feet into
clogs, and tiptoed outside.

"What took you so long?" he asked as she eased
the door shut behind her. Then he stepped out of
the shadows.

"What do you want?" Elizabeth answered his
question with one of her own.

"To talk, Elizabeth, just to talk." He took her
hands, pulling her gently down the garden path
toward the summerhouse. Built with hip roof and
large windows to catch the summer breezes off the
river, the structure had not been used since autumn. A closed-up, musty smell enveloped Elizabeth when she followed Alexander into the
building. Moonlight streaming through the windows outlined the furniture, whose protective linen
coverings, Elizabeth had long since appropriated
for the hospital.

"She's not going to disclose your identity, if
that's what concerns you." Elizabeth kept her back
toward him, not near ready to face him.

"It's not, at least that's not why I came."

"I see." Elizabeth traced her finger along the
woven edge of a chair. She could sense him move
up behind her, feel the warmth of his breath on

her neck.

"What you told your cousin . . . I know 'tis a falsehood, but I thank you for it."

Elizabeth said nothing as his hands grasped the indentation of her waist.

"It was a lie, wasn't it?"

Squeezing her eyes shut against the pain, Elizabeth told him what he wanted to hear. "Of course. I could think of no other way to stop her, and you did save my life."

His hands slid up her ribs, grazing the sides of her breasts before cupping her shoulders. "Don't fall in love with me, Elizabeth, please. It would only bring you pain in the end."

"Don't concern yourself, Major." Elizabeth let her head fall back against his hard chest. "Passion is all I feel for you . . . all we share."

"Ah, there is that, isn't there?" His words were muffled against her hair. As if to prove the point, Alex's palms cradled her thinly clad breasts. She moaned, her head lolling to the side as his thumbs teased the tight nipples through the linen. And then even that barrier was gone as he untied the drawstring, and pushed the fabric down her body. The chill night air caressed her flesh, turning her into her lover's arms.

There was something wild and sensual about standing in his embrace nude and him fully dressed — something that fanned her passions to new heights. He denied her love for him, denied loving her, but he could not deny their passion. His lips met hers, and Elizabeth opened her mouth, meeting his tongue in a provocative dance. She'd feed his desire, show him with her lips, her arms, her body, what she could not tell him with words.

Elizabeth slid her hands under his broadcloth waistcoat, caressing his shoulders as she slipped the jacket from his body. "Share your passion with me, Alexander," she whispered against his lips as his mouth closed over hers.

Chapter Sixteen

General William Howe was leaving Philadelphia and returning to England. His replacement, Sir Henry Clinton, had already arrived in the city. Rumors circulated and grew almost hourly among the Loyalists as to the reason for the change in command. Though not privy to all information, Elizabeth imagined the expanded scope of the war to be at least partially responsible.

Word had reached Philadelphia on May fifth that France had declared itself an ally of America. Her first thought upon hearing the news had been of Alexander. He would be pleased . . . the war would continue.

There was also talk that the British were to abandon Philadelphia. If they did, there was little doubt Washington's army would reclaim the city. And where would that leave her father and all the others who'd been loyal to the king? Elizabeth could do naught but speculate—and worry.

But not today. Today she was too busy to dwell on the possibilities.

The tinkling of glass caught her attention, and Elizabeth turned from the window to watch the two soldiers who were lowering the prismed luster in her dining room.

"Please be careful," she warned as one, a heavyset fellow whose tunic held his girth with difficulty, let the rope slip. Why the task of packing delicate glass chandeliers had fallen to one so clumsy, she had no idea.

"Allow the men to finish their job, Elizabeth."

Elizabeth glanced over at Robert Littleton, ignoring his unctuous smile, then turned back toward the window. Perhaps he was right. She should let the soldiers work. What difference did it make if a glass crystal shattered, as long as the colonel and his men left quickly.

Colonel Littleton had arrived with the small detail twenty minutes earlier to collect the chandelier Jonathan Lancaster had agreed to lend for the Meschianza. The elaborate affair, organized by General Howe's officers to bid him farewell, was to be held on the morrow.

Elizabeth had received her official invitation this morning. Emblazoned with Howe's crest and a ribbon bearing the motto, *Luceo Descendens Aucto Splendore Resurgam*—I am shining as I set, but I shall rise again in greater splendor—it asked for the favor of her presence at Knight's Wharf near Poole's Bridge tomorrow at half past three.

Elizabeth pulled back the drapes, watching the rain drops drip off the roof, land in the puddles with a splash.

"Don't fret, Elizabeth." Littleton had moved over to the window, and now stood so close to Elizabeth that his words were for her alone. "I'm certain the weather will clear so you can enjoy your fete."

Elizabeth, who was not looking forward to the party, and hoped the rain would continue, chose to ignore him, a reaction that made him bolder. He pressed against her, trapping her between his body and the glass window panes. A quick glance at his smirking face and at the men now packing the luster in a wooden crate filled with sawdust, showed her that there would be no help from that quarter. With her father gone, to who knows where, Elizabeth felt a shiver of vulnerability race up her spine.

"It's too bad I won't be able to attend the festivities tomorrow, I could have carried your favor in the tournament."

"You'll be absent from the Meschianza?" Elizabeth asked sweetly, trying to pretend she didn't notice his hot breath fan across her cheek.

"I fear so, lovely lady." His hand twirled a lock of midnight black hair. "Duties dictate that I be

331

elsewhere. Will you miss me?"

"Actually, I was just beginning to think the day held some promise after all."

Flashes of pain scorched her scalp as his hand yanked on her hair. Through a sheen of tears, Elizabeth saw the soldiers lugging the heavy crate from the dining room, leaving her alone with the colonel.

"You have a sharp tongue, Elizabeth," he hissed close to her ear. "Not a very attractive trait in a woman, and one I fear you may live to regret."

Elizabeth raised her chin, ignoring the revulsion she felt with his nearness. "More threats based on lies, Colonel?"

"Ah, my lovely Elizabeth." He traced his finger down her cheek, grabbing her chin when she tried to twist away from his caress. "Threats perhaps; however, I think you'll find these based more in fact than you realize."

"What are you talking about?" Elizabeth ground out the words.

"Now I see I've captured your interest."

Elizabeth gritted her teeth as his free hand trailed down her bodice, clamping on her breast. "I seriously doubt anything about you shall ever interest me." His hand tightened, and Elizabeth bit her lower lip to suppress a scream.

"We shall see, Elizabeth. We shall see." After one more vicious squeeze, he left the room.

May eighteenth dawned, as Robert Littleton had predicted, fair and pleasant with only a bit of wind to mar its perfection. A gust tugged on the end of Elizabeth's silver-edged gauze turban as she and her father stood amid the throng of people at Knight's Wharf. It was past four o'clock, and still they waited to board one of the flatboats that would carry them to the Meschianza.

Looking out across the river, at the boats bedecked with streamers and bunting, Elizabeth realized the event was as pretentious as she'd imagined it might be. From the moment she'd been chosen one of the Ladies of the Blended Rose, an honor she'd have gladly declined had it not been for her father, Elizabeth had dreaded this day. She and thirteen other young ladies—selected, so she was told, for their youth, beauty, and fashion—were to carry the colors of their brave knights in the jousting tournament.

"Do you suppose they will ever get us all boarded?" Elizabeth queried.

"Have patience, daughter. General Howe and his brother Lord Howe have just embarked on the *Hussar.*"

"Yes, I thought I noticed the general's paramour crossing the gangplank."

"Elizabeth!"

"Sorry, Father," Elizabeth added with a wry smile. Mrs. Loring, General Howe's mistress, was

333

not considered suitable conversation for her. Elizabeth brushed some dust off her gown. Fashioned of white silk in the polonaise style, its bodice gently molded her slender body. Cut daringly low at the neck, it was tied around the waist with a wide sash trimmed with the same silver edging as adorned her turban.

Elizabeth hoped the procession of boats would move faster once they were underway on the river, but she was disappointed. Everywhere she looked streamers and bunting waved in the breeze, from the houses and wharves lining the waterfront to the sloops and warships they passed in the river. As the flotilla passed the sloop, *Fanny,* strains of "God Save the King" drifted across the water. At the warship *Roebuck,* Howe and his guests were treated to a nineteen-gun salute. When they finally reached the Wharton Mansion, Walnut Grove, it had taken the slow-moving procession two hours to cover one mile.

As Elizabeth walked up the sloped lawn toward the two arches specially constructed for the occasion, she spied Alexander. Although not surprised to see him here—after all, he must be anxious to know the truth of the rumors concerning a British withdrawal from the city—the sight of him filled her with warmth.

He glanced up from perusing the captions on the arched columns and smiled. And then he strode toward Elizabeth and her father. Dressed in a puce silk suit of the latest cut, his long legs encased in white stockings, he appeared the epitome of an English dandy. However, there was nothing foppish about the muscular body beneath the stylish clothes, nor in the determined step he used to cover the ground. Elizabeth felt her heart quicken just watching him.

"Mistress Lancaster, you're looking lovely." Alexander stopped before her, and Elizabeth forced herself not to laugh at his stilted speech as he turned to greet her father.

"This is certainly a magnificent event," Alex said, making a sweep with his hand. "Sure to go down in the annals of history as an example of Great Britain at her finest."

Elizabeth followed his gesture, noting the lavish and ostentatious decorations, so out of place in this war-torn country. "Oh, I quite agree, sir," she said with a smile.

Alexander returned her grin. "And you Mistress Lancaster. I see you've been chosen as a Lady of the Blended Rose. Such a great honor."

"I'm truly humbled." Elizabeth swept him a deep curtsey, hoping her father wouldn't notice the mischievous twinkle in Alexander's eye.

"As well you should be, mistress."

"Come daughter. I think it time you found your seat to preside over the tournament."

"Yes, Father." His firm grip on her arm allowed for naught but her to follow him.

"Mistress Lancaster." Alexander's voice pulled Elizabeth's gaze around.

"Yes?"

"Who is your brave knight. Perhaps I shall cheer for him."

She couldn't remember. Elizabeth pulled her arm free, and stared back at Alexander. He was her knight, her brave and chivalrous warrior, and she could think of no other.

"She wears the colors of Captain Cathcart," her father answered. "His motto is 'Love conquers all.'"

"A noble sentiment," Alex mumbled as he watched Elizabeth walk away. "Though not a very realistic one."

The joust began as soon as all the ladies and guests were seated in the pavilions, newly constructed for the festivities. The white knights, resplendent in their costumes of white silk, declared their ladies the wittiest and fairest of all. Retrieving the gauntlet, accepting this challenge, were the black knights, equally handsome in black satin, who declared their ladies of the Burning Mountain outshone all others.

With a blast of trumpets the antagonists, in the manner of tournaments of old, rode at each other, first with lance, then pistol, then swords, and finally in hand-to-hand combat. After the fourth encounter, the judges of the field declared the honor of all the ladies had been upheld, and ordered the fighting to cease.

Afterward, Captain Cathcart, who'd performed admirably during the contest, escorted Elizabeth along a gravel path, through a flower garden heady with spring's bounty, and into a ballroom. In that room illuminated by thirty-four branches of spermaceti candles, the knights and their ladies opened the ball.

Captain Cathcart was a pleasant enough young man, tall and militarily precise in his movements, however Elizabeth found her eyes searching the crowd, looking for the blue gaze she longed to see. When she found it, discovered it locked on her, she couldn't hold back the smile that brightened her features. Surely he felt more for her than simple passion.

At ten o'clock there were to be fireworks. Slaves garbed in oriental costumes opened windows to make certain all the guests would have an unrestricted view. The orchestra, seated at the entryway at the head of the staircase, played a reel as Elizabeth reached for a glass of punch resting on the green baize-covered table.

She'd finally managed to disengage herself from Captain Cathcart, but she couldn't help feeling guilty. After all, if she really were a Tory belle, she'd be having the time of her life, grateful to her dying day to the captain for choosing her as his princess. The trouble was, she didn't know who she was anymore.

Was she a staunch Loyalist, daughter of one of the colony's leading supporters of the king? Or was she a woman with rebel leanings, a woman whose lover was a Patriot spy? Elizabeth sipped the cool liquid, lost in her dilemma. If only she could talk to someone about her problem, but there was no one.

Rebecca wouldn't even receive her. Twice Elizabeth had visited where her cousin was staying, and both times she had been told that Rebecca wasn't seeing visitors. But when Elizabeth had spoken with Sarah Chamberlain at the theater two nights ago, Sarah had mentioned what a delightful tea she'd had with Rebecca.

Talking with Hannah would do no good. She'd never understand Elizabeth's feelings for Alexander. And Father acted as if he disliked the rebel major. Of course he'd have good reason if he knew Alex's true identity, but he didn't. Because if he did, Alexander Knox would be hanging from the nearest gibbet.

If only she could discuss her feelings with Alexander . . . But she couldn't. He'd made it painfully clear he wanted no entanglements. She'd even lied about her love for him to keep him from knowing.

The orchestra stopped playing, and Elizabeth sensed movement behind her. She turned, expecting to see dancers shifting toward the windows. What she saw made her breath catch painfully in

338

her throat.

Colonel Robert Littleton, his scarlet uniform looking oddly out of place amid the silks and satins of the merrymakers, strode into the room. Accompanied by six soldiers Elizabeth assumed to be grenadiers assigned to keep the uninvited from the fete, he marched straight ahead, his gaze fixed on something across the room.

It wasn't until the colonel was almost even with her that Elizabeth discovered what — or who — warranted his complete attention.

Alexander stood, his back to them, engrossed in conversation with one of General Howe's aides. He had no way of knowing what ill wind blew his way, and he wouldn't until it was too late — unless someone warned him.

Elizabeth's mind raced. Running to him was out of the question. By the time she wended her way through the milling crowd, Littleton would already be there. She could scream, but she doubted he'd hear her across the room. If only Alexander would look this way, he'd be certain to see Littleton motioning the soldiers to fan out across the ballroom.

Frantically, Elizabeth's eyes darted about, searching for some way to make Alexander notice the colonel. The idea came to her the moment she saw the punch bowl. Leaning forward, using all her strength, Elizabeth tugged on the crystal bowl. Sangría-laced punch sloshed over the glass sides, staining the sleeves of her white gown, but Elizabeth paid no heed. With one final heave, she pulled the dish over the edge, jumping back as it shattered onto the floor.

The crashing of glass, and accompanying gasp of the crowd interrupted a very interesting story about Howe's plan to surprise one of Washington's generals on the morrow. Alex looked around in annoyance. Whoever had been clumsy enough to drop something may have cost the Patriots. He wasn't certain he could work the aide around to this subject again without arousing suspicion. But as he glanced toward the cause of the disturbance, Alex's irritation quickly turned to concern. Elizabeth, her beautiful dress stained and ruined, stood in a puddle sparkling with shards of glass.

Alex started forward, forgetting the crowd of revelers who stared at her in awed surprise, conscious only of a need to make certain she was all right. The expression of horror on her face stopped him. Reluctantly his field of vision widened, till he noticed the man beside her angrily swiping at the wine on his breeches. Wine as red as his tunic.

Recognition hit Alex instantly. He'd tried to give Colonel Robert Littleton a wide berth all winter, but by the scowl on the British officer's face as their gazes clashed, the time to avoid a meeting had passed. It didn't even take Alex's quick inspection of the ballroom, his discovery of the armed grenadiers, to convince him that flight was his only option.

Within moments of the crash, Alex pushed by Howe's startled aide, running toward the nearest window. Grasping the sides, Alex leaped through the opening just as the first fireworks exploded overhead in a kaleidoscope of color. The thick shrubbery surrounding the house cushioned his fall.

As Alex started running across the lawn, zigzagging his way toward the throng of uninvited guests still ringing the grounds, he hazarded a look back toward the window. He couldn't help grinning at what he saw. Instead of Colonel Littleton silhouetted in the frame, poised for pursuit, there were elegantly dressed ladies and men. Because they didn't realize what was happening, or they simply didn't care, the Tories were aiding his escape. Apparently watching the fireworks that exploded all around him took priority over catching a spy.

"My God, daughter! What happened here?"

Elizabeth looked up from where the slaves were mopping at the wine punch with rags. Someone had summoned her father from the faro room. "I . . . the punch bowl fell."

"That's rather obvious. How did it happen? Are you all right?"

"Yes, I'm fine. Just wet . . . and sticky." Elizabeth wiped her hands on the front of her gown.

"But how did it happen?" Jonathan Lancaster insisted.

"I . . ."

"No one is quite sure," Captain Cathcart who had rushed to Elizabeth's aid answered. "It appeared to have occurred just as the fireworks began. I theorize someone knocked into the table in their zeal to get to a window to watch the spectacle."

Lancaster studied Captain Cathcart for a moment, then turned his attention toward his daughter. "Is that what happened, Elizabeth?"

"I . . . I suppose so." Now that it was over, Elizabeth's nerves were frazzled; besides, her main concern was whether Alex had gotten safely away. She wished the fireworks would end so she could hear what was happening.

"You don't know for certain how you came to be covered with wine?" Her father sounded as if he doubted the story.

"Well . . ."

"It happened very quickly, Mr. Lancaster."

"I see. We should be getting you home, Elizabeth."

"Yes, Father." It amazed Elizabeth that so few people did know what had occurred. If anyone had watched her pull the punch bowl off the table, she hadn't noticed and no one had spoken up. Everyone simply seemed to assume, like Captain Cathcart, that Elizabeth was the victim of someone's clumsiness. Few people had even remarked about the man who'd jumped out the window.

Of course, not everyone believed in Elizabeth's innocence. Colonel Littleton had paused in front of her on his way toward the door. "You will regret this, Elizabeth." That was all he'd said. But it was enough. He knew what she'd done, and, more importantly, he knew why.

It wasn't till later that night, lying clean, thanks to a bath, in her bed, that Elizabeth began wondering if Littleton had planned this attempt to capture Alexander all along. His statement that he'd be occupied elsewhere during the Meschianza came back to haunt her. Had he plotted even then to capture Major Knox? And if he knew about Alexander, did he know about her also? Perhaps she'd underestimated Colonel Littleton.

He'd said she'd regret her actions. Elizabeth sat up in bed, wondering what form that threat would take. Littleton hadn't returned to the house this evening. She hoped that meant Alexander was still free. Whatever Littleton might do to her, she'd never be sorry about what she'd done to help Alexander.

Most likely their paths would never cross again. With his identity known, Alexander couldn't stay

343

in Philadelphia. If were lucky, he'd escape to the Patriot lines and she'd never see him again. Elizabeth sighed, supposing this was her sacrifice for the war effort.

She climbed out of the high tester bed and walked toward the window. After the time he'd stood below, insisting she come down Elizabeth often stood thus, looking out, wondering if he might be somewhere in the garden. But she knew he wasn't there tonight.

Hunger made her leave her room. She'd missed the dinner at the Meschianza, and a bath had been her first priority when she and her father had arrived home in their borrowed coach. But now her growling stomach reminded her that she hadn't eaten since breakfast.

Wrapping a shawl around her shoulders, Elizabeth took up her bedside candle and started down the steps. She'd assumed her father was asleep in bed, the hour being late, but when she passed the library, a faint ribbon of light shone from under the door. Shaking her head at his carelessness, for she was certain he'd fallen asleep in his chair, Elizabeth reached toward the knob. Another deep grumbling from the region of her stomach made her pause. First she'd find something to eat, then she'd awaken her father, and help him to bed.

Jonathan Lancaster crossed his legs, leaning

back in his favorite chair. Moonlight streaming through the French doors mingled with the candle's glow, bathing the room in soft light and shadows. For a moment, before speaking, he observed the man who paced the library like a caged mountain lion. "Would you be seated, Major. You make me weary just watching you."

"Sorry." Alexander Knox crossed the room and sprawled in the chair closest to Lancaster's. Impatiently he swiped a lock of hair from his forehead.

"That's better," Jonathan began. "I'm glad you came. I didn't know how to get in touch with you."

Alex rubbed his eyes. "After tonight you won't have to."

"You're leaving Philadelphia, then?"

"I've no choice. Samuel Brown is already on his way to Valley Forge. I managed to get to him before Littleton did."

"Good." Jonathan leaned forward, resting his elbows on the polished surface of his desk. "And you'll be following him."

"Yes. Another agent will be contacting you soon. But before I leave, I want to know if you've heard anything about a surprise attack tomorrow."

"Exactly the reason I hoped you'd come. The British hope to capture Lafayette."

"The marquis?" Alex was on his feet again, ignoring Lancaster's annoyed expression. "When? Where?"

"Well, if you'd sit down . . ." Jonathan swept his hand toward the chair Knox had vacated. "Never mind. Lafayette is in the vicinity of Barren Hill, commanding a detachment of about two thousand men. General Grant is to march tomorrow night and attack from the rear. Howe in the meantime will close the trap by blocking Lafayette's retreat through Germantown."

"So this is to be Howe's last hurrah?"

"So it would seem. Not a bad way to end his stint in the colonies, capturing the Marquis de Lafayette."

Alex nodded. "Washington feared Valley Forge would be his target, but I suppose this appeals more to Howe's sense of the dramatic. Capturing the marquis just as the French join the war does seem a bit like poetic justice."

"We have the Meschianza to thank that it's not a *fait accompli*. Howe postponed the attack till after the celebration."

Alex grinned. "I fear their fun-loving ways may be the downfall of the British." He started toward the French doors, planning to exit as he'd entered. By dawn he could cover the twelve miles to Barren Hill and warn Lafayette. What needed to be done was clear, still he paused. "Lancaster?"

The older man stopped snuffing the candles, and looked up. He'd obviously thought their conversation over.

"You may want to consider leaving Philadel-

346

phia."

"Do you think Littleton suspects me?" Jonathan questioned.

"Not you. Elizabeth." Alex retraced his steps and leaned across the desk. "The shattered punch bowl tonight was no accident. I'm sure of it. It was meant as a warning. . . . a warning I heeded, but one, unless I miss my guess, Littleton noted as well."

"I wondered." Jonathan rubbed his chin.

"Elizabeth could be in grave danger if what I suspect is true." The realization had nagged at his mind all night. He hated to think of Elizabeth in jeopardy at any time, but that she was in this circumstance because of him . . . Alex gripped the polished mahogany. "Do you understand what I'm saying to you?

Alex heard the doorknob turn before he noticed fear spring into Jonathan Lancaster's eyes. With an economy of motion, Alex backed into the shadows, drawing his pistol and aiming it toward the opening door.

"I thought certain you'd be asleep." Elizabeth pushed open the door with her hip, balancing a silver tray in her hands. "But I made you some tea, anyway. What's wrong?" Something in her father's expression concerned her. She rushed toward him. "Are you ill?"

"No . . . I'm . . ."

Elizabeth had no idea what made her turn at

that moment. But she did. And stared straight into Alexander's eyes. For the second time that day she felt wetness seep through her clothes as the tray and its china cups and saucers clattered to the Turkish rug sending hot water and tea leaves flying. "What are you doing here?" Elizabeth's hand flew to her mouth when she noticed the gun. "No, Alexander. Please don't shoot him."

It took Alex a moment to realize what she meant. He only knew that Elizabeth stared at him in horror. When he did notice that his gun was turned toward Elizabeth and her father, he lowered the pistol, jamming it into the waistband of his breeches.

Elizabeth slumped against the desk in relief. She couldn't imagine what reason Alexander would have to hurt her father. "Why, Alexander? Why have you come here?"

"Yes, why don't you tell her, Major Knox. I'm certain we'd all find the tale interesting." Robert Littleton stepped through the French doors.

Alex spun around, grabbing the gun butt and yanking it from his breeches, but it was too late. Moonlight gleamed off the brass barrel of Littleton's pistol as he shifted his aim from Alexander to Elizabeth.

"I wouldn't, Major. It would be a shame to destroy one so lovely as Elizabeth, especially after she so heroically aided your escape this evening; however, that's what you'll force me to do if you don't hand over your weapon."

Reluctantly Alex leaned down placing his gun on the floor, all the while keeping his eyes trained on Littleton.

"Kick it over this way. Carefully," Littleton warned. When Alexander had done as he asked, Littleton leaned against the door frame. "Now, Major, I believe you were going to answer Mistress Lancaster's question or would you prefer that I do it?"

Alex said nothing. He glanced at Lancaster, wondering if he kept a loaded pistol in his desk, wondering, too, if the man would have the presence of mind to use it. So far Littleton had been content to let the older man sit, his hands hidden from view. Jonathan caught Alex's eye, and Alex knew the answer to his question.

"Not willing to elaborate, Major Knox?" The hint of an evil smile shaded Littleton's mouth. "Or perhaps you think there is some secret to keep. But, believe me, I know everything. I'll admit you had me fooled for a while, Lancaster. You make a very convincing Loyalist, but I finally unraveled your little scheme." Littleton's gaze drifted to Jonathan Lancaster.

"I don't know what you're talking about, Littleton." Alex successfully regained the colonel's attention, though the gun was still pointed at Elizabeth. "You've captured me, and I'll come quietly. Now let's leave these innocent people alone."

"Come now, Major. You'll have to do better than that. We all know that Lancaster here is one of your main agents in the city."

Alex heard Elizabeth's gasp, as did Littleton. "Very convincing, Elizabeth. I could almost believe you knew nothing of this. Unfortunately, no one else will believe it after I tell them how I captured the three of you together. I wonder if the court-martial will decide to hang a female traitor."

"You bastard!"

Elizabeth watched in shock as her father jumped out of his chair, a pistol in his hand. At the same time, Alexander leaped through the air toward Littleton. "Get down," he yelled at Elizabeth, moments before the first report split the night air. The noxious fumes of gunpowder drifted on the smoke-filled air as another shot sounded. Her body finally obeying Alexander's command, Elizabeth fell to the floor, echoes of her own scream sounding in her head.

Chapter Seventeen

"My God!" Elizabeth scrambled to her feet, yanking the wet nightrail away when it stuck to her legs. "Alexander," she cried, dropping to her knees beside him. Littleton was sprawled on top of him, and as Elizabeth watched in horror, blood began oozing onto the floor, soaking into the rug.

"I'm all right," Alex answered, giving the body covering his a hard shove. "But I don't think the colonel can say the same."

When Littleton was rolled over, his brown eyes staring unseeing at the ceiling, Elizabeth noticed the source of the blood. A jagged hole just below his gold gorget, marred the perfection of the uniform. "Is he . . . ?" Elizabeth grabbed hold of Alexander's arm, unable to voice the question.

"I think so." Alex pried the pistol out of Littleton's lifeless fingers. "How's your father?"

"Oh, no!" Elizabeth pulled herself up, trying not to look at the dead British officer as she stepped over his legs. How could she have forgotten about her father? It was just that when the gunshots had ceased, and she'd opened her eyes, all she'd seen was Alex and Colonel Littleton . . . and the blood.

"Alex, he's been shot." Elizabeth leaned over the unconscious figure slumped in the chair. "Alexander!" She cried, her voice fraught with panic.

"I'm right here, Elizabeth." He grabbed her shoulders, moving her aside. "Let me see."

Elizabeth wiped ineffectively at the tears that dampened her cheeks. How could she fall apart like this? She'd always been so dependable at the hospital. She took a deep breath, ignoring the tang of death in the air. "I should be doing that," she said to Alexander.

"Just let me have a look first. Here." He reached up, thrusting the pistol and his powderhorn into her hands. "Do you know how to load one of these?"

Looking down at the weapon Elizabeth shook her head. Candlelight reflected off the still-warm barrel. "No . . . I . . . no one ever showed me.

"Never mind." Alex lowered Jonathan to the floor, ripping the heavy silk brocade of his jacket so he could look at the wound. "Just keep a watch. Let me know if you see or hear anything."

"Like what?" Elizabeth peered out the French

doors, seeing nothing but darkness. She strained to listen, but could only hear the rending of silk and Alexander's mumbled curses.

"Anything. Maybe Littleton had men with him, stationed outside." He stood up, taking the gun out of her hands. "Your father is alive, but he's losing a lot of blood. Do you have something I can use as a bandage?"

Elizabeth's eyes darted around the room, lighting on her flowered scarf lying on the floor. "Here." She handed it to Alexander. With a gentle motion, she touched her father's cheek. "Is he going to be all right?"

"I think so." Alex tightened the scarf around her father's shoulder, tying it in a knot as Jonathan regained consciousness. Alex answered the question in the older man's eyes. "You've been shot, but you're going to be fine."

"Elizabeth?" His pain-stricken words tore at her heart.

"I'm here, Father." Elizabeth took his hand. Jonathan's eyes fluttered shut. "Shouldn't we get him to bed, send for a surgeon?"

Alex examined Elizabeth and for the first time noticed her frightened expression. She wasn't accustomed to seeing men shot, not to mention in her own house. But Alex feared her ordeal wasn't over. "Elizabeth," he said tearing her attention from her father, "we can't stay here."

"But—" Elizabeth tried to make sense of his

353

words. "We can't leave my father."

"No. He'll have to come with us."

"But his wound." Elizabeth touched the make-shift bandage that was rapidly turning red.

"Listen to me." Alexander pulled her to her feet, giving her shoulders a gentle shake. "I think Littleton was alone. At least, no one has stormed into the house demanding to know about the shots, but we don't know who else he told about your father . . . or you."

Elizabeth raised imploring gray eyes to his. "Why didn't you tell me about my father—that he was a Patriot?"

Dropping his hands to his sides, Alex looked away. "It wasn't my place to do so, Elizabeth," he said softly. Alexander had been dreading this moment ever since the colonel had exposed Jonathan Lancaster's secret. He knew how betrayed Elizabeth felt. But there was no time for explanations now. "We need to be leaving before someone notices he's missing." Alex motioned toward Littleton.

Elizabeth nodded. What he said made sense. She just couldn't believe this was happening. "Where are we going?"

"I'm not sure." Alex crossed the room, snatching a pillow off a chair. He tucked it under Jonathan's head, and retrieved the other gun. Quickly he poured in powder and rammed the shot home.

Elizabeth sat back on the floor, leaving her

354

father's side reluctantly when Alexander reached for her hand.

He resisted the urge to pull her into his arms. "You need to get some clothes on. Dress in something serviceable like a riding habit or, better yet, something belonging to one of your servants. Where are they anyway?" It occurred to Alex that if they were here, they would have come to investigate the noise.

"Father gave them the night off to watch the fireworks. I'm surprised some of them aren't back by now."

Taking this piece of information as another reason for haste, Alex urged Elizabeth to hurry.

"And, Elizabeth . . ." She had started toward the door, but stopped at the sound of his voice. "Take this with you." He closed the gap between them, folding her hands around the gun butt. "If you should need it, just aim and squeeze the trigger."

"But I never—"

"Just do it, Elizabeth, and I'll be there as quickly as I can." He brushed back an ebony curl.

"What are you going to do?"

"Get rid of the body first, and clean up the blood. Then I'll hitch up something for your father to ride in. Do you have a wagon?"

"Yes. Amos uses it to haul wood and fodder. But wouldn't the coach be more comfortable for father?"

"Possibly, but it would draw more attention, and

355

that's something we don't need right now." Alex gave Elizabeth a quick hug, and found it as comforting for him as he'd intended it to be for her. "Come back to the library as soon as you're ready, and bring some linens for bandaging."

Elizabeth picked up the candle she'd left on the stand in the hall and, hiking up her skirts, scurried up the stairs. I mustn't think about what has happened, she told herself repeatedly. If she did, panic was sure to follow. She would simply do what had to be done. Take things one step at a time—but she wouldn't think. Elizabeth glanced down to where the pistol dangled from her hand, and felt a wave of nausea. Resolutely she ignored it, setting her sights upon the well-trod steps.

She bypassed her bedroom, turning instead toward the attic steps. Jane's room under the eaves was cramped but clean. Elizabeth quickly searched through the small clothespress, grabbing a coarse cotton shift. Shedding her ruined nightrail, trying to ignore the bloodstains smeared upon it, Elizabeth pulled on the underclothes. She quickly donned a short sack of calico material and a wool overskirt. After tying a kerchief around her neck, Elizabeth stuffed her hair into a ruffled mob cap.

Hurrying from the room, she descended the steps, stopping off in her own room to grab an armful of blankets and linens and her cloak before heading back to the library.

"Good girl," Alex smiled up at her when she

reentered the room. "See, Jonathan, I told you she'd be quick about it. Now I'm going to carry you out to the wagon," he explained as Jonathan, obviously in pain, tried unsuccessfully to raise himself.

"Father!" Elizabeth ran to where Alexander leaned over Jonathan. He was awake and gave his daughter a wan smile when she sank down beside him.

"I've been trying to talk the major here into letting me stay. You'll stand a much better chance of making it through the lines without me." Jonathan's voice was weak, and he had to pause several times, his pale face grimacing in pain.

Elizabeth's gaze shot to Alexander.

"It seems your father is hesitant about joining us on our little adventure, but I've assured him we wouldn't attempt it without him."

Elizabeth knew Alexander deliberately kept a light tone to his voice. She met him in kind. "The major's right, Father. We simply won't let you miss the fun. Fooling the British, that's what you two are good at, isn't it? Well, I think we should continue the charade." Elizabeth politely omitted that they had fooled her, too.

Taking her word as the deciding vote, Alex eased his arms under Jonathan. "Bring the bedding and that lantern," he ordered Elizabeth as he hefted her father up.

By the time they had Jonathan settled on the

357

hay in the wagon bed, he'd lost consciousness again. His face, in the flickering lantern light, looked deathly pale. "Are you certain he'll survive being jostled around in this wagon?" Elizabeth asked, pulling a blanket up to his chin.

"No." Alex jumped down from the wagon. "I'm not sure, Elizabeth. But I am certain of the consequences if he stays in Philadelphia, and I think your father would rather die of a British bullet than hang from one of their ropes."

A shiver of fear ran down her spine as she recalled General Warner's words of so many months ago. Hanging was a "fitting punishment for a traitor," he'd said. At the time she'd assumed he meant Alexander. Now she knew both the men in her life might meet that fate. Her gaze met Alexander's. "Let's go," she whispered.

The streets were quiet, which surprised Alex. A major breakout of American prisoners from the gaol had been planned for tonight, and, from what Samuel had said when he'd stopped at the house to warn him, the attempt had been successful. Alex touched the pistol stuffed under the old coat he'd found in the stable. He hoped it wouldn't be necessary to use it, especially with Elizabeth near, but this was not a good night to flee Philadelphia.

Besides the prison break, the Patriot general, McLane, had harassed the defense lines by setting fire to large kettles of combustibles. Little more than an annoyance to the British, this tactic had helped create a diversion for the prisoners. Unfortunately, Alex theorized, it also fortified the numbers of troops manning the redoubt that guarded the city.

Slapping the reins, Alex prodded the horses to quicken their pace. They were heading north along Second Street, toward the Germantown Road. He glanced beside him at Elizabeth. Except for occasionally turning to look behind her, where her father lay in the wagon bed, she stared forward, her expression hidden from his view. Even if she faced him, Alex doubted he could read her expression in the weak, oscillating light thrown out by the lantern. Still he wanted to know that she was all right.

"Do you remember where you're to say we're headed?" he asked.

"To our farm in Mount Airy," Elizabeth recited, repeating part of the story Alexander had given her when they'd first climbed onto the wagon seat.

"And what's your name?"

"Betsy O'Malley. You're my husband Jake, and we're on our way home after enjoying the fireworks."

"And why are we getting such a late start?" Alex prompted.

"Because my father got separated from us, and it took us hours to find him. By the time we did, he'd tipped too many grogs. So now he's sleeping it off in the wagon. Alexander we've been through all this once," Elizabeth added with annoyance, grabbing the seat as they bounced over a deep rut in the road.

"I know, but there can be no hesitation when we're questioned."

"You're right." Elizabeth turned to look at him. "I suppose I'm just frightened."

Threading the reins through the fingers of one hand, Alex reached out, drawing Elizabeth close to his side. "You'd be foolish if you weren't. I know I am."

"You?" Huddled against his chest, Elizabeth looked up at him in surprise. He'd seemed to handle any dangerous situation she'd seen him in so calmly. It had never occurred to her that he might fear anything.

"Sure. If this old coat weren't so thick, you'd hear my heart racing like a thoroughbred's."

Elizabeth thought she could detect the beat of his heart, but it sounded steady to her. "I'm not sure that's a very reassuring thought."

"Nothing wrong with a healthy dose of fear, Elizabeth. It keeps you alert. When you scoff at danger, don't prepare yourself for all the possibilities, that's when you get careless."

"And caught."

"Yes." Alex's voice was reflective. "And caught."

"Is that what happened tonight?" Elizabeth asked as his jaw brushed against her forehead. He looked down at her.

"Maybe. It could be I underestimated Littleton. But one thing's for certain. I only make one mistake a night. We'll get out of Philadelphia all right." Alex wished he felt as confident as he sounded.

As they approached the British lines, Alex reached into the wagon for the slouched, felt hat he'd grabbed off a peg in the tack room. Stuffing it on his head, he hoped it made him look like a farmer. "They probably won't ask you anything," he assured her as he pulled on the reins, stopping the wagon beside a British soldier.

"I'll be ready if they do," Elizabeth whispered though she wasn't certain if he heard her.

"Halt!"

Elizabeth thought the order unnecessary since Alexander had already stopped the wagon, but the sergeant seemed the type to follow regulations. His uniform was neat and pressed, and even though the hour was late, his bearing was precise as he raised his lantern, peering into what he could see of Alexander's face.

"What business do you have out on the king's road at this hour of night?"

"And haven't I been asking myself the same question?" Alexander began, his voice taking on an Irish tilt. "Tired I am, bone tired, and no rest in sight before the sun sets on another day, but here I am facing a journey that would drive a

361

sober man to drink. And why, you might ask. Because my wife's old man can't pass by a tavern without tipping a few ... the old goat."

The accent surprised Elizabeth, though as Alexander continued to speak, she didn't know why it should. She had heard him master the speech of the dandiest of British fops. The sergeant was fooled by him, Elizabeth was certain of that. He acted quite annoyed, looked like he wished this wagon and its occupants would just disappear from his sight. Perhaps with a little more persuasion, he'd give in to his disgust and send them on their way.

"Just who are you calling an old goat?" Elizabeth screeched mimicking the tone she'd heard Polly use when chasing the cat from the kitchen.

Alex forgot the British soldier as his head jerked around toward Elizabeth. She was supposed to be quiet, yet there she sat caterwauling at him like some fishmonger ... or poor Irish farmer's wife. Cocking his brow, he couldn't resist a grin as he yelled back. "Your da that's who. If it wouldn't a been for his grog-guzzling ways I'd be in me bed this very moment instead of sitting on this hard wood listening to a shrewish wife."

"Shrew, am I?" Elizabeth shrieked. "And me the God-fearing mother of your five babes, and quickening with another. You're a mean man, Jake O'Malley." Slapping her hands over her face Elizabeth made loud sobbing noises.

"Oh, Betsy, love, 'twas not my intent to make you cry. Hush now, girl." Alex patted Elizabeth's knee.

Elizabeth wailed louder, putting her heart into the act, especially when she heard moans from the wagon bed. This wasn't the time for her father to wake up.

"Enough!" bellowed the sergeant. "I'll not listen to this blubbering another minute. Be on your way, farmer, and take that woman with you. My God, man, try to teach her some manners. That bawling would wake the dead."

"Yes, sir. That I will, sir," Alex said, slapping the reins. "Hush now, Betsy love. I'll have you home before you know it."

Elizabeth's only response was muffled sobs.

When they were out of earshot of the last British soldier, Alex turned to Elizabeth. "Five babies?"

Feeling the tension drain out of her, Elizabeth laughed. " 'Twas the first number that popped into my mind."

"I see." Alex shook his head. "Well, you were very convincing. I almost believed you myself."

"Thank you." Elizabeth settled back in the seat, stifling a satisfied smile.

"Oh, Elizabeth?"

"Yes?" She turned to meet his quizzical stare.

"About what you said . . . I mean . . . carrying the sixth baby." Alex cursed his stammering. "You aren't, are you? With child, I mean?"

"No, Alexander, I'm not," Elizabeth answered, noting his relieved expression. In her mind, she couldn't blame him. It had been a worry of hers after each time they'd been together. But in her heart she resented his obvious relief. Each time she'd realized she wasn't carrying his child, a sadness had swept over her. She wanted his children—wanted him. But he hadn't even cared enough to confide in her about her father.

Elizabeth looked into the darkness beyond the puddle of light from the lantern. The landscape appeared barren, the British had cut many of the trees close to Philadelphia for firewood. She tried not to think of the deceit the two men had played on her. Elizabeth had trusted both of them, had thought they trusted her. Yet they had been playing a deadly game, had unwittingly involved her in that game, and she'd never known.

Elizabeth glanced over her shoulder, trying to discern her father's features. No more sounds came from the wagon bed, and Elizabeth hoped that only meant he'd fallen back to sleep.

"How much farther are we going?" She could imagine the pain her father's wound must be causing him with every jolt of the wagon on the rough road.

"There's an inn right outside of Germantown where you'll be safe for a while. I think I can get someone to help your father, too."

Relieved as she was to hear this, Elizabeth hadn't missed the lack of reference to himself. "Won't you be staying with us?"

"I'll get you settled. Then there's something I must attend to."

"I see." Well, she knew secrets were his trade. Had she honestly thought he'd start confiding in her now?

She was angry. He could tell by the the tilt of her chin, which was all he could see because of her hood. "It's better you don't know."

"Do you think I will warn the British?"

"Listen, your father didn't want you involved in this, and neither do I."

Elizabeth clutched the seat to keep from falling as she turned on him. Her eyes shone with angry silver sparks. "Don't speak to me of avoiding entanglements. My father's wounded, I was threatened with hanging, I'm fleeing the British, going I've no idea where. I am involved! I've been enmeshed in this situation since the day I met you, probably before, if truth be known. I've no idea how long my father has been a Patriot."

"From the beginning."

"Ah, so he's lied to me for years—even before you started."

"Elizabeth."

"Don't use that patronizing tone with me Alexander Knox. I feel betrayed!" And with that, Elizabeth slumped back against the hard wood

365

seat, all her fire spent.

"Elizabeth." Alex reached out to touch her, but she turned away.

"I don't want to talk about it, Alexander. What's done is done. Right now I have to think about taking care of my father."

They kept their peace, each deep in thought as they passed through the sleeping hamlet of Germantown. Alex turned the horses left at Market Square down Schoolhouse Lane, heading west toward the junction of the Wissahickon and Schuylkill rivers. After they'd gone another hundred rods or so, they turned again. This time the narrow, tree-lined lane led to a stone dwelling. A sign swung over the front door, illegible in the darkness.

Jumping from the wagon, Alex patted the head of the mongrel dog that barked at him, before striding to the front door. His pounding sounded uncommonly loud in the predawn quiet. In a few minutes, a yellow glow appeared in the window directly over the entrance. The sash was thrown open, and a cadaverous head topped by a sleeping cap thrust through the opening.

"Hell's fire and damnation! Who's there pounding on my door, waking decent folk from their slumber?" The candle the man held in his bony hand cast eerie shadows on his sunken cheeks.

In spite of her newly formed resolve to be brave, Elizabeth found herself cringing back

366

against the rickety seat. But Alexander backed up till he could peer up at the window. "You've some travelers below, in need of a meal and a place to rest."

"Travelers, eh? What will you be taking with your meal, travelers, coffee or tea?"

Alexander's laughter boomed. "Ebenezer McGill, you haven't the strength to force English tea down my gullet."

The skinny body leaned out over the sill until Elizabeth feared he might tumble from the second story. "Is that you, Alexander?"

"Who else would agree to stay in your run-down excuse for an inn?"

Instead of the reaction Elizabeth expected from this insult, the man in the window howled with laughter. "You've got the right of it there, Alex lad."

By the time the door swung open, Alex had lifted Elizabeth down from the high wagon seat. She immediately climbed into the back, searching for signs of life from her father. Alex leaned over the side. "How is he?"

"Alive, but the wound's still bleeding."

"We've got a wounded man here, Eb," Alex said to the man who stomped out into the yard, nightshirt flapping around skinny legs. "Can you send someone for Doc Webster?"

"Now that might be a tad difficult." Eb held his candle high, looking first into Elizabeth's face, and then down at her father. "Seeing how he died nigh a month ago."

"Hell." Alex bit the word through his teeth.

"That'd probably be the best place to look," Eb quipped. "What happened to him?"

"Took a British ball." Alex vaulted over the wagon's side. "Help me get him upstairs."

Elizabeth, carrying the lantern, led the way up a winding stairway to a small room. Four beds, covered with rough wool blankets, lined the walls under the eaves. Unable to stand because of the slanted ceiling, Alex lowered Jonathan's body onto a cot. As Elizabeth said, fresh red blood stained the scarf they'd used as a bandage. Alex started to unwrap it, and Jonathan moaned.

"Let me see what I have in the way of medicines. Doc Webster left some stuff here last time he passed by in exchange for feeding him and his horse."

"I'll get the linens from the wagon," Elizabeth said, trying to fight the helplessness she felt.

When she opened the front door, she noticed the first touches of mauve tinting the eastern sky, but there was no wagon, nor were there horses, in the yard.

"Your bedding's over there on a chair." Eb motioned back into the hall. He'd pulled on a pair of breeches, tucking his nightshirt into the top. "My boy took them out of your wagon before he hid it over by the gorge. No sense letting them lobsterbacks and Tories know we got company."

Elizabeth could hardly argue with that sentiment as she hurried upstairs with her pile of linens. Alexander had cut away her father's coat, and was gently probing the bloody wound with his fingers. He glanced around when she walked in.

"The ball is in too deep. I can't get it out." By the feel of it, the ball had lodged in the joint of the shoulder. Alex doubted Jonathan would ever have full use of his arm, that is, if he lived. Judging from the loss of blood, Alex wasn't certain of that.

"We'll have to pack it then. He can't lose much more blood." Elizabeth began shredding sheets, scraping as much lint off the linen as she could.

"What do you have in there?" Eb had followed Elizabeth into the room, and it was to him that Alex addressed his question.

Eb looked in the basket, removing brown bottles, and squinting his eyes to read the labels. "Here's some tartar emetic and snakeroot, but I can't find any ointment or poultices."

Alex moved aside, and Elizabeth began packing the wound with lint and shredded linen. When she was finished, Alex helped wrap Jonathan's shoulder, binding his arm against his body.

"That's all we can do for now. When the fever comes on him you'll be thankful for the basket Doc Webster bartered." Alex stood, rubbing his tired eyes. He'd give a lot for a couple hours of sleep, but it didn't take the crowing of Eb's old rooster to tell him that a new day had dawned. A day that would see Howe marching from Philadelphia in pursuit of Lafayette. It was no coincidence that Alex had headed north when he'd left the city. He'd covered over half the distance to Barren Hill already, but he still had to get there in time for the Americans to escape the trap the British had devised.

"Do you have a fast horse you can lend me?" Alex pretended he didn't notice the questioning glance Elizabeth shot his way. But after Eb left he moved over to where she sat on a Windsor chair beside her father's bed. "I'll be back in a few days, maybe sooner."

"You needn't hurry on our account. We'll be fine." Elizabeth fought to keep her voice calm.

"I wouldn't leave you now if I didn't have to. A lot of lives may depend upon my reaching Lafayette in time."

"So that's where you're going?"

Alex nodded. "I would have told you before except —"

"You didn't want to get me involved."

"That does seem a poor excuse under the circumstances." Dropping to his knees beside the chair, Alex enfolded her clasped hands in his. Dressed in a rough wool skirt and loose calico blouse, her shiny, midnight black hair escaping her mob cap and curling charmingly around her face,

370

Elizabeth looked as natural and beautiful in this attic room, surrounded by homemade furniture and dressed in servant's clothes, as she did in her fanciest ball gown.

Without thinking he lifted her hands to his mouth. "I'm sorry I got you into this. Sometimes I think if I hadn't raided Landon Hall—"

"Or if I hadn't argued with you about taking Colonel Littleton." Elizabeth closed her eyes, biting her bottom lip.

"Don't think about him, Elizabeth."

"I can't help it. I'd grown to detest him. I never mentioned it to anybody, but he threatened me several times before last night." Elizabeth felt Alexander's hands tighten on hers. "Oh, he never did anything, but—"

"You should have told me."

"Maybe you're right." Elizabeth shrugged. "But anyway, I hated him. Yet, I can still close my eyes and see him . . . The last word was caught on a sob.

"Don't, Elizabeth," Alex whispered as his hand traced the gentle curve of her cheek.

"I'm sorry." Elizabeth raised large luminous eyes, meeting his gaze. "I suppose I'm not being very brave."

"You've been very brave. I can't imagine what this has been like for you. And back there at the redoubt, with the guard." Alex chuckled. "You were wonderful. I never knew you could lie like that."

"You should have." Elizabeth's heartbeat quickened. He didn't think she could lie, but she'd told him the biggest untruth of all when she'd pretended she didn't love him.

"What do you mean, 'I should have'?" He'd stopped laughing, but his eyes still twinkled with blue devilment.

"I lied to you, Alexander." He was going away, maybe never to return. If there was one thing she'd learned in the past few hours, it was never to take life for granted. She wouldn't take love for granted, either. "Do you remember that night in my garden?" She knew the exact moment he guessed what she was going to say. "I lied about not loving you. I do."

"Elizabeth, I—"

"Horse's saddled." Eb blustered his way into the room. "I found you some clothes to wear. Had the missus pack you something to eat, too."

"Thank you, Eb." Alex spoke to his friend, but his eyes remained locked with Elizabeth's. "I'd better leave."

"I suppose so."

"We'll talk when I get back." Alex stood, took the bundle from Eb and strode out of the room.

A short time later, Elizabeth heard the pounding of hooves. Rushing to the gable window, she peered through the panes, watching as Alexander rode away.

Chapter Eighteen

Elizabeth's head fell forward, the sudden motion waking her. For a moment she looked around in confusion. The guttered candle sputtered in the malodorous wax, throwing grotesque shadows upon the slanting walls. Her eyes focused on her father, sleeping on the cot beside her chair, and realization flooded her senses. Standing, arching her back to assuage the stiffness, Elizabeth reached into the candle box. She lit the new taper from the dying flame of the old, before the room was thrown into total darkness.

More from habit than conscious thought, Elizabeth dipped a piece of toweling into the pail on the floor. Wringing out the tepid liquid, she wiped the cloth across her father's forehead. Forehead, gaunt cheeks, cleft chin—it had become a pattern over the five days and nights she'd sat by his side, fighting the fever that ravaged his body.

There had been little to break the monotony during that time. Eb had offered to take her place the first few nights, but when she'd refused, had stopped asking. Her father's and her own presence in the small attic room was not common knowledge. Eb's son knew, though she never saw him, and Mrs. McGill had been in the hideaway several times to collect soiled linens and bring meals, but she was a singularly quiet woman, who spoke only when spoken to. There were other patrons at the Inn—Elizabeth had seen them through the dirty window—but as she never left the room, she had no idea who they were.

Elizabeth sighed, closing her tired eyes. Each day she'd hoped for Alexander's return, and each day she'd been disappointed. Now she began to wonder if he'd come back for them at all. Perhaps he'd been needed by the army or . . . Elizabeth stuck the cloth in the bucket again, sloshing water onto the wide plank floor. She refused to believe anything had happened to Alexander.

Again the cloth worked its way across her father's face. But this time, as it trailed along the grizzled whisker's that roughened his cheek, Elizabeth's fingers touched his skin. Used to fiery heat, they encountered instead, cool flesh.

Her body jerked forward as she reached for his forehead with her free hand. It no longer burned. Tears scalded her sleep-deprived eyes as she realized the fever had broken. She listened to his breathing. That, too, had lost the fitful, restless quality of the last five days. Pulling the blanket under his chin, Elizabeth gave a prayer of thanks.

The cot against the far wall was rumpled from the last time she'd used it, catching a few hours' sleep between seeing to her father's needs. It beckoned her with all the power of a lover. Elizabeth swiped back a lock of hair. It needed brushing. Even without a looking glass, she could tell it tumbled around her head in unruly curls. But she hadn't the strength to use the brush Mrs. McGill had brought her.

The footfalls outside the door caught her off guard. She'd heard no one on the steps, but then, she realized, her mind had been wandering. It was too late for Eb to visit, and she couldn't imagine who else it would be.

Anxiously, Elizabeth reached under her pillow for the pistol Alexander had left. Grasping the handle, she whirled around, aiming it at the entrance just as the door opened.

"My God, Elizabeth, don't shoot me!"

"Alexander!" Dropping the gun onto the cot, forgetting her fatigue, Elizabeth ran toward him, throwing her arms around his narrow waist. She nuzzled into the buckskin jacket, loving the smells of leather and horse and him.

Kicking the door shut with his foot, Alex leaned his rifle against the wall and gave in to the urge to wrap his arms around her. Damn, this wasn't what he'd planned.

As soon as he'd ridden away, and most of the time he'd traveled toward Barren Hill, he'd thought about what she'd said to him before he left. She loved him. If he hadn't been so busy being relieved when she'd denied it in the garden, he'd have known that for the lie it was. It had taken almost riding into a British patrol to convince him that he had to stop thinking of her admission—and Elizabeth.

Damn, he thought again as he cradled her more firmly against his body. She felt so good pressed against his heart, and after what he'd been through he needed something that felt good. But this was never going to work. Riding back, pushing his horse and himself mercilessly to get to her as quickly as he could, Alex had finally admitted to himself that he loved her. But it didn't make any difference—couldn't make any difference. Or so he had told himself until he'd opened the door and seen her.

"I was afraid you'd been hurt or . . ."

Alex looked down at Elizabeth, and in the flickering candle glow her eyes shone silvery bright. "I told you I'd be back. How's your father?" He twined his fingers through her hair, smiling when they caught in a tangle. He'd never seen her look quite so unkempt, or so lovely.

"The fever broke, just tonight. Oh, Alexander, I

think he's going to be all right."

He hugged her tighter, thankful for the good news. "But what about you?" Alex trailed his thumb under her eyes, noticing, even in the dim light, the lavender-tinged shadows. "You look tired."

"I'm fine. I am," she insisted when he cocked his brow. "But tell me of you. Did you warn Lafayette?"

"Yes." Alex brushed his lips across her forehead in a whisper-soft kiss. "However let me sit down before I tell you about it. Perhaps you're not tired, but I am."

Alex flung his powderhorn and haversack off his shoulder. Stripping off his jacket he sat on the nearest cot, leaning back against the whitewashed wall. He pulled Elizabeth down with him. It seemed only natural for her to snuggle against his broad chest, for the steady beat of his heart to form a backdrop for his tale.

"I found the marquis' camp late on the morning of the nineteenth."

"The day you left here?" With some exasperation, Elizabeth realized she'd lost track of the dates.

"Uh-huh," Alex agreed, letting his fingers caress the soft warmth of her arm. "As your father had said." Alex paused, shifting so he could look down at her. "He's the one who gave me the information."

Elizabeth returned his stare. "I thought as much."

"Well, anyway, the marquis was in an indefensible position, with part of the British able to block his retreat across the Schuylkill as Howe advanced on him from Germantown."

"But he did escape, didn't he?" Elizabeth wriggled around, staring up at Alexander. All she could see was the bold curve of his jaw. Though it was roughened by a day's growth of black whiskers, she still found it fascinating.

"Oh, yes." Alex chuckled, stopping when he heard movement from the cot across the narrow room. Jonathan Lancaster stirred in his sleep, but didn't waken. When Alex spoke again, his voice was little more than a whisper. "Luckily for the Americans, Howe had given command of the force to block Lafayette to General Grant. As usual, he took his sweet time, wasting a lot of it in indecisions and in being just plain overly cautious." Alex words were tinged with contempt for the inept general.

"Lafayette was able to cross at Matson's Ford before Grant reached it. When Howe heard the news, he marched back to Philadelphia."

"So there was no battle?"

"A few minor skirmishes, nothing more." Alex slid down further on the bed. He'd had very little sleep over the past six days, and the mattress, despite its thinness, felt almost as good as holding

Elizabeth. "There was a confrontation between some of Howe's dragoon's and a detachment of Oneida Indians who were with Lafayette."

"Indians?"

"Sure there are some working with the American army, though I think Washington discourages it. The British use them a lot in the north. Anyway, from what I understand, not much happened in this encounter. Some war whoops, and a lot of fleeing."

Elizabeth smiled at the scene Alexander painted for her. "Did you stay with the marquis?

"No." Alex yawned. "As soon as we'd crossed to the west bank of the Schuylkill I rode for Valley Forge. I had to apprise Washington of what had happened in Philadelphia, and to ask him for a short leave."

"A leave?" Elizabeth's heart fluttered as she thought of Alexander being away from the war—and danger—even for a little while.

"Yes, my dear Elizabeth, I want to see you and your father to safety."

Elizabeth snuggled closer. He must care for her at least a little. "And did he grant you your leave?"

"Not exactly."

"What?" Elizabeth sat up, her hair tumbling across Alex's chest as she stared down at him in disbelief. "Does he have any idea of all you did in Philadelphia? Why, if it hadn't been for you he'd have been defeated at White Marsh, and Lafayette . . . well, we know what would have happened to him. And my father. You yourself said he told you about Howe's plan. Doesn't Washington know that or doesn't he care now that my father can no longer be of any service? And—Oh . . ."

Alex's hands snaked out, weaving into her hair, grasping her head, and pulling her down. His lips met hers, forcing them apart, capturing her surprised gasp.

Elizabeth's mind froze as liquid heat spiraled through her. Her fingers explored his chin, the rumpled hair framing his face. He positioned her more firmly atop him, deepening the kiss, invading her mouth with his tongue. She returned his passion, luxuriating in wild pleasure as their tongues teased and tasted, tantalized and delighted.

Her breasts were crushed against his muscular chest, and his hands left her hair to caress her back, the swell of her buttocks. The force of his need was strong. Elizabeth could feel it rock-hard, burning through the fabric that separated them.

Her breath came in ragged gulps when she raised her head, effectively stopping the kiss, but not the passion that flamed between them. "Why did you do that?" she asked. His eyes shone midnight blue, darkened as much by desire as the dim light filtering through the curtain of her hair.

"Because I've wanted to since I walked in this room," Alex growled, as he lifted her onto the ticking beside him. He told himself he was out of his mind to kiss her like that with Jonathan Lancaster lying not five feet away. Of course, he hadn't meant to get that carried away. Still, experience should have taught him better. "Besides, I couldn't think of any other way to quiet you long enough to explain about Washington.

"He does appreciate everything your father has done. And everything I've done," he added when she started to protest. In spite of himself, Alex enjoyed having her as his champion. "I have all the time I need to see you both to safety. But it isn't exactly a leave because General Washington would like me to monitor Tory activities in the areas we travel."

"Oh, Alexander, I could help you. I could—"

"Enough," he hissed. "You've done enough, Elizabeth. I don't want you to get any more involved than you are at this moment. Do you understand?"

Luckily, Elizabeth didn't have to answer since Alexander yawned again, apparently taking her agreement as a foregone conclusion. Mumbling something about not sleeping for days, he closed his eyes, and the next thing Elizabeth heard was the muffled sound of his snoring. With a tired sigh of her own, she rested her cheek on his linen shirt, using his chest as her pillow, and fell asleep.

* * *

"Elizabeth."

The voice of her father, rusty from disuse, woke Elizabeth the next morning. She opened her eyes, staring across the broad expanse of Alexander's chest. Sunlight streamed through the small window panes, highlighting the dust motes dancing in the air. Her gaze latched onto her father's. His eyes were lucid for the first time since they'd arrived at the inn. In her excitement she tried to sit up, forgetting, until the weight of Alexander's arm hindered her, how intimately they were lying. Guiltily she pushed his arm aside and climbed over Alexander's body, waking him in the process. She ignored his groan of protest as her knee slid into a sensitive area of his anatomy, and scurried off the bed.

"Are you feeling better?" Elizabeth sank down beside Jonathan's cot. "You look so wonderful today. How is your shoulder?" She brushed a wisp of gray hair off his brow.

"One question at a time, daughter. But first may I have some water."

"Of course." Elizabeth poured some water from the pottery pitcher. Trying not to notice Alexander, who sat on the edge of his cot, rubbing his hands across his face, she lifted her father so he could drink from the dented pewter cup. "Is that better?"

"Much. Where are we?"

Patiently Elizabeth explained where they were,

and how they'd come to be here. Her father remembered the incident with Littleton, but not much about their flight from Philadelphia.

"Has he been here the whole time?" Jonathan asked when Elizabeth finished her narrative.

"Oh, no, he—"

"I arrived here late last night from Valley Forge. Before that I was at Barren Hill." Alex interrupted Elizabeth with his own account. He did not doubt what Jonathan was thinking, what any father would think if he woke up to see his daughter sleeping with a man. But he refused to act guilty. After all, nothing had happened—last night.

"Lafayette?"

"Safe. He and his men managed to ford the river before Howe could spring his trap. I was relating my adventures to Elizabeth, and it appears we fell asleep."

"I see," was Jonathan's succinct reply.

Elizabeth continued to stare at the cup clutched in her finger while Alexander spoke. When her father responded she hazarded a glance toward the rebel major. He appeared the soul of sobriety, but as he reached to take the mug from her hand, he winked, giving her a grin that showed his dimple, even through the bristly, black whiskers.

"We should be leaving here as soon as you can travel." Alex set the cup on a homemade pine table and turned back to Jonathan.

"I'm ready to leave now." Jonathan tried to

heave himself up with his good arm.

"Father!" Elizabeth helped him back down to the cot. His face was racked with pain.

"I think we should wait another day," Alex said. "According to Elizabeth you've had a fever for almost five days. You need a little time to build up your strength. And I'll wager your daughter has had precious little rest. Tomorrow will be soon enough. I'll go see about having some breakfast sent up, and arrange for some horses."

"Alexander." Elizabeth stopped him before he left the room. "Where are we going? You never said last night."

"I've a small plantation, a farm really, in Maryland. Unless either of you can think of someplace else, I'll take you there." He hoped they did have someplace to go, but when they both agreed with his plan, he knew they didn't. Having Elizabeth at his home, even if he weren't there, was not going to help him forget her. And it certainly wouldn't help her forget him.

More and more he was convinced forgetting would be for the best. He didn't want her sitting around his plantation at Oak Hill, as his mother had done, listless and tearful. Alex glanced back, watching Elizabeth. Her back was to him as she pulled a blanket over her father. An ebony curl escaped her cap, falling over her ivory-smooth cheek. He caught a glimpse of her gray eyes as she impatiently tucked it back. He could not let her waste away, waste away waiting for a man who might never return. A knot twisted in his stomach as he turned and left the room.

The next morning dawned clear and warm. After two good nights' sleep, Elizabeth felt renewed. As she packed the wagon with their meager belongings, the scent of lilac drifted through the air, and spying the bush Elizabeth had the strongest desire to bury her nose in the fragrant purple blossoms.

But she didn't. Though red-breasted robins sat diligently upon nests in trees freshly graced with spring's new leaves, this was a land at war. Alexander had reminded her of that earlier this morning when they'd discussed their plans.

As before, they were to travel as farmers, husband and wife. Her father, who looked much better after another fever-free night was to rest in the back of the wagon, a victim of yellow fever if anyone asked. "That should help persuade people to keep their distance," Alexander had commented. Then he'd chuckled.

Elizabeth fluffed the straw, covering it with a blanket before heading back into the inn. On impulse she veered to her right, snatching a lilac sprig before opening the door. Feeling a little foolish, she stuck it in the ruffle of her cap.

Alex glanced up when she entered the attic

room. "I'll help your father down to the wagon. Will you grab my musket and canteen?"

They headed south on Manatawney Road, bypassing the more heavily patrolled Germantown Road. Fording the Schuylkill, Alex skirted Philadelphia, picking up the main road to Chester below the city.

Tired as she was of sitting on the hard, unsprung seat, Elizabeth voiced no protest as Alexander pushed on long after she'd have stopped for a rest. The sun was well past its pinnacle when he halted the horses near a grove of birch trees. Elizabeth climbed into the wagon bed, anxious to check on her father, while Alex unhitched the horses and then watered them at the small brook that bubbled through the trees.

Sitting on flat, moss-covered rocks, they ate the bread and beef Mrs. McGill had packed for them.

"Is your shoulder hurting you?" Elizabeth watched her father grimace as he leaned against the bedding she'd stacked behind him.

"Not too badly, daughter."

"I realize you've had a rough ride of it. As soon as we reach Chester, we'll get back on the main road, and things should be a little smoother." Alex filled his canteen in the swirling water.

"I'm not complaining, Major. The farther we get from the chance of running into British patrols, the better I'll feel."

"Eb told me this morning that rumor is strong

386

Clinton is leaving Philadelphia. Some of the troops have even been ordered to transfer their gear to boats in the harbor."

"Do you think that's how he'll leave, by sea?" Jonathan bit off a piece of bread, shaking his head when Alex offered the canteen.

"Possibly, though I think he fears French warships could dot the horizon at any moment. My guess is he'll march overland to New York."

"He'll be vulnerable," Jonathan pointed out.

Alex's grin reminded Elizabeth of the first time she'd seen him. "That he will."

After they'd eaten, and the horses were rested, Elizabeth climbed back onto the wagon seat, and their journey began anew. Alex had been quiet earlier as they'd ridden, the conversation he'd had with her father being the most she'd heard from him all day. If memory served her right, he'd hardly said a dozen words to her since she'd fallen asleep in his arms night before last. Elizabeth was determined they would not ride the whole way to his plantation in silence.

"It's a lovely day, don't you think?"

Alex cast her a sidelong glance from beneath his slouch hat. "I suppose so."

"Spring is definitely upon us."

"Is that why you put that flower in your hair?" Alex jerked his head toward her hat.

Elizabeth touched the wilting blossoms with her fingers. "I couldn't resist."

"We're not on a picnic, Elizabeth."

"I know that." Did he think she'd forgotten Colonel Littleton, the flight from Philadelphia, and her current situation.

"And as soon as I get you safely to Oak Hill, I'm returning to the army." Alex wasn't sure why he'd said that. He'd been thinking too much about her admission of love, and his realization that he felt the same. Maybe he just wanted to confirm things in his own mind.

"I know that, too."

He nodded, slapping the reins, urging the horses to quicken their pace. Elizabeth sighed, looking out over the newly wakened landscape, trying to pretend his silence didn't hurt her.

She'd tried to let him know how much she loved him, but he obviously didn't feel the same. By not so much as a look had he referred to her admission of love. Well, he told you how he felt months ago, Elizabeth thought. You simply chose not to believe him. Now you must.

It was dusk when they stopped for the night, not yet dawn when they started their trek again. Elizabeth had slept in the wagon with the stars for a tester. There had been a chill in the air, and she'd longed for the warmth of Alexander beside her, but he'd taken a blanket out on the ground. If he'd slept at all, she would be very surprised. He hadn't said he'd keep watch, but she was fairly certain that was what he'd done.

"Will you show me how to load a pistol?" They were riding along, when Elizabeth broke the silence.

"Why?" Alex didn't interrupt his contemplation of the horse's swaying tails. The closer they got to Maryland, to his leaving her, the more his mood soured.

"Because I want to know." Elizabeth's voice held an edge of exasperation. "I would say it's a skill that might come in handy in times such as these. Besides, if I knew, I'd be better able to help you keep watch tonight."

"Elizabeth."

"I'm not made out of glass, you know. Well, I'm not," Elizabeth repeated when he glanced at her skeptically. "I'm sure I could load *and fire* a gun if someone would show me how."

"I don't want you to have to shoot or load a pistol."

"But you can't always control what happens, can you?" Elizabeth glared at him, daring him to deny the obvious.

He didn't. "I'll show you how to load it when we stop to rest the horses."

"Good," she said, a smile curving her lips.

"But I won't teach you how to shoot it, we don't have the ammunition to spare."

"Fine. I'll practice without the benefit of ball and powder."

He made a good teacher, patiently showing Elizabeth how to clean the barrel, then measure out powder, and ram the ball home.

"Do you think you can do it now?" he asked, handing her the other gun.

"I think so." Elizabeth took the pistol, quickly mimicking what he'd done.

"Very good." His raven brows were cocked above indigo blue eyes. "Are you certain you haven't done this before?"

"Quite certain." Elizabeth lifted the gun, sighting down the barrel at an oak tree several rods away.

"Here. Let me show you how to do that." Alex wrapped his hand around Elizabeth's.

"Are you sure we can spare the powder?" Elizabeth leaned back against his hard body, tilting her head, and smiling at him innocently.

"It probably would be a good idea for you to know how to shoot," was all he said.

Elizabeth's first few shots were far from the mark, but on the fourth she hit a holly tree not two feet from her target. On the sixth, roughened bark chipped away as she hit the oak.

"Oh, Alexander!" she squealed turning toward him excitedly, her face radiant with excitement.

Without thinking Alex lifted her up, twirling her around in a swirl of linen petticoats and wool. Laughing with her, he put Elizabeth down, hugging her against him. It wasn't until his eyes met Jonathan's disapproving gaze — Elizabeth's father was resting against the wagon wheel — that Alex realized he'd forgotten his resolve to distance himself from Elizabeth.

It took five days to reach Alex's home, traveling the road along the Delaware River, crossing the Brandywine toll bridge to Wilmington and then the Christiana Bridge into Maryland. By late afternoon of the fifth day, Alex rang the bell to hail the ferryman on the far side of the Chester River. A few miles farther, and Elizabeth got her first glimpse of Oak Hill.

They approached the main house along an unkempt lane full of rain-swept ruts. Lined with towering oaks, spring-green with new leaves, the driveway, despite its need of repairs, held a certain charm. But it was the house itself that Elizabeth found most appealing.

Built in the telescoping style, with each new addition fanning out from the original structure, it gleamed shining white in the early afternoon sun. Though not nearly as large as Landon Hall, its steep, gabled roof, and plentiful windows made it a much superior dwelling in Elizabeth's opinion.

"Alexander, it's beautiful," Elizabeth said as he slowed the wagon in front of the door.

Alex examined the building he'd rarely lived in since his mother died. "It's in a sad state of repair, I'm afraid. I've a manager, and some tenant farmers take care of the fields, but the house . . ." Alex let his words drift away. He hadn't considered the condition of the property when he'd suggested

Elizabeth and her father come here. Now, as he surveyed the peeling paint and overgrown lawn, he questioned his decision.

The inside appeared scarcely better. As they walked into the front parlor Alex kept reminding himself that there was a war going on, and he had nothing better to offer Elizabeth. And, at present, she had nothing better either. The American's were certain to confiscate her home in Philadelphia as soon as they entered the city, as they would the homes of all the Tories who would flee in the wake of Clinton's withdrawal. It would take time before General Washington could restore the Lancaster property to its rightful owner.

"Father, do you really think you should be walking about?" Elizabeth cringed with each step Jonathan took.

"Stop fussing, daughter. I'll sit when I'm tired." He settled onto a dusty settee. "As it so happens, I'm tired now. But you two go on. I can tell you're anxious to see the rest of the house, Elizabeth."

The dining room looked out over a garden thick with tangled vines. Oddly shaped boxwood, allowed to go untrimmed for years, lined the crushed-shell paths.

"My mother loved the garden. She used to sit . . ." Alex scanned the vista. "There." He pointed to a wooden bench under a sprawling crepe myrtle. "She'd sit there for hours staring at the roses."

"Did your father sit with her?" Elizabeth found

the prospect of solitary contemplation of flowers somewhat boring.

"Father was rarely here."

Elizabeth caught the hint of derision in Alexander's voice. "Where was he?" she questioned softly.

"At war . . . sometimes. He fought with Washington in the French and Indian War," Alex explained. "But even before that, he wasn't one to stay at home for long."

"I see." Walking over to the fireplace, Elizabeth trailed a finger along the scallop-shell pattern carved into the mantel. She examined the portrait hanging above. "Is this your mother?"

"Yes." Alex stood behind Elizabeth, memories flooding him as he looked at the portrait. "This was painted not long before she died."

"She's so young." Elizabeth stared at the frail woman in the painting. The blue eyes were all that linked her appearance with her virile son's. "Did she succumb to fever?"

Alex turned away. "No. She simply died."

"But I don't understand. People don't just die."

"Well, she did. Look at her, Elizabeth. She was a lady." Like you, he almost said. "This plantation belonged in her family. She had everything until she fell in love with my father. Even before the war with France, he was always away. 'Chasing dreams', my mother used to say."

"But you don't believe that."

"He had no right to marry her, then abandon

393

her like he did." Alex turned to Elizabeth, staring into her serene gray eyes, imploring her to understand. "Even as much as he was gone, she still loved him. When word reached her that he'd died, she lost her will to live. She had nothing."

Elizabeth touched his buckskin sleeve. "She had you."

"Apparently that wasn't enough."

Elizabeth's heart went out to the boy Alexander had been, to the man who still suffered. But his story had explained some things about his actions. At least she hoped it had. "I'm not like your mother, Alexander. And you are not your father."

Her words seemed to penetrate his mind slowly. He looked at her, his blue eyes dark in the gathering afternoon shadows. "I do nothing but leave you."

"Not by choice, Alexander. Don't you see—"

"Damn it, Elizabeth! We all have choices." The power of his words forced her to step back. He followed till the paneled wall stopped them both. "I've money enough to hire someone to take my place in the army, but I won't. The fact is, tomorrow morning I shall mount my horse and ride away. And there is a very good chance I'll never return."

His nearness compelled Elizabeth to tilt her head to look at him. He glared, but his anger did not frighten her. "Don't you think I think I'm aware of that?"

Alex swept the hair off his forehead. "I don't know what you want from me."

"The truth, Alexander. I want to know the truth of your feelings for me." His large body pressed against her, forcing her spine to the wall.

"You want the truth?" His arms shot out, bracing the paneling, bracketing her head. "I love you." He shouted the words at her. "Is that the truth you wanted to hear? I love you. I think I've loved you since the moment I saw you, and tomorrow . . ." Alex's voice gentled. "Tomorrow I must leave you."

Elizabeth touched his cheek, moved by his admission. Turning his head, Alex brushed her fingers with his lips. "Oh, Elizabeth, I do love you, and it hurts so much."

"I know." She accepted his kiss as it was offered, with tenderness. Her lashes fluttered shut, fanning her dewy soft cheeks as he tentatively explored her lips. He nibbled and cherished, his breath warm and sweet upon her face.

But a fire this hot cannot simply smolder forever. The touch of his tongue, bold and wild, proved the spark that ignited their passions. The explosion of emotion left them breathless as the kiss deepened, and desire flamed.

Elizabeth's hands clutched at his broad shoulders, clung to the strong pillar of his neck. Her knees weakened, and if it were not for the press of his hard body and the unyielding wall, she would drift to the floor on a euphoric cloud.

"God, Elizabeth." His voice rasped in her ear as his mouth traced its delicate curve, then trailed down her silky throat. He touched her everywhere, his frenzied hands unable to get enough of the feel of her.

Dizzy. He made her dizzy with intoxicating need. He thrust forward, the hard proof of his desire burning through the fabric separating them to fuel the yearning ache in her. Elizabeth pressed against him shamelessly, shattered by the force of her desire, her breasts crushed, aroused and hard against his muscled chest. And her mouth, when he claimed it again, opened to accept and meet his marauding tongue.

Fragmented, she was hopelessly, blatantly inflamed. She was jolted back to earth by the sound of her father's voice.

"So this is the dining room." Such innocently spoken words had never affected her quite so intensely. Alex pulled away slowly, steadying her as he removed the shelter of his body. Elizabeth felt color flush her cheeks.

"Sir, I—

"The garden appears overgrown." Jonathan interrupted what was to be Alexander's explanation. "Do you suppose I could lie down? My wound makes me tire easily."

"I'll help you upstairs."

"That's quite all right, Major. I'm certain you

have other things to do. My daughter is all the assistance I need."

It was a dismissal. Alex glanced at Elizabeth, but she offered a tentative smile and waved him away. "I'll be in the stables if you need me." He paused a moment to make certain Elizabeth realized the words were meant for her, and then left the house.

Her father waited until she had stripped the bed in the first room on the second story, remaking it with linens she found in a cupboard, before he mentioned what Elizabeth knew was on his mind.

"You surprise me, daughter."

"I can't imagine why." Elizabeth tucked the blanket under the mattress.

"What is Major Knox to you?"

"I love him."

"I see." Jonathan sat on the edge of the bed, easing himself back. "And the major. How does he feel?"

"The same."

"He'll only hurt you, Elizabeth. When you need him, he'll be off somewhere."

Elizabeth knew he spoke of himself, of the wife he'd left to have her child—and die—alone. But he hadn't wanted to leave her mother, any more than Alexander wanted to leave her. If she could accept the circumstances that forced separations, why couldn't he?

She opened her mouth to try to explain, but

397

before she could, her father sighed. "He's not the man I'd have chosen for you, however you have my blessing to marry him."

"There will be no wedding." Elizabeth looked away from her father's shocked expression. "He's leaving in the morning."

"Without marrying you."

"Yes." Alex had admitted his love for her. Elizabeth had no intention of pushing him into marriage before he was ready.

"And you're satisfied with being his mistress?"

Elizabeth stared at her father, raising her chin defiantly. "I'm satisfied with the love we share." Turning on her heel, she walked out of the room.

Chapter Nineteen

No moon silvered the view as Elizabeth stared out the window. Her room overlooked the garden. She'd noticed that earlier, but now she could see only darkness. Restlessly she turned, surveying the bedroom. In the warm glow of the single candle, the walls shone a soft white. They contrasted with the dark green of the molding, the rose red of the fireplace bricks.

The day had been long and tiring. Even after their arduous journey, Elizabeth had insisted on beginning the monumental task of preparing the house for habitation. Alexander had ridden off to inspect his fields, and interview his tenants. He'd returned near dusk, accompanied by three girls, daughters of local farmers, whom he'd hired to work in the house at Oak Hill.

Elizabeth sighed, looking at the high tester bed, knowing by all rights she should be sound asleep by now. But she couldn't sleep, couldn't do anything except think of Alexander leaving on the morrow. Leaving . . . possibly never to return.

She could go to him. The need to be with him had nagged at her all evening and into the night. Uncertain why she didn't, Elizabeth paced back to the window. Alexander had acknowledged his love for her, but she couldn't shake her father's words. There had been no mention of commitment. Did it matter? Elizabeth leaned her forehead against the cool glass, closing her eyes.

She knew the answer the moment she heard the latch lift, felt the draft of the opening door. She turned to face Alexander. Dressed in the clothes he'd worn that day, buckskin breeches and loose linen shirt, he stood before her.

Alex stepped into the room, closing the door behind him. "I couldn't stay away." His voice sounded husky with desire as his eyes raked her slender form. She wore only her shift, and her thick ebony hair fell in a tumble of curls around her shoulders.

"I don't want you to." Elizabeth moved forward, meeting him midway across the room as he enveloped her in his muscular arms. Her fingers touched his silky hair, the warm flesh of his neck, and she suppressed a sob. How long would it be before she knew the joy of being held by him again? She took a deep breath, imbibing the virile, outdoors smell of him. She wouldn't think of the endless tomorrows that stretched before her—not tonight. Tonight would be theirs.

Alex buried his face in her neck, his words muffled in the profusion of midnight hair. "I don't want to leave you tomorrow. If something should happen—"

"Shhh." Elizabeth pulled back, covering his lips with her hand, feeling her knees weaken when his tongue wet her palm. "Nothing will happen. Please don't think that way. I can't stand it."

Pulling her closer, Alex shut his eyes, her words ringing in his head. She couldn't stand it if he didn't return. It was happening just the way he'd feared. And there was nothing he could do about it. "Elizabeth," he whispered, "don't hide from the truth. You must face—"

"What, Alexander? What must I face?" She clutched his shirt, balling the fabric in her fists. "The fact that you're going off to war? That I may never see you again?" She took a deep breath. "I don't want to face that tonight. Let reality come crashing down upon me tomorrow. But please don't speak of it tonight."

His hands trailed up her arms, cupping the curve of her jaw, forcing her to look up. With a gentleness that denied the urgency they both felt, his lips found hers. He would abide by her request . . . for now. But before the morning . . . before he rode away from Oak Hill—they would talk. He would extract a promise from her—a promise to forget him.

His thumbs traced the sensitive skin beneath her ears, the innocent motion stoking the flames of passion within her. She moaned, her mouth opening to the fire of his tongue, needing the warm moist length of it inside her. He moved slowly, sensually, arousing her with the strength of his control. She felt it in the trembling of his muscles as she slid her hands under his shirt. His smooth skin tightened beneath her touch, the sensation sending shivers of desire rushing through her.

Elizabeth leaned into him, her legs weak, unable to support her. Her breasts crushed against his chest, and they swelled, tingled with anticipation. Her stomach pushed against his hardness, and she ached. "Please, touch me," she begged, her lips grazing his whisker-roughened jaw.

"I will," he promised. "I want to touch you everywhere, kiss you everywhere." His warm mouth feathered down her neck, nudged away the coarse cotton shift, pressed hungry kisses to her soft shoulder. "You smell so good." He moved lower, his teeth nipping gently at the soft skin below her arm. "And you taste so good." His words vibrated against the upper swell of her breast.

Her nipples tightened, their torrid tips pebble hard, anticipating his course. With a quick yank on the drawstring, the shift opened, exposing her breasts to his appreciative gaze. "And you are so beautiful." The breath from his hoarse voice fanned across her skin. He brushed his knuckles over her breasts, the deep indigo of his eyes darkening as her body responded to his touch.

Her bones melted, and she draped back across his supporting arm as his mouth captured her nipple. His teeth tortured, exquisitely. His tongue soothed, and she gasped for breath when he drew hers into his mouth, sucking the tender flesh.

"Alexander." She clung to his shoulders, her fingers digging into his hard muscles. "Oh please, Alexander." Elizabeth begged for release. The coil of desire inside her tightened unmercifully. She writhed against the knee he pressed between her legs, collapsed into his chest when he picked her up.

He lowered her onto the bed, yanking off his shirt and breeches before lying down beside her. He'd wanted to take it slowly—to fill her with as much passion as he felt. But desire proved a double-edged sword. For with every craving he'd evoked in her, his own yearning had multiplied. Now, as his open mouth locked with hers, catching her breathless sigh, he felt near crazed with raw need.

His fingers strummed down her body, combing through her damp curls, plunging into the moist heat. His rhythm intoxicated her. She arched against his hand, quivering on the precipice. He drove her wild. His body slid down hers, the heat of his mouth taking up the frenzied cadence, and Elizabeth lost all touch with reality. Colors, dazzling in their brilliance, exploded before her eyes. She trembled, tumbling, soaring toward the enchanted land of lovers.

"Alex . . . Alex," she cried, her hands clasping spasmodically on his shoulders.

"I'm here, Elizabeth." He leaned his elbows on the pillow, staring down into her passion-drugged face.

She reached up, touching his cheek. "It's so beautiful, Alex. Share it with me."

He thrust upward, loving the wonder in her eyes as his length filled her. "Always, Elizabeth. We'll share it always."

Alex pulled back, then plunged harder, deeper, groaning when her legs locked around his hips. He thrust again and again, losing control of his movements, beyond knowing anything but the sensual sensations sweeping through his body. He felt her shudder, knew her pulsing rhythm matched his own as they climaxed together.

"God, I love you."

Elizabeth opened her eyes to stare up into Alexander's face. He appeared stunned, as much by his words as by what they'd just shared. She wasn't surprised. Her head still reeled with the intensity of their lovemaking. And she knew Alex didn't like to admit his feelings. Though she didn't know exactly why, Elizabeth felt certain his leaving her was part of the reason. But knowing he loved her wouldn't make his leaving any harder. It couldn't be any harder.

She smiled up at his startled face. "I love you, too."

Rolling off her, Alex pulled Elizabeth into the crook of his arm. He hadn't meant to bring up love again. But then, after all that had happened between them, there could be little doubt the emotion existed. Alex took a deep, cleansing breath, hating the topic he intended to broach, knowing her reaction to it from earlier.

"Elizabeth?"

"Hmmm?"

"I'll try to come back to you."

"I know you will." Elizabeth ran a lazy finger through the silky hair on his chest.

"But if something should happen . . ."

Elizabeth's hand stopped. "Don't —"

"I know you don't want to talk of this, but there are things that need to be said. Please."

Elizabeth heard the desperation in his voice. She leaned forward, resting her chin on the flat of her palm, staring down at him attentively. "What do you want to tell me, Alexander?" She tried to sound calm, to pretend her heart wasn't racing at the very thought of something happening to him.

"I'm not speaking of this to upset you." Alex touched the quivering pulse at the base of her throat.

Elizabeth said nothing, simply waited for him to continue.

405

"It's just, if something should . . . if I can't return, I don't want you to mourn. I mean, I want you to get on with your life, as you were doing before we met."

Minutes passed. The candle on the bedside stand flickered, and still Elizabeth stared at Alex in amazement. "I'm to pretend I never knew you, never loved you?"

"Damn it, Elizabeth. You don't understand at all." Alex sat up, throwing his legs over the side of the bed in exasperation.

"You're right, I don't." Rising to her knees, Elizabeth touched the muscled planes of his back. "Why would you say such a thing, Alex? How can you think I would not . . ." She leaned her cheek against his shoulder. "This is because of your mother, isn't it? Because of what you told me earlier today."

"Hell, yes, it's about my mother. You didn't see her as I did, day after day, sitting on that bench. . . . I can't bear to think of you sitting there."

"Alex, look at me." Elizabeth touched his chin, guiding it around. "A part of you will always live within me. Nothing can change that. It was too late to even try the first time I saw you. But I'm not like your mother. I wouldn't just drift away."

Alex studied her, searching for the truth. Her eyes never faltered, and even in the dim light he could see the firm resolve of her dimpled chin.

She was a fighter. She'd shown him that in her own persistent way. And she was determined. "Come here." Alex pulled her across his lap.

Elizabeth cuddled against his warm chest, brushing aside the hair that tickled her nose. His heart beat a steady tempo in her ear.

"I talked with one of my tenants about watching out for you. He should be over next—What's the matter?" Alex would have had to be deaf not to hear her groan.

"Must we speak of that now?"

"I guess not. Why, are you tired?" Alex's fingers traced a curl that had fallen down between her breasts.

"No." Elizabeth peeked up from under her lashes. "Are you?"

He grinned—that devilish grin, complete with dimple, she'd loved from the start. "Not even a little bit." As if to prove his point, Alex tumbled back against the pillow, pulling her with him.

She wriggled along his hard length, a teasing light shining in her eyes. "Are you certain sleep is not what you want? You do have a long ride ahead of you tomorrow."

"And you, my darling, Elizabeth," Alex clutched her bottom, pressing her more firmly against him, "shall have a long ride tonight."

"You're shameless," Elizabeth giggled.

"And you're beautiful." Grabbing handfuls of soft hair, Alex dragged her lips down to his hungry kiss.

Much later Elizabeth lay with her back snuggled to Alex's chest. "Are you asleep?" His breath sent tiny tendrils of hair near her ear aflutter.

She shook her head, settling deeper into the spoon of his body. "I wish I had something to give you. Something you could remember me by."

"Do you really think I need anything for that?" His hand tightened on her breast. "Besides, I already have something."

"What?" Elizabeth turned into his embrace. "I don't recall ever—"

"Just a minute." Alex brushed a kiss across the tip of her nose before getting up to fetch his breeches. He reached inside a pocket before climbing back into bed.

The mattress dipped beneath his weight, and Elizabeth looked up, searching his hand. He opened it slowly. "Do you remember this?"

Elizabeth stared at the scrap of ribbon nestled in his palm. It had been red at one time, that much she could tell, but dirt and wear had dulled the color. She touched a frayed end with her finger. "Should I?"

Alex shrugged, closing his hand over the fabric. "It's yours. You had it in your hair that day by the marsh."

"And you kept it all this time?" Elizabeth looked up at him with undisguised wonder. She did remember tying her hair in a scarlet ribbon to

408

match her riding habit, and when she'd returned to Landon Hall it had been gone, but she'd had no idea . . .

"I didn't plan to at first. I simply noticed it in the dirt after you'd ridden away. A vision of one of those deserters returning and finding it popped into my head, so I scooped it up." Alex rolled onto his back, watching the shadows dance across the underside of the canopy. "A few times I started to throw it away, but . . ." Alex sighed, deciding he might as well finish the story now that he'd begun. "But after I'd been shot at Brandywine, I realized just holding it made me feel better. Not my leg, of course." He didn't want her to think him daft. "But it made me think of the marsh. I could almost smell the salty water, hear the birds singing in the trees, see . . . you."

"That's beautiful." Elizabeth's eyes misted over.

"Are you going to cry?"

"No," she lied, swallowing back her tears.

"Good, because I didn't tell you that to upset you." Alex pulled her down beside him, resting her head on his chest.

"I'm not crying."

"Good," he repeated, combing his fingers through her hair, ignoring the dampness he felt against his skin.

Elizabeth's eyes jerked open. She'd been asleep.

As hard as she'd tried to stay awake, to savor the remaining minutes with Alexander, fatigue had overcome her. She sat up, aware that she was alone on the bed, fearing he'd gone, and then saw him staring out the window at the grainy predawn. He'd dressed in the buckskin pants and shirt he'd had on the past night, adding the leather hunting shirt that made up his uniform. He looked ready to leave.

"I didn't mean to wake you." Alex looked at Elizabeth. The sheet he'd covered them with lay puddled around her waist. Her creamy rose-tipped breasts aroused him even after their night of lovemaking. He turned back toward the window. "I want to get an early start."

"That would probably be best."

Alex nodded, tracing his finger along the windowpane. "There's money in the drawer by the bed. Jonah, the man I told you about last night, kept some of it for me. I want you to use it as you see fit."

"Alex, I . . ."

He turned, holding up his palm in a gesture of silence. "Just do it, Elizabeth." He smiled, shaking his head. "No arguments this morning, please."

Elizabeth returned his smile. She would need money; she and her father had left Philadelphia with nothing but the clothes on their backs — in her case, the borrowed clothes on her back. "All right, no arguments."

410

"Good." Knowing he'd be unable to keep his distance if he continued looking at her, Alex examined again the paling sky. Subtle tints of rose streaked the pearly gray. Nature's reminder that time passed. He really should leave.

He was going to leave. Elizabeth could tell by the set of his shoulders, the words left unspoken. "Can you tell me where you'll be?"

"No."

"Still don't trust me?"

Giving up all pretense of staying away from her, Alex went to the bed, sitting on the edge. "I'm not telling you, my pretty little Tory." Alex laughed. "Because I don't know. I'll spend a couple of days gathering the information Washington wanted. What's wrong?"

"I wanted to help you do that."

"So I feared." Laughing again, Alex gathered Elizabeth against his body. The expression on her face was scathing. "Anyway, after that I shall return to headquarters, then go where they send me. Probably New York."

"But New York is . . . so far away," Elizabeth finished lamely. She'd almost blurted out that it was occupied by the British, but realized just in time how silly that would sound. Of course he would go where the enemy was, where it was most dangerous.

Alex held her to his heart for a moment. "I must go," he said.

Elizabeth clutched at his hunting shirt. The leather felt smooth and soft in her hands. She forced herself to release it.

"No tears." Alex held her shoulders, looking into her face. She seemed on the verge of crying, and he doubted he could control his own emotions if she were to start.

"No tears," Elizabeth promised, her voice straining past her constricted throat.

He kissed her then—a warm sweet kiss, full of love and the promise of tomorrows. Over too soon. Elizabeth watched as he strode from the room.

Hurriedly pulling on her clothes, Elizabeth ran down the stairs. She didn't have to wait by the parlor window long before he came around front, leading one of the horses Eb had lent them. Alexander vaulted into the saddle, looking back at the house before he rode away.

Elizabeth waved, but she didn't think he saw her. Probably just as well, she thought, wiping tears away with the back of her hand. Slowly she sank to the wide-planked floor. She'd promised not to cry, yet the tears would not stop. "I lied, Alex," she whispered on a sob.

Wind, sharp-edged with the promise of winter, whipped around Elizabeth, and she leaned lower over her mount's neck, urging the horse to pick up its pace. The stallion's nostrils flared, his hooves pounded the sandy road. Obviously he was anticipating a warm barn and a measure of feed, much as his mistress looked forward to the roaring fire that awaited her at Oak Hill.

She'd spent the day in Chestertown finalizing arrangements to have much of the corn grown on Alexander's plantation this past summer sent to Washington's army. She'd also gone to town hoping to hear news of the war's progress. There had been little—news or progress.

For all last year's excitement about the French alliance, they had proved to be of little help thus far in America's fight for independence. Her father had explained to Elizabeth that with France's entrance into the conflict, the scope of the war had changed. King Louis of France had to worry about his possessions in the Caribbean as well as assist his allies.

The honk of snow geese sounded overhead, and Elizabeth reined in her horse, searching the azure sky till she spotted the familiar V formation. Heading south, they stopped often to feed on the corn left in the fields after the harvest.

Leaning over to pat her horse's neck, Elizabeth started back down the road toward home. She had heard from Alexander rarely since he'd left over a year ago. There had been a post last July, written after the battle of Monmouth. He'd been safe . . . then. And last spring, right after planting, a soldier had stopped, bearing a message from Alex. But since then there'd been no word.

Horse and rider turned off the main road, galloping down the lane, under the brown canopy of rustling dried oak leaves. Elizabeth smiled when the house came into view. She'd come to love Alexander's plantation—to think of it as home. In reality it was the only place that could claim that title. Her father's house in Philadelphia had been confiscated and sold by Congress, as had many of the homes of prominent Tories who'd fled the city with the British forces. Jonathan Lancaster assured his daughter that the situation would be cleared up as soon as the war ended. Washington would come forward, announcing Jonathan Lancaster's part in the war effort.

Elizabeth dismounted, and led her horse into the stables. Before the war, Oak Hill had been known for her fine horses. Now there were only a few left, and most of them so old the army didn't want them. After dragging off the saddle, Elizabeth rubbed her mount down. She'd learned to do many things for herself since coming to Oak Hill and throwing herself completely into the task of running the plantation. Alexander's tenants planted and harvested the fields, but with the help of the hired girls, Elizabeth took care of the vegetable garden, the weaving, and the running of the household.

Heading toward the house, she took the path

through the garden, looking with pride at the weeded flower beds, and neatly trimmed box-woods. Even the hearty chrysanthemums were dead now, but this summer the oasis of flowers had provided a pleasant place for her father to sit. Elizabeth bent down, picking up a shell, tracing the fluted edge with her fingertip. Jonathan Lancaster hadn't fully recovered from his wound, and Elizabeth wondered if he ever would. The ball lodged in his shoulder pained him, leaving his body weakened and his arm nearly useless. She sighed, tossing the shell back onto the path.

"Elizabeth!"

She looked toward the house, waving when she saw her father standing by the door. Beside him stood a tall young man Elizabeth didn't recognize until he doffed his hat and the afternoon sun caught fire in his red hair.

"Jacob?" A smile brightened her face as the youth bounded toward her. "Jacob," she repeated when he stood before her. "You've grown so tall." Elizabeth grabbed his hands. "Look at you. I never thought to see you again after that day in Philadelphia. How have you fared?"

"I've done all right, I reckon. Still in one piece."

Wishing she could rumple his bright head, Elizabeth opted for squeezing his hands. "So I see. How did you know where to find me?"

"Major told me."

Elizabeth's heartbeat quickened, and she looked

past Jacob, toward the house. "He's not with you—"

"No, ma'am, he ain't."

"Oh." Elizabeth suddenly realized that though she'd been rattling on, asking questions, Jacob had had very little to say, and he'd yet to smile. "Jacob, is something wrong?"

"Yes, ma'am. I'm right afraid there is."

"What is it?" Elizabeth gripped Jacob's hand, but still he said nothing, and his silence sent shivers of fear down her spine. "It's not Alexander. He's not . . ."

"I'm sorry, ma'am." Jacob's voice quivered. "I got a letter for you. I was told . . ." Tears welled in his eyes. "He wanted you to have it."

Elizabeth watched Jacob unfasten his jacket, fumble inside his shirt till he found the folded parchment. Fear coiled inside her as she took it from him. Her fingers trembled as she broke the seal and opened the post. The writing was Alexander's—she'd recognize the bold script anywhere. Hope kindled. If Alexander were dead he couldn't have written to her.

Elizabeth searched Jacob's face for an answer, but he looked away, leaving her with naught to do but read Alexander's words.

My dearest Elizabeth,
When you read this letter, you'll know I'll be unable to return as I'd hoped. Though

416

service to my country was important to me, I deeply regret the part it played in our separation. I'm not usually one to belabor "what ifs," yet I can't prevent longing thoughts of what our life might have been together.

Please do not grieve overlong on my account. I've faith in your strength, and your ability to struggle forth. Before leaving the area last spring, I visited my solicitor in Chestertown. The title to Oak Hill is in your name. I beg you accept it as the last loving gift of a man who could offer you nothing else.

I love you, Elizabeth, with my all heart. And your love, so sweet and unselfish, helped me to withstand the hardships of war.

I remain in this life and the next, your most loving servant,

Alexander

Elizabeth felt a hand on her arm, guiding her, and the hard, cold garden bench as she sat down. She heard the distant honking of geese, the soothing quality of Jacob's voice. But none of these sensations registered in her mind. Alexander was dead. That was the only reality that mattered.

How long she sat there, flooded with memories of Alexander, she didn't know, but Jacob finally brought her back to the present.

"Are you all right, Mistress Lancaster?"

He sounded so concerned, looked so worried when Elizabeth glanced up, that she instinctively nodded as she swiped at her tearstained face. She'd never be all right again, but there was no use telling that to Jacob. Fumbling in her pocket, she found a handkerchief, and tried to wipe her eyes. It proved a useless task, as fresh tears only replaced the ones she dried.

"How . . . how did it . . . ?" She couldn't get the words out.

"Hanged."

Elizabeth's body jerked involuntarily at Jacob's reply.

"He give me that letter a long time ago. Said if anything was to happen to him, I was to hightail it to you. Give it to you. I thought it pretty silly at the time. 'No lobsterback's gonna catch you,' I said. You know how he sorta had that way about him, like nothing or nobody could hurt him?"

"Yes," Elizabeth agreed. How many times had she thought of him as invincible? Such a foolish notion.

"Well, anyway, I was with him in New York, posing as his groom, I was. Major Knox, he didn't want to take me with him when I chanced upon him in Valley Forge last year, but I told him I'd desert and follow him if he didn't."

"I imagine he became very angry at that." Elizabeth smiled through her tears.

"Hell, yes . . . I mean . . ." Jacob fumbled

418

about, and his face bloomed as red as his hair. "Begging your pardon, I meant to say, yes, he sure did. Threatened to whup me good for not obeying orders, but he didn't. He took me with him. Said I'd probably get in less trouble with him watching out for me."

"He was like that," Elizabeth added between sobs.

"Yes, ma'am, he sure was. But I didn't need no looking out for. Just sorta minded my own business, thinking things were going real good till that night about a month ago."

"What happened?" She had to know all of it.

"Well, it was late. I was already in bed, but I heard the major come in. He'd been at one of them assemblies. He went into his library and shut the door. I figured he was getting a message ready to send to General Washington. That's what he usually did. Sometimes he'd slip out of Brooklyn himself; sometimes he'd send one of the men he had with him.

"So there I was, all ready to fall asleep, when there came this god-awful pounding. Before I could pull me britches on, lobsterbacks came swarming into the house. The major, he put up quite a fight, but weren't no use. There was too many of the bastards. Besides, when he saw me ready to join in, he stopped, and told me it was all right.

"Well, I knowed it wasn't, but I didn't know

how bad it was till the trial. Seems one of them double agents turned the major over to the British. They had him dead to rights, even found one of them messages on him. 'Course it was in code, but that didn't seem to matter to them." Jacob paused. "Sentenced him to hang."

"When . . . when did it happen?" Elizabeth felt so close to Alexander, she couldn't believe that he'd been dead all this time and she hadn't sensed it.

"Don't know. I left New York soon as his trial was over."

Elizabeth's fingers tightened around the arm of the bench till they hurt. Looking down, she realized she sat on the same bench where Alexander's mother had wasted away her life. Elizabeth jumped up. "You mean you didn't actually see him hang?"

"Aw now, Mistress Lancaster, don't go getting your hopes up. If he is alive, they're fixing to hang him, and there's nothing we can do about it. They wouldn't even let me see him."

"But he could still be alive?" Elizabeth's heart pounded against her ribs, and her breathing quickened.

"Yes, but . . . Now where are you going?"

Elizabeth's shoes crunched over the shell walkway. Her skirts swirled around her legs as she paused, tossing her answer over her shoulder. "I'm going to New York!"

Chapter Twenty

"You've surprised me, Mistress Lancaster, or should I say Madam Weston? I didn't know our prisoner was married."

Elizabeth gave General Warner her most dazzling smile, at least she hoped it was, and nodded her head. A fine sprinkling of white powder from her hair dusted her richly brocaded gown, and Elizabeth brushed it away with her borrowed lace handkerchief. Despite his words, the general, who, Elizabeth had discovered upon reaching New York, was in charge of the Provost, didn't look surprised. He leered at her décolletage.

"Then my husband is still alive?" Elizabeth asked, trying to disguise her trepidation.

"Temporarily." General Warner leaned back in his chair. "Tell me again how you and your father became involved with a Patriot spy."

"I'm still not convinced that a mistake has not been made. I can't imagine Alexander bothering himself with anything so tedious as spying. Perhaps he simply—"

"There was no mistake. We caught your husband red-handed, so to speak."

"Oh, well." Elizabeth loosened the death grip she had on her handkerchief, and swished it through the air. It wouldn't do to let the general realize her true state of mind. "Obviously, I don't know Alexander as well as I thought. He seemed so gallant." Elizabeth smiled again, launching into her well-rehearsed lie. She had gone over it so many times on her trip from Maryland—hoping only for the chance to use it, the chance that Alexander still lived—that she related it smoothly.

"When we discovered—my father and I—that the rumors of the British leaving Philadelphia were true, we nearly panicked. You know what a staunch Loyalist my father is." Elizabeth paused. This was one part of her story that worried her. If Colonel Littleton had imparted information about Jonathan Lancaster's true loyalty to his superiors before he died, Elizabeth knew she might be arrested on the spot. But apparently Littleton had kept his knowledge to himself, for General Warner agreed and urged her to continue.

"Father feared we'd be left behind, so when Alexander suggested we accompany him to his plantation in Virginia, we accepted."

"I didn't know Weston had a plantation in Virginia."

"Neither did I. However, it is there, and it is frightfully large."

"And rich?" General Warner's smile revealed his large protruding teeth.

"Precisely."

"Thus the reason for your concern."

"Well, I am Alexander's widow, or shall be when he's hanged, and I think it only fair that I should reap some benefit from this affair. After all, when word gets out that my husband was a spy . . ." Elizabeth trembled daintily.

"I suppose I could let you see him, briefly. That is what you want, isn't it?"

"Yes." Elizabeth's heart thumped wildly against her ribs, but she kept her voice calm. "If I could only talk to him, I'm certain he can be convinced to write a will naming me his beneficiary."

General Warner stood, rounded the heavily carved mahogany desk, and grasped Elizabeth's hands. It took strength of will not to yank them away. Elizabeth knew the general thought her a self-serving, greedy wench, and, worse, admired her for it. Before her revulsion became more than she could bear, Elizabeth thought of Alexander's words that day they'd been in a carriage filled with

423

contraband medicines and been stopped by a British patrol. *It doesn't matter what the British think, as long as we fool them.*

She'd fooled General Warner, and because of that, he would allow her to see Alexander. What difference did it make if he forced her to endure his disgusting company a moment longer?

"You will let me know if there is anything else I can do for you while you're in New York?" His pale blue eyes seemed to bulge more than usual as his gaze slid over her. "Your husband's execution is set for day after tomorrow. Perhaps we can dine together that night, and celebrate your freedom?"

"I'd enjoy that," Elizabeth lied, as the general left the room to arrange for her visit to the New Jail. All the while her mind worked feverishly. She had arrived in New York with only a day to spare. How was she ever going to get Alexander out of prison before the sun set tomorrow? Elizabeth shuddered to think about what would have happened had her trip north taken longer.

She had Hannah to thank for the speed of her journey, at least from Philadelphia to New York. Elizabeth had arrived on the Evanses' doorstep four days after she'd received Alexander's letter. She'd been tired and afraid, emotionally spent. Her decision to go to New York had caused a terrible fight with her father, who, physically unable to accompany her, had refused her permission to leave.

She'd left anyway, dragging Jacob with her for protection and moral support. And all the while, she'd lived under a cloud of desperation. What if her trip proved futile? What if Alexander was already dead? Ignoring her doubts and fears, she'd poured out her story to Hannah. And to her utter relief, Hannah had helped her. Not only had she arranged for Elizabeth to travel the rest of the way in the company of three Friends making the journey to Long Island, she'd managed to procure a gown and garments suitable for a wealthy Tory to wear.

Elizabeth smoothed the embroidered skirt with her hand, wondering again where Hannah had found the dress that fit her with only a minimum of padding.

"Captain Murphy will escort you to the Provost." General Warner reentered the paneled room with a tall thin man of about thirty years at his side. "I want you to remember, my dear, that the most notorious traitors are imprisoned at New Jail. These men, for the most part, are desperate and have nothing to lose."

"I shall heed your advice, General," Elizabeth said as she rose.

"Got you a visitor, Weston."

Alexander broke off his study of a spider's progress between the corner angles of his cell's

425

ceiling, and raised a skeptical brow at his jailer.

"I'm supposed to make sure you're presentable to receive company."

After swatting at some of the vermin infesting his body and cell, Alex stacked his hands beneath his head, and focused again on the spider. He'd been in this gaol for almost a month, and never, not even during his trial had he been allowed a visitor. He didn't believe they'd allow him one now.

"Get up off that bed, you lazy traitor and straighten yourself up."

Alex shifted on the filthy straw, an idea filtering into the recesses of his mind. He'd kept track of the days by making small scratches in the wood with his thumbnail. If his calculations were correct, his hanging was to take place day after tomorrow. "Is Cunningham giving me a chance to redeem my eternal soul before I meet my Maker?" he asked referring to Captain Cunningham, the notorious provost marshal of New York.

"Don't know who 'tis you'll be seeing, any more than I know why anyone would have an interest in the likes of you."

"Now, now, Baldwin," Alex chided, ignoring his jailer's rank. "Don't you know all men are equal before the Almighty?" Slowly Alex pulled himself up, favoring the leg injured during his capture. Amazingly, even without medical treatment the bayonet wound hadn't festered.

Brushing disheveled, coal black hair from his

forehead, Alex took the three steps to the barred door. As much as he'd liked to have spurned anything Cunningham had to offer, Alex couldn't ignore the need he felt to speak with a clergyman. Not that he intended to bare his soul about his spying. No matter how good for it confession might be, Alex had no intention of admitting his actions or taking the chance of implicating anyone else. Still, a prayer would help him face what was to be.

Unbidden, his thoughts strayed to Elizabeth. Thank goodness she was safe in Maryland. He knew she'd be upset when she received his letter, but at least she'd have Oak Hill. Alex sighed, rubbing his hand down the bristly beard that covered his jaw. He hoped Jacob would be able to get the letter through to Elizabeth. Alex knew the boy hadn't been captured the night he'd been taken, but what happened after that?

Maybe he could send a message to her through the minister. Alex stopped in midthought. Had captivity dulled his brain? He would do nothing that might lead the British to Elizabeth or her father. He'd just have to go to his death hoping Jacob could deliver the letter to her.

Alex leaned against the iron grate, fixing his eyes on Baldwin. "I suppose I'm ready. Unless you had it in mind to offer a hot bath and clean clothes."

"Always the funny one, ain't you, Weston? Well,

we'll see who's doing the laughing day after the morrow."

Alex's snort of disgust followed the jailer as he disappeared around a corner. The man was right. Alex traced the keyhole with his finger. In two days he was going to face the death of a traitor, and there didn't seem to be much he could do about it. As much as he'd tried, he had been unable to figure a way out of his predicament.

"Alexander."

Alex's mind remembered the sweet melodic sound of Elizabeth's voice before it comprehended that she stood before him, separated from his touch only by the flat metal bars.

"Elizabeth?"

Nodding, unable to speak around the constriction of her throat, Elizabeth stared at the man she loved.

"What . . . what are you doing here? Are you all right?" Alex's fingers reached through the rusty bars.

"Yes, yes, I'm fine." Elizabeth glanced quickly at Captain Murphy who'd accompanied her into the hall, and then back at Alexander. His clothes, tattered and stiff with dried blood, covered a body, though no less tall and broad of shoulder, grown whipcord thin. Elizabeth longed to touch the hollows of his cheeks, brush aside the ragged, uncombed hair, and minister to the swollen, split skin below his left eye. "What's happened to you?"

428

Alex's laugh held no humor as he gingerly traced the bruise. "Cunningham's idea of persuasion."

"Oh, my poor darling." Elizabeth curled her fingers around his, fighting back her tears.

The warmth of her hand soothed him as nothing else could. Alex longed to hold her in his arms, to know again the softness of her body, the tenderness of her caress, the heat of her love. . . . Reality hit him as he pressed forward, his chest encountering the cold unyielding iron.

"What are you doing here?" He kept his voice low, yet the question contained barely controlled irritation. "How did you get here?" Alex's eyes scanned her, taking in the expensive dress, the styled and powdered hair.

"I've come about your plantation." Elizabeth spared a hasty glance at the British captain who stood within earshot.

"My what?"

"Your plantation." Elizabeth answered in a clear, loud voice. "As your wife, I think you should deed it over to me."

Eyes narrowed, Alex studied the woman who claimed to have wed him. He still didn't know how she came to be here. If she'd received word from Jacob, she already knew Oak Hill belonged to her, if she hadn't then how did she know where to find him? He noticed the nervous twist of her head toward the British captain as she moved

429

closer to the bars.

"Give me a name to contact," she whispered. "Someone who can break you out of here."

"Oh, no, you won't," Alex ground out. "There's nothing you can do here, and you'll just get yourself hurt if you try. Now go home."

"I knew you'd be this way," Elizabeth sobbed, throwing herself into the act. "Even if you shall gain no benefit from your wealth, you would deny me." Leaning toward Alex, she hissed, "Give me a name, or I'll break you out by myself."

"Damn it, Elizabeth." A moment ago he'd wanted nothing more than to caress her slender neck, now he feared, given the chance, he'd throttle it. What did she think she was doing? The gaol was heavily guarded. Escapes were few, and seldom successful. He didn't care for himself. If given a choice, he'd rather die attempting a breakout than hanging at the end of a British rope. But he refused to risk taking Elizabeth down with him.

The captain moved farther down the hall, in an obvious attempt to distance himself from Elizabeth's incessant and noisy crying. Alex took the opportunity to latch his fingers around the hand that clung to the bars. He tightened his grip, forcing her eyes to meet his, her fake crying to cease.

"Can't you see you're making this harder for me?" he asked, love shining in his eyes.

"I only want to help you," Elizabeth pleaded.

"I know you do, sweetheart. But you can't. Nobody can. And that's why I want you to go home."

Closing her eyes, Elizabeth turned her head, her chin dropping in dejection. Somehow she'd thought if she could only reach Alexander in time, all would be well. Together they'd find a way out of this situation. But he wasn't going to help her. Knowing he refused for her safety didn't make the decision any more bearable. If anything, it strengthened her resolve. If only he'd give her a name, someone she could contact. General Washington came to mind, but she'd never make it to his camp and back in time.

She wished she'd allowed Jacob to come to New York with her. He'd know some Patriots. But she'd convinced him to visit his family, assuring the lad that she'd be able to free Alexander. And now she couldn't. All because Alexander wanted her safe in Maryland. Inspiration came quickly.

"I don't know how to get home." Elizabeth stared at him with guileless gray eyes.

"Well, how did you get here?" Alex asked, glad that she seemed to be thinking reasonably.

"I accompanied some Quakers, friends of the Evanses. But I left them as soon as we reached the city, and I don't know where they are."

Alex brushed hair off his forehead in frustration. The British captain moved closer as Alex said in a hushed voice, "There's a man on Long Island

431

named Daniel Hershey. He can help you get back to Maryland."

Elizabeth pressed against the bars. "How can I find him?"

"Go to the Pig's Eye Tavern and ask for the proprietor. That will be Daniel." Alex paused, searching her face. "You'll go to him?"

"Yes. Immediately."

"And you'll go back to Maryland?"

"Yes." Lowering her eyes, Elizabeth added silently, When you can come with me.

"Good." Alex's face relaxed into a smile. It really had been wonderful to see her again, even if he had to worry about her reaching Maryland safely. "Now," Alex murmured, "I think you should go. The guard appears restless."

Elizabeth's gaze followed Alexander's. "I suppose he won't allow us much more time together."

"I love you, Elizabeth."

These words, so unexpected after Alexander's apparent anger at her presence, brought Elizabeth's eyes around to meet his. Though the rest of him appeared battered, his eyes were still the vivid blue of the late afternoon sky. "I love you, too. I—"

"Your time is up, Mrs. Weston." Captain Murphy's hand fastened on her elbow. "General's orders."

"Just a moment longer?" Elizabeth pleaded.

"Go with the man, Elizabeth. And don't forget about going home."

Nodding, Elizabeth swallowed back a sob. She refused to believe it would end this way. But he was right. She should leave. Already deep into her plan of contacting Daniel Hershey and somehow bringing about Alexander's escape, Elizabeth gave him a watery smile before following the British captain out of the hall.

Three hours later she sat in a small backroom, surrounded by the odor of strong spirits. Barrels of whiskey and rum lined the walls of the cramped room. Elizabeth picked up her fork, but in reality all she accomplished as her gaze locked on the gentleman across the rough-hewn table from her was to stir the stew around on her pewter plate.

"Not hungry?" Daniel Hershey leaned back, balancing on the legs of his chair.

"I suppose not." Elizabeth dropped her fork. "Though 'tis very good."

Daniel waved the compliment away.

"Well, are you going to help me or not?" Elizabeth had explained her plight to the wizened old man when she'd first arrived at the Pig's Eye Tavern. At the time he'd been very noncommittal.

"Breakin' someone out of New Jail is nigh impossible," he said eyeing Elizabeth over a tankard of grog.

"So I've been told."

"Planning an escape from the Old City Hall

433

would be easier."

"But Alexander isn't in the Old City Hall," Elizabeth fairly screamed in exasperation.

Daniel simply raised his brows at her outburst. "I imagine there must be ten guards."

"Two sentinels posted at the front door, two more on the first barricade, and two more at the foot of the stairs. Alexander is on the second floor, so that means there are six guards to pass. I took note of things when I visited there earlier today," Elizabeth said in explanation.

"All right." Daniel rubbed his chin. "So there are only six guards. That still leaves locked cells."

"I shall see that they're unlocked."

"And Alexander isn't even armed."

"He will be." Elizabeth gripped the table's edge, leaning toward the older man, her expression stamped with determination. "I'll see to getting a pistol to Alexander, and getting him out of his cell. What I need from you are two horses, some provisions for traveling, and a diversion."

"A diversion?"

"Yes, anything. I'd thought perhaps a prison break would be helpful, or a fire, maybe even a combination. Anything to draw attention away from the New Jail. Can you handle that?"

He'd agreed. Elizabeth lay on a narrow cot in the attic of the Pig's Eye trying to calm her racing heart. The night was pitch black, and she told herself this was a good omen. Tomorrow night, when she and Alexander stole through the countryside, the lack of light would slow their pursuers.

Elizabeth closed her eyes, trying to summon sleep, but she knew it was a useless endeavor. Tomorrow she would break Alexander out of his British prison—or she'd die trying. Clasping her hands together in the darkness, Elizabeth began reciting prayers from her childhood.

"Elizabeth! I didn't expect to see you until tomorrow evening." General Warner rose from behind his desk as she swept into the room. "This is a pleasant surprise."

Smiling, Elizabeth extended her hand, gritting her teeth when his sickeningly moist lips touched her skin. "I simply had to try one more time," she cooed. "That beast I married is all you said he was, and more. Why do you know that he laughed at me when I suggested he sign over the deed to his plantation."

"That is a shame, my dear. However, there is a strong possibility that England will confiscate the property anyway."

"Not if it belongs to a staunch Loyalist." Elizabeth paused, meeting General Warner's gaze with a meaningful one of her own. "And a British general."

435

Watching the general's bulbous eyes narrow with avarice, Elizabeth couldn't keep a smile from tilting the corners of her mouth. "You do understand, General Warner, how very grateful I would be if I could manage to procure Alexander's plantation?"

The general offered Elizabeth a chair, leaning over her shoulder as she sat. "Your *gratitude* interests me very much, my dear; however, I must point out what you yourself said. Your husband isn't likely to sign his property over to you."

"Ah, but, General, that was yesterday." Elizabeth ignored his hot breath on her shoulder, the skimming of his fingers along her silk sleeve. "Today he is one step closer to the grave, one step closer to quitting this life with nothing to show for his existence."

"I imagine he is rather desperate at this point."

Elizabeth smiled her agreement though she had no doubt the general's assessment of Alexander was false. She imagined he'd face death the same way he'd faced every other adversity in his life — with strength and dignity. But that wasn't the picture she wished to paint for Warner. "I'm certain he is nearly frantic. And that's why he'll be so eager to accept what I shall offer him."

"And that is?"

"An heir. A small replica of himself that shall remain when Alexander Weston is no more." Elizabeth watched the general's gaze descend toward her flat stomach, and she prayed he'd believe she could convince Alexander she was with child.

"Is there to be an heir?" Warner left Elizabeth's side and leaned against the corner of his desk.

"The truth of it matters not," Elizabeth said with a shrug of her bare shoulders. "Convincing Alexander that he is to be a father, that he needs to make certain his child is provided for, is important." Her heart beat frantically as she voiced her request. Without the general's agreement to her next words, she might not accomplish Alexander's release. "That is why I need to be in the cell with him — alone."

"Alone!" General Warner stood up. "You seem to forget this man is a dangerous spy."

"And you seem to forget that I'm carrying his child. He won't do anything to me, and I'm sure that with a little persuasion on my part we can both profit nicely from Alexander's unfortunate demise."

Warner studied her long and hard, and Elizabeth forced herself to appear calm, all the while wishing she could scream. She was no good at this lying and deceit. No wonder Alexander had implied that he'd rather fight battles than engage in spying. But, unlike her, he was good at fooling people. Elizabeth was sure that at any moment the general would jump to his feet and have her thrown into prison.

"I'll want it in writing."

The general's words startled her. "I . . . don't understand."

"My share of the plantation's profits. I'd like the agreement in writing before I allow you to see Weston."

Elizabeth's heart soared. She could get to Alexander. "That seems only fair. What percentage did you have in mind?"

"Fifty."

Fifty? General Warner was greedier than she'd assumed. Not that it really mattered what percent she offered of a nonexistent plantation belonging to a nonexistent person. Apparently the British hadn't discovered that Alexander Weston was in truth, Alexander Knox. But she would hardly tell General Warner that, and so she protested the percentage as she thought Weston's near-widow would.

"As you wish," she capitulated when Warner insisted again upon half the profits. Elizabeth wished only to leave his odious presence, to free Alexander.

"There's one more thing." Warner dipped a quill into the inkwell.

"Yes?" Elizabeth asked when he paused, the freshly carved point poised above the parchment.

"I've long admired your," Warner's pale blue eyes lowered, making no pretense of hiding the direction of his gaze, "beauty," he finished.

His stare made Elizabeth feel soiled, but she

ignored the urge to cover her bodice with her hands.

"Since we shall be financial partners, I think we should consider expanding our relationship." He replaced the quill in its holder and stood up. Pulling his tunic down over his ample stomach, he rounded the desk, never once taking his lecherous eyes from Elizabeth's breasts.

Panic swelled within her, and Elizabeth nervously wet her lips. The thought of him touching her made her stomach churn, but there was a more urgent reason for her near hysteria. Hidden in the wire baskets of her hoops were two loaded pistols. They were impossible to see. She'd turned and twisted in front of the chipped mirror at the Pig's Eye Tavern to be certain of that. But they could be felt.

Elizabeth rose and moved toward the window, keeping a few paces in front of Warner's advancing form. "That is my wish also, General." Elizabeth turned, offering her hands, which he immediately clutched in his own. "But surely you can see why we must wait, deny our own desires, just one more day."

His lids lowered skeptically over his watery eyes, and Elizabeth searched her mind for a viable reason for her statement. "I'm a married woman." It sounded desperate, even to her, but apparently General Warner accepted her excuse of propriety because, though he didn't back away, he did stop pressing her against the wall.

"Perhaps you're right. One more day will make no difference."

Stifling a sigh of relief, Elizabeth followed him back to his desk. With a flourish she signed the document, thereby agreeing to split the profits of a nonexistent plantation in Virginia with Joseph Warner.

"Now may I see Alexander?"

"Get the hell away from the door, and stay away."

Seeing that he was nearly as far away from the cell door as possible in his cramped quarters, Alex thought this a rather stupid request. But though he excelled in cruelty, Baldwin hadn't shown Alex he had much common sense.

"What's going on?"

"Don't worry, I ain't tak'n you for your meeting with the hangman yet." Baldwin chuckled. "I'm letting someone else in your cell."

Alex watched the guard insert a heavy metal key, heard the clang as the lock sprang.

"You can bring her on in here now," Baldwin called up the hall as the cell door opened.

Turning to follow the guard's gaze, Alex caught a quick glimpse of rose silk before Elizabeth propelled herself through the door and into his arms. "What the. . . ?" He'd thought her on her way

440

to Maryland. The realization that she wasn't filled him with anger and concern.

"Don't talk," she whispered, grabbing his hand and pressing it against her hip. "Just hold me."

Chapter Twenty-one

The shape and hardness could only belong to a pistol!

Alex pressed his hand tighter against the bulk and peered down into Elizabeth's guileless gray eyes. "It's mate 'tis in my other hoop," she whispered when his expression confirmed his awareness of what she'd hidden beneath her skirts. "And I've a knife lashed to my right leg."

Though Baldwin had relocked the door, and disappeared down the hall, Alex pulled Elizabeth into the cell's corner before speaking. "I thought you promised to return to Maryland?"

"And so I shall, but only when you do." Reaching up, Elizabeth traced the bruise on his cheek with loving fingers till Alex caught her hand in his strong grip.

"Persist in your foolish ways, Elizabeth, and you shall not return at all," he scolded, his voice low but steady.

"Is it so foolish to deny the British their hanging of you?"

Eyes narrowed, Alex drew Elizabeth's fingers to his lips, kissing them gently before releasing her hand. "Give me the weapons then, and be on your way. I shall come to you. . . . Why are you shaking your head?"

"We leave together," Elizabeth insisted. "Don't start arguing, and please just listen to me." Elizabeth bent over, searching through layers of petticoat, extracting one gun, then the other. "They're primed and ready," she said, handing them to Alex. He immediately stuffed them into his breeches, billowing his shirt over them.

"I contacted Daniel Hershey," Elizabeth began after untying the knife, "and he arranged for two horses to be waiting for us on the street. He will also try to create a diversion in the street, but we can't be certain of that."

"When?" Alex took the knife, sliding it into the top of his boot. Not at all comfortable with exposing Elizabeth to danger, he nonetheless knew further objections were useless.

"Daniel was to give me three-quarters of an hour from the time I entered General Warner's office. It's been almost that now," she added.

"Guard! Damn it, Baldwin, get her out of

here!" Alex pulled Elizabeth behind him. "A little of that hysterical crying you're so good at faking would come in handy now," he said for her ears alone.

Not needing to be told twice, Elizabeth was sobbing loudly by the time the guard fumbled the key into the lock. "What the hell is going on here?" he yelled, throwing Elizabeth an exasperated look.

"I want her away from me. A condemned man has some rights, doesn't he?" Alex shouted, pretending to push Elizabeth away as she clung to him.

"Come on lady," Baldwin said. "And stop that infernal caterwauling.

"But you don't understand," Elizabeth cried, loosening her hold on Alexander's arm and clutching Baldwin's tunic. He smelled of unwashed flesh and last night's dinner, but she ignored the odor as she stared up at him wiht tear-filled eyes. "He's my husband, and—"

The dull thud of pistol butt crashing against skull cut off her tirade, and Elizabeth watched as Baldwin slid down in a rumpled heap at her feet. "Is he dead?" she asked, stepping back.

"I have no idea." Alex grabbed her hand, pulling her through the unlocked cell door. "Stay behind me. Do you understand?" he added when she didn't respond.

Powdered curls escaped their pins as Elizabeth

nodded vigorously. Pressing her back against the stone wall, Alex brushed a tendril off her forehead. Despite her daring actions, Elizabeth now looked frightened, her wide gray eyes apprehensive. "We'll make it out of here, Lizzie," he said, touching the small cleft in her chin. "And then we're going to have a long talk about your impetuous nature."

"I am not impetuous," Elizabeth began indignantly, but Alex's fingers touched her lips, instantly silencing her. The rustling sound of men moving about caught her attention as Alex moved forward cautiously.

Peering around the corner into the main hallway, Alex saw soldiers pouring out of the guardroom at the foot of the stairs, some buttoning their jackets as they went.

"What is it?" Elizabeth whispered.

Instinctively, Alex backed up, then looked out again. "The guards are hurrying off for some reason."

"I wonder if it has something to do with Daniel Hershey?" Elizabeth wrinkled her nose. "I smell—

"Smoke," Alex finished for her. "Stay here. The guards at the bottom of the stairs are still at their posts." Without waiting for a reply, Alex crept down the stairs, careful to muffle his footsteps on the stone steps.

The first guard never knew what hit him as Alex knocked him senseless with the same gun he'd used on Baldwin. Unfortunately, the noise he made falling to the floor alerted the other soldier, who raised his musket, aiming it straight at Alexander's heart.

They both heard Elizabeth's anguished cry at the same moment. The guard's mistake was to take his eyes off Alex long enough to determine the cause. Instantly, Alex leaped at him, knocking him to the hard floor. The scuffle that ensued proved more difficult than Alex anticipated. Weeks of near starvation and an injured leg had weakened him and slowed his reactions. He barely missed receiving the full impact of the soldier's meaty fist. The blow grazed Alex's chin, snapping his head to the side, allowing the soldier to roll on top.

Alex's well-placed punch sent blood spurting from the redcoat's nose. Stunned, the soldier was unable to block the next strike. Alex saw enraged fury on the face just inches from his own, smelled the blood and fear of the man as he reached for the soldier's neck. As Alex applied pressure, frantic fingers closed around his, then, suddenly, went limp.

Heaving the dead weight off him, and struggling slowly to his feet, Alex stared into Elizabeth's eyes. "You didn't roll over this time," she said, thinking of that day in the marsh when she'd knocked Alexander unconscious by mistake.

Alex's gaze dropped to the musket she clutched in her hands, the one she'd used to club the

British soldier on the back of the head. "Lucky for me," he quipped before snatching her hand and racing toward the door.

The smell of smoke grew stronger as Alex cracked open the heavy oak door reinforced by iron crossbars. "What's going on?" Elizabeth whispered when he pulled his head back inside.

"I can't tell for certain, but it appears the guards are fighting a fire around the side of the building. I can see the beginning of a bucket brigade."

"What about the horses?"

"They're about a hundred paces to the right, beside a mounting block." Alex leaned his back against the door, staring down into her upturned face. He knew she would balk at his next suggestion, as surely as he knew he would force her to accept it. "I want you to walk out of here and mount a horse. No one should question your right to leave."

"What about you?"

"I'll follow as soon as you've safely turned the corner."

"Oh, no." Elizabeth shook her head. "We leave together or not at all."

Clutching her shoulders, Alex forced her eyes to meet his. "Would you listen to me? The only chance I have is speed, outrunning them, getting on that horse and out of musket range before they know what's happening. I can't do that with you slowing me down."

"I won't." Elizabeth tried to convince him, but his hands tightened on her, drawing her closer.

"You couldn't help but cause me delay, Elizabeth. Look at your skirts. Think about mounting. Do you want me to take the time to lift you onto the horse's back while bullets whiz past me—past you?"

"No, but—"

"Then do as I say. Take your time. Walk slowly to the horses, use the block and mount. Don't show any haste until you round the corner, then ride as fast as you can for Long Island. I'll meet you at the Pig's Eye Tavern."

"But what if I make the guards suspicious and they come in here?"

"They won't."

Elizabeth searched his face with tear-brimmed eyes. She knew he couldn't be certain of that, just as surely as she knew his motive was her safety rather than his own. But there seemed to be nothing she could do. He looked at her with calm determination. He would not budge, and with each passing second their chances of escaping decreased.

"All right." Elizabeth took a deep breath. "I'll wait for you at the tavern." She straightened her dress and reached for the iron door handle.

"Stay calm," Alex warned, brushing a curl behind her ear. "And they won't suspect a thing.

They're still busy with the fire." Stepping away from the door, he touched her chin. "Don't be afraid."

"I'm not," she lied, giving him her best simile of a brave smile.

His answering grin made her eyes tear up again. Would this be the last time she'd ever see it?

"One more thing, Elizabeth," he said pulling open the door and gently pushing her outside, "don't turn back for any reason."

Sunlight and smoke assaulted her eyes simultaneously, causing her to squint as she stepped out onto the sidewalk in front of the New Jail. She tried to ignore the soldiers she could hear off to her left as she made her way slowly toward the horses. Thirty paces, forty, she walked, her body tense for the moment the guards would notice her and call out an order to halt. Her steps seemed to consume no ground at all, and Elizabeth had to resist the temptation to lift her skirts and break into a full run.

Finally she was close enough to the horses to see their thick eyelashes, the flaring of their nostrils as they breathed. Her own breath had caught in her throat, but she stepped onto the mounting block, pulling herself onto the saddle. Elizabeth swung her leg over the horse, hoping no one noticed the way her skirts rode up, but knowing astride she could ride faster.

With the same forced patience she'd used to

control her steps, Elizabeth walked her horse along the street. Body tense, looking neither left not right, she was nonetheless aware of her surroundings. Crisp autumn air, thick with the smell of smoke, chilled her skin. She heard the British soldiers busily fighting the fire, the crowds of passersby who'd gathered to see the spectacle, the plodding of her horse's hooves, but there was no command to stop.

Turning the corner, knowing herself out of view of the guards, Elizabeth breathed a sigh of relief. It caught in her throat as the first report of gunfire splintered the morning calm. Tugging on the reins, turning her protesting horse in a tight half circle, Elizabeth started to dig her heels into his flank.

Don't turn back for any reason. Alexander's words ricocheted through her mind. *For any reason* . . . As she clutched her horse's mane, fraught with indecision, Elizabeth jerked at the sound of the second shot, the third. *Don't turn back.* The command rang through her head as clearly as if Alexander stood beside her. Ignoring the tears streaming down her face, Elizabeth turned her mount, and headed for Long Island.

"Is there any word?" Elizabeth asked Daniel Hershey as soon as he entered the back room of his tavern. The striped homespun skirt she'd changed into swirled around her ankles as she clutched the edge of the handmade table.

"Not of Alexander." The proprietor poured himself a mug of grog, and took a healthy swig, wiping his mouth with the back of his hand before continuing. "The lobsterbacks are in an uproar about the trouble this morning. Half a dozen or so prisoners managed to escape during the confusion. They finally got the fire out." He paused in his story to take another gulp from his mug. "Word is that a General Warner is nigh foaming at the mouth over the deceit of some woman."

Elizabeth's shrug conveyed her lack of interest in whatever that loathsome man might feel. Sinking into a chair, she voiced the only question that did concern her, "What has become of him?"

"Well now, the British ain't bragging about killing or recapturing him, least not that I could discover, so he's probably holed up somewhere. He'll show up."

"But it's been four hours!" Elizabeth dropped head into her hands, sorry for her outburst. It would do no good, and she knew Daniel to be as aware of the time as she.

When she'd arrived at the Pig's Eye she'd recounted the escape to Daniel in detail. Of course, he'd already known some of it. He and some fellow Patriots had piled empty boxes and straw in the ally beside the New Jail and set them afire.

After she'd told him about Alexander, Daniel

had out to see if he could find any word, and Elizabeth had set about readying herself for their escape to Maryland. It had taken her little time to brush out her hair, tying it back with a ribbon, and change into a homespun gown, the type she'd become accustomed to wearing at Oak Hill. That finished, she'd had nothing to do but wait and worry.

Elizabeth felt Daniel's comforting hand on her shoulder before she was aware he'd moved. "Now, now," he began though he were talking to a small child. "Maybe you should get some rest. I'll keep an eye out for your man, and if there's any word, I'll be sure to wake—"

"I couldn't possibly sleep." Elizabeth covered his hand with hers. "But thank—"

The rusty hinge on the back door squeaked, and Elizabeth twisted around in her chair. Before Alexander even stepped into the room, she'd jumped up and run to him. It felt so wonderful to be pressed against his solid strength that for a moment she didn't realize he held her with only one arm. He swayed against her, nearly knocking her off balance, and that's when Elizabeth discovered his wound.

"My God, what happened?" She clutched his arm, gentling her touch when he flinched.

"One of the British got off a lucky shot." He grinned at her, but that didn't hide the tiny white lines of pain that bracketed his mouth.

Leading Alexander to a chair, Elizabeth nodded her thanks to Daniel, who had poured water into a pottery bowl.

"I don't think it's too bad," Alex said, gritting his teeth as she stripped off his shirt. "Are you all right?"

"Yes." Elizabeth dabbed at the bloody hole in his upper left arm with a wet linen rag. "But then the British weren't shooting at me."

"When they saw me and started firing, I was so afraid."

"Well, who wouldn't be?" she asked indignantly.

Alex grinned again, his blue eyes meeting hers. "I was afraid for myself, of course, but mostly I worried you'd turn back."

"You told me not to."

Alex's howl of laughter startled the calico cat sleeping on the windowsill. "And just when have you ever done anything I've told you?"

"Today," Elizabeth said, leaning over and pressing a quick kiss to his warm lips, then pulling back before he could grab hold of her and prolong it. As much as she would enjoy giving Alexander a thorough greeting, now wasn't the time. Besides, Daniel still moved about the room, and he'd been joined by his wife, who set about piling a pewter plate high with a thick stew. She set it in front of Alex, sharing a shy smile with Elizabeth when he dove into the meat like a starving man.

"I'm not finished with your arm," Elizabeth

453

said, though by the way he wolfed down his food, she wondered if appeasing his hunger wasn't more important at the moment.

"Don't worry," Alex said around a bite of the most delicious potato he'd ever eaten. "I don't want it bandaged till after I've deloused myself anyway. Besides, it's only a scratch."

Admittedly the musketball had passed completely through the fleshy part of his upper arm, however, Elizabeth would hardly call the gaping wound a scratch. But she didn't want to argue with him—not when he sat near her, alive and free. He glanced up and, catching her staring at him, gave her a broad wink. Elizabeth felt the heat from the blush that spread over her neck and face. His grin told her Alexander noticed it, too.

"If it's all right with you, Daniel, Elizabeth and I will rest here today and start south as soon as it grows dark," Alex said, pushing away his empty plate. "That ranks as one of the best meals I've ever eaten," he added to Mrs. Hershey after her husband had assured him he would be welcome at his tavern.

Later that afternoon, as Elizabeth lay down on a cot in the Pig's Eye Tavern, she discovered how tired she was. There had been little time, or inclination, to sleep since the day Jacob had arrived at Oak Hill. But now that Alexander lay, sound asleep, on the cot across the room, she could relax.

Elizabeth stole a glance at him. He looked more like himself since his bath. He'd shaved, and combed his clean dark hair back into a queue. Elizabeth smiled as he sighed in his sleep. A few more good meals would fill the hollows in his cheeks, and their ride to Maryland would help return the color to his face. Her eyes drifted shut as she thought about how happy she was to have him back from the grave.

"Wake up, sweetheart."

Elizabeth opened her eyes slowly to see Alexander leaning over her. The lengthening shadows seemed to wrap them in a cozy web. "Is it time to go?"

"I'm afraid so." Alex brushed a raven curl off Elizabeth's forehead, letting his fingers linger to trace the curve of her jaw.

"How is your arm?" Warm and soft from sleep, Elizabeth's voice drifted over Alex like honey.

"Stiff and sore as hell. But it will be fine," he said, never giving the afflicted limb a glance as he gazed down into her gray, velvet eyes. "Thanks to you."

"I didn't—" Elizabeth began, but his lips, pressed gently to hers stopped her protest.

"You did," he whispered against her mouth. "You not only took care of my arm, you saved my life."

"You've saved mine a time or two," she responded, her arms snaking around his neck.

"I have, haven't I?"

Feeling his grin against her neck, Elizabeth smiled. She loved this arrogant side of his nature. Of course, she decided as his lips traveled lower down the bodice of her gown, she loved every part of him.

"I'd better stop." Alex straightened and took a deep breath.

"Why?" Elizabeth felt deprived of his warmth.

"Because, my sweet Elizabeth, in another moment I won't be able to stop. And much as I long to make love to you, I think we'd better put as much distance between ourselves and the British as possible."

"You're right, of course." Elizabeth half-rose, leaning on an elbow. "What's wrong," she asked when he gave her a disgusted look.

"Well, you could have argued, just a little."

Laughing, Elizabeth swung her legs over the side of the cot, feeling around on the floor with her toes for her sturdy leather shoes.

Using back streets and alleyways, she and Alexander made their way out of New York without incident. At dawn the next morning they stopped at the home of the same Friend who'd offered hospitality to Elizabeth and her companions on their journey to New York. Checking Alexander's arm, Elizabeth was glad to see it wasn't festering.

Then, each having been given a room with a comfortable bed, she and Alexander slept the day away while the family went about their normal activities.

Though generous with their food, even packing provisions for the travelers to take on the trip south, the Quakers seemed wary. Elizabeth mentioned this to Alexander as they started out the next evening.

"The area has seen it's share of trouble," Alex explained as they crossed a well-worn bridge over a muddy stream. "We're between the British and American lines. A no man's land. Freebooters, Tory and Patriot sympathizers, roam and pillage almost at will."

Elizabeth twisted on her horse, searching Alexander's face in the gathering dusk. "The Patriots cause trouble against their own?" she asked in astonishment.

"I fear 'tis more booty than principal that rules both the cowboys and the skinners." At Elizabeth's questioning look, he explained further. "Cowboys or refugees are the names given themselves by the Tories."

"The Patriots call themselves skinners?"

Alex nodded. "Fanciful names for cowards and thieves who prey on the weak and innocent. Our host told me he'd lost his best milk cow to one of the groups less than a sennight ago. He's uncertain which side deserves his ire."

"But can't something be done? Certainly if General Washington—" Elizabeth stopped when she noticed Alexander shaking his head.

"These men do their deeds at night, so no one is certain exactly who they are. It could be a neighbor for all they know. Besides, we are too close to the British outposts for Washington to risk sending more than a small detachment to protect the locals."

"So the people living in this area become yet another sacrifice to the war?"

"I'm afraid so." Alex leaned over, patting his horse's neck. "There will always be good and evil men. War tends to magnify the attributes of each."

By daybreak a steady drizzle had soaked them to the skin. They begged shelter from the first house they saw. The widow who lived in the small stone dwelling seemed reluctant to have them until Elizabeth offered to pay. After that she acted quite gracious, serving them a hearty breakfast of griddlecakes and ham before they rested.

The rain had stopped by the time Elizabeth woke. A late afternoon sun shone in the window of the widow's bedroom. Making use of the water in the pitcher and bowl, she dressed quickly in the clothes she'd hung by the fireplace to dry. Alex had already rolled up his pallet when she entered the kitchen, and after a supper of mutton stew, they set out again.

They reached Philadelphia by late morning the following day. Now under Patriot control, the city was once again the capital of the new nation. Riding through the streets on their weary mounts, Elizabeth observed how very little it had changed. There was not a redcoat to be seen, of course, but other than that, the people went about their business much as they had when the British had occupied the city.

Alex led the way to an inn, asked for the best room available, and he and Elizabeth were led upstairs to a bedroom with a large poster bed. A bed Elizabeth couldn't take her eyes off.

"This is all right, isn't it?" Alex asked when he noticed her staring at the coverlet. Perhaps he'd taken too much for granted in asking for one room. But being with her, knowing again the warmth and comfort of her presence, interfered with his judgment. It had been nearly a year and a half since they'd parted at Oak Hill. For him, the time had only served to increase the love he felt for her. However, a lot could change in over a year. Perhaps she'd realized her mistake in loving him. Of course, she'd come to New York to rescue him, but could that have been to repay a debt? She'd even mentioned the times he'd saved her life.

Alex moved up behind her, cupping her shoulder in his hands when she still didn't answer. "I can sleep elsewhere if you want," he whispered into the thick mass of curls behind her ear.

"No!" Elizabeth swirled around, clutching his jacket with her fingers. "No," she answered more softly as his arms wrapped around her, pressing her more firmly against his body. "It's simply . . ." Elizabeth's gaze met his and locked. Lost in the indigo blue of his eyes she continued, "I want you so much, it scares me."

"Oh, God, Elizabeth." Alex's arms tightened around her slender form. He couldn't get her close enough. His lips grazed the corner of her mouth, her chin. "It has been all I could do, staying away from you until we were safe." Alex's breath came in choppy gasps as his hands explored the straight line of her spine, pressed against the swell of her buttocks. "I came close to shocking the Quakers we stayed with by insisting upon sharing a room with you."

"And those nights on the road, many a time I looked over at you, barely able to make out your form in the darkness, wanting to pull you off your horse and drag you into the bushes."

Laughing because of his words and because his whiskers tickled her collarbone, Elizabeth admitted, "I would glady have joined you in the bushes."

"Really?" Alex lifted his head, his eyebrow cocked in surprise.

"Really." Elizabeth laughed again.

"I'll have to remember that for future reference," he quipped. "But then I knew it wasn't safe." His hands tangled in her hair. "And I love you too much to ever purposely expose you to danger."

Elizabeth melted into his kiss, savoring the firm lips that played along hers, the bold thrust of his tongue as it plunged into her mouth. The taste of him was familiar yet captivatingly new and exciting. She relished it, her breasts tightening, and her body set aflame by the power of her desire.

"Alexander?" Sultry and sensual, her voice drew his attention from the smoothness of her silky black brows.

"Hmmm?" His tongue teased, wetting the tiny indentation in her chin.

"Are we safe now?"

Alex's laughter didn't keep him from scooping Elizabeth into his arms, sending her petticoats flying above her stockinged knees. "Safe as we'll ever be in this war, my sweet Lizzie. Certainly safe enough for me to demonstrate how much I've missed you."

Quilted coverlet and soft feather mattress engulfed Elizabeth as she and Alexander landed on the bed. Wrapping her arms around his neck, clutching the whipcord muscles of his back, kissing him with all the pent-up longing of countless months, she lost touch with reality. He was here, touching her body, making her heart sing with gladness. His smell, so unique and arousing, wafted about her. His breath mingled with hers, fanned the tip of her ear, the flesh above her

461

bodice.

"Oh, Elizabeth . . ." Alex nestled his face in the valley between her breasts, feeling her heat through the cotton fabric. "I missed you so much. There were times, I wanted nothing more than to ride away from it. The war. The spying. The constant intrigue. I just wanted to be with you." His eyes met hers. "But I couldn't. As much as I wanted you, needed you, I couldn't desert my country."

Elizabeth wove her fingers through his hair, brushing the silky strands off his forehead. "And I would never ask that of you."

His shifting weight settled atop her. "I love you." His words were simple, yet the sincerity of his feelings sent tingles through her.

"And I love—"

A pounding at the door, followed by an insistent "Major Knox" sent Alex rolling to his feet. He instinctively grabbed for his pistol, aiming it toward the sound. "Who is it?"

Fear gripped Elizabeth as she lay on the bed, twisting the quilt in her hands. Even without Alexander's reaction, the shock of hearing his real name after all this time was enough to send her heart racing.

"It's me, Ethan Henshet. You sent me with a message to Colonel Kincaid when you first got here. I got an answer for you."

Alex lowered the gun, and opened the door a crack. Passing the boy a coin, part of the money

462

Elizabeth had brought with her, Alex took the sealed parchment. "Colonel Kincaid is my intelligence contact in Philadelphia," he explained to Elizabeth who sat on the edge of the bed, her legs dangling over the side. "I thought I should let him know I'm in the city. Damn!"

Elizabeth watched Alexander scan the message, surprised by his sudden outburst. "What does he want?"

"Me—now" was Alex's succinct reply.

"Is something wrong?" Elizabeth slid from the bed and went to his side.

"Not really." Alex grinned. "It's just that I had other plans." He bent, giving Elizabeth a kiss. "I suppose I'd better go," he added reluctantly as his lips trailed along her cheek. "This shouldn't take long."

After he'd gone, Elizabeth sat on the small chair in front of the window staring out at the bare maple branches. Her life had changed so drastically in the last two years. When the war began, she'd thought it but a futile rebellion to be squelched by the British in a matter of months. It had affected her very little. Now . . . She leaned forward, resting her elbow on the deep windowsill. Now she believed the English would be defeated, would go home and leave the new country, her country, in peace.

When, that was the question . . . and at what further cost to those she loved?

Suddenly uncomfortable with the train of her thoughts—the memory of how close she'd come to losing Alexander, the possibility that she could still lose him—Elizabeth sprang to her feet. She'd visit Hannah while waiting for Alex's return.

She found the young Quakeress supervising the hanging of the heavy bed curtains and drapes for winter.

"Elizabeth," Hannah ran to her, squeezing her in a hug. "Thee had me so worried. Is thee all right? And thy Major Knox? Did thee save him?"

"Yes, yes," Elizabeth answered, returning her friend's embrace. "All is well with me. Alexander is meeting with Colonel Kincaid at this very moment."

"I'm so glad." Hannah led them out of the bedroom and down the stairs to the parlor. "Is thee staying in Philadelphia long?"

"I don't know," Elizabeth admitted. "We'll probably return to Oak Hill soon. Several of Alexander's tenants agreed to watch out for Father, but I don't like to leave him any longer than necessary. He hasn't been well since. . . ." Visions of that awful night when Colonel Littleton shot her father filled Elizabeth's head. "Since we left Philadelphia," she finished lamely. There was no need to burden Hannah with all that had happened.

"What of *your* father?" Elizabeth asked, changing the subject. "You mentioned that he was home, but I'm afraid I didn't have time to hear the details before I left for New York."

Hannah smiled, smoothing her plain gray skirt. "Congress released him and the other Friends in April a year ago."

"But he didn't sign the oath?"

"Thee knows he wouldn't. Apparently Congress has had a change of heart, for they rarely press the issue."

"Well, they certainly shouldn't. Not after all your family has done for the revolution."

Hannah shrugged. "We do what our conscience wills us to do."

"What has become of the Loyalists?" Elizabeth asked a question she'd speculated about ever since she'd learned of Clinton's departure from the city. At one time she'd thought she and her father would be among the stranded refugees.

"Many of them left with the British. For weeks people scrambled for places on His Majesty's ships in the harbor. Others stayed."

"Do you know what became of my cousin, Rebecca?"

"I believe thy cousin sailed for Canada with many of the others."

Elizabeth left Hannah soon after, promising to visit again, if possible, before she left Philadelphia. Alexander waited for her in the common room of the tavern, nearly pouncing on her when she walked through the door.

"Where have you been?" he hissed in her ear as

he guided her up the stairs to their room. "When I returned and you weren't here, and I couldn't imagine where you'd gone. . . ." He let the rest of his words fade away as he closed the door and searched her face. "Why are you laughing?"

Elizabeth tried with little success to squelch her mirth. "You sound like a mother hen."

"A mother hen, am I?" Alex backed Elizabeth against the door. His face remained sober, but his blue eyes danced with devilment.

"Well, perhaps not a hen." Elizabeth laughed as his arms bracketed her body. "Maybe more like a rooster."

Alex threw back his head in laughter. "I'll teach you to compare me to a barnyard animal," he said, his fingers circling her ribs, tickling her.

"No. Stop," Elizabeth pleaded, batting at his hands.

"No more referring to me as poultry?" he questioned, his fingers inches from her waist.

Elizabeth shook her head, her raven curls spilling over her shoulders.

Alex traced a silky lock, brushing his knuckles against the side of her breast as he twisted the end around his thumb. "And no more running off."

"I didn't run off," Elizabeth argued. "I went to visit Hannah. Will you ever believe I can take care of myself?"

"Now, Lizzie," Alex began, his hands once again reaching for her, tickling the last thing on his mind. "I know what you can do. Hell, I owe you my life. But that didn't stop me from worrying when I didn't know what had happened to you."

"I'm sorry." Elizabeth wound her arms around his neck. "I should have left word downstairs." She certainly could empathize with his concern.

"And I should have tried to stay calm." Alex nibbled on the tip of her ear, nudging her thick, lavender-smelling hair out of the way with his nose.

Calm was the last thing Elizabeth felt as his exploration continued down the stem of her neck. Her voice was a breathy whisper as she asked, "What did he want?"

"Who?" Her breast fit his palm perfectly.

"Colonel Kincaid." Elizabeth leaned into his hand.

"He said they won't be able to use me as a spy anymore."

"What?" Elizabeth's indignation pierced the sensual cloud surrounding her. "You're a wonderful spy. He'd be hard pressed to find anyone who could fool the British the way you have." In her ire, Elizabeth failed to realize she argued against the very thing she'd hoped for.

Grinning, Alex watched the silver flash of her eyes as she defended him. "He agrees with you."

"He does? Then why?"

"I've become too well known." Alex unhooked the top button of her bodice.

467

"Famous?"

"Infamous," Alex corrected, making quick work of the remaining fasteners.

"What are you going to do now?" Elizabeth's eyes fluttered shut and her head fell back as he pushed the fabric from her shoulders. His lips, warm and moist, caressed her skin, sending flames of desire leaping through her.

"Now?" Cocking an obsidian brow, Alex waited for Elizabeth's eyes to meet his. "You have doubt as to what I plan to do now?"

His next moves left little question as to his design, for he slowly, sensually stripped the gown and shift from Elizabeth's body. Nor were her intentions in doubt as she lovingly pulled off his shirt and breeches.

Lying on the down-filled mattress, Alex's lean, hard body pressed to hers, Elizabeth felt the tender ache of longing build inside her. She loved him, knew, at that moment, she'd never love anyone else.

His hand swept down her body, touching her fevered flesh, driving all but him from her thoughts, her being. Their lips met lightly, tenderly. Then, as passions long denied welled within them, more urgently. Tongues stroked, caressing, plunging deeper as the fire grew, feeding on itself.

"Elizabeth." The rough-edged word, barely above a whisper, sent tingles down her spine. His knee nudged her thighs and she opened for him, wrapping her legs around his narrow hips possessively.

"I love you." His declaration sang through her soul as his magnificent body thrust into her. She stretched, then instinctively her body tightened around him. "I've dreamed of this so many nights."

Opening her eyes, Elizabeth stared into the blue of a summer afternoon. His hooded eyes searched her face, mirrored her own desire. He moved, and a dizzying breath of air caught in her throat. He moved again and her body arched toward him, convulsing, clenching him spasmodically.

What modicum of control he'd possessed fragmented, and he climaxed with unleashed power. Still joined, Alex rolled them to their sides, facing each other. He brushed damp curls from her cheek, smiling when she looked at him, her gray eyes luminous with the wonder of their union.

"Marry me." The words astonished Alex as much as he could tell they surprised her. Not that he hadn't thought of making her his wife — often — but he'd hoped to couch his proposal in sweet sentiments, not blurt it out. "Please," he added.

"Is that what you want?"

Alex's thumb made small circles on her shoulder. He simply couldn't stop touching her. "I didn't think so at first. I wanted to protect you from the pain if something should happen. But I can't do that, can I?"

"No." Elizabeth traced his whisker-roughened

jaw with her finger.

Alex took a deep breath. "I want us to be together as much as we can." He paused. "I want to know you'll be waiting for me when this war is over." Resting his chin on the heel of his hand, he asked again, "Will you marry me?"

"Yes."

"Yes?" His dimple deepened as he searched her face.

"Did you expect me to say no?"

"No. I don't know." Alex flopped over on his back. "I never asked anyone to marry me before." Wrapping his arms around her, Alex pulled Elizabeth on top him. "I don't have to join my men until spring."

"You can stay at Oak Hill this winter?" Elizabeth rested her arms on his chest, hardly able to believe they'd be together.

Her hair formed a gossamer curtain separating them from the outside world, the world of war and reality. Sifting his fingers through the silky mass, Alex pulled her closer. "Three whole months."

"A lifetime," Elizabeth whispered as his lips met hers.

Epiloque

"What's this, Momma?"

Elizabeth Knox brushed a wayward curl under her straw bonnet and looked down to where her son sat in the freshly plowed dirt. He clutched a swirled shell in his chubby little hand. "That's a snail, Jon," she answered.

"Oh." He poked at the shell several times, then squinted up at his mother with indigo blue eyes. "What's a snail?"

Laughing, Elizabeth scooped up her son, snail and all, ignoring the rich Maryland soil that clung to his bare legs and feet. At two and a half years, her child was as inquisitive as he was brave. It would never have occurred to him to be afraid of the snail, just as he wouldn't stop questioning her until his curiosity was temporarily satisfied.

"A snail," Elizabeth began, "is a tiny animal that lives in our garden. And he carries his house around with him."

The boy's eyes grew large with wonder. "Like our house?"

"Something like ours," Elizabeth agreed glancing toward Oak Hill's gabled roof and welcoming porch. "But, of course, his is much smaller, so he can take it with him wherever he goes."

Her son seemed to ponder this new piece of information as he turned the hapless snail over in his dirty hands. "Like Papa's house?" he finally asked.

"Yes, sweetheart. Very much like your papa's house." Elizabeth's footsteps crunched along the shell path as she left the vegetable garden she was planting—with her son's "help"—and walked toward the wide front porch. "Only your father doesn't live in a shell."

"Tent," Jon burst out, obviously proud of himself for remembering the word.

"That's right." Elizabeth sat on a step laughing as her son scurried off her lap and placed the snail on the wooden porch. She tried very hard to make his father a real part of young Jonathan Alexander's life. Considering that Jon had only seen Alexander once, and that nearly eighteen months ago, it was not an easy task. But she read and reread the few letters that managed to find

472

their way to Oak Hill, and she told their son stories.

Stories about Alexander's life in the Continental Army were Jon's favorite. He'd sit on her knee and listen as she told him of marches and battles and of how much his father wished he could be with his son.

Elizabeth leaned back against the whitewashed pillar, watching as Jon prodded the reluctant snail with his finger, and thought about the last time Alexander had been home.

It had been late October of 1781. The snow geese were flying south, their honking a constant companion as they stopped to feed in the fertile marshes along the bay. There had been a great siege fought in Yorktown, Virginia, and the British general, Cornwallis, had surrendered his troops to a combined American and French army. Elizabeth had heard the news not long after Captain Tilghman rode through the area. He was on his way to carry the message from General Washington to the Congress in Philadelphia.

An American victory. Elizabeth could not stop the surge of excitement that ran through her when she heard of one, no more than she could overcome the fear that Alexander might have been injured, or worse. Trying to overcome her anxiety, Elizabeth had thrown herself into taking care of the plantation and their son.

Her father would have enjoyed knowing about

473

Washington's defeat of Cornwallis. But Jonathan Lancaster had died the previous winter. He'd never really recovered from the wound inflicted by Colonel Littleton. When a fever had hit him, during a particularly bad cold spell, he'd lacked the strength to fight it. Elizabeth still missed him dreadfully, and thanked God that she had Jon.

Then Alexander had come home. He could only stay a sennight, but at least she'd known he was safe. Elizabeth smiled, remembering the first time Alexander had seen his infant son asleep in the same cradle he'd used as a baby. Tears had shone in his eyes as he'd rubbed the fuzzy black curls, and he'd reached out and hugged Elizabeth to him.

Alexander had thought the war would end soon, but it hadn't. Though most of the fighting had stopped, a formal peace eluded the two countries, and had for over a year. Recently, however, Elizabeth had heard rumors that perhaps all the waiting would soon be over.

Alexander would hardly recognize his son now, Elizabeth thought as she opened her eyes to check on the boy. The snail was there, slowly sliming its way across the porch, but her son was not.

Standing up, she shaded her eyes against the bright sun, and looked for her precocious offspring. Spotting him about ten rods down the oak-lined drive, she yelled for him to stop. "Come back here, Jonathan Alexander." Elizabeth descended the porch steps.

Tossing a glance over his shoulder at his mother, Jon toddled on. "Horse, Momma," he called back.

Looking beyond her son, Elizabeth saw the horse and rider coming, galloping through dappled sunshine filtered by new oak leaves. She grabbed up her skirts and ran, her bonnet, caught by a satin bow around her neck, flying behind her. Passing her bewildered son, she met Alexander as he leaped from the horse.

Laughing, she grabbed his wife by the waist, lifting her and twirling her around and around as she peppered his face with happy, excited kisses. His lips met hers, hungrily, passionately, as he stopped turning and let her soft body slide down his.

"Momma?"

The single word spoken in a child's voice caught Alex's attention, and he looked down into eyes as blue as his own.

"Jon," Elizabeth said, reaching down, but Alexander was quicker, and gathered his son up between them. "This is your papa, sweetheart."

"Papa?" Jon mimicked as Alexander shifted him to one arm. The other he draped around Elizabeth's shoulders as they walked toward the house.

"Yes, your papa." Alex hiked his son higher. "And I've come home." Alexander's eyes met Elizabeth's, shining bright with love. "To stay."

Author's Note

Spies did play an important role in the American Revolution. Many of the events portrayed in this book actually occurred. Learning from his experience in New York, Washington had his Philadelphia spy network in place before the British entered the city in 1777. Depending upon trained operatives and the patriotic citizens, he kept close tabs on Howe's movements during that long winter.

It was a woman, a Quaker housewife, who listened at a keyhole as the British planned their surprise attack, thus saving Washington's battle-weary troops at White Marsh. Howe's attempt to capture the young Marquis de Lafayette also failed because of American spies.

Though fictional characters, Alexander Knox

and Elizabeth Lancaster epitomize the men and women who, through their bravery and sacrifice, fostered the birth of our nation.

ZEBRA ROMANCES FOR ALL SEASONS
From Bobbi Smith

ARIZONA TEMPTRESS   (1785, $3.95)

Rick Peralta found the freedom he craved only in his disguise as El Cazador. Then he saw the exquisitely alluring Jennie among his compadres and the hotblooded male swore she'd belong just to him.

CAPTIVE PRIDE   (2160, $3.95)

Committed to the Colonial cause, the gorgeous and independent Cecelia Demorest swore she'd divert Captain Noah Kincade's weapons to help out the American rebels. But the moment that the womanizing British privateer first touched her, her scheming thoughts gave way to burning need.

DESERT HEART   (2010, $3.95)

Rancher Rand McAllister was furious when he became the guardian of a scrawny girl from Arizona's mining country. But when he finds that the pig-tailed brat is really a voluptuous beauty, his resentment turns to intense interest; Laura Lee knew it would be the biggest mistake in her life to succumb to the cowboy—but she can't fight against giving him her wild DESERT HEART.

Available wherever paperbacks are sold, or order direct from the Publisher. Send cover price plus 50¢ per copy for mailing and handling to Zebra Books, Dept. 2916, 475 Park Avenue South, New York, N.Y. 10016. Residents of New York, New Jersey and Pennsylvania must include sales tax. DO NOT SEND CASH.

GOTHICS A LA MOOR – FROM ZEBRA

ISLAND OF LOST RUBIES
by Patricia Werner   (2603, $3.95)
Heartbroken by her father's death and the loss of her great love, Eileen returns to her island home to claim her inheritance. But eerie things begin happening the minute she steps off the boat, and it isn't long before Eileen realizes that there's no escape from *THE ISLAND OF LOST RUBIES*.

DARK CRIES OF GRAY OAKS
by Lee Karr   (2736, $3.95)
When orphaned Brianna Anderson was offered a job as companion to the mentally ill seventeen-year-old girl, Cassie, she was grateful for the non-troublesome employment. Soon she began to wonder why the girl's family insisted that Cassie be given hydro-electrical therapy and increased doses of laudanum. What was the shocking secret that Cassie held in her dark tormented mind? And was she herself in danger?

CRYSTAL SHADOWS
by Michele Y. Thomas   (2819, $3.95)
When Teresa Hawthorne accepted a post as tutor to the wealthy Curtis family, she didn't believe the scandal surrounding them would be any concern of hers. However, it soon began to seem as if someone was trying to ruin the Curtises and Theresa was becoming the unwitting target of a deadly conspiracy . . .

CASTLE OF CRUSHED SHAMROCKS
by Lee Karr   (2843, $3.95)
Penniless and alone, eighteen-year-old Aileen O'Conner traveled to the coast of Ireland to be recognized as daughter and heir to Lord Edwin Lynhurst. Upon her arrival, she was horrified to find her long lost father had been murdered. And slowly, the extent of the danger dawned upon her: her father's killer was still at large. And her name was next on the list.

BRIDE OF HATFIELD CASTLE
by Beverly G. Warren   (2517, $3.95)
Left a widow on her wedding night and the sole inheritor of Hatfield's fortune, Eden Lane was convinced that someone wanted her out of the castle, preferably dead. Her failing health, the whispering voices of death, and the phantoms who roamed the keep were driving her mad. And although she came to the castle as a bride, she needed to discover who was trying to kill her, or leave as a corpse!

Available wherever paperbacks are sold, or order direct from the Publisher. Send cover price plus 50¢ per copy for mailing and handling to Zebra Books, Dept. 2916, 475 Park Avenue South, New York, N.Y. 10016. Residents of New York, New Jersey and Pennsylvania must include sales tax. DO NOT SEND CASH.